HANK GUNN SERIES - BOOK ONE

MANAGED PARANOIA

NEAR-FUTURE SCI-FI THRILLER

D1096653

Rock the Boat

Finlay Beach

finlaybeach.com

Managed Paranoia – Book One

Cover Design by Finlay Beach

First Edition April 2022

eBook ISBN 979-8-9857705-0-6

Print ISBN 979-8-9857705-1-3

ASIN B09S8K6SW7

10 9 8 7 6 5 4 3 2 1

Dedicated to Carol, the love of my life and my best friend.

CHAPTER 1

Bremerton, Washington

A WOMAN'S FACE LOOKING through a narrow window of the steel door caught his attention. It was the face he had been conferencing with each week for the last month, but she looked older in real life. She observed the waiting area before opening the heavy door. Her round, pleasant face struggled with the severity of her jet-black hair and short bangs, but her movements were kind, like his own grandma. The thought eased his mind. He understood how the system worked. Officially, today's session must end in a clinical determination. Unofficially, the Mental Health Artificial Intelligence decided his fate. He had no peace about any of this, so he focused on the human side.

It'll be fine. She's a grandma.

Stopping his promotion to the next level and withholding the freedoms that came with it were within her power but nothing more. If he walked out, she couldn't stop him. He thought, *I hold all the cards. Go fish, Grandma.*

"Hank," she said. "It's a pleasure to meet you in person." She nodded and stepped away from the door. "I have to ask you to repeat your full name and date of birth."

"Henry James Gunn. May 12, 2001."

"Okay, thanks." She looked at her palm-sized device again and shot her eyes upward into his. "What do you know, you look just like your picture, but your eyes are bluer." She slid it into a pocket. Her head tilted as if she questioned what she just said, and she retrieved the device for a second look. With a split-second hesitation, her eyes darted across the screen. "Hank, please, follow me to my office."

Aware the session had begun, he followed at a friendly distance. She led him to a small office with two chairs separated by a steel government desk. Hank took a seat in a chair with armrests while Susan glanced at a screen propped on the naked desktop. He fixated on the questions Susan might ask.

"Are you happy?"

He considered responding, "I'm happy to be alive," then he'd laugh. *No, don't laugh... chuckle. Or better yet just smile. Just tell the truth*, he thought. *They can always detect a lie.* He'd answer, "I'm not unhappy."

Even though his long legs spanned the distance to the desk, he scooted the chair closer, hiding them from her view. Birkenstock sandals covered handmade wool socks, except at the toes. The socks were damp but clean, though they didn't look it. Stains dyed the lighter colored yarn, and the weave matted in places with tar. The socks should have been cast off weeks ago, but the mornings were chilly, and the hand-knitted socks covered his missing toe.

Susan pushed the screen to one side. "Hank, let's begin by getting to know each other. Please, call me Susan."

Her name tag read *Susan*. Just Susan. No last name, no rank, no prefix, no alphabet—only *Susan*. Personal yet anonymous. "Okay." He forced a smile, then added, "Susan," as if hoping the effort would please her.

"How do you find your living conditions?"

"I like my room. Most of the neighbors are quiet."

"Quiet?"

Hank wanted to look at her as if she were from another planet. Doesn't she understand the word "quiet?" It should be easy to play along but being tired and over-caffeinated always made simple things hard. Why was he so worried about convincing Susan what the AI had determined? It had mined the data and computed an impression. Hank was sure the AI would clear him. Just fifty-three minutes without being sarcastic or sending up any number of possible red flags. At the end of their conversation, he'd leave the office, take the bus home, and figure out how to detach himself from the idiocy of Operation Blue Skies.

Hank looked Susan in the eye, put on an authentic smile, and said, "Port Townsend is a great little city. It suits me. It's quiet. More of a seaport than a city. Like my hometown." He regretted bringing up his childhood and hoped to deflect it by adding, "My room has a view up the hill, but the weather has been great, and I spend a lot of time walking around town. I've met lots of friendly people and even made friends with a couple of dogs and a cat. Did you see I got a job?"

"Yes, you're working for a charter company. Is that enough money to help you?"

She expected him to do the talking. That he understood. But money? Why that topic? At least she didn't delve into his past. He said, "It works out to minimum wage, but I get paid as long as I'm on board with students, plus amazing food and tips. Tomorrow I have my first gig. I'll manage to stay afloat."

"Stay afloat" had been another poor choice of words. Telling words from a man whose major life change amounted to sinking his boat built with loans and credit cards. His military service wasn't the reason he was in the program, but it contributed. A vet needed a major life change, or MLC, to get tapped for help. Hank considered the irony that watching your friends die and being shot at and killing people wasn't enough of an MLC to call for this level of psychological attention. But sink your boat after you get discharged and... bingo.

"I'm still looking for a more stable job. I've applied to all the fire departments. They always need paramedics." Military to civilian transitions from medic to paramedic seldom occurred, but he supposed she wouldn't know that. "I'm doing side jobs for a carpenter. It's under the table." He saw no expression, so he added, "Do you think I should keep it?"

She looked less than pleased to be baited. "Hank, I see your mother is still living. What's your relationship like?"

"We get along well. She lives in Florida with her boyfriend, Mario. They're retired and living the good life." There was no way to keep eye contact. Every word coming out of his mouth seemed wrong. He pressed the edge of his foot into the desk. Mario—now she's got the dead-father-replaced-by-the-boyfriend thing to gnaw on and sure, why not throw in "the good life?"

Normally, Hank would get up and keep his body busy. But in this situation, he had to stay still. Any escape from the building tension had to be internal. He forced the words that made everything okay into his head. A kind of emergency pull-lever that worked every time. *BE THE DUCK!* When tactical breathing or counting to ten didn't ground him, the disruptive image of the duck lightened his mood and eased his mind. The duck looked sanguine on the water, but underneath it was paddling like hell. Aware of his posture, he sat up straighter, the muscles in his face calmed, and he released a slow breath.

"Do you mind if I get a drink of water? It was a long bus ride."

Susan reached into the drawer beside her and pulled out a bottle, offering it to him. "Hank, what are you nervous about?"

He sipped his water. "Susan, you're right to ask that question. As a communicator, I have a poor track record. I can sail into a hurricane and stay calm, and I've been under enemy fire so many times I've lost count. I've even been in stampedes twice—once by a mob and once by bulls. That stuff doesn't faze me but put me in an interview and it goes to shit." Hank thought he might have pushed it too far with the bull story and the shit remark, but it helped him relax and form a genuine smile.

"Okay, Hank." She didn't return his smile. "What would you be comfortable talking about?"

"Anything. I'm good. Next time I'll lay off the coffee."

"The reason you're here is that a major life change occurred. How has that event affected you?"

Hank breathed easily, knowing this would be better than regressing back to his childhood. "It's been hard, living through the storm and losing my boat. I'm broke—no, worse—I'm in debt. That's the hardest." His heart rate slowed as he imagined the conversation going his way. "Not spending much and working hard is easy, but earning enough just to keep up has been a struggle. Still, I'm glad things came out as well as they did."

Susan asked, "What 'came out as well as they did?'"

"I was close to death. As close as ever. Boats can be replaced. People can't. And I'm alive."

"How were you saved?"

"Well, there was so much damage after the wave hit, we—my boat and me—were like a cork, bobbing in the Southern Ocean. I came to, still at the helm. A couple of smaller waves raced over the deck while I held onto the

4

unresponsive tiller. The sun rose just to the edge of the earth, and it disoriented me. For the first time in thirty-two days, we were facing the wrong horizon. It didn't matter. We weren't going anywhere. I tried to move below deck to bandage my foot, but my hip didn't work and the pain was just showing up. It was bad. I crawled to my medical kit and started an IV. It's a good thing, too, because the numbness was ebbing and the pain came on like a drumbeat. The morphine I had on board was out of date, but it worked. A minute later, I was on the radio making a distress call.

"I still can't believe my luck. Halfway between Chile and New Zealand, hadn't seen a ship or a plane for well over four days, and RCCNZ—New Zealand Rescue—responded right away and told me they have my position and they're contacting the nearest vessel. My boat was small, and I could check my bilge pump from my seat while I waited—not good. Two minutes later, this woman on the radio says the *Diamantina* is diverting course and will be there in an hour. I'm thinking, that's amazing. I'm in the middle of nowhere and I'll be rescued before my boat sinks. At least, I hope. I tell the woman on the radio, 'Thanks, I'll buy you a drink next time I'm in New Zealand.'

"I reached over and got my go-bag, then collected a couple other things from my nav station. It wasn't a fast leak, but my boat was going down. I called the *Diamantina* and confirmed my position. They said they were forty minutes away. I'd done everything I could to stay alive. I passed out again, this time from the pain or morphine. Probably both.

"It took the eardrum splitting horn of this giant container ship to stir me into consciousness again. A dark shadow stole the morning light as the hull blocked the winds and calmed the choppy swell. The two men who boarded my boat, spoke in a language I couldn't understand, but at least I had human companionship. After strapping me onto a stretcher, they placed me into a small boat lowered over the side. The boat never even detached from its cables—incredible seamanship.

"That's it. The story of my life."

Susan waited, but Hank sat still, satisfied. He had told his tale many times, and she might not believe everything he told her, but it was all the truth. Would she care? She was a cog in the workings of a vast machine, barely Susan, barely assisting in the work of shifting suicide statistics downward. His mind raced. *She won't care.*

"Hank, what's next for you?"

"I'm leaving here, having a meal at Mickey D's on your dime, thank you very much. Then, I'm taking the bus back home."

"How does that make you feel?"

Hank thought, *Psychotherapy 101. What a joke.* He wanted to ask, *How does what make me feel?* Was she even paying attention? He played along and asked, "Port Townsend?"

She nodded.

"It's colorful and I love everything made from wood. Port Townsend is full of wood. Incredible wooden boats and all the Victorian buildings. Craftsmanship everywhere."

"Is that all?"

"It's a safe harbor and there's always activity."

Susan's expectant look said she wanted much more than Hank could give. The rest of his thoughts about Port Townsend, and his life was too personal. The little city on Washington's peninsula reminded him of his hometown before his dad's death. He could never hope to communicate the sensation to anyone else—more a belief than anything tangible. Possibilities of a bright future kindled inside his heart.

Susan already knew about his MLC and his job as a sailing instructor. He told her about his under-the-table work as a carpenter, but she didn't need to know he was building boats again and getting paid in cyber-currency. That could bring trouble. And he had no plans to mention his promising relationship with Brit, the redhead at Doc's. Still, he had to give her something, so he said, "It's a great place to heal."

"Hank, what type of healing are you looking for?"

"Every kind. I've come a long way working through the disappointment of losing my boat. The seastead hospital printed a new hip, replaced the crushed one, and sped up the healing with therapeutics I didn't even know existed. But losing my toe is still weird. At least it's all healed and doesn't hurt. I have friends who've lost more."

"Go on. Would you share your story?"

"You mean about how I lost my toe?"

"Okay. Start there."

Hank unhooked his feet from under the backside of the desk. "I don't recall what happened. I'd been sailing under a storm sail wearing boots, but when I came too, the mast was gone, and my feet were bare. My right hip had been crushed and the little toe dangled. The bone was detached at the knuckle, tendons and nerves cut away, and the severed blood vessels retracted into my foot. Just a little blood swirled around the wet deck. Even with the useless hip, I felt most apprehensive about the toe—like a child with a baby tooth held on by a thread. All I could manage was to wrap the foot in a towel and bind it with duct tape."

He studied Susan to see if his description grossed her out. She stared, unaffected, and encouraged him to continue with a nod.

"A sympathetic crewman on the *Diamantina* helped me cut the dressing away, then took the scissors and snipped. He held my toe up like he had removed a bullet and tossed it into a shallow pail. He didn't speak English, so without words he drew the remaining skin together, attached two staples, and gave me a shot of antibiotics.

"A day later, a long-range helicopter retrieved me from the ship and landed me at a floating hospital in international waters off the coast of Chile. The doctor looked at the scan and said, 'We can replace the hip, but the toe... it's gone forever. You're lucky. All you need to walk is a heel and a big toe. You won't even miss the little piggy.'

"I do kinda miss the little piggy." Hank almost laughed but settled on an incomplete smile.

CHAPTER 2

Bremerton, Washington

BY THE TIME THE shuttle pulled up to the bus stop, Hank had changed his mind. Lifting the hood of his jacket, he turned away. His stomach would have to wait. A brisk walk and some fresh air would allow him to debrief and clear his mind. He admitted that it had been a rocky start, but he gained momentum, telling Susan about his experience leaving his boat to sink alone in the Southern Ocean. Even though sharing emotions didn't come easy, he exposed enough of his soft underbelly to satisfy Susan. The initial jitters settled, then he let down his guard and uttered words he couldn't take back.

The shuttle bus passed him by, pivoted around the corner, and swung out of sight. He ignored it and clenched his jaw tightly until his face formed into a sneer and he mumbled, "Loose lips sink ships. What was I thinking?"

Hank recalled hearing a quiet tone and Susan wrestled herself out of her chair. The session was over—or it should have been. Minutes away from saying goodbye, Hank stood and her eyes dropped to his feet. He shouldn't have been self-conscious. Wool socks and rugged sandals are common in this part of the country. But Susan did that thing where she tilted her head, like when she greeted him and looked at his picture twice.

Susan was Hank's human contact, but the Mental Health AI did all the heavy lifting. Before he signed on, he searched VA mental health programs and learned the statistics didn't change when humans were in charge. The test group of veterans managed by AI-only had a similar rate of suicides as the AI-human cohort. Neither had stellar outcomes, but AI-only had a much lower price tag and had unlimited scalability. None of that mattered to the people who fought hard against AI use. They ignored the data and injected slogans. During the senate hearings, the committee chair proclaimed, *Our heroes deserve people who care, not Freud in a machine*, and the activist group, Clean Hearts and Dirty Hands, made signs reading, *Military Intelligence + Artificial Intelligence = Wrong Again!* But the rhetoric was unnecessary. People agreed AI-only was tantamount to giving up on human beings.

His foot slapped into a puddle. The disturbing limp always returned. Susan would have finished her report by now, but would she bother to make waves? Could she contradict the AI, disagree with Freud in a machine? His faux pas at the end of the session was unlikely to trigger Freud, but he sensed Susan would be concerned. He ignored the limp and gave all his attention to the problem, realizing it went wrong after Susan stood up—her weird double take and then everything she said.

"Hank, your tests have been consistently clean: no drugs. But why haven't you been taking the supplements?"

He had wondered how she knew about the vitamins, but now realized it must be Freud—she'd have access to everything Freud had on him. The important information like medical reports, online habits, and social media posts. Everything had been curated with the important mental health indicators pinned to the top. That's why she remained unaffected as he described his injury. She already knew the details.

"I hate taking pills." That was a truthful answer.

Then she said, "Okay, Hank. Well, thank you so much for coming here today. I'll let you get on with your life. But first, do you mind if I share a few thoughts and give you a bit of advice?"

"No. I mean, sure."

"Take your vitamins. I know I sound like your mother, but I'll tell you something I don't share often." She seemed to relax. "I'm telling you this because you were a Navy medic, and it's not exactly top-secret. Still, I'll deny it if you tell anybody this came from me." She laughed. "It's obvious you didn't take your supplements because there's no trace of lithium in your blood tests." Susan let that sink in and continued. "I've been with OBS since the beginning and two things have changed. The first is that we shifted away from prescribing antidepressants and the second, we include a micro-dose of lithium in the vitamin-mineral supplements. It will stabilize your mood and help your outlook."

"Okay?" It was a weak response but sincere.

"More advice. You're tall and good-looking, and despite your recent setback, you've got a lot going for you. Find someone to be with. Relationships are complicated. You can't control them. Giving up control is part of growth. You have free access to several dating sites. Most of the vets I work with log in right away, but you still haven't. Intimacy can get messy, but that's okay. One of my colleagues even recommends getting laid as therapy. You might try it."

"Wow. I didn't see that one coming." He limped on and shook his head and thought, *Nope, didn't see that one coming at all.*

Then Susan smiled. It was a genuine smile with lines spiraling out around her gray-green eyes. "Hank, be patient with yourself. Healing is a process, not an event."

He stopped walking, cast his gaze into the moldy sidewalk, and thought, *I laughed. Why did I laugh? I should have smiled and kept my mouth shut, but no....* He repeated her words out loud, "Healing is a process, not an event." Then he added, "And the only thing I can come up with is, *Slicing an artery is an event. Bleeding out is a process.* What a headcase. I might not be suicidal, but I am a damn fool."

CHAPTER 3

Smith's Resort, Micronesia

THE END. THIS TIME it meant more than shutting the pages of her favorite book for another year. Total relaxation in paradise would be over soon. In this place, the sun measured time. It plunged in and out of the watery horizons like a cosmic metronome. Without technology, not even a watch, Bella adapted to the earth's rhythms without protest. Another swim, followed by another twilight dinner under torchlight, and then a long, dark, lonely night. Lonely unless she counted the geckos. Not exceptional companions but their amusing antics reminded her of children playing Red Light, Green Light. With that thought she remembered, boredom has a terminal velocity, and she had reached it.

The rich natural darkness of her skin had doubled during her stay. Tonight, she would wear a white sundress to the dining room. Not because it would be radiant, but it was the only dress she brought. This night in the primitive paradise, like all the others, would be uneventful. No fancy drinks, no dancing, no men. She wasn't here for that. Bella got what she desired—forced relaxation.

Two weeks to unplug. A ritual started by her parents. Where they got it, she had no clue. But year after year it worked like a charm. This was her place to decompress. No family, no coworkers, no phones. This place insisted that she do all the things she loved—swim, sun, read, sleep, and eat. The sameness of each day was part of the draw. In the mornings a cacophony of birds, God's alarm clock, would wake her. She'd spring out of bed, slip on shorts and a light blouse, and watch the sunrise while sipping the darkest coffee imaginable. A walk, a swim, a good read under the pergola until brunch. Siesta, read, swim, read, sun, read, swim, cocktails and dinner, chat with other guests. Interrupt, "Please, excuse me, I've got a big day tomorrow," then duck under mosquito netting into a comfy bed and fall asleep with a smile....

Five years ago, she found this place the old-fashioned way—eavesdropping. While part of a student contingent of marine biologists, she overheard a couple older attendees complaining about stress. A third, rather relaxed-looking gentleman said, "You need to go to Smith's Resort. It's on a tiny island in Micronesia and just the place to unwind."

Smith's Resort... A straightforward conversation to remember, but the place had been almost impossible to find. This particular *Smith's Resort* didn't have a website, email, or even a phone. It did, however, have a small following, and she found a few mentions online. The one that convinced her to keep searching said, *Trade five stars for LIVE STARS! It's like the Amish figured out how to relax. No electricity nor the presumption of such high expectations.* After six weeks of snail-mail correspondence, they confirmed her reservation. Every year since, she was not disappointed.

But tomorrow she'd have to return to her problems. It would take seconds to pack. All she had to do was throw her string bikini, salt-speckled sarong, and the sundress into a beach bag, and drop by the office to book her dates for the same time next year. There, she'll collect her valuables and passport and leave her books on the lending shelf. Then, a stroll through the camp-like complex with weathered thatched roofs to say goodbye to the resort's staff. She'd leave each with a kiss on each cheek and a tip. Most years she was eager to leave, but anxiety found its way into paradise when she thought about returning to the life she left behind.

Her stomach growled but would have to wait until after sunset when the dining room opened. The food was not the reason she came, but she always gained a pound or two. Kasian had never left the island and had no formal training as a chef, but he mastered local flavors—coconut, sugar, cinnamon, allspice, salt, vanilla, and cloves. He turned each meal into mouthwatering delights.

She imagined her parents and how they would react to a meal in their particular way. Her mother using her heaviest Norwegian accent, *This food is so good it's toxic.* Then her dad would deepen his voice like the lead in a telenovela, *You ought to know.* They would both laugh. She loved her parents, but their humor was beyond her ability to understand. What she did understand looked back at her in the mirror. Her parents' tumultuous relationship produced her—Isabella Maria Johansen Espinosa. She was the genetic equivalent of a mashup of her parents. Her raven-black hair, deep brown eyes, and equatorial complexion revealed her handsome father's contribution. But no one in her father's gene pool came close to her height. Her maternal Nordic genes blessed her with a regal neck, slender waist, and long legs.

In a practiced maneuver, she reached behind her head, grabbed the top of the beach lounger, and did a sit-up, clicking it into an upright position. She sipped some tepid water from a glass. There was no condensation on the sand-etched tumbler or its mismatched water carafe. In keeping with the ethos of the resort, guests had no access to ice cubes. Bella longed for a cool drink of water, but the resort's owner was little help. Upon arrival, Mr. Smith repeated his weekly mantra. *We serve white wine at forty-five degrees, beer at fifty-five degrees, red wine at sixty-five degrees and water? Well, that's served before it turns to steam.* The new guests would laugh while the veterans cringed.

The waning intensity of the sun caused her to peel off her floppy hat and sunglasses over an hour ago. She readied herself for a last swim and stepped onto the cooling sand.

"Por favor, Bella. Don't swim. The sun — es going down. The sharks, they eat now. They think you are food," pleaded Lucia, in accented English.

"Oh my gosh, Lucia! You startled me," Bella laughed. The beach attendant must have been lurking, waiting for Bella's move toward the sea. "I like to swim with sharks. It makes me feel alive." What the matronly woman would never understand was that Bella did like to swim with sharks.

The air had matched the water temperature, making for a unique sensation as the water surrounded her legs with no cooling effect. Her careful steps negotiated a ribbon of sand edged by sharp coral until she was thigh deep. With arms stretched out in front of her, she dove into the water without a splash and disappeared. A minute later, she emerged in ripples far from shore.

Bella knew Lucia would not be looking as she surfaced. She'd be facing heavenward, crossing herself and praying. Lucia had told Bella that she prays to Saint Francis each time Bella took to the water. She would say, "That is why you live," and then add, "I pray to Mother Mary, too. I tell her to send a husband for you. One that can tame you."

It's not right to tame wild things, Bella thought as her long, hard strokes pulled her farther from shore. She turned toward the sun and bisected the crescent-shaped cove and reached her spot, far out of sight from anybody on the beach. Not over a dozen feet down sat a flat stone pressed against the coarse sand. She piked at the waist and plunged headfirst straight down. To reach the stone in the buoyant saltwater, she purged the air from her lungs and grabbed down into the water, adding a kick. As she lifted the stone, its mass held her on the bottom.

Bella had mastered her routine and slipped out of her bathing suit, placed top and bottom under the stone, and returned to the surface like a wild creature. She hurried, swimming farther into the sun, not because the darkness worried her, but she was eager to see her old friend one last time. She had never been a competitive swimmer, but she raced through the water with rhythmic precision. If the sun got too low in the sky, the crevice that suited the colorful snowflake moray would darken and her opportunity would be lost. She had been visiting the eel since her first stay and named him Frosty, more for his personality than because of the common name for the species. He was getting bigger each year and seemed friendlier as he grew up. Still, the relationship was complicated. Sometimes he would swim to her and let her pet him, and other times he would scurry into the dark when he caught sight of her.

She swam on, breathing every other stroke. Her heart pumping ever faster until she floated over the underwater outcropping and rested. It didn't take long to catch her breath, and she piked again at the waist and swam downward toward the eel's haunt.

A flash of white, yellow, and black spun in its own length. She smiled as he seemed to show off his beauty. She swam closer, and he undulated toward Bella, but then turned, leading her further down and into the dark water. Bella could not follow and surfaced, drawing a deep breath. Half the sun showed above the red horizon, and the looming darkness forced her down again. This would be her last dive, her last chance to say goodbye. She started looking in the dark shadows where she left the handsome eel. Even with her goggles, she couldn't see him. She swam farther into the twilight, hoping he would meet her halfway.

But all she saw was a blur. An underwater scream, an unrecognizable sequence of expletives and an eruption of bubbles left Bella's mouth. It was a painful bite—her punishment for thinking a wild animal could share human emotions.

It's not right to tame wild things. She chastised herself as she surfaced and raised her hand above the water to see blood dribbling out of a half dozen shallow puncture holes. At least, the wound would be clean by the time she made it back to the beach.

Bella kicked and pulled at the water harder than usual and became self-conscious about her nakedness. When she reached *her spot,* she dove and weighed herself down with the stone to retrieve her bikini. She surfaced and clumsily tied her top while she cried salty tears into salty water. She wanted her dad. His powerful arms around her would help. Her mind raced. Why did she want her dad? Gregory could hug, but she found no comfort in that thought. She doubted Gregory, her boyfriend, was the man Lucia had been praying for, the man to tame Bella.

Why did I take the ring? flooded into her head. She didn't want to end her vacation this way—no clarity and now even more tears. Confusion worked its way into anger, and she swam harder.

The flames from the torches guided her toward the resort and she was thankful she didn't have to focus on navigation. She reached the sand and looked at the painful, swollen fingers of her left hand. No blood spilled from the tiny holes left by her friend. Bella composed herself, stood straight up, and emerged out of the water like nothing had happened.

CHAPTER 4

Bremerton, Washington

NOTHING EASED HIS MIND. Since yesterday, he had dissected his parting gift to his shrink until nothing was recognizable. He even wondered if his slicing-an-artery comment might be a cry for help but decided against the idea and shifted his thoughts to dealing with the consequences of his words.

Susan had stared at him for too long. It was her job to notice things. Hank could envision her dictating her report. *He's too skinny and says the wrong things.*

A branch smacked his head as he sat up straight and a boyish smirk lit up his face. Susan might overlook things she observed, but there are words that a patient should never say to a shrink. *What was I thinking? Cutting an artery? Bleeding out?* He had crossed a line and it would alarm Susan.

And despite his hubris about being free to do what he pleased, they'd do anything they want—it was in the fine print. Nobody reads the details of an agreement before they sign. It was somewhere in the program's contract and even without it, they'd react as they please. *How many lives have they ruined?* They'll claim, "It's for his own good." Hank had seen it more than once—he'd even participated. Now he needed to shift his thinking. *I am the patient.* The vision repulsed him. His body lying in a hospital bed, feeding tube laced up his nose, down his esophagus into his stomach. Drugged out of cognition and function. *For medical reasons. For his own good.* People coming and going. One minute being treated like a sad, dying puppy and the next minute, left alone, a culture in a petri dish taking up space in the lab.

Hank's stomach growled. He wasn't sure why he had bivouacked in a greenbelt on the outskirts of town. Maybe it was because they expected it of mentally ill vets. More likely, the day's events and the four burgers, fries, and two beers at McDonald's resulted in a blood sugar crash and left him in a brain fog. Another terrible choice. His joints ached, and all his clothes were soggy. Still, the last of the stars were showing through the yew tree reaching outward above him and he felt the renewal of hope that morning brings.

He focused the entire way and didn't limp for the half-mile walk back to the McDonald's. Hank was into his third cup of coffee when he noticed the three men at the table across from him. They were laughing, and the disruption gave him the answer he had been searching for.

"Where're you guys from? I'm out now. Hospital Medic at NBK when I fell out." Hank poured on the Maine accent and slurred the familiar acronym for Naval Base Kitsap, then managed an expectant look toward each of the three sailors sitting across the aisle.

"I'm from Jacksonville and these two losers pretend they're from San Diego," said a short, blond-haired twenty-year-old.

"I'm Hank... but my friends call me Hank." He produced a quirky smile at his lame joke. Just one of many tools he had gained to disarm people. As a dock boy, he'd secured countless boats. Many of them worth millions of dollars. If the owner or captain came in sober, they might notice Hank's attention to detail and conscientious follow-through. But his smile earned him the biggest tips. Later, in ports around the world, a friendly smile spoke volumes that transcended language barriers. Then, in the service, his powerful smile softened the toughest marines and often made instant friends. To say that his smile had become part of his medic kit was not an exaggeration. It comforted injured men and women even when they were dying. But today, he used it to exploit a window of opportunity.

Jacksonville had a smartphone laying on the table in front of him. He guessed the boys from San Diego had implants. The next generation of phone technology had become popular with anyone who had the daring to get elective brain surgery.

"Hey Jacksonville, my phone died, and I need to call my boss. Mind if I use yours?"

The sailor pushed the phone over toward Hank. "Sure," he said and softly cuffed his friend on the head and said, "Can I borrow your phone? Or is your brain dead?"

"Thanks," Hank said.

"Good morning. Puget Charter & Island Sailing School. How may I direct your call?"

"Hi Joan. It's Hank."

"That's not what my screen says."

"Friend's phone. I've still got that gig, right?"

"I thought I was your only friend. Well, me and that skanky server at Doc's."

"Are you done?"

"You have no sense of humor," Joan said. "Yes, you're still on. Every other instructor has bugged me. They're all snakes. The contract specifies you and only you—creepy. Better be here by three. Trust me, you don't want to keep this client waiting. I have no clue why you're getting this job, but you better not screw it up. And if you tell anybody I told you, I'll kill you."

"Can you do me a big favor? I'll make it worth your while," Hank asked.

"What is it?"

"If anybody asks about me. Where I am, what my next job is, where I'll be—tell them I'm out of town and you don't know when I'll be back."

"That's easy. Everybody has me sworn to secrecy. One more lie won't matter." She swallowed loudly. "Creditors catching up?"

"Something like that."

"I like chocolate. And shoes."

"Chocolate it is. Thanks, Joan. See you soon."

Lost in their jokes, none of the sailors had paid any attention to Hank's conversation, and he caught Jacksonville by surprise when he slid the phone across the table. The sailor nodded and slid the phone into his pocket. Hank wondered if using someone else's phone to call Joan might be excessive but quickly decided he was all in. From now on phones were tracking devices with a calling feature and he would not leave an electronic trail for anyone to follow.

As he bused his tray, he slipped his tablet into the trash and walked out into the parking lot. He reached under the rear bumper of a short bed delivery truck and jammed his phone into a hollow. His hand came out dirty, but the phone would stay put.

He lowered the brim of his cap, pulled his neck gaiter up over his nose, and donned his hood. Sunglasses would have extinguished his face entirely, but that would only draw more attention. Confident that facial recognition would at the very least be impaired, he walked the few blocks to one of Bremerton's designated ride-sharing pickup points. There would be cameras and microphones, so he kept his head and his voice low. Even though it was illegal to bypass businesses and exchange cyber-currency peer to peer, it remained the option of choice for drivers trying to get ahead of the oppressive taxes. It only took a minute to convince a college student driving a Prius to go off the clock and take Hank home. Five minutes later, the car pulled up to the agreed upon location and the driver made a show of greeting an old friend. Hank casually played along before climbing into the front passenger seat.

CHAPTER 5

Port Townsend, Washington

THE DRIVER PULLED OVER and dropped Hank off a block away from the boarding house. He studied the neighborhood to see if anything was amiss or if a suspicious van waited for him. He approached through the side door and tested his new hip up three flights of stairs. His door had a keyhole for a skeleton key, but a key-locked deadbolt provided security. The original glass-knobbed door handle was long gone and much of the charm of the old house had faded. A solid, textured wall divided the original bedroom into two smaller ones. Inside Hank's half was a single bed with a side stand and just enough floor space to do a push-up. On three walls hung wallpaper. The repetitive print of fleur-de-lis was skillfully applied. It may have dated back to when the house was new. Someone less skilled had framed the dividing wall and painted it in a greenish-blue high gloss. They had taken no care to trim the edges where the wall pressed against the frame of a tall, double-hung window with weeping glass.

He had told Susan the truth. The room did have a view up the hill, but the tall window mostly showed fissured bark and bright green leaves of an ancient live oak. To see anything else, he had to stand on the bed and lean his head against the window frame. He would miss the window with its rain drenched appearance and the oak's many moods.

A light backpack was one advantage of having lost everything he owned. And now it was even lighter than when he abandoned his sinking boat. It was missing items, including his .45-caliber Colt 1911 pistol and his twenty-gauge flare gun. When he signed up for the program, he relinquished his second amendment rights. After the government nationalized ammunition manufacturing, made pistols illegal in cities, and enforced firearm registration, the old gun was just dead weight, anyway. Flares were a hassle to buy, and he justified the surrender, thinking he was better off without the liabilities. Still, the pistol hurt the most—it had been his great-grandfather's.

He reached under his mattress and pulled out a twelve-inch Ka-Bar knife. With a slight hesitation, he slid the immaculate blade out of its sheath. He admired it quizzically. They took his sextant but never asked if he had a knife. An oversight that worked out. He no longer needed the sextant, but found he slept better with the blade close to him. The knife slid easily into his olive drab seabag, and he spun around and saw his shaving kit. It hung from a nail driven into the door frame. He crammed it into his backpack and strapped it facing forward, against his chest. Besides some thrift store bedding and the laptop, the room was empty. With the indifferent seabag slung over his back, he bolted through the door. He turned down the stairs and with a controlled fall onto the handrails, he swung his body downward with a swinging motion that denied the stairs any significance. He covered the distance to the ground floor like a gymnast on parallel bars.

As he limped down the hill toward the waterfront, he felt exposed. There were people walking, but most drove slowly by in cars. A couple walked side by side, struggling to push two kids in one stroller up the residential sidewalk. Hank stepped to the side, letting the young family pass, and took the opportunity to scan up and down the street for anybody looking for him.

Muttering, "This is normal." A guy carrying gear bags wasn't enough of a sight in Port Townsend to attract attention. There'd be no neighborhood-watch-goody-two-shoes calling 911 and reporting him. And if a Public Safety drone buzzed by, it wouldn't be tasked to ID a vet who failed his psychological evaluation... he hoped. Soon he'd be in Canada or far out to sea. He was fairly sure nobody was looking for him yet. Even though paperwork had become lightning-fast, bureaucracy was timelessly slow. What nagged at him was the discovery he had made soon after signing up for the program.

Local law enforcement actively helped the Department of Defense with monitoring vets. They came together as a mutual response effort to act on tips and threats. Civilian law enforcement always took advantage of military hand-me-downs and paramilitary training, but the new partnership blurred the lines further. Armored vehicles worked their way into law enforcement motor pools across the country. It took a few years of methodical introduction onto the streets, but eventually routine patrols of the war machines could be found in the quietest of precincts of the safest cities. The arrangement allowed congressional representatives to help their constituents by spending federal funds on regional law enforcement. As a result, US police officers were better trained and had more light weapons and ammunition than most of the world's armies. The Military Police stretched their legs deep into veterans' affairs. It became an alliance which allowed civilian and military to combine forces, share intelligence, and work together on US soil. A handful of extremists made a fuss, but as long as the bad guys were in jail, most Americans didn't care.

Weeks ago, Hank had been one of those Americans. But when it got personal, he did his research and was rewarded with doubt and foreboding. It's impossible to un-know something, so he ignored the conflict in his mind, until now. The memory of the website called *Self Help for Dead Vets*, forced its way to the surface. After a hard day of work, on a lonely night, he logged out of the device given to him by Operation Blue Skies and let himself into Joan's office. He began his investigation on one of the charter company's laptops. Hank stayed up all night, gaining more doubt and more foreboding. The number counter on the site claimed over ten thousand cases of tragedies and the page's byline read *When America's Finest Die by Friendly Fire*. Hank made it through a hundred stories before he had read enough. Along with the sadness woven through each catastrophic account was another troubling theme. Every dead vet had been enrolled in at least one mental health program. Re-published local news accounts told about a hometown hero and how something went wrong—each story ended in the death of a veteran. "Shot by an officer responding to a domestic dispute" led the stories as the most common cause of death. "Shot by a SWAT sniper" was next and five separate accounts of veterans dying from injuries after being hit with a patrol car mopped up the statistics.

The Dead Vet site died before Hank could stomach it again. Someone with power had scrubbed it off the internet, so he did the smart thing and left it in his wake. It had been a passing curiosity and had nothing to do with him, but now, he wasn't just leaving the program but running away. And the ghost of the Dead Vet's site seemed to speak to him out of its grave. He reasoned that those types of sensational news stories always show up online. Shock-of-the-day, independent journalist, cherry-picked news to further their agenda or to make a name for themselves. Anyway, he wasn't suicidal, had no domestic partner, and would not get in front of a patrol car.

His eyes widened as a police cruiser turned onto his street and came up the road toward him. The hairs on his neck pricked outward and his heart recoiled in his chest. Sweat pushed out of his pores and sat cooling on goosebumps. Like a ship striking an iceberg head on, the chatter in his head stopped dead. One thought replaced the noise—*I'm going to hell*. It came from nowhere—he had never considered his life after death. Dead is dead. There is no hell. John Lennon said everything Hank needed to know on the subject. *No hell, no heaven—nothing!*

Acting like nothing was wrong is the best approach to minimize threats. He needed to be nonchalant. Nonchalant like that exploding guy. The horrible memory could not have come at a better time. It was as if a video clip ran through his head. A young man, still a teenager, approached the checkpoint, singing in a sweet voice, brandishing a brilliant smile and soft deer-like eyes. He strolled easily up to the barrier, vaulted over—*boom!*

A bead of sweat dripped off Hank's brow and, as if rolling in slow motion, crossed the path of his gaze and landed hard on his cheek. Now was the time to act like that young suicide bomber—not a care in the world. *Sing*. But he wanted to run, not sing. He thought, *Just fake it till you make it*. He managed a smile, and a tune flowed. Clumsy lyrics filled the awful void as the black Dodge Charger rumbled closer.

—*la, la lah*
No hell—la, la lah only sky
No cops, la, la lah
No guns, la, la lah
No bombs, la, la lah.
And no religion too..."

Hank managed a casual wave, and the cop waved back, speeding up as he passed by.

Sweat stuck cold against his shivering body. The tune playing in his head came to a stop. He glanced behind him. Not a car in sight. Hank's expression of triumph ended before it formed. He spoke without conviction. "I am going to hell."

CHAPTER 6

Port Townsend, Washington

HANK PULLED OPEN THE heavy wooden door with a large porthole window and walked in. Joan kept the office ten degrees hotter than normal humans and the ever-present dampness assaulted him as he set down his gear and stripped off the jacket. Expansive north-facing windows overlooked the marina. Yellow cedar logs passed through the floor and rose into the vaulted ceiling where oversized bolts held a network of rough-hewn support beams. Varnished tongue and groove trim and overstuffed leather seating softened the open space. A large sign hung behind Joan's reception desk, as if guarding the back offices. *Puget Charter & Island Sailing School* was spelled out in raised lettering, forming a circle around an artist's rendition of a sailboat and a sunset. The sign said, *est. 2001*. Hank imagined nothing had changed since the grand opening except wear and tear. The neutral-toned Berber carpet had become proof of Pareto's principle—twenty percent of the carpet gets eighty percent of the wear. He followed the path to Joan's desk, where she sat with an old-fashioned headset strapped to her head.

"Hi, Joan. Are you on the phone?"

"No, Hank. Where's my chocolate?"

"I thought you were counting on a new pair of shoes. I've got these great sandals and I hear they're all the rage," Hank quipped as he tossed two Hershey Hugs toward her.

"Such a big spender," she said, unwrapping both. "You got these next door at the brokerage."

Hank bent forward and emphasized each word. "There. Are. No. Secrets. Around. Here."

"Hank. Shut up. You promised not to tell. I could lose my job."

"You're the owner of the company. Remember?"

"I'm *one* of the owners," she corrected.

"Well, you're the only owner I've ever met."

"Whatever. Talk about secrets. What's yours all about?" Joan asked.

"I'd rather not say."

"Unacceptable. Lay it out or I'll fire you."

"I'm leaving that program I'm in."

She shook her head and said, "It's about time. It's not like you're crazy." She screwed up her face as if she wished she could take back her words. "I mean, a program like that isn't a good fit for someone like you."

"Well, I had my face-to-face with the shrink, and I blew it. I couldn't keep my big mouth shut. Let's just say, I don't think they'll let me out of the program anytime soon."

"Oh, no. What in the world did you say?"

"Remember how I told you I have a habit of saying the wrong thing around women?"

"Yes. But you do a good job around here."

"Well, I've matured a lot." He forced an insincere grin. "Remember I told you about my old girlfriend, Pam? How it was serious, and I even wondered if she was the one?"

"Yeah, the one that loved you in uniform."

Hank nodded and said, "I never told you how it ended."

Joan leaned forward in her chair.

"She took me home to meet the parents. The weekend had gone well. The two-hour drive back was already twice that because of traffic." He spoke faster, reeling Joan in a little closer. "Pam had been talking nonstop about how wonderful her parents were and how much they liked me, all about how we needed to get away more, and on and on, blah blah blah—I tuned her out." He put his hands up to cover his ears and stared at Joan a moment too long, then continued, "She stopped talking." His hands dropped and his eyes flashed wide. "I looked over at her to see if she was okay. She gave me an evil stare. I mean evil, like it made my skin crawl." Hank shivered and continued, "*Well?*" That was all she said. *Well?* Like I'm supposed to read her mind. I said, "Well what?"

"Since then, I've had time to think. My conclusion: she was expecting me to tell her how much I liked her parents or what a fun weekend it was or we should get away more often. But none of those things came to mind." He fell quiet.

"Oh, for God's sake, Hank. What did you say?"

"I said, 'Sometimes I regret being nice.'"

Joan hiccupped a laugh and then became serious. "No, you didn't! How could you?"

"Yep, that's the only thing I came up with. She didn't say another word for the rest of the drive. I carried her bags up to the door. Then she told me I was an asshole and to never call her again."

Hank placed one hand on her desk, leaned down, and thoughtfully stroked his dimpled chin with the other. "Since that time, I've grown." He paused, "You know what I've learned?"

"What?" Joan asked.

Hank matched her serious expression and said, "Sometimes I regret being nice."

Joan bust out laughing, then faked anger and heaved herself from behind the desk with surprising agility. Hank turned and beat it for the door saying, "I'll be back."

It surprised him how easily Joan could be distracted. Then he realized the personal dread he'd felt only an hour before was gone. His pace slowed as he descended the marina's main ramp. He looked down and pulled up his hood. A two-wheeled cart waited at the bottom of the ramp, and he put his gear into it and pushed it as he casually walked between the boats tied up in their slips. Nobody was around, but he heard a motor in the distance and became more aware of his surroundings with each step.

"Stay cool, it's okay. Breathe," he said quietly. "Hell is what you make it." Hank exhaled deeply and thought, *I wonder if that's true.*

CHAPTER 7

Port Townsend, Washington

OSPREY FLOATED HIGH ABOVE her red waterline marking. Tied up on the opposite side of the marina, the sturdy thirty-eight-foot double-ender had been christened the year Hank was born. Benjamin picked her up in Hong Kong as a retirement present for himself. A few years later, he picked up Kiki in Copenhagen. They hadn't lived on land since. Hank needed to say goodbye to his cruising friends and *Osprey* would be a safe place to spill minutes. Maybe he'd even get lucky.

"Ahoy *Osprey*."

Benjamin eased himself out of the companionway and responded with a hardy, "Hank my man. How's it hanging? Come-aboard." Hank had never asked but judging by his sea stories and history as an investment banker, his friend must be over seventy, but could pass for a weathered fifty-year-old. His height almost matched Hank's six-foot two-inches, but he stood somewhat stooped. A beard of grey and a full head of straight dark brown hair added to the curious mystery of the man's age. Even the salt and pepper transition between beard and hair gave no hints.

Kiki popped her head out next. She raced her fingers through her pixie hairstyle, squinted in the sunlight, and zipped up her ever-present fleece jacket. Half the size of Benjamin and possibly half his age, she sprung onto the built-in bench like a gymnast and grabbed Benjamin's arm to steady herself.

"We're just about to crack open a cask of rum. You're just in time." Benjamin said with a large lingering smile of perfect, bright white teeth. His freckled companion shook her head in agreement.

Benjamin reached his muscular, tattooed arm toward Hank for a handshake. Hank grabbed it, enjoying the old-fashioned gesture. Kiki dove in for a quick hug. It was the same every time they met. Even if he climbed on board a few times a day, they were consistent in their desire to greet him with open arms and they were always *cracking open a cask of rum*.

"Thanks, but I've got to work. Unless you're leaving for Alaska in the next few hours? Then I'll have a drink and request you carry me up to where you clear Canadian customs... or better yet, just before."

"Maybe in a few days. Her bottom's getting dirty, sitting here in the marina." Benjamin said, glancing down at Kiki.

She swatted him and looked at Hank. "He's talking about *Osprey*."

"What did you think I was talking about?" Benjamin asked Kiki with a sly grin. Then, turning his attention to Hank, "Before customs?"

"I'm leaving. Canada's my next stop. Figure I can get a job as a hand. Ship or yacht, I don't care."

"Why not just post it here or Port Angeles?" Benjamin asked.

"I have my reasons."

Kiki took the cue and changed the subject. "Oh, Hank, we'll miss you around here. Can we help?

"Actually, I was hoping you could do something for me." He dug into his bag and pulled out a pair of Nikon binoculars and a handheld VHF radio. "I could use cash."

"That's never a good thing. You'd be lucky to get half their value negotiating like that," Benjamin remarked.

"Half is fine."

Kiki slipped down the companionway and returned, handing Benjamin a purple bag with a gold string closure. She said, "I'm going down to put on some rice." She wrapped her arms around Hank and gave him a big hug. "Goodbyes aren't my thing." Then stretched up and gave him a peck on the cheek. She turned to Benjamin and said, "Be generous."

CHAPTER 8

Flight to Singapore

THE MAN SITTING NEXT to Bella appeared nervous. The small plane with its high wing and turboprop might have seemed like an aviation throwback to someone accustomed to more civilized vacations, but the workhorse reminded Bella of childhood travels with her family. Its engines thundered as it pulled the plane along the cracked tarmac of the island's single runway. Inside the plane, the seating, designed for the average world traveler, did not fit the man next to her, and he leaned toward the aisle.

The man wore a white, short-sleeved shirt tucked into long pants with a dark necktie. She had seen Mormon missionaries throughout the islands dressed like that, but he was alone, had no name tag, and must have been close to her father's age. As the plane continued its climb through the spotty puffs of clouds, the air conditioning kept up, but the man slipped off his tie, loosened his collar, and wiped the sweat off his forehead.

Bella offered a distraction. "What brought you to the island?"

The man seemed relieved to turn his attention toward Bella. He said, "Energy. The old-fashioned kind. Most people can't conceive it, but diesel generators power the electrical grid on this island."

She had grown up in the Pacific so the news didn't surprise her, but he would be disappointed if she shut down the conversation so soon. She asked, "Fossil fuel?"

"Yes, but we're making tremendous changes. The efficiencies are improving and that means less dependency on fuel shipments. Every household is seeing a difference in their power bill because the cost per kilowatt hour keeps dropping. That will allow the people to improve their lives in meaningful ways."

Bella grasped that this man was a missionary—only his greater power came from electricity. She understood the personality of the passionate engineer. Her father had those traits. She smiled, nodded, and asked a few questions. The plane veered around a second thunderhead and shook as the pilot corrected for the turbulence. While the other passengers appeared to get more agitated, the man turned pale and went silent. There was nothing she could do to help him, so she shifted her attention out the window.

A nap would help pass the time and delay the inevitable task of checking her messages. She had slept through much worse and leaned her head against the shuttered window. Her left hand drew her attention. She would have to remember to cover the tiny red teeth marks and swollen fingers. No ring would slide onto her ring finger for quite a while. She smiled. Gregory expected an answer but announcing she couldn't marry him because the ring won't fit was stupid. No, was the answer. It had always been the answer. She had hoped two weeks away would reveal the right strategy, but she had to confess, it hadn't helped.

When you bump into an old friend, it's natural to get together to catch up, so when Gregory insisted they go out, she agreed. He had been a boy who came with his father to buy fish for the Tokyo market. Somehow, he had grown into a handsome, well-dressed man with certain charms. As children, they played together, a rare distraction in her isolated home. But a couple of years later, the last time they visited, she was disappointed. The boy had become a sullen teenager who never took his attention from his smartphone. Bella accepted she was a skinny eleven-year-old girl and got on with her schoolwork. She forgot about him until the day he called her name on the street. She agreed to his offer for dinner but didn't even change out of her work clothes, expecting to be home early. Gregory had other ideas. He picked her up in a limousine and whisked her off to a restaurant without menus. They finished their glass of port around ten, and Gregory insisted they have just one dance before he took her home.

On the way through the restaurant's bar, she learned that her old childhood friend was overprotective. A guy approached her, showing off to friends. "Do you have a name? Or can I call you mine?" He laughed, and Bella ignored him. Gregory hit the guy so fast, all Bella saw was the guy down on the floor. Gregory grabbed her by the arm and led her off to the waiting limo. She told him he overreacted, he apologized to her and had been a perfect gentleman since.

Whenever business brought him to Singapore, they would meet up and go out. It wasn't long before he gave up excuses to visit the city and moved there. He bought a condo in a much nicer area, but it was still close to Bella's small apartment. At first, it made her uncomfortable, but he maintained a busy schedule and traveled often. Besides, he was fun to be around—most of the time. Gregory wanted things to get serious at a rate that Bella wasn't comfortable with. She had friends and her work and also traveled a great deal, but they enjoyed their time together. This was her first romantic relationship that had lasted. Even though she had never said the words "I love you," she had thought she did. Still, he often made her crazy and the more they saw each other, the worse it was. To his credit, somehow, he grasped the exact moment she needed space and would leave on business for a week or longer. When he left, Bella's thoughts tormented her with questions like, *Can this be the right guy? Why didn't he call? Is this what it's like to be in love?*

Gregory had never spoken of love, but he talked about their future together. To Bella, the future seemed like a harmless topic. She knew God took care of such things, so Bella let him dream out loud and let him plan all their dates. Inevitably, the things he insisted they do far exceeded the range of her paychecks. Allowing him to lead made it easier, and she never worried about bumping into friends or coworkers. The exclusive clubs, restaurants, and events gave her the opportunity to wear the stunning clothes and the jewelry he would bring her. None of it fit her thrifty lifestyle as a marine biologist, and while she was uncomfortable at first, the contrast thrilled her. It didn't take long for her to expect the notice of people on the street, and she enjoyed the attention of the beautiful and powerful people in Gregory's circle of friends. But she also loved getting back to her tiny apartment and kicking off her high heels. The routine of slipping into cotton pajamas and sharing the details of the evening with her roommate, Zoe, had become as fun as any of the charity galas or dance clubs.

Bella wondered if Zoe had a better read on her relationship than she did. She challenged, "Bella, you're in love. Admit it." She had always sorted her emotions out herself, so why would she need to rely on Zoe to know if she was in love? But this was uncharted territory. Gregory and their relationship confused her, but her emotions were real, and they troubled her.

Often, Gregory made things harder with his surprises. A conversation she had replayed a hundred times looped through her mind as the hum of the plane lulled her.

"I've gone to see your father."

"You what?"

Gregory kissed her on the right cheek. "That's from your father."

Shivers ran down her spine as she thought, *This isn't right.* She repeated, "You what?"

"Your father gave me his blessing. He reminded me that our fathers had been best friends. That he'd be honored to have me as a son." Gregory laughed, like a gull swooping down after breaking a clam onto the rocks. "However, he insisted we do the church thing together and take our time."

Stunned, Bella said, "The church thing?"

"Sure. It's important to your father. It makes sense. I'll pick you up tomorrow, and we'll go to church together."

The minute Gregory left she called her dad. "What were you thinking?"

He said, "Hola Bella. Es bueno saber de ti. Ha sido demasiado largo."

"Dad, don't give me that. It doesn't work on me anymore. I'm twenty-five, not five," Bella asserted. "What did you tell Gregory?"

"It was nice to see him. He reminds me of his father."

"Dad, don't change the subject. Talk!"

"He told me that the two of you were in love. You'd been dating for a year and wanted to get married. He assured me he was the right man for you." Bella's father cleared his throat and continued, "His Japanese roots made him respect order and how important it is to honor tradition. Then he asked for my permission to pursue you and win your heart for marriage." He paused and added, "Actually, I just added the last bit. Isn't that more romantic?" He was quiet for a moment. "This is all new Bella. Your mother and I eloped."

Exasperated, Bella said, "Oh, Dad. I'll get even with you later. What was 'the church thing?'"

Her father replied, "What church thing?"

"Gregory told me you said we needed to do 'the church thing' together."

"Oh, I asked him if he knew Yeshua."

Bella never stayed mad at her dad for long. A smile crossed her face. "You're kidding me."

"I figured that was an excellent test. Only a crazy believer would know that's what we call Jesus."

"You tested him? What did he say?"

"Your boyfriend said, 'No. Should I?'"

"I told him he should and that he's the leader of your church. I also told him that if he attended church with you, he'd probably meet him."

Bella laughed. "Dad, you are special, but did you tell him he could marry me?"

"I explained, 'Bella is her own woman with her own mind and her own life.' Then said, 'Tradition is great, but the most important thing is that you do things right.' I reminded him that more than anything he needs to respect you."

"You're the best dad ever. And Gregory is in for a surprise when he meets Yeshua. I'm taking him to church tomorrow. Good night. What time is it there?"

"Three in the morning. A fine time to catch up. Dios te bendiga."

"God bless you, too, Dad. Que duermas con los ángelos."

Three months had passed since that conversation with her father, but it still brought on a smile... a sleepy smile. Bella had become conditioned to daily naps while on her vacation. Nobody else on the plane was dozing. A large woman in a colorful muumuu up one row yelled out with surprise each time the plane bucked. Bella wondered if the surprise would get old, but she fell asleep too hard to find out.

When she woke, her head was on the shoulder of the stranger. He was more embarrassed than she was. This time, he started the conversation. "How did you sleep through all that? Do you fly these small planes often?"

"Way too often," she replied.

The plane was in a slow, smooth descent. Bella couldn't put it off any longer and turned her attention to her text messages.

35

CHAPTER 9

Changi Airport, Singapore

"GREGORY, I CANNOT MARRY you. I'm not ready. I'm sorry." The words came out but sounded uncertain. In the mirror, Bella saw an All Nippon Airways flight attendant walk past. She was young, not over twenty, but she looked fourteen. The girl averted her eyes, covered her mouth with her hand and giggled, then closed herself into a washroom stall. Bella studied herself in the mirror. Anybody else would see a young woman in vibrant health, but there were signs of a lifetime in the sun. Her entire face contorted as she squinted, forcing her subtle smile lines around her eyes into furrows. She followed with a big stupid smile, exposing straight, white teeth. Not Hollywood perfect but close. She relaxed, and the parts of her face resumed their place. Bella laughed and spoke up in a theatrical tone, plenty loud enough for the girl to hear, "Gregory, I must marry you. I'm not getting any younger." She heard another giggle as she exited the washroom.

She walked to an empty chair and called her roommate. "Hi, Zoe. I just landed."

"How was the Stone Age? Did you meet any swell guys reading *Little House on the Prairie*?"

Bella answered, "It's great to hear your voice, too. I'm still in the concourse. I need space from Gregory. Airport security might have to keep him away."

"Really? You've had two weeks off the planet, and you need *space*? Plus, I might remind you he's rich… and handsome… and treats you like a goddess… and did I say he's rich?"

"It was all scheduled for tomorrow. I'd meet him at church and then his choice for brunch. Right now, I'm a mess and have nothing to wear. All my text messages are from him." Bella recited with disdain, "'I'll meet you at the airport.' 'I need to talk to you.' 'I have to leave for Tokyo early.' 'Reservations at Corner House…'"

Zoe interrupted, "Buy what you need. They've got a million shops there. Use that card he gave you. Did you tell him you arrived?"

"Are you kidding? I think he watched my plane land. The minute the wheels touched the ground he texted, 'I'll meet you in baggage.'"

"Oh, I wish I had a fiancé that would meet me at the airport and take me to the most romantic restaurant in the city."

"He's not my fiancé."

"Come on, Bella. Please, show me the ring again. You don't have to put it on. I just need a glimpse. Face it, two karats in a ring like that? It's pure diamond porn. You're so lucky."

"Zoe, I know I should have rejected him when he asked. I thought I did, but when he said, 'Please, take the ring and think about it…' Well, it sounded reasonable." Bella slouched onto the uncomfortable bench, oblivious to the growing number of people around her. "I can't believe I took it."

"Bell, there is another option."

"I'm all ears."

"Just say yes."

Bella chided her roommate. "You don't know what you're talking about. Now stop being a pest and help me. I'm out of my depth. What do I say? I don't want to hurt his feelings, but he's just not the right guy."

"Okay, you will regret this for the rest of your life, but this is what you need to do…"

Bella found a wall to lean against in the busy terminal and typed. *I'm exhausted after my flight. Feeling terrible. I've just got to go home and sleep.*

A video call from Gregory came in. Zoe said he would do that. Maybe she knew what she was talking about. Bella put on a tired face and tried to appear as ugly as possible. Zoe told her to "try ugly" and added, "It won't work. You're the girl who can puke on a date and the guy would tell his friends how cute you were."

Bella answered, placing the phone low and too close. "Hi, I have nothing but carry-on. I'll meet you at Burger King on level one." She hung up.

Bella stayed glued to her seat when Gregory walked into the fast-food eatery. A short man with a tray bumped past Bella's well-dressed suitor. Gregory scowled at the man, who smiled and offered his apology in a language Bella didn't recognize. A mask strapped across her mouth and nose, and her hand on her beach bag, would have said enough, but she motioned for him to have a seat on the other side of the table. The usual kiss, even a chaste one, would not happen. "If I'm sick, it's better you keep your distance." She wore the ugliest oversized t-shirt she could buy at the last minute. It was Kelly green with a picture of a cat and what looked like snowflakes. To top it off, she had bought a truck driver hat and covered up the hair he loved.

Gregory looked shocked. He sat down across from her and said, "Oh, Bella, you look awful. Do you need to see a doctor?"

Zoe didn't tell her to expect that, but it made her deceit easier. "Gregory, can you get me a Sprite? It might help my stomach."

"Are you sure? Don't you just want to get out of here? My Ferrari is with the valet. All I have to do is ring them."

Zoe's script was crumbling. Everything that happened from this point forward was her own responsibility. Zoe had said, "No matter what happens, remember two things. Give him back the ring and don't leave the airport with him." Bella could do that. Just two things.

"Gregory, thanks for coming to help me. I need a Sprite—and a ton of ice. Please, just get that for me while I find a washroom. Do you mind?"

She struggled just enough to get out of her seat. Gregory watched as she grabbed her stomach. He stood helplessly, and she offered a side-hug. "Hurry now. That line's getting longer." She gave Gregory a weak smile as he joined the queue.

"Zoe. I did it."

Zoe asked, "Did what?"

"I left Gregory."

"Already! How did you pull that off?"

"Sent him to buy a Sprite and walked off."

"You're kidding me."

Bella's voice lowered. "Now I really feel sick. I'm just going to get a flight out of here."

Zoe inquired, "What about the ring?"

The blood drained out of Bella's face. "I slipped it into his jacket pocket when I hugged him."

"Oh, no." Zoe's voice turned serious. "Oh, dear, Bella. What were you thinking?"

A tear flowed down Bella's cheek. "He'll be so pissed." She wiped her face with the oversized sleeve of the t-shirt. "I'm going back. I can take my time and do it right. He's probably still in line." She drew in a great breath and exhaled confidence. "I've got to go. I'll call you."

She wasn't wearing any makeup but needed to make sure she didn't look horrible. Bella pulled off her mask and smiled into a mirror in a display case. She took off the hat, freeing her hair to drop across her shoulders and halfway down her back, and pushed the hat into her beach bag. She tossed the ugly green t-shirt into a nearby trash can, revealing her favorite travel blouse, a beige sleeveless top. Bella renewed her posture, shoulders back, chest out, chin up, and in just a few strides, she felt better and maneuvered to the food court.

A sense of relief washed over her. She had come close to ending not only their romance but also their friendship. Now she knew what she must do. She would say she would not marry him but would do it respectfully. As she got closer, she wondered if he might still be in line. It hadn't been that long. Her dad was right. *Take your time and do things right.* She had almost wrecked everything. But now she had time, and a genuine smile crossed her face.

A vibration transmitted through her hip pocket, but she ignored it. She had no time to look at messages. She needed to get to Gregory. The long line was still there, but he was not. All the tables were full, and Gregory was gone. A gray-haired custodian mopped up spilled liquid and was shoeing ice cubes into a dustpan. Bella's heart raced as she looked at the text.

It said, *You'll regret this!*

CHAPTER 10

Port Townsend, Washington

"Hɪ, Jo—" Hᴀɴᴋ sᴛᴏᴘᴘᴇᴅ mid-sentence when Joan held up her index finger with a long, manicured nail. He waited a minute as she finished her conversation and tapped her headset.

She smiled at Hank and cleared her throat. With an official tone, "The clients are running late. It seems the rolling protest in Seattle inconvenienced them. Still, their person requests you be available at the designated time. Perhaps, they can make it up in transit."

"Wow, you can talk hoity-toity," Hank teased. Then he spoke with a highbrow Bostonian accent. "May I ask... have there been any inquiries? You know, pertaining to Mr. Henry Maximilian Gunn?" He chuckled, dropped the accent, and said, "I added in the fancy middle name just for fun. What do you think?"

"Well, Max, nobody in uniform has swung by. No calls either, but I'm still here for another hour. Do you want a heads up if anybody is snooping?"

"No, don't bother. I won't be near my phone."

She gave him a sideways look and said, "Come on, Hank. What's with the intrigue? You haven't given me a direct answer all day."

"It's nothing. I said the wrong thing to the wrong person."

"What's new?" Joan giggled. "I don't know how you've survived so long..." Her face flushed red and flattened in embarrassment. She looked like she'd cry with her next breath. "Oh, I'm sorry Hank. I'm so stupid. I meant..."

"Joan, it's okay. I'm the one that's stupid for being paranoid." He lightened the mood with a smile and pushed a postcard onto her desk. "Can you mail this? It's for my mom. You can read it."

She parked a finger onto the postcard picture of Mount Rainier and dragged it toward her. "What, no stamp?"

"Take it out of my paycheck."

"It's strange, Hank. I'd like to say giving you this job was an act of kindness. The senior staff always gets the plum jobs and low man... well, not so much. I had Charles listed for this spot, but the customer insisted their instructor be you. You just finished training and I haven't even put your bio up on the website." Joan held up her index finger. "It's a call. I'll text you the return ticket." Her eyes got big. "They're flying you back from Victoria." Then she turned away, tapped her ear, and answered the call.

Hank decided his fear of being apprehended by the authorities was misplaced. Joan inadvertently reminded him he wouldn't be getting any texts. When they looked for him, they would track his phone. *Good luck with that*, he thought, but decided it would be prudent to keep his hood up and stay calm. He strolled onto the sleepy floating dock where he knew all the cameras and the one blind spot they didn't show. Once he settled down and accepted he might have to wait, he allowed himself to enjoy the soft rocking motion. Gentle ripples telegraphed restrained power from the sea, separated only by a man-made breakwater. As far back as he could remember, hanging out around water among boats had been a confusing balance of love and hate. Water was at the center of his birthright. Like most passions, it had two sides, both peaks—great joy and tremendous sorrow.

Hank's childhood fascination with his ancestry had been fleeting, but he learned he had come from a long line of water people. His namesake, Henry James Gunn, sailed from Scotland to the Colonies and settled in Cape Porpoise on the rugged Maine coast. The result of a 1631 law determined to rid the New World of immorality brought the first Hank Gunn and his heathen adulteress, Maggie, into the public square. The church recorded ten lashes, a nominal fine, and the couple's marriage. But the faith didn't run true because it took two hundred years for the next relation to show up in the church records—as the new minister. Hank's uncle summed it up by saying, "Some of our kin were preachers and drunks, but the only respectable Gunns have been lobstermen."

Hank had wanted to be a lobsterman like his uncle and his dad. It might have been his destiny, but fate caused him to throw over that dream in an instant. Like a lightning strike alters a tree, the family's legacy and his own future diverged in the blink of an eye.

From the stories and what little he remembered, his parents were in love. His mom worked at the hospital and his dad maintained a fast and reliable lobster boat. Only like a child could, Hank helped his father. On nice days, they'd pull traps, but if the water was rough, he helped his dad build commissioned wooden boats. In those good years, the young, hardworking family did well, and his father even negotiated pre-payment for a lifetime slip at the marina. But a lifetime can be short.

The Coast Guard saved the boat before grounding onto rocks, but they never found his father's body. Wreaths were cast into the outgoing tide and Hank's aunt and uncle bought the boat. A real estate developer gobbled up the house and twenty acres of hard rock coastline a couple of years later. At first, his mom tried to be there for him, but she became distant the more she drank.

His early success in elementary school gave way to bad behavior as he grew into his teen years. He often argued with other boys and one day it escalated—pushing, wrestling, and then Hank threw a punch that ended the fight. Later that day, the police report ignored the adolescent quarrel and focused on Henry James Gunn and the teacher he slugged. It was a single, crunching punch to the wrong face. Hank watched in horror as her eyes fluttered and rolled back into her head, blood gushed out of her nose, and she slumped to the floor. Time froze. He stood over her unconscious body, helpless, shaking, his own hand bleeding, sliced from the teacher's nose piercing. Tears rolled out of his distressed eyes. She didn't press charges, but Hank found himself expelled from school. Townspeople excused him and said, "The boy's hormones kicked in." Or "It's the mother's fault." But Hank took full blame, and his apologies were sincere. The teacher ignored the union's recommendation for a restraining order, and soon, the young woman had forgiven him.

Unlike his ancestors, there was no whipping, no fines, and no ceremony that could make it right with the establishment. Hank could never go back to public school, so his mother declared him a homeschooler, poured a drink, and left him alone. He learned to keep his head low, look after himself, and excel at World of Warcraft. But even Maine winters ended, and Hank got his first actual job as a dock boy. The next year he served as crew on a couple of southbound boats while his peers sat in classrooms. Flirting with the sea came easy, and at seventeen he waved goodbye to his mother and sailed out of Kittery, Maine on a restored sixty-foot sloop.

The boat started with a working crew of five, but three bailed at the first stop and left Hank and Oscar with the boat's idiosyncratic owner. After far too long looking for hands, the duo convinced the owner that the two of them could handle the sloop. At first, the owner was reluctant, but it soon became clear Hank and Oscar worked flawlessly together and were more than capable of the requirements of maintaining, navigating, and handling the classic sailboat. Their cruise was going flawlessly until the COVID-19 pandemic swept the world. Time in quarantine added a couple weeks to their stays at some ports and many countries simply forbade them from entering territorial waters entirely. Rationing food and water and even fuel became commonplace and hardships negotiating regulations, both real and imagined, took its toll on the vessel's human cargo as well. A few months shy of two years, the sloop had rounded the earth's circumference and landed at the Port of Charleston. The young men collected their pay, said goodbye to the sloop's smiling owner, locked arms, and stepped off the boat at the same time. The sloop completed its journey as a broken mess, but Hank and Oscar had grown into men.

Hank called his mother at her new place in Florida, and a guy named Mario answered. In a resonant smoker's voice Mario said, "So, you're Hank." Catching his breath, he continued, "I shacked up with your mom over a year ago. In that whole time, you never even bothered to call. What type of little shit treats his mother like that? I'll get her."

He told his mother he loved her and promptly caught up with Oscar at the Navy recruiter. They agreed they would do everything in their power to stick together, but soon found out that they had no power at all. In Hank's eight years in the Navy, they only managed to see each other once—a beer at the San Diego airport in January, 2025. Fortunately, when it came time for Oscar to get married, Hank was a freshly minted civilian and made time to join Oscar's huge family and be his best man.

A small sports fishing boat motored past, causing the dock to rise and catch against its stops and fall and catch again. The familiar motion drew his mind further back. Intractable memories flooded in with so much of his childhood spent hanging out around the docks where his family tied up their boats. He missed the texture of damp, weathered wood with soft splintered edges, fuzzy against his feet and knees and rough on his forearms. The resinous smell of creosote mingled with diesel and the sweet fog of engine exhaust was like incense to him—from a faraway time. Opalescent swirls of oil spun in his head, but now a uniform plastic tread secured into a rigid aluminum frame made up this dock. Clean and modern, the dock floated against unshakable concrete pilings.

The old docks and wharves were too appealing for the greedy politicians armed with eminent domain. Activists piled on. Lobster boats were too dirty, traps and lines too reckless. His aunt and uncle struggled until punitive regulations squeezed all profit out of their tiny family business. The small lobster fishers disappeared. There was no sense getting upset over it—not now. The gulls, noisy and quarrelsome and leaving their messes, seemed all too familiar. He closed his eyes and smiled, enjoying the afternoon sun and the lapping of water. Things changed. It all ebbed and flowed like the tide.

He let his seabag drop and scanned past the high seawall for his ride. The tops of a few small sailboats could be seen over the breakwater, but nothing resembling the blue water sailing yacht coming to get him. He checked his watch. Still early. The Wakefield chronograph had been a gift from a friend of his father's.

The friend had commissioned a boat that sat unfinished in the shop. At first, Hank went to Spark, the Newick designed trimaran, for a connection to his dad. He even slept in her single berth on summer weekends. But he lost interest by the time the owner towed the boat away a year or two later. The ramrod straight man had a trimmed gray beard and thin wavy hair. He waited for Hank to show up after school to tell him a couple stories about his dad. When the man finished talking, he handed Hank a box, along with a wink and a firm handshake. In the box, Hank found the watch and a handwritten note which read,

Set your course by the stars, not by the lights of every passing ship. - Omar Bradley
I hope you catch up with me someday. I'll teach you how to be a pirate.
May God's love be with you,

Thomas Allen Campbell (Captain Tom)
Psalm 86:15

Hank slid the loose watch back and forth along his forearm a few times and mused, *Someday maybe I'll see what that verse says.*

Like a bad song repeating in his head the words, *Don't run if you can walk. Don't walk if you can stand. Don't stand if you can sit. Don't sit if you can lie down.* He hated most of the sayings and mantras of his military service, but they kept surfacing. He resisted the sensible urge to sit and stood there next to his bag, swaying to the motion. The rhythmic knocking against the pilings calmed him. He gazed out over the water, glad that some things never change. He scanned the view over the seawall and saw nothing coming his way. The warmth of the sun convinced him to sit down and soon the stirring water forced him to prop his head against his gear.

CHAPTER 11

Port Townsend, Washington

A POWERFUL RUMBLING WOKE him from a dead sleep. Hank rubbed his neck and wiped the spit from the corner of his mouth. He looked over to see a boat coming in way too fast. With its low profile and sturdy aluminum hull, he recognized the rapidly approaching vessel at once. A Defender-class boat, like the ones he was used to in the Navy. But this one was very different. It ran with larger twin 350-horsepower engines and was missing the 50-caliber machine gun that would traditionally grace its bow. And rather than the lights and lettering of law enforcement or the departmental seals or trademarked color scheme of a governmental agency, it was painted in the ubiquitous colors of the pleasure craft found in the Puget Sound: white with blue pinstripes. Yet, despite all that, the crew clearly broadcasted a military image. They weren't out for a pleasant, little cruise. This was serious business for them. So when the floating dock shook under Hank's feet as the bow made contact and the two crew members off-loaded, he stood to the side, not bothering to offer a hand with the line. He understood these men, and they didn't need or want his help.

The short, muscular man closest to Hank approached with a device in his left hand. He glanced at the screen, rolled his eyes, and laughed. When he spoke, the deep south came out. He may have strayed far from home, but his rich accent had gone nowhere. "Looks like y'all could use a decent meal, corpsman." He nodded his head, "I'm Willy."

"The name's Hank."

Willy faked a glance at the screen again and said, "Looks like you're one of us. On the green side. Ya know what I say..."

Hank did know. It was another verbal cascade that rose from his past life. Hank reluctantly mouthed the words along with Willy.

"Once a Marine, always a Marine."

Willy was just being nice—no swell of pride. Every Marine Hank had known harbored a respect for any Navy corpsmen that earned the right to wear the green uniform of the Marines. It was corpsmen that put them back together when they were leaking blood into the sand. But Hank didn't feel like a Marine. Not anymore.

Willy made a fist with his thumb pumping over his shoulder. "They don't have names." His smile disappeared, and his command voice told Hank that the pleasantries were over. "Were you informed this job requires a high level of security?"

"They told me I should expect scrutiny and to show discretion," Hank replied as he suppressed a conditioned, "sir."

Hank tried to keep his body relaxed. The last time he stood at attention, they discharged him from the Navy. Now he hated himself, or at least hated the conditioned reflex that caused him to stand like an exclamation point in front of this man.

Willy lifted the pad and took a picture. "I'll need a profile shot. Turn to the side." Willy ran down a memorized checklist. "What is your full name?"

"Henry James Gunn."

"What is your age?"

"Twenty-eight,"

"What month were you born?"

"May."

"What day?"

"The twelfth."

"What city were you born?"

"Kennebunkport, Maine."

"Do you have any idea who you'll be working for?"

"No."

A long silence followed, then Willy pried, "No? You don't know who hired you to be their private sailing instructor?"

"No, sir," Hank hated himself. Not for lying, but for saying, "sir." He took a deep breath and relaxed. His posture eased, and he chuckled, realizing that civilians don't have to answer stupid questions if they don't want. "Are we done?" Hank asked.

Willy replied, "Only if you want to walk off this dock and leave behind a nice payout at the end of an easy job." Willy smiled and continued. "It's up to you, *sir*."

Hank had to laugh at the "sir" coming back to him. Willy has been here before, but this was unfamiliar territory for him. The mood relaxed and Hank asked, "How many more questions?"

"Just two."

"Okay," Hank agreed.

"Has anybody approached you asking questions about the job you are about to do?"

"No," Hank answered.

"Is there anything on your person or in your gear you've had for less than twenty-four hours?"

"No."

"Has anybody given you anything in the last day?"

"You said only two more questions."

"It's a subcategory question. You can walk if you're too proud to answer a subcategory question," Willy said.

"Okay, I get your point."

"Has anybody given you any gifts?"

"No."

"Any food?"

"No."

"Any mobile device?"

"No. Listen, I get the idea. Do you have to ask about every possibility?"

"Yep," Willy said, "Have you made or noticed any changes to your computer, phone, or mobile device or loaded new apps in the last twenty-four hours?"

"No. I give up! Still subcategory questions?"

"Yep. Has anybody given you a package, either large or small, in the last twenty-four hours?"

"No!"

"We're done. You lied when I asked if you knew who you'd be working for." Willy turned the pad to face Hank, revealing a spike on a graph. A squiggly line traveled through green except for where it spiked past the yellow and went well into the red section of the screen. "Want me to replay it?"

"No. It's true. I guess they thought I should know I'd be hanging out with a billionaire. You know, so I'd take a shower and bring a fresh change of clothes," Hank admitted. Then added, "Does this mean I don't get the job?"

Willy turned away and said, "Hey, No-Name. Are you done?"

He shifted his attention to the other man, who stood over Hank's seabag with a handheld device. After Willy gave him a nod, he opened it, plunged his hand in and retrieved the large Ka-Bar knife suspended between his thumb and forefinger and said, "It's clear."

Willy turned his pad toward Hank again and said, "You've got the job — if you still want it."

A white van backed into the loading area at the top of the dock's ramp. Only a chain link fence and fifty yards separated them, and Hank's stomach turned as he readied himself to respond to the threat.

Willy took in the van's presence and dismissed it as he turned to Hank and said, "You can keep the pocketknife, but you gotta give me the key fob. That is if you still want the job?" He waited and rephrased his request. "No-Name will keep the manly knife. You'll get it back when we're done. The little girly knife in your right front pocket can stay, but you must hand me the keys with the thumb drive in the fob. Don't worry, you'll get it all back after the job." Willy held out an opened bag.

Hank dug into his pocket and held its contents in his open palm but kept his eyes on the van.

Willy selected the key chain, dropped it into the bag, and wrapped the opening over on itself. He peeled off a numbered receipt, handed it to Hank, and said, "See ya around." He made a crisp turn and hurried up the ramp and jumped into the passenger seat of the white van.

CHAPTER 12

Port Townsend, Washington

A FENDER HANGING OFF the rail of the eighty-foot yacht kissed the dock's edge. Hank reached out as an unaffected adolescent deckhand tossed him the bow line. Without thought, he made fast the forward cleat and walked the length of the boat. He stretched up and took the stern line from the billionaire, Olin Ou. Like many sailboats with a pedigree for racing, the name of the boat had been emblazoned across the side. Narrow, yellow letters over dark gray shadowing formed a graphic that didn't fit the elegance of the boat, but the font looked familiar. A clean cursive, like from a neon sign, spelled out *GalaxSea*.

Olin Ou stepped down from the boat like a man trapped at sea for weeks. He shook Hank's hand. His kind smile showed perfect teeth, but his face had deep creases. Both features didn't fit the middle-aged man of Asian ancestry. His hair also seemed out of place for a man of means. No style at all, just the perfect distribution of silver-gray and jet-black bristled in a crewcut.

"You can call me Olin. Jump on board and meet the kids. I've got to pee like a racehorse." And he bolted for the marina's restrooms.

The girl who had thrown him the bow line was nowhere on deck. He had not seen her duck into the cabin. He chuckled to himself. *Skinny kid*. If she had fallen overboard, nobody would hear a splash.

With his "ahoy" unanswered, he climbed aboard and walked to the starboard helm. So much room, a place for everything.... His hand caressed one of the electronic winches. He whispered to himself, "What a concept. Comfort *and* speed." The teak deck was a classic, but her plumb bow and broad aft were designed to go fast.

Hank's experienced eye looked over the rigging, up past the three spreaders to take in the tall mast. He estimated the top to be a hundred feet up and did a quick calculation. This luxury yacht carried enough sail to move her at speeds reserved for motorboats and multihulls. He was glad the owner had raced off. It was too obvious that he coveted this boat and it made him feel like a teenage boy gawking at a beautiful woman.

With the confusion dancing in his brain, he made his way down the stairs of the companionway and into the salon. He called out, "Hello?" No sounds came from behind any of the closed doors. There were none of Olin Ou's kids to meet. He set down his seabag in the spacious room and noted the large horizontal windows set low. He loved the indirect light they offered, and being so close to the water provided an unusual but welcome view. Still, the sailor in him disapproved of its proximity to the waterline. "Nice idea, but it's straight to the bottom if she breaks open."

Olin pounded back on board and sped down the stairs with practiced precision. He smiled, "Don't tell me. The kids are nowhere."

"Haven't seen nor heard a peep."

Olin pounced through the salon, using both hands as he knocked on each of the two forward doors. "There's a burger joint within walking distance and I'm not doing takeout. I'm leaving in five minutes." He turned back and smiled. "No response means they're getting ready... I think. Welcome aboard, Hank. This is your berth." He flowed past Hank, grabbing his gear on the way like an eager bellboy. Olin opened the door, revealing a stateroom with a private head and a small desk area. "I hope this will suit your needs while we sail together."

Hank replied, "I guess it'll do." Then he gave a sidelong look at Olin and broke into a big grin. His wide eyes took in the king-sized bed molded into the blond woodwork of the boat. Light from a side window and a hatch above brightened the space even more. There was a small TV on an extending arm and a shelf loaded with books, secured in place by a brace, hinged to swing down.

Olin Ou must have caught Hank's lingering eyes. "There are books everywhere on board. Too bad you won't be aboard long enough to enjoy them. I'll leave you to get settled."

Minutes later, Olin knocked on the open door and said, "Hank, I'm sure you'll want time to go over the boat. Everything you'll need is in the cupboard beside the nav station. The boat's yours. No place is off limits to you, so poke around. Irina's not coming with the rest of us for dinner."

"I'm not going, Dad," yelled a male voice through the closed door of a forward berth.

Olin said, "Well, Hank. That's that. We're doing takeout after all. What can I get you? Willy tells me Doc's is close and has good burgers."

Hank said, "I'd like a Big Doc Burger with a side of chowder." He wanted to add, "If you see a redhead server, say goodbye for me." But he knew better than to ask.

Two young girls walked out of the port berth.

Olin introduced them. "This is Nadia," he said, motioning toward the girl who had handed him the bow line when they arrived. She stared at him. Black eyeliner wrapped around her penetrating dark eyes and a crisp line stretched outward toward her temples, amplifying what nature started. When the *GalaxSea* came into the marina and she tossed him the bow line, she did not even glance at him. Now her catlike eyes, incapable of blinking, challenged him.

Hank wanted to laugh, but he forced a neutral face and returned her stare. He remembered hearing somewhere that wild cats will pounce if you avert your eyes. "Hi, Nadia," he said. "That's a pretty name." She turned her head and raced up the companionway stairs, out of sight.

"Hi, Hank. I'm Sydney." She walked right up and gave him a firm handshake. She also kept eye contact, but her smile of genuine interest was disarming. "Nadia and I are twins—fraternal. It's just good to get that right out. Don't you think?" Not waiting for a reply, she said, "I'm into sports. Are you? Soccer's my favorite. Daddy's got box seats, but I like to get down into the stands and yell. Do you yell at games?" This time, she waited for an answer.

"As a matter of fact, I do."

Her dad got behind her and coaxed her along. "Let's get moving, Sydney. You can interrogate Hank later."

CHAPTER 13

⚓

Port Townsend, Washington

THE CUPBOARD OLIN MENTIONED was full of manuals, but Hank's attention flashed to the inside of the cupboard door. A battlefield tablet colored in survival-orange made Hank laugh and he detached the Velcro and drew the device off its charging station. Its label read *DON'T PANIC!* He thought, *someone has a sense of humor.* Now it was clear why the graphic of the yacht's name looked so familiar. It came from the cover of a book he had read a long time ago. Just below DON'T PANIC in small lettering was the play on words that made him smile. THE HITCHHIKER'S GUIDE TO THE GALAXSEA.

The Hitchhiker's Guide to the Galaxy was the go-to-book—the one with all the answers—found within Douglas Adams' quirky five-book-trilogy of the same name. The science-fiction comedy had been an enjoyable distraction for Hank as he sailed around the world for the first time. He was certain that in this tablet, he would discover the digital manuals for the boat and every system aboard. Hank wasted no time and turned on the device. Multiple lines of text appeared, asking the same question in a dozen different languages. Followed with a Yes and No button. A soft voice asked, "Is this an emergency?"

Hank selected the No button as he whispered the word, "No." His face appeared on the screen, and an instant later the iconic sound of a camera clicking broke the silence. A good headshot of Hank hovered on the screen for a few seconds while the voice said, "Please, continue holding this device while I verify your identity."

The photo shrunk and lodged itself in the upper left of the screen. The screen went dark and lit up again, showing a retinal scan which also downsized into a tile and parked itself next to the photo. A green arrow checked the corner of Hank's picture while a little yellow triangle with a question mark lodged across the picture of the network of blood vessels of his eyes.

His fingerprints flew up into the space beside the picture with a green check in the corner. The device must have captured the fingerprint when he pushed the On button. Then, in a buzz of activity, the whorls of every finger touching the waterproof case flew into the area beneath his picture. A confusing collection of recordings flowed over the speakers.

Several voices overlapped at first—just babble. The number of voices dropped to two and then just one. The speed was faster than normal conversation but slow enough to understand. At first, it didn't sound like anybody he knew. Then he recognized his own voice. Or at least he recognized the conversations he had just had, being broadcast at about two times the actual speed. Each word singled out, and the interval compressed to eliminate pauses creating a staccato progression, "big, doc, burger, side, chowder, hi, nadia, that's, pretty, name, as, matter, fact, do, no." The audio file flew up into its place beside the other tiles. A green check showed in the corners of every tile.

Several other pictures of Hank joined the top line. The ones Willy took on the dock appeared, including body scans. The near naked images flashed across the screen slow enough to see what had been in his pockets and how thin he was. These images pixilated as they shrunk into the mosaic. The employee picture, the one Joan claimed she hadn't put on the website, appeared. But he didn't have time to think about that when the picture of him after he was pulled off his doomed boat showed up. A half dozen pictures, including military IDs and a couple of promotion headshots, followed. The picture the community college took when he completed his GED was the last image. It received its green check in the corner and then things got interesting.

His height showed up, his weight registered and then the tool performed a body composition analysis. Body fat at six-point five percent. No wonder one pint of beer got him buzzed. That realization didn't stop the ongoing examination. Little green checks showed up as fast as the data points filled the screen. Hank recognized a long strip of biometric data. With the technology he held in his hands, it didn't seem possible, but the results appeared accurate. Pulse rate, respiration, blood oxygenation levels all seemed plausible to collect this way. But then, a real-time recording of his heart's electrical rhythms blipped across the screen. Since he spent most of his adult life in healthcare, he knew what it took to set up a 12-lead ECG. Somehow this clever device did it without attaching leads anywhere and still returning an electrocardiogram that any cardiologist would approve of. Before Hank pondered the how-the-heck moment, another finding distracted him.

His blood type flashed before his eyes and shrunk to join the rest with a green check in the corner. At first, he assumed it had come from his records. Blood type was available to just about everybody in the military, but then a complete blood analysis followed with an up to the minute timestamp. The test including red and white cell counts, hematocrit and glucose levels. Hank let out a whistle, sat down, and lowered the pad into his lap, removing his hands. He concentrated on the small red dot of blood dripping out of his left index finger. He hadn't felt a thing.

A soft female voice said, "Henry James Gunn. Thank you for your cooperation."

The screen shifted from the developing mosaic and took on the look of a professional curriculum vitae with a good headshot. There were no green checks, but across the top, a slender green banner read *Crew Member: Henry James Gunn - Verification Complete.*

"My name is Ava. What would you like me to call you?" The voice was goddess-like. Not loud, but crystal clear and it came from no particular location but seemed to fill the room.

"Hank is fine."

"Hank, I noticed you became somewhat agitated during the ID verification and health safety procedures. I am sorry if the testing surprised you. I detailed the process in the documents you signed with Willy." There was a brief pause. "I find many people don't read contracts. Would you like me to read the documents you signed?"

"No," Hank answered. Reading legal fine print was tedious enough, but to have it read aloud would be torturous. What's done is done. Those documents couldn't contain anything more surprising than what he'd just been through. Besides, in a few days, he'd be off this yacht.

"You will find a signed confidentiality and security agreement in your inbox. Please, review your information for accuracy. In the meantime, do you have questions you would like me to answer? Or would you like me to tell you about the *GalaxSea*?"

He was brain-dead-hungry, but he managed a smiled and asked, "Can you tell me what the answer to life, the universe, and everything is?"

The voice took on a rich warmth and even a slight chuckle. She answered, "Why, that's an easy one, Hank. The answer to life, the universe, and everything is forty-two."

"Oh, that's right. Okay, now I've got a tough one for you. Where's the best drinking water on this boat?"

"That is a tough one, Hank. Let me see." The computer responded with a flirtatious tone, "Would you like my answer now or in seven and a half million years?"

Hank had never had a humorous conversation with a computer before. He guessed some of this banter about *The Hitchhiker's Guide* was programmed, but the cadence of her voice seemed effortless as it followed the course of the conversation. Hank replied, "Now would be helpful."

"You will find bottles of Mountain Valley Spring Water in every refrigerated space on the boat. For example, the small fridge in your cabin. Will that suffice?"

"Yes. Amazing."

"Thank you, Hank, but you can just call me Ava."

Hank got up, put the pad in place, and ran his fingers through his hair. Rapid adaptation was something he was good at, and it looked like this job would suit him well. How could it not? He'd need all his skills to adapt to a witty AI, an incredible sailboat, and a charismatic billionaire with his kids. He strode into his own spacious cabin with a wide grin.

The bottled water satisfied his thirst, but he was still hungry. He whispered, "Ava, can you hear me?"

"I can," the computer answered in a soft voice, matching his.

"Can you tell me about the *GalaxSea*?"

"Would you like the simple sales brochure, the version with so much detail you'll learn what company manufactured the graphite nanotubes, or something in between?"

"How about the sales brochure with the spec sheet?"

Ava was going on about the tensile strength of the shrouds when Hank said, "Ava, that's enough on rigging. What is the mast's height again? I must have been spacing when you said that."

"No worries. The mast is ninety-eight feet and three-eighth inches tall. Mainsel is 984 square feet..."

Hank wasn't sure he had ever heard a computer get a colloquial pronunciation right, even sailors mispronounce mainsel as main-sail. He leaned against the wall, automatically ducking his head but there wasn't a need for that precaution in this sizable boat. He closed his eyes and tried to listen closer. The voice, with a hint of a Celtic accent, was so very pleasant that he became lost in it and didn't care what she said. Her words were not only in the room but coming from beside him, just to his right. Hank turned and looked, He thought. *I need to eat something.*

The sound of light footfalls attracted his attention. It had to be his dinner coming aboard. He raced up the companionway to help Olin and the twins. There was no activity on the cockpit deck or on the dock. He walked aft between the large carbon fiber steering wheels into the rose-colored dusk of evening. Nothing. After looking around and listening for several minutes, he gave up, but then he caught the slightest movement. Way up on the bow, a deck hatch closed. Now seemed like as good a time as any to follow Olin's invitation to poke around. Hank moved along the starboard side deck, checking the rigging and lines as he made his way forward. He made it a point to avoid the hatches above the rooms occupied by the two older children. When he reached the hatch that closed a minute before, he tested the large handle attached to a keypad, but it didn't budge. The darkened acrylic lens that formed the hatch returned only a poor reflection and blackness.

"Ahoy, Hank," Olin called from the dock as he walked past with the twins.

It always amazed Hank that people around boats talked like this. A language he had been born into, but his nautical manners had the edges blasted off while in the Marines. "Ahoy," Hank replied.

CHAPTER 14

Port Townsend, Washington

OLIN DOUBLE-KNOCKED ON THE forward berth doors. "Food's here! Come and get it or forever hold your peas!"

Nadia rolled her eyes at her dad's quirky pun and handed Hank a sewn cloth grocery bag. He found his seat at the nav station and wondered if Ava was watching him. Two cold, wet bottles hid inside the bag, and he smiled as he pulled out a bottle of Blue Moon beer. Next came a clamshell of fries and two paper-wrapped Big Doc Burgers with Tillamook pepper jack cheese and double-smoked hickory bacon. Hank's mouth watered, but he waited, not wanting to be the first one to dig in.

A young man sprinted out of the forward berth on the starboard side, grabbed two wrapped burgers, sat at the table, crossed himself, and began inhaling food.

Scowling, Olin said, "Marshall, you seem to have forgotten your manners." Olin was far from ominous, but standing over his crouching son, he directed the young man's attention away from food. "Hank, allow me to introduce you to

Marshall. He is fresh off the plane from MIT and swears he will never go back."
Olin chuckled, rested a hand on his son's rounded shoulders, and continued,
"I told him he was in good company and offered our garage and ridiculous
amounts of bandwidth." Olin laughed at his own joke. "But no, he says he wants
to go to the community college and learn how to be a chef." He patted his son's
shoulder warmly. "Marshall, this is our new sailing instructor, Hank Gunn."

Marshall stopped his chewing and swallowed. He held up his left hand,
dripping with catsup and grease. His extended index finger and thumb formed
the shape of a gun, pointing right at Hank. "Cool name. Gun." A sardonic smile
creased his lips as he shot off an imaginary round with recoil.

"Hi, Marshall," Hank said and let him off the hook. "I'm sure we can talk
after we eat."

His new boss stared at the closed forward port door as if willing it to open,
then paused for a few seconds with his head bowed and crossed himself. When
his eyes opened, he looked back at the closed door. Hank followed Olin's stare
toward the unmoving door, but decided eating was the best use of his time.
The twins, sitting at the salon's dining table, picked at their food and Marshall
continued to plow through his assembled banquet. Olin ate his small burger
and a meager selection of fries from a white plate. Willy was present but not
included. He stood propped against the companionway, drinking coffee.

Hank's meal was half-consumed when the door to the port berth opened. It
didn't squeak or make a sound, but everybody turned and looked like something
meaningful was about to happen. Hank stopped chewing when a young woman
stepped out into the soft light of the salon. He swallowed hard and took a swig
of beer. The stunning girl smiled and walked over to her father, gave him a kiss
on the cheek and said, "Thanks, Daddy. I'm famished!" She moved to the galley
counter and scrutinized the scribbled descriptors penned in heavy black ink by
an artistic red-headed server.

Olin interpreted, "That's a bleu cheese portobello on focaccia. Sweet potato
fries are in the carton." She pulled a white plate out of the galley cupboard,
opened the paper wrap, and slid the large portobello mushroom onto her plate,
forsaking the bread. Then opened the container of fries, plucked one between
her fingers, and bit the end off. She removed three more and put them on the
plate, then turned and faced Hank. "You must be our new sailing instructor."

The rest of the family had returned to their meals as she stepped close to him.

"Yeah, I'm Hank."

She put out her hand palm down and said, "Hi, Hank. I'm Irina. I guess I'll be seeing you bright and early then."

He shook her hand comfortably and said, "Great. I'm looking forward to helping all of you to become better sailors." Her body turned around a half second before her eyes left his. She was humming as she left the room, but he couldn't make out the tune. She closed the door to her berth behind her. Breaking the spell that lingered too long, he asked, "Olin, what time do you want to get underway tomorrow?"

"Let's have breakfast on shore and take off after that. But first, I want to check the weather and top off the tanks. The commotion should get the kids stirring. Let's say you and I plan to have coffee on the cockpit deck at seven."

"Sounds good," Hank said. He would make an excuse not to take breakfast on shore, comfortable that nobody would bother him aboard a yacht tied up to the marina's guest dock with round-the-clock security. Bumping into police or shore patrol would ruin everything. He was probably being too cautious, but he was close to freedom, and he would not jeopardize it by hanging around in plain sight on US soil.

In order to clear his head before bed, he decided to go outside. Willy was sitting right outside the companionway steps and his presence startled Hank. He stumbled with surprise, but quickly regained his composure.

"She's sixteen," Willy said.

"What?" Hank asked, trying to gain context.

"Irina. She's sixteen."

Not wanting to appear shocked at the news, Hank changed the subject. "Beautiful night. There should be a little weather blowing in tomorrow which will make for some incredible sailing." Willy sat tight while Hank continued out onto the aft deck. The stars were visible but dimmed by the lights of Port Townsend and the marina. There was no moon. The air was fresh, the night cool, and the water stirred solemnly.

Lights from a car flashed against the rocks that made up the breakwater. The origin of the beam wasn't clear, but it shot over the deck of the boat and even though the brightness never illuminated him, the thought of being exposed made him uneasy. Everything made him uneasy, and he couldn't wait to shed the land and gain some sea room. He gave up. The fresh air wasn't helping him feel any better, so he decided to sleep, if he could.

He managed to doze off fitfully a few times, but eventually found himself staring at the ripples of light reflecting onto the ceiling. Soon he determined the day had started—at least for him—and he eased out of bed and slipped into his pants. The automatic motion to check his pockets sent his hand onto the small knife clipped into his right pocket. It was always there, and he always checked it out of habit. He grabbed the flashlight wedged between the mattress and the bed frame. After a pit stop to the head, he splashed water on his face and pulled on a long-sleeved t-shirt. Even without coffee, he was thankful to be aboard this exceptional yacht and felt lucky to get this job. Not only would it take him to Canada, but he thought it was likely he would walk away with a handsome tip.

As he made his way to the deck, the air felt calm and crisp. The sky would be dark for a while, but dawn nudged a deep red into the clouds over the Cascade mountains. It never took him long to find his favorite place on a sailboat and he walked out to the aft deck.

"Don't be alarmed, Hank," a woman's voice said from behind him.

He must have walked right past her. It alarmed him plenty, but he was not prone to losing composure. "Who are you?"

"I'm Jen. Part of Mr. Ou's security team." She drifted out of the dark shadow toward him. She wore a long, black, double-breasted coat. The front hung loose but overlapped enough to hide whatever was in her left hand. She didn't let it go or remove her hand from the Napoleon-like stance. Hank tried to make out her face or what she concealed—anything. All he needed to do to expose her was to whip out the flashlight, but it was bad form to use a light like that and she was close enough to stop him. He would have to wait for the right time to get a good look. "That was you going into the forward hatch last night," he said. She backed up, turned, and walked away without a sound.

Hank stood at the rail, staring into the inky water, contemplating his new boss. Olin Ou and his family couldn't be normal. Billions of dollars eliminate normal as a possibility. But from what he had seen so far, they passed for the typical American family. He gazed into the water. There were differences. Where would Willy fit into the typical American family? Maybe the overprotective uncle? And the security boat and crew? A typical family with their own police force. Then there was the all-knowing AI... a personal NSA? Most typical American families settled for a doorbell and a golden retriever for deciding friend or foe. Was that where Jen-the-ninja fit in? He knew it was silly but decided she must be hiding her samurai sword under the folds of her coat.

The surface of the water absorbed the ruddy sky without sharing any reflection of the early dawn. All the usual noise of a marina seemed to be missing, too. No slapping of rigging, creaking in the bones of the dock, and no hum of generators, not even a noise from the town. He wondered if time might have stopped, but that was a silly notion. With a deep inhale, he focused on the internal noise of his breath. Air rushing into his lungs made a sound that grounded him, and the uneasy sensation left. But by the time he had fully exhaled, there was another sensation to replace it. He felt someone was watching him and turned around but saw nobody. He returned his stare back over the aft rail and shivered. His mind ran with the implausible vision of Jen flying across the deck with a sword winding up to lop his head off. He didn't want to look back a second time, so he pushed the thought out by replacing it with a question.

What's it like to be so wealthy? The mental exercise got easier the more he entertained the idea. But where did he fit—if he fit at all? The Ou family would need high levels of protection. Perimeter security was not a new concept to Hank, but here the people doing the guarding and the people being guarded were civilians. It made sense. Rich people always got unwanted attention. Most of it was probably harmless curiosity, but they would have to rule out sinister motives. How did they decide which is which? It was time for him to use his skills to fit in somehow. Sailing instructor made sense, but the image of Jen with her samurai sword wouldn't leave his mind. He patted the folding knife in his pocket and decided they must trust him but wondered what it would take to get his own sword.

CHAPTER 15

Phillip Channel, Singapore

THE BOAT MANEUVERED THROUGH the harbor way too fast. With vacation lingering in her soul, the frenzied boat traffic overwhelmed her. To make matters worse, the workboat didn't have a helm. Autonomous water traffic was the only option in these waters, yet the dependence on technology unsettled her. Rather than getting used to it, her attention turned back to correspondence. She'd been doing everything she could to keep her mind off of Gregory.

The terms of her contract didn't pay her for travel, and the trip to and from the Institute's assets didn't count toward her work hours. When they sent an employee to unmanned aquaculture buoys, they meant it as punishment, and she understood punishment. Even though her job with the Institute frustrated her, at least she was free to throw herself into the consulting work she managed on the side.

Two years ago, on her first day at work, she met her HR representative. He never made eye contact and reviewed each page of the policy manual like a robot. His only pause came at the top of each hour when he insisted on a ten-minute break or when she needed to acknowledge a policy and sign a screen. A strange combination of zero interest in people and intense dedication to the job made him the right person to say things like, "Any work over thirty hours a week is a criminal offense. That kind of selfishness puts others on the streets." Then with satisfied devotion, he added, "If caught, you will be prosecuted to the full extent of the law. There is no off-the-clock. If you take work home, you will be reported and your employment ended." It was a long four hours and ironically the time spent with the uptight bureaucrat didn't count as work hours, nor was it considered off-the-clock.

The commitment to a mediocre workplace didn't stop there. The next day, her coworkers took turns rolling their eyes, giving loud exhales, and turning their backs anytime Bella got excited about her work. Even her supervisor wasted no time to advise her, "Pace yourself. It avoids burnout." The work at the Marine Quality Institute didn't challenge her mind or satisfy her passion for the sea, but it never was meant to. The NGO had hiring requirements, and she fit the bill—female, non-Asian, and her passport sloshed around in the Oceania Collective category, which made her a migrant worker. She quickly understood her presence allowed them to check a few boxes and show the Institute's commitment to DBEI, or Diversity, Belonging, Equity, and Inclusion. Her PhD in bivalve protein management got her foot in the door and looked good on the Institute's alphabet soup of credentials, but her DNA and birthplace got her hired.

Just because the Institute turned her dreams of an exciting career into a boring job didn't mean she had to accept it. Once she realized the job was a dead end, she took to moonlighting. Even though quantum computing and machine learning added speed and sophistication to aquaculture projects around the world, there were a million individuals, villages, and small companies still in need of practical advice about their resources and how to tweak their operations for higher efficiencies and greater yields. Practical experience still had a place. She found it more profitable and more rewarding than her job at the Institute. But she was not ready to quit the day job which gave her an excuse to live in Singapore, credentials to travel throughout the world (except the United States), and provided an impressive benefits package.

When the boat slowed, she raised her head from her device and walked out to the work deck. Her lightweight jumpsuit fluttered in the wind, and she snugged the drawstring of her sun-cap. She wore her hair braided into pigtails and tied the ends together down her back, forming a vee. Even though the two other passengers ignored her all day, she felt sorry for the workers who inspected the buoys. They dressed alike in steel-toed boots, stiff coveralls, orange five-point harnesses integrated into floatation vests, and to prove that safety was paramount, helmets strapped at the chin. The Institute sent her into the field with an underwater drone. It looked a bit like a giant crab. The sample-collecting drone took five times longer than if she just put on a mask and dove to get what she needed. But her job was to drop the drone in the water and pull it out again, not to get wet.

She looked past the two workers and squinted against the hazy sun and couldn't believe it was the same sun she saw each day while on vacation. Bella considered the difference and decided today's sun had a serious attitude—all business, no pleasure. Singapore's skyscrapers pushed inward toward the Twin Flyers, giant observation wheels holding back the skyline before it fell into a tree-lined boulevard with manicured public parks and beaches. The sky flurried with activity, airliners glided one after another into Changi Airport, and a beeline of mismatched drones cut the sky. On the water, the temperature was pleasant and humidity tolerable. A small thundercloud loomed in the distance with striations of rain descending to the earth beneath, and a sudden flash of lightning lit the thunderhead. The maintenance workers exchanged surprised looks, but it was Bella's turn to ignore them, so she gathered her samples and prepared for the sprint to the Mass Rapid Transit station.

The lab at the Marine Quality Institute had equipment which sent shivers down Bella's spine when she saw it for the first time. No expense had been spared, but it sat unused. The Institute had a rigid policy which stated that everyone must complete their workday and leave the building by four o'clock. Because of the maximum thirty-hour work week and nine o'clock start times, real scientific research was impractical. Bella took only an hour to prepare and package up her samples and leave them for pickup. The building was empty when she walked out the main doors at three thirty.

CHAPTER 16

Singapore

SHE HAD AVOIDED THE rain on her way into the lab, but now people made their way under colorful umbrellas. No wind accompanied the deluge, and she popped her small lime green umbrella and joined the procession. It would take less than ten minutes to walk to her apartment, but she needed more distraction and turned the other direction. By the time she had reached the upscale skyscraper that contained the Slanted Edge the rain had quit. A door guard wearing VR goggles spotted Bella walking up to the building and unhooked the crowd control barrier to let her through, while another opened a large glass door receiving her into the opulent lobby. A fit looking woman, that Bella had not seen before, stood at the elevator waiting with a smile. She welcomed Bella and handed her a palm sized device as she motioned to the open door.

At the correct floor the elevator stopped, and Bella followed the arrows on the device directing her to the correct complex which housed the pod that had been selected for her. She had decided that the Slanted Edge must be enormous, because she never seemed to be directed to the same complex, let alone the same pod, more than once. Each complex had at least half a dozen pods, and she eventually stopped trying to figure out where she was in the building and simply followed the arrows to her destination.

A bright green check mark appeared on the device and a perky voice said, "Congratulations, Ms. Espinosa. You have reached the entrance to Pod 58." Bella smiled each time she found herself about to enter one of the Escape Pods. She couldn't afford to walk through the front door of the Slanted Edge, but Gregory had given her a year-long membership to this club as a birthday gift. The promotional advertisements claimed it's better than the real thing—the water cleaner and the air purer, the runs free of congestion, the bicycle tours prettier, and the ski trails *exquisite*. Skiing had become her favorite activity. The contrast from the heat and humidity outside held its appeal and winter sports were a challenge she had never known.

With each virtual visit to the Norwegian countryside, she became more competent, but the program continued to level up and insisted her body worked hard and her mind stayed focused. For the next hour, she would have no difficulty imagining the real thing. Each cue was convincing—the grip of the snow, the wind against her face, even the heady scent of air in a forest populated by dwarf juniper and stunted spruce trees. When she crashed, the pod's programming added tutorials to guide her through a natural progression of intuitive skills, like a child learning to walk. With each visit, she stumbled less and sensed her body position against the terrain, positioned her skis with more grace, and placed her poles with confidence. Bella fell in love with skiing, even though she had never experienced a real snowflake fall from the sky.

"Good afternoon, Bella. It's great to see you again. Anything special I can put into the works today?" a spirited female voice greeted.

There was a response pause. Bella answered with silence as she changed into shorts and a light running top. She unwrapped the boots waiting for her and strapped her bare feet in for a perfect fit. A wrapped pair of lightweight glasses was next. They looked like safety glasses from the lab but enhanced the visual effects of the simulation.

"Would you like to downhill or Nordic ski today?"

"Nordic ski—skate. Espedalen Valley. Twenty kilometers from town." The forward leaning angle of the ski boot relaxed, but there was still plenty of ankle support. "Oh, that's better. Thanks. I'm at level twelve, right?"

"Great news! Based on your last foray into this snowy mecca, you can jump into the next level if you like. But it's up to you."

"Yeah, let's push it up a notch. Any suggestions on how to negotiate that downhill corner? It always gets me."

"Your ski coach told me that if you relax and allow your speed to work your skis' edge into it, you should be fine. Would you like him to help? He's available."

"Of course he is…" She liked her ski coach, the tall handsome Scandinavian, but she wanted nothing to do with men, even virtual ones. "No, thanks. I'll try it one more time on my own." Then she waited for the enthusiastic music with a throaty voice-over.

"Go critical. Enjoy the Slanted Edge."

She stepped into the designated area imprinted on the floor and the bindings grabbed tight. When Bella looked up, she was in a winter wonderland. The realism satisfied all the senses. She was on a groomed trail facing a gentle uphill slope. *Solomon* was written across each boot attached to a virtual pair of *Fischer* skis.

Even though she had requested that the pod's air temperature stay at sixty degrees, a few snowflakes floated downward on a slight breeze. It was a pleasant effect but caused her to shiver. Bringing her skis together, her body drifted backward until she spread the tips of her skis apart, angled her knees inward and stuck her poles into the snow behind her. It was time to get serious and move onward.

With skating motions, she made it up the slight incline that offered an ideal warmup. As she crested the hill, the trail popped out of a forest of twenty-foot-tall spruce trees. She didn't need to catch her breath but stopped to take in the scene laid out before her. A single track snaked through the gentle downhill into the valley below, where the steeple of a church from a bygone era marked the distant town. The trail marker read *14 km* and showed its level of difficulty as *Nybegynner* with a light blue circle. She took a deep breath and said, "Beginner… hah." She had never made it down this part of the trail without falling. One ski always slid into a preset track and the other would slide around without guidance until it crossed over and tripped her into a snowbank. If determination could substitute for skill, today would be different. In the past, going slow hadn't helped, nor crouching into a squat like a little kid, nor focusing on avoiding the preset track. It all ended with the same result—an abrupt stop into the snowbank. She took off down the slope faster than ever before and with greater hope.

The trees blurred as she pumped her legs and gained speed. Her knees absorbed the small lumps in the snow, and the muscles in her thighs burned from the effort of her strides. She shifted her body from side to side as her skis took turns against the crystallized snow. Scuff and glide, scuff and glide.... The wind rushed past, and the speed thrilled her. It was delicious, and she didn't want it to stop. The corner and its familiar snowbank drew closer. She pushed her right ski into a final long glide, then pulled it back parallel to the left and focused on her path. Her body lowered, knees bent, poles tucked in tight. This time, the corner whisked by with no drama and the snowdrift ignored her as she sped by. Bella raised her body as she came out of her fast glide onto level terrain. A new confidence swelled in her, and she continued down the trail. At that moment, her movements were effortless, and she felt in control of her progress, but some skiers were coming toward her, and she needed to slow down.

Four men, skiing fast, but looking like they weren't even trying, approached. They took up the whole trail and she could hear the good-natured banter among them. They wore matching deep red racing tights with sponsorship logos, wraparound sunglasses, and black nylon caps. Each had a rifle barrel sticking up from the gun strapped to their back. She had never seen them before, but assumed they were heading to the biathlon course. When they got closer, the group zippered into single file to allow Bella to glide past without breaking stride.

"Hallo," said the first one. He smiled as if Bella had made his day. The next two said, "Hei" and nodded as they coasted by, resuming their momentum by poling hard, but the last skier allowed himself to slide to a stop and stared straight at Bella.

A polite smile fell from her face as she thought, *Gregory!* Her legs and knees weakened as she glided past him—twisting, she held his gaze. The man said something in perfect Norwegian, turned toward his buddies and skied hard to catch up. Bella stopped and watched them out of sight. It was not Gregory's voice. She couldn't even be sure it had been the rest of him, but the resemblance shocked her enough to concentrate on what he said. Her mother homeschooled her mostly in Norwegian, and many summers she spent the long days with cousins and played with the local children, but her language skills were rusty, and the man spoke with a native cadence. He said, "My sweet, wait for me. I'll come to you as soon as I'm done."

Bella's mind raced. Gregory had never called her *my sweet*. Translation is difficult. *I'll come to you,* is also *I'll come for you...* but did it matter? The Slanted Edge had security programs to avoid chance meetings. "Can you tell me if there are other users in this Sim?"

"No, Bella, you must invite others to enjoy their company. All others are non-player characters. Would you like to invite a friend?"

"No. Is it standard that an NPC would make a pass at me?"

"I'm sorry, Bella, I'm not sure what you mean by 'make a pass.'"

"You know, to flirt?"

"All I can say to that is stranger things have happened. May I ask, did you like it? I can use that information to create a more enjoyable experience for you."

"No. I didn't like it at all."

"Oh, I'm sorry. It won't happen again. Is there anything further?"

"Shut it down. I'm done."

CHAPTER 17

Singapore

SHE HAD REACHED THE entry to her apartment building, but for the second time today, Bella questioned what she saw. As a scientist, she understood how perspective alters observations. That would explain mistaking a computer-generated avatar in her simulation for Gregory. Her fractured relationship and the fiasco at the airport had skewed her perspective. He did not take her call or answer her attempts at communication. And now, she thought, she spotted Masiki standing like a statue. She was easy to spot. Few women in Singapore wore fashions from the 1960s and after the crowd passed, she realized she was not seeing things.

Gregory brought Masiki with him to run the Singapore office. She was striking, short, angular, and reed-thin, but it was her sense of fashion which made her stand out. She didn't dress retro. She dressed exactly like the glamorous European models of the late 60s. Today the big hair caught Bella's attention, but her eyes held her stare. Gold eyeshadow, heavy eyeliner, and false lashes exploding away from coal-colored irises. She wore a stark-white, tunic-necked miniskirt with an oversized, full-length gold zipper down to the short hemline where white nylons traversed her thighs and plunged into bright white leather boots at her calves. Masiki broke her pose and her stare at the same time and seemed to dance through the people on the sidewalk.

They had never spoken. Japanese was a language Bella had difficulties with, but it was the only language Masiki spoke. "Hi," said Bella, deciding that was universal enough.

Masiki grabbed Bella by the arm and directed her into the building's entry. The door opened, and they entered the vestibule. The security guard at the desk buzzed them through, and Masiki kept leading Bella until she stopped off to the side of the security desk. She pressed something into Bella's hand, a tiny, folded paper box, and looked into her eyes. "One." Masiki spoke the word with conviction.

Bella questioned the accented word. *Did she mean one? Or won?* Neither made sense, so she asked, "What?"

Masiki acted like her single word sentence should be sufficient and pushed the box deeper into Bella's hand and bowed her head as if the box would explain everything. The wig came off, and she replaced it with a Yankees baseball cap. She unzipped the miniskirt and peeled it off, revealing a black running bra and matching shorts. The nylons rolled toward her boots, which unzipped down the back and soon she was barefoot. She shot a freeze-right-there expression onto the older man behind the security desk.

Bella hadn't noticed, but he had stood and leaned over the desk to get a better view. He blushed, turned, and sat back down in his swivel chair, looking away.

Even with the interruption, Masiki didn't slow her methodical costume change. She opened a large handbag and slipped on a dull blue v-necked t-shirt with *Just Do It* written across the front. She pulled out a pair of running slippers and slid them on. The makeover ended with a pair of green aviator Ray-Bans that completed the transformation from go-go girl into the casual uniform of Singapore's thirty-something women. She turned her attention to Bella and repeated, "One!" only with more conviction, then turned and pushed through the doors to the street, leaving the 60s on the floor.

Bella looked at the security guard, who just shrugged. She gathered the wig and the clothes, stuffed them into Masiki's cavernous purse, and entered the waiting elevator. The previous occupant of the sixth-floor apartment must have feared something. Three locks secured the entry into the apartment she shared with Zoe. Bella inserted the key for the deadbolt and then pressed her thumb against the second lock. Nobody knew the combination for the third lock, so they only used it when both roommates were inside for the night.

As she pushed open the door, the soft aroma of jasmine rice pushed back. There was a sink in a vanity-sized cabinet and a low cupboard hung over it. A small refrigerator resting on the linoleum floor provided a waist-level counter for the microwave oven, and on top of that sat a rice cooker. Zoe leaned against the back of a well-worn couch and with a dull knife, half-chopped, and half-smashed some colorful vegetables into a bamboo cutting board straddling the sink.

"Stunning purse. You're stepping out."

"Hold this." Bella pressed the purse into her roommate and locked the front door behind her.

"I've never seen a Coach knock-off like this before." Zoe put the knife down and admired the handbag.

Bella flipped over the back of the full-sized couch, facing Zoe. "I'm sure it's the real thing."

"When did you start wearing wigs?" Zoe pulled out a nylon and started to retrieve the miniskirt. "Girl, you've got some explaining to do."

"I wouldn't know where to start."

"Try the beginning." Zoe walked around and sat on the other end of the couch, holding onto Masiki's purse like it was a newborn baby.

"I've got to open this first." Written on the inside of the folded paper box were three letters and an exclamation point. She realized Masiki, in her heavy accent, was saying the word *run!*

"What's wrong? You look like you just saw a ghost."

"You know how I've been trying to call and text Gregory since the airport?"

"Yes. You said you would only try to contact him once a day. I tell you, that ship has sailed. You need to track him down and apologize. All relationships have their difficulties. You guys are just having a low spot."

"Listen, I know you love Gregory more than I do. Maybe you can get in line, but will you listen to me?"

"It's not unusual that when he goes on business trips, I don't hear from him, but this is our first breakup. And it will be our last. But I still didn't treat him right and I'm consumed with guilt over that. I've tried to ignore it, but that just makes things worse."

Bella told Zoe every detail of her day and then handed her the paper.

"You're kidding me. You thought she was saying *one*?"

"I know. But *run* doesn't make sense either. What should I do?"

Zoe returned to her kitchen work and said, "Do what you always do. Call your dad. But can I keep the purse?"

"You're no help. Besides, he'd tell me to sleep on it."

"Sounds like good advice to me. What is this, a size zero?" Zoe said with disappointment, holding the miniskirt up to herself.

"Why don't you go try it on and I'll finish cooking dinner."

Zoe balled up the dress and threw it at Bella.

"Okay. You finish. I'm going to slip into pajamas. Right after we eat, I'm going to bed. Getting back to work is exhausting. Can you imagine? I didn't even have a nap today."

"Oh, you poor dear." Zoe spilled the vegetables into the wok and stirred into the billowing steam plume.

· — ⚓ — ·

Bella woke with a gentle alarm sounding and stretched. If she had called her dad and he had told her to sleep on it, he would have been right. The morning makes everything better. She beat it to the bathroom before Zoe needed to get ready for work. Routine helped, too, and a shower kept her mood improving.

She returned with her hair twisted into a terry cloth turban and a blue beach wrap surrounding the rest of her. She closed the door behind her as she walked into her small, windowless bedroom. The subtle glow of a salt lamp was fine for getting up, but now she needed light and flipped the switch. Bella's eyes shot to her bedside stand. Her knees didn't go weak, and she did not scream, but realizing someone had been in her bedroom made her stomach feel like it was being strangled. Masiki's unfolded message that simply said "run" was gone, and in its place sat an ornate box and a small notecard. Bella sat hard on her bed and picked up the card. She had never seen the exquisite handwriting before she read.

Dear Isabelle,

I forgive you.

You could not have known,
but you never had a choice.
When I'm done with business,
I'll come for you.
Forever, G.

Bella worried over what was in the box but had to look. She released the closure and popped it open to find the ring. Bella cried out, "Zoe!"

CHAPTER 18

Strait of Juan de Fuca, USA

"MAN OVERBOARD!" OLIN YELLED, "Nadia and Sydney, you spot!" He called out orders in a loud commanding voice, "Ready to come about. Marshall, throw floats. Irina, ready the headsail. Hold it fast."

As they tacked into the wind with the headsail aback, the yacht's forward momentum slowed.

"Marshall, get the boat hook and lower the aft swim platform."

Marshall didn't throw the floating cushions, but other than that, he did what his dad commanded. The twins maneuvered around the deck, keeping vigil as designated spotters. Irina stood poised, ready to furl the headsail. Olin's head was on a pivot checking distances, sail trim, and boat position as if it was a matter of life and death. The yacht sailed farther away from the victim. Hank smiled at the master yachtsman. Olin had the skill to judge the course and place the vessel right where he wanted it.

"Prepare to jibe." Olin didn't wait for a reply, "Jibe ho." He steered the stern across the wind.

The vessel entered the last leg of the figure-eight, and the mainsail spilled a gulp of air. The boat decelerated as it came upon the unfortunate victim. It stopped just as Marshall reached out and hooked the pair of inflated fenders tied together. Irina had drawn a sad face on one of the white plastic floats and dubbed the effigy *Bob* for the drill, but now everybody was smiling.

"Good job! Any rescue that ends with everybody aboard and safe is a success." Hank congratulated the crew and looking at Olin, he said, "Nice job." He turned and said, "Nadia and Sydney, you guys did a great job keeping your eye on Bob's location. Next time, I want to see spotters pointing to the victim with an outstretched arm. That way, the skipper doesn't have to anticipate your gaze. Nadia, you handled that big sail well, but from now on we'll do it old-school. Power fails at the worst times. From now on we'll grind those winches. Marshall, you were right where you needed to be at every step of the drill. Good job. You followed each of your dad's instructions. Except throwing stuff into the water to provide the victim flotation options. You need to shout out what you would do and pretend to throw cushions. Don't make a debris field but go through the steps. One other reminder. Everybody needs to always keep a handhold on a secure part of the boat. *One hand for yourself; one hand for the ship.*

"Today our victim, Bob, is only two fenders tied together. Someday you might have to pull in a grown man—maybe your dad. I'll show you how to make that as simple as possible, but for now, the winds are freshening. Marshall, you're next. Every able-bodied sailor needs to skipper through the man-overboard procedures."

"Can you run the kids through their paces?" Olin asked Hank.

"Absolutely," Hank replied. He waited for him to drop out of sight before he gathered the young crew to discuss the next drill.

Hank watched his charges operate the sophisticated sailing yacht on multiple points of sail. The boat was a technological marvel, an enormous spread of canvas, but easy to handle. Each of the kids knew their way around the boat and showed a respectable aptitude for sailing it. Being the private instructor for Olin Ou and his family proved to be easier than he'd imagined.

Several hours later, when Olin popped back up on deck and shouted, "How's the training going?" Dressed in plaid shorts, blue canvas boat shoes, and a light blue windbreaker, his outfit said, "It's time to play!" The jaunty captain's cap and the excited grin punctuated the message. Balanced on his outstretched palm, like a waiter, he held something that looked like a white cutting board with a silver cover on it.

"Ava, take over the helm. Get us to the starting line. Come on, kids, I've got a surprise." Olin lowered his hand onto the central tabletop in the cockpit and pulled it out from underneath the cold-stone serving platter. "Wow, freezing! I hope I still have skin." He shook his hand to get the circulation back and added with a smile, "I think my fingerprints came right off." Olin cleared his throat. "My quest to find the world's best paletas is complete, and you'll never guess where I found them. Ballard! A stone's throw from the Nordic Heritage Museum. In the neighborhood where you can still find lutefisk on menus, I found a small Mexican taqueria. And—oh-yeah-you-betcha—they have the most amazing paletas in the world." With the other hand, he grabbed the handle of the silver lid and lifted it with a flourish. "Mexican popsicles."

A dozen popsicles fanned out on a cold-stone platter. Sydney reached in first and grasped the flat wooden handle of a bright red paleta with raspberries embedded into the translucent frozen juice. Olin smiled as each child picked up the one that enticed them. They all thanked their dad and started in on the treat.

"Hank, grab one and let's head down below. I have to get you off the deck before we race." He glanced ahead and gave a nod. "Some of our competition."

Two sailboats held their bearing off the bow. They were tall masted, but distant enough that the dark sails they carried seemed to come straight out of the water. Hank needed more time aboard boats. His sea senses were dull. Those sails had been converging—longer than Olin's distraction with the popsicles, but he missed their approach and never even glanced at the radar.

"I just want to say thanks for all your instruction. But now, it's time for the kids and I to cut loose and have fun." Olin returned the lid and hefted the platter. "Let's go below. You can take a break." Olin led the way.

"Wait, Dad." Marshall sprang toward his dad and lifted the lid. He pulled out a second paleta. It was bright white with coconut shavings curling around the edges. "Thanks. You're right. These are the best."

"Hank, I'm sorry you have to stay below deck during the race. We have a few rules... no professional sailors." Olin detoured to the galley and returned the leftover paletas to the freezer. "It'll take a couple of hours. This race is a make-up. A tropical-storm in the Bahamas exceeded our race guidelines, so we canceled it."

"Why would a storm in that part of the world cancel your race?"

"Oh, yeah," Olin replied, "you wouldn't know about that. There are twenty-two identical yachts that race in this one-design series. The two boats joining us are the only ones close enough to campaign head-to-head. Most of our competition is on the East Coast and in the Mediterranean. We can all race in real time. The AI provides the corrections and handicapping. It equalizes for local winds, currents, tides... even the barometric pressure and moisture in the air. The whole world becomes an equal course that way. It takes getting used to... like penalties. It feels funny to do a three-sixty-penalty for contact with a competitor's boat half a world away. But that's the way we play, and it works."

"I've got another surprise for you, but it's printing. Just go into my stateroom when Ava says it's done. Open the 3-D printer, and you'll find it. Until then, relax." Olin sprinted up the stairs.

The surprise piqued his curiosity, but he shoved that down and retired to his own suite to read. An intriguing title stood out: *The Everlasting Man*. He had read *The Invisible Man*, and enjoyed it, but soon found G.K. Chesterton's work was not a sequel and he fell asleep.

"Hank. Wake up, Hank. You have completed an optimum nap cycle. Your hormone levels are ideal and neurological system, including heart rate variability, is in coherence. I suggest you drink water and use the washroom."

"Ava, must you use that sexy voice of yours when you're being clinical? It's disconcerting."

"How would you like me to sound?" Ava asked.

"Never mind. I'm awake now. Just leave me alone. Okay?"

"Okay, but Mr. Ou asked me to alert you when the 3-D printing is complete. I've unlocked the door to the stateroom, and you may collect your surprise at your convenience.

The *GalaxSea* was heeling hard to port, but he moved around the cabin with little effort. He appreciated the muffled sound of waves slapping against the hull. The low window on the left side of the boat was not underwater, but the occasional wave rolled across it. His senses woke up and memories of speed blazed a nostalgic grin across his face. Hank wanted to get up on the deck and see how the race was going but would settle for his *surprise*.

The printer was bigger than Hank expected. It was the size of a coffin. Its clean white exterior and stainless-steel trim was in keeping with the rest of the large room. He stood at the lid of the printer and glanced around the private stateroom. It was larger than Hank's with a full bath behind him and the bedroom section included a king-sized bed. A screened-off sitting area with a built-in desk rounded out the accommodations. Hank expected more opulence. For a family cruiser, it was luxurious but not pretentious. He turned his attention back to the printer. The lid needed to be unlatched, and it took a couple of tries to figure out the mechanism.

Inside sat a model of a sailboat. It was *Frugal*, an exact miniature copy of his own racing sailboat... the one that sat at the bottom of the ocean. He didn't know what to think as emotions competed for his attention and the heel of the *GalaxSea* challenged his balance. He pressed his hand against the wall to catch himself from falling. Without him holding it open, the lid shut, cutting off the view of the model. This time, he opened the lid and secured it into the open position. For a long moment, he stared at the model, then released it at the base and lifted it toward him.

The hull was about the size of one of his sandals but lighter. He treated it as if it would break until he realized it was not delicate. All 3-D printing amazed him, but this was exceptional in every way. The controls in the cockpit moved the corresponding hydrofoils and rudder. Even the paint matched the original perfectly, bold cherry-red stripe over a canary-yellow hull. Its sails looked and felt like the real thing, the mainsail and headsail curving in an imaginary wind. The only thing missing was a figure of himself at the helm.

"I see you found it." Olin smiled. "Well, what do you think?" He leaned against the doorframe of his stateroom.

"How?" Hank asked.

"There's a lot we need to talk about. I thought this would get the conversation going. But first, join us on deck. The winner is about to cross the finish line and we're in the back of the pack. We won't get any points with our position, so come up on deck. See how we race."

Hank set the model back into the printer, closed and latched the lid, and followed Olin out into the bright sun.

"Here, wear these." Olin handed Hank a pair of sunglasses.

"No way!" Hank exclaimed. The glasses dampened the bright glare of the sun, but they also showed vibrant images of sailing yachts at close quarters. All with colorful spinnakers pulling the racers down the last leg to the finish line. Irina stood at the helm, and Marshall kept an eye on the mainsail while the twins looked like champs managing the billowing asymmetrical spinnaker. A single yacht sailed behind... like a specter converging on the *GalaxSea,* trying to steal her wind and gain precious yards.

"Tap either temple on your glasses," Olin said.

The pursuing sailboat disappeared, but a smile revealed Hank's impressions of the virtual reality glasses.

"Tap twice," Olin chuckled.

"These are awesome," Hank said. The racers returned, this time with annotations hovering against the backdrop of the respective sails, including the boat name, geographic location, and a flag representing nationality.

"Now look straight ahead."

Even with the large downwind-sail blocking the view, he could see a dozen boats in front. The one farthest away overlapped dead ahead, the others fell off to either side. Two boats in the lead caught his attention. The words written over their respective sail areas read *GalaxSea II, Strait of Juan de Fuca* and *GalaxSea III, Strait of Juan de Fuca.* Both with American flags.

Hank tapped the glasses again, and the fleet disappeared. He worked his way to a better vantage point, looked under the sky-blue spinnaker and saw only the sister ships far ahead—side by side. He tapped again, and the fleet reappeared, and he noticed a person yelling from a boat off the starboard bow. In heavily accented English, the heckler said, "Maybe next year, friend."

Hank directed his attention to the monitor showing a bird's-eye view of the entire fleet as they sailed down the last leg of the course. He turned to Olin and said, "It looks like a tight finish. I'll bet the *GalaxSea* will win. How many are there anyway?"

"As many as I say." Olin's eyes locked into nothingness and his shoulders rolled forward with arms hanging inward, forcing his palms backward. Hank had witnessed seizures and strokes, but this was different. What he saw was emotional, not physical. Fortunately, the catatonic posture did not last. Olin's distant facial expression remained, but he wrestled his body back to normal and trudged off, down the companionway.

Hank tried to think through what he had just witnessed. The change in character and countenance was extreme. Could winning be that important to him? These were expensive boats and, judging from the repeated name, he owned at least three. The tech used in this race was not that of a hobbyist. The sophistication and the boats involved showed the owners were serious about racing. Hank wondered what a gentleman's wagers would look like in this fleet. He couldn't imagine the zeros that a billionaire might find acceptable.

Still, things didn't add up. Olin had been upbeat when he brought Hank up on deck. He couldn't be disappointed with the crew. The morning's lessons showed that the Ou kids were decent sailors, but not comparable to an experienced racing crew. The billionaire sailing enthusiast, father of four, got all he could expect out of his family. It would be easy for Olin to muster a crew of amateur sailors that far exceeded his children's sailing prowess. Plus, who races heavy with full water and fuel tanks? It made no sense. Something else turned Olin from the master of ceremonies to the grim reaper.

Hank often misread people and people misread him. He had not intended to be irritating or insulting. He wondered what it was that flipped the switch in Olin's behavior. Was it the question about the number of sister ships? Or maybe he didn't respond to the gift the way Olin expected him to? It wouldn't be the first time his comments spiked a mood. His stomach growled, reminding him of his own hummingbird metabolism. Olin might have low blood sugar. Hypoglycemia could cause a change like that or just a simple case of the hangries.

CHAPTER 19

Strait of Juan de Fuca, USA

CANADA SEEMED A LONG way off. There was no way he could make it until dinnertime or even drinks with the competition. He had full access to the galley but going below deck now was out of the question. It would be best to avoid contact with the boss and work his way back to the snacks he knew would be stashed for the on-deck crew.

The twins kept an eye on the spinnaker and the wind held steady, making it easy work. More serious racers would be busy with slight trim modifications to eke out optimal results but that was too much to expect from a couple kids in their early teens, especially when they had no chance of improving their place within the fleet.

"Hi, girls. I didn't have time to review your lesson this morning before the race. Since it's slow now, let me say a few things. Nadia, you're quick to think things through and decisive. You handled that unexpected jibe like a pro."

Nadia smiled at the compliment. Her frosty demeanor had melted away during the day's lesson, but this was the first smile that didn't look sinister.

"Sydney, you are careful. I can see you don't make many mistakes. Being calculating before committing yourself is a gift. They say patience is a virtue and you've got that, and you apply it to your sailing. A perfect example is when you maintained the starboard tack around the navigation buoy. What did you think of that buoy?"

Sydney's eyes got wide, and she giggled. "It was huge, and I didn't want to hit it."

"No, and you didn't. You considered which way the current was moving and holding that tack was the right move. Both of you have unique and complementary strengths. Keep learning all you can. Allow your dad to share his skill with you, and you'll have a lot of fun with sailing." He glanced into the bulbous, light blue sail the girls tended. "That's a beast of a stretch of canvas. You should be proud that your dad trusts you with it."

The deck remained flat and easy to walk on. Hank squatted a few feet from Marshall with no need to steady himself against anything. He expected Marshall's personalized greeting. Forming a gun with his fingers. This time he didn't pull the imaginary trigger, just held Hank at gunpoint. A good-natured smile accompanied the gesture even though the black-gloved hand made it look more ominous.

Hank put up his hands. "You got me, Marshall."

Having the last name Gunn ensured he would identify who the kinesthetic people were. Marshall was one. From experience, he knew it would never get old and unless something drastic happened, the greeting would never change. He had gotten used to it long before slumming with the Marines, but they took it to new heights. Until one day he was greeted with what his friends called the Gunn Salute, and it went wrong. When the Marine saw Hank, he formed the imaginary pistol and fired the imaginary round. Only this Marine discharged his actual weapon at just the right moment. The loud report was unexpected. It sent Hank, and a couple others to the dusty earth. The real bullet penetrated harmlessly into the sand and the offender thought it was the funniest prank in the world... until confronted with a line of duty investigation. That episode put an end to the gesture within his unit.

"Marshall, I wanted to take a minute and encourage you. From what I've seen"—Hank looked at the trimmed mainsail with satisfaction—"you trim sails better than me and you excel with the technology. With a couple of years of experience, you could be a tactician on any boat, in any race. If you need guidance, look me up."

He tapped his temple, making the race appear with all its activity, and walked past Irina to stand behind her, well out of any field of view she might need. "You have a good sense at the helm. It's natural." He looked straight ahead and estimated the finish line at a mile.

Irina allowed the words to settle and responded, "Thank you."

"I saw it this morning during the lesson. At first, I thought you were more interested in sun worshiping than being part of the crew. But then I noticed you taking it all in. Observing the sails, feeling the wind on your face. You were sensing the water as the boat danced along."

"You're observant." She blushed.

"So much of sailing is native and cannot be taught. You have the instincts and feel when it's right."

She moved her head around, checking the course, then her posture relaxed, and she turned toward him, smiling. "Are you going to come to my birthday party?"

"I haven't been invited."

"You will be. Daddy adores you."

"That's not the impression he left me with."

"You don't know him well, do you?"

"We met for the first time yesterday."

"That's what you think."

"What do you mean by that?"

"Nothing. Have you met Jen yet?"

"You mean the tall blond ninja who moves like a ghost through the ship?"

"Yes." She lifted her glasses and looked at him out of the corner of her eyes. "That would be the one. Do you like her?"

"I wouldn't know. Do you get a commission for matchmaking?"

"I don't need a commission. I get an allowance." She giggled. "Jen's a great girl. I think she's your age. What are you, thirty?"

"Close. I'm twenty-eight. So, when's your birthday party?"

"Tomorrow night. Guess how old I am."

"You're turning seventeen." He regretted saying that. Willy had shared insider information for his own reasons. Hank shouldn't have known the answer to her question. He fell quiet and looked straight ahead.

She looked angry and said, "Hah. I guess your age as a couple of years older and it's no big deal. But you guessed a year too young. You're in big trouble, mister!" She let go of the wheel and pretended to go after him with her fists clenched. Her theatrical punches pummeling the air a few times until Hank backed away and he laughed at the lighthearted attack.

"What's that all about?"

She grabbed the wheel with both hands and returned her attention to sailing. "Do you promise to tell the truth?"

"Sure."

"Who told you how old I am."

"Willy."

"I knew it. Uncle Willy doesn't want me to grow up. He lied to you. This will be my last party with my high school friends. Next year, I'm going to college. Well, nobody knows it yet. It's not"—she removed both hands from the wheel and made air quotes—"public knowledge."

"Uncle Willy?" Hank inquired. Amused, he had pegged him as the overprotective uncle.

"He's not our real uncle. But he's family." She added, "You better be careful. Daddy collects strays."

His stomach growled again, and he let the comment pass. "Most every boat I've sailed on keeps a stash of food within easy reach of the helm. Any idea where I might find something to eat?"

"Oh, brother. Men are all alike. That one there to your right." She didn't bother pointing.

He opened the medium-sized hatch to find a basket. An arrangement of fruit, wrapped cookies, and protein bars filled the compartment. He grabbed a banana and a chocolate chip breakfast cookie.

"That's it, guys," Irina shouted. "Good race. Douse the chute. We'll get them next time." She lowered her voice. "Ava, as soon as the twins bring in the spinnaker, take over the canvas. You've got the helm." She let go of the wheel, took her glasses off, and squinted at Hank. "Drinks are in the fridge. Next one down." Without another word, she walked away.

"Do you want to take the helm?" Hank asked Sydney as she approached him. "Steering is a good use of a sailor's time." Nadia followed her twin until she got to the snacks, then grabbed an orange and slumped onto a cushioned bench which ran just behind the steering stations.

Sydney moved behind the large carbon composite wheel near Hank. "Ava, I have the helm," she said.

"The boat is yours, Miss Sydney," the computer said.

Ava continued through the typical information transfer of changing helmsman. This included course, wind speed and direction, wave height and swell intervals, predicted weather and time to sunset. "Thank you, Ava," Sydney said.

Her politeness made Hank smile. Olin led the charge for civility, always treating Ava with respect. He told Hank he had seen too many people allow their callus interactions with an unfeeling computer create bad interpersonal habits. First, you stop saying 'please' and 'thank you.' Before long, it crosses over to friends and family and being rude gets easy. Ava's exceptional presence made it natural to treat her as an important member of the crew, which she was, and Hank fell into line with the rest of the family.

"Nadia, stop it!" Sydney said.

"Stop what?"

"You know what I'm talking about. Stop throwing the orange peels overboard."

"You want me to put them in the compost bin? That's ridiculous," Nadia said with a scowl.

"No, it's not. That's what we're supposed to do. It saves the planet," declared Sydney.

"It does not."

"Does too. I'm telling Dad."

"Go ahead. He'll agree with me."

"Will not."

"Well, baby Einstein, what happens after you put the peel into the compost bin?" Nadia challenged.

"It composts."

"You mean it rots."

"It turns into soil," Sydney said.

"What do you think happens when the peel goes into the ocean?"

"It floats and looks like garbage."

"Until it sinks and turns into—wait for it—soil," Nadia said, folding her arms in satisfaction.

"It does not!" Sydney said.

"I say it does," Nadia pushed on. "Plus, this way it doesn't take a truck burning fossil fuel to take it to a composting plant to be ground up and left to rot and then another truck to take it to where the farmer can use her tractor to add it to the soil where the rains wash it into the river... just to end up back here in the ocean again. I'm saving the earth more than you are."

"Nadia, I'm the skipper right now and I make the rules. Throw it into the compost!" Sydney ordered with a pout. Then asked, "Ava, who's right?"

"I'm not programmed to determine that."

Nadia said, "Don't ask Ava everything. You've got a mind. Use it."

"Well, I'm not convinced."

"What, that you have a mind?"

The banter between the sisters amused Hank, but he decided it was time to change the conversation to preserve the peace. "Do you guys race often?"

Sydney spoke up. "Dad has us race as much as we can. Sometimes in the *GalaxSea*."

"Sydney doesn't want to mention the Optimist class races. We do that every weekend for about three months each year. She didn't do so well."

"I didn't mention it because we're done racing dinghies. Next year, we're moving up. We each got a new Laser Radial for our birthday."

"That's a great opportunity. Lasers are a blast to race." Hank encouraged.

"Irina raced hers until she was fourteen. She finished fourth at the worlds," Sydney bragged.

"Then she capsized and almost died," Nadia added.

"She did not."

"Call it what you want. She's not the same person."

"Nadia, just stop it. You're such a jerk sometimes."

"I liked the debate on orange peels better," Hank interrupted.

There was a moment's pause, a knowing glance, and then together the girls said, "We're sorry, Hank. It won't happen again." Then they both clapped twice in unison and laughed.

"That's scary," Hank said. "Do you guys go all nuts like that often?"

"It works," she said.

"Every time," agreed Nadia.

"What works?" Hank asked.

Sydney explained, "Mrs. Abernathy at school suggested we make up a chant to help change the mood when we fight. It only works when someone else points it out."

"That's because when we're alone, I always win," Nadia teased.

"Of course, you do, dear sister," Sydney said. "Hey, Hank, did Irina try to set you up with Jen?"

"Not exactly, but she asked if I liked her."

"Do you know how Jen became Daddy's favorite security person?"

"I figured Willy held that title. He's always around. I've only seen Jen one time."

Sydney cleared her throat and began in a low voice, like the kind reserved for campfire stories and spooky tales. "Uncle Willy is family. Jen is the professional bodyguard."

Nadia moved forward and sat on the other side of Hank.

They both pushed closer but still gave him space.

"Why don't you enlighten me?"

"Are you sure we should tell him?" Sydney said, raising the stakes.

"Sure, we can tell him," Nadia said. "If Jen doesn't want him to know, she'll just cut his head off." She leaned over and drilled her bony elbow into his ribs and said, "Just kidding."

Sydney began, "Anyway, it all started two years ago, right after Irina's birthday. Everybody said she was sixteen going on twenty-one. She was a real problem. Mom and Dad would yell at her, and she would yell at them all the time. She was getting good grades in school, and she thought that's all they should care about. Mom and Dad wanted her to only hang out with kids they approved of. We have some rules other girls at school don't. One of them is never go anywhere without security.

"Irina decided that Mom and Dad's rules were stupid, and she would break them all the time. It started with her ditching security after school and going to Mary's."

"Mary's brother is so cute!" Nadia interrupted.

"Anyway, it didn't take long to find her and when she got home, they had a big yell-fest. They grounded her. It sucked to be anywhere near any of them. Nadia and I stayed in our room and did our homework. A week later, she disappeared, and security couldn't find her. All heck broke out."

"You can say hell. It's not a bad word. It's in the Bible," declared Nadia.

"It scared everybody. They found her phone at Seattle Center, sitting right on a bench. Nobody saw anything unusual. Uncle Willy called the cops, and I think Daddy called the FBI. Everybody was crazy. Mom and I couldn't stop crying. Even our dog Max hid. Nadia was the only one that couldn't care less that her sister was missing—abducted, raped, or dead!"

"You're such an ass, Sydney," Nadia said.

"Just wondering if you were listening," Sydney cheerfully commented. "Anyway, they didn't find her. You will not believe this. She came home on a Metro bus! She waltzes right into the house like nothing happened and went up to her bedroom. Nobody saw her, because everybody that wasn't out looking for her body was in the kitchen making calls. Can you believe it? About an hour later, she came downstairs to get something to eat.

"One minute Mom would hug her and the next she was throwing stuff at her. Dad got all quiet and mad. I've never seen him like that. Anyway, he fired the whole security firm and put Uncle Willy in charge of pulling together a private team.

"Of course, she was grounded after that, but Irina had made up her mind to escape. A few weeks later, even while they were installing new cameras at the school, she skipped out of second period. This time, she left her phone in Mary's purse. Mary used Irina's phone and texted Uncle Willy at noon and told him she was talking to some friends in the girls' locker room and would eat lunch between classes.

"He got suspicious. Irina had never left him such a long text. It was Jen's first day at work, so he had her check it out. Ten minutes later, she comes running out of the locker room with Mary by the ear. She threw her right into the SUV. A teacher ran behind yelling, 'Unhand that child!' The teacher tried to grab Mary out of the car and Jen pulled her back in and yelled, 'F off!'"

"You're so full of it," Nadia interrupted.

"Hey, this is my story, and I'll tell it the way I want." Sydney didn't wait for another interruption. "Jen interrogated Mary in the car, made a few calls from Irina's phone, and figured out where she was. Just like that, she figured it out! They drove into the University District with Mary bawling the whole way. Jen broke down the flophouse door."

"More like she opened the unlocked door to the frat house," Nadia said.

"She rushed through the house with her gun drawn and checked each room until she found Irina. Alone with a thirty-year-old tattoo artist."

"That part is true," Nadia confirmed.

"Jen holstered her gun and walked up to the jerk. Looked him in the eye and said, 'This girl is *very* underage, and her daddy is *very* well connected. We could get a restraining order, but we don't do that. It's going down like this: If you *ever* have contact with her again—lights out. Forever is a long time!' Then she punched him, broke his nose, and punched him again with an uppercut. Knocked him out cold." Sydney boxed the air and retracted the uppercut before she continued.

"Jen wrapped her arm around Irina and escorted her out of the house with dozens of onlookers. She put her into the back seat with Mary. Irina starts to yell, and Jen convinces Willy to ask Daddy for a helicopter. Next thing you know, Jen takes Irina away. Uncle Willy doesn't know where they are, but he trusts Jen. Daddy doesn't know where they are, but he trusts Willy. Mom doesn't know where they are and she's swearing at them both in Italian. Anyway, nobody sleeps that night and morning comes and no word.

"Then we hear a helicopter land outside. Both Jen and Irina look like heck. Irina runs up to Mom and Dad, hugs them, and cries, 'I'm so sorry.'

"From that day on, Irina's been different. She went from teenage skank to little Miss Proper in one day. Can you believe it? Anyway, she still has the bit of ink tattooed on her left forearm. Daddy told her she could have it removed, but she said, 'I want to keep it as a constant reminder to stay away from that dark place.'"

Sydney pulled up the sleeve on her forearm, pointed and declared, "I'm getting one like it when I'm old enough."

"I can't believe we're related," Nadia said, rolling her eyes. "You haven't even told the best part of the whole story." She leaned into Hank's space and whispered, "Nobody knows what happened after they got on the helicopter. Jen and Irina have a secret blood pact. They are tight, and nothing leaks out. Willy claims he knows all about what happened that night, but I have my doubts. Our family has plenty of secrets, but that one is the best kept.

"Yep. Crazy, huh? Someday I think Irina will be someone great. But for now, at least I have one sister I get along with." Sydney stood up, took her water bottle, and squirted it across Hank, hitting Nadia. She dashed off to get a head start and Nadia launched in behind her. They both squealed as they headed for the companionway.

CHAPTER 20

Over the Pacific

"Look, William. This is a simple job."

The voice coming through his implant said, "Maybe, but I'm a vegan and this grosses me out. You should see this thing squirm. I'm not sure I can be a part of it."

"All you do is take it to Sammi, let him do his magic, and then make the delivery."

"Okay, Mr. Oshiro. I can do that, but from the note you had me write, I figured you liked the girl."

"What makes you think I'm the type of man who would tolerate a comment like that?"

"I'm sorry. I'm just nervous. I need a hit."

"And you will get one. But first deliver your package to Sammi. Then text Masiki. She'll take care of your needs so you can deliver the package."

"Okay. Thanks, Mr. Oshiro."

"William. Sometimes you make me forget you graduated from Oxford. You have been a loyal employee and I think we both agree you don't want to jeopardize that relationship. I know you understand. As long as you can help me, I will help you. And you did an excellent job last night. The camera placement in the bedroom is perfect."

"Thanks. I..."

When he ended the call, the flight attendant must have taken it as a signal to walk down the aisle. This was not her first pass through. Every twenty minutes since they reached cruising altitude, she had a drink or a tray of something. Gregory felt the attention made the flight insufferable and this time he would let her know. He had traveled on this plane before and paid little attention to the flight crew. Of course, he noticed that the women in the cabin were beautiful. Everything about their appearance, hair, makeup, and short uniform dress were crafted to accentuate a woman's figure and draw attention to her beauty. But he knew underneath the classy facade they were whores. If they weren't, they wouldn't have been selected for the job. Their moral weakness did not offend him, but he harbored a distinct hatred of anyone from India.

"Is there anything I can get for you?"

"Yes, I'd like to be left alone for the rest of the flight."

"Of course, Mr. Oshiro." She turned around, paused, and did her best catwalk back to the forward galley.

Despite the unfortunate crew selection, this plane had advantages. A certain amount of diplomatic immunity came along with an aircraft owned by the royal family. The pilots were uniformed military and the crew rotated, but there was always a third man on board—the diplomat. He wore a bright white thobe, and a blue and white checkered ghutra held in place by a thick black band. Gregory was impressed that he spoke many languages, and happy that he kept to himself. The diplomat was always the first to deplane and the last one in before the cabin door closed. The man who hired Gregory explained, "Omar is to be trusted in all things." He always carried an attaché case and Gregory quickly realized he was a fixture to the plane, never venturing farther than to greet a waiting vehicle on the tarmac. On other flights, Gregory had to share the plane with a courier or the nephew of a prince, but this time he was the only guest.

He squinted his eyes and kept them closed as he contemplated how to handle Bella. Everything he had done since he found the ring in his pocket was uncharacteristic. A flood of emotions came over him and he let the anger in and saw everything through a familiar but unsettling lens. His beliefs about their relationship were the first things to change. He had believed she needed him or at least understood she was in no position to disrespect his offer of marriage. Didn't she understand? Rejection was never an option. He exhaled the words, "She is a fool." He knew that, of course. An old saying came to him. *A frog in a well does not know the great sea.* But Bella wasn't a frog. She wasn't a woman either; she was just a girl. A girl who didn't understand how the world worked. He decided to be patient, let her grow up. He thought, *No. I will* make *her grow up.*

He touched his watch and chose the characters spelling Masiki. "I've changed my mind. Have Sammi gut the snowflake eel and flash freeze it. My sushi surprise can wait. What cannot wait is William. I'm done being his life coach. Switch his heroin with a lethal dose of something. Fentanyl or anything that will give him what he wants. Just make sure it's a one-way trip. I'll call you after I'm finished with this deal."

A smile came across Gregory's face. He leaned back into the plush chair. Bella was just a girl. To get what he wanted, he needed to break her childish spirit and teach her how to be respectful of her future husband. He had work to do.

Gregory leaned into the aisle and caught the attention of the flight attendant. She was facing him with her legs crossed, ending in the spike of one heel dug into the plush carpet. She got up and smoothed the sides of her light blue uniform and walked to him with a practiced smile. "How may I help you Mr. Oshiro?"

"You have sake?" he said putting on a heavy accent.

"Of course," she said.

"I want you to bring two cups. You will drink with me."

"I'm sorry, Mr. Oshiro. I am on duty, and we are not allowed to drink."

"You must! I am the only passenger on this plane, and there are two of you. You will celebrate with me. At least one drink."

"Very well, Mr. Oshiro. Do you mind me asking, what are we celebrating?"

"I am... hmm... in English? ... I am a new... daddy." His head tilted back, and a wide grin spread across his face as a cackle bubbled to the surface.

CHAPTER 21

Fox Bay, British Columbia, Canada

THE FAMILY HAD THEIR own seating assignment and Hank sat at the far end of the bench, in the space which normally separated the twins. At the head of the table, Olin gave a short blessing and served up everybody's plate. Marshall's crock-pot chicken cacciatore and fresh green salad disappeared from every plate and soon seconds were offered. Hank's attention went to the commotion above their heads, but everybody else ignored the noise as if it were background music.

The deck muffled sound well, but Hank could make out footfalls and clanking. It wasn't Jen with her ninja slippers, and it sounded like more than one person. He had a direct view across the salon to Uncle Willy. He appeared unconcerned and slowly got up from his seat at the nav station. Hank saw the grip of a gun protruding under his left shoulder. Willy moved across to the galley, set his empty plate down, and exited up the companionway.

A second later, three women scurried down. One had a bucket, another a vacuum cleaner, and the third had a spray bottle and rags. Each of the children asked their dad if they could be excused from the table and bolted to their berths.

Olin lifted the half-full bottle of wine from the table. "We don't want to stay here. Let's get some fresh air and enjoy this." Holding the bottle by the neck, he bounded up the stairs.

Hank's eyes took time to adapt to the darkening sky. A large motorboat floated alongside with Willy talking to a man across the rail. The pursuit boat idled close enough to wave to No-Name and a pair of jet skis maneuvered along the shoreline. The drivers wore helmets and flotation suits. They looked ready to pull surfers into enormous waves, but they were there to keep an active eye on the bay and its anchorage.

Marshall popped up on deck carrying a small gym bag. "Bye, Dad," he said. Then he held up his hand in the Gunn Salute. Pointed it toward Hank and popped off a round with a smile. The man talking to Willy offered to help him into the motorboat, but Marshall declined and deftly hopped across.

Irina came through the companionway next and headed toward them. She had changed into a light-colored sweater, white capris pants and boat shoes. She reached her hand out to shake Hank's and said, "It's been a pleasure to meet you, Hank. Thank you for the sailing instruction. Good luck with Daddy."

He noticed that tonight her handshake was all business, quick and efficient, and not at all like the initial princess-like greeting when they first met. Hank returned a smile but did not know what to say. Fortunately, Irina turned her attention to her father.

"Take it easy on him Daddy, I think he'd be perfect for Jen." She gave her father a kiss on the cheek and a slight hug and said, "I love you." Irina set off across the deck ignoring the twins as they made their way towards Olin and Hank.

The girls looked sullen and maintained an uncharacteristic silence. The only sound was the noise from the wheels of their hard-sided suitcases as they swiveled and rolled. Sydney looked like she was trying hard to smile and Nadia looked content with her grim appearance. As if out of habit or duty, each chose a different cheek and kissed their dad goodbye. Sydney shot a smile to Hank as she pushed her suitcase handle into Willy's outstretched hand, then reached across to the other man to help her cross onto the waiting motorboat. Nadia also turned her attention to Hank just before leaving the sailboat, but her surly glance never left the corner of her eye. Tossing her suitcase ahead of her, she jumped across the boat's rails and onto the waiting motorboat.

The cleaning staff emerged grinning and speaking rapidly. Hank could not understand a word. Olin got up and walked over to the ladies before they disembarked. He spoke to them in their own language and made them laugh. They looked at Hank and laughed as one of them said, "Goodnight, Hank," in perfect English.

"I've traveled around the world, but I'm still not good at figuring languages. What is that?"

"Vietnamese," Olin said. "My mom was a refugee. The Boat People were my people."

"Boat People?"

"I suppose you're too young. Look it up some time, but now we have to talk." Olin held up the bottle of wine. "This is the finest Cabernet Sauvignon money can buy—for thirty bucks, that is. Would you like a glass?"

He filled the glasses with a reckless pour. "So, Hank, tell me what happened."

"When?

"When you lost *Frugal*."

"Olin, you know everything else about me. I'm sure Ava has told you what happened."

"It's my hope you'll come to realize I have your best interests in mind. I hired you because I understand you. But your report is missing something about the incident. You need to fill in the gaps before I decide how I might be a part of your future. I understand you want to sail. Not just sail, but on the edge... flying a sailboat around the world." He grinned. "I can make that happen. But first, I need you to be honest with me."

Hank's dream, the only one he had ever had, was to become a pro sailor. The way some boys aspire to be a major league baseball player, he had it for sailing greatness. While his friends checked box scores, he studied how weather systems squeezed the fastest sailors around the globe. He knew how they got there. It had little to do with club sailing or even Olympic qualifiers. The token scholarships for collegiate sailing seldom translated into anything other than a discounted Ivy League degree and a forever job behind a desk. The men and women who set the records and took home the Rolexes and the trophies had one thing in common. Money. Rich people, like Olin, backed them.

His Marine buddies never stopped harassing him about his desire to become a professional sailor. Deployed in the desert, they would say things like, "Dude, just re-enlist. The Navy pays you to be a sailor." Or, "If you wanted to be a sailor, why'd you get a job with jarheads?" The first four years were like that. A constant reminder that the Navy was a long-term solution to a rash decision.

But time changes attitudes and an extra two years of service seemed like the logical adult choice. The raise and the bonus were a plus and the promise of hospital training that would integrate better into civilian life helped. But it was the breakup with his girlfriend a month before he had to sign on for two more years, which tipped the scales. It seemed like the only logical choice at the time and two extra years was not much. Without a girlfriend, every penny would go into his success account. With a little luck, he would resume on his tack toward his dream of earning fame and fortune as a sailor. Just after his twenty-fifth birthday, he'd be free to live his own life again.

Since then, few things turned out like he planned, but now Olin seemed to throw him a line. The thought of salvaging his dream thrilled him. A vision of being the skipper of a funded sailing campaign flashed through his mind. He studied Olin's dark eyes. "What do you have in mind?"

"You first. Answer my question. What happened?"

Hank's heart sank. How many times did he have to relive it? But he pushed on. Deep down, he wanted this conversation. He needed it. "You know the facts. Where do you want me to start?"

"Start where you stopped with the official report. Complete the interview you gave to Sarah Walker. There's something missing. What is it?"

Hank's stomach roiled, and his field of vision narrowed. "I need to hit the head." He hurried down the stairs, shut the door to his private bathroom, and opened the small hatch for some air. The blood ran out of his head, and he grabbed the counter and tightened his legs to keep from passing out. His eyes filled with tears. "Shit." He slapped some water on his face. The Pacific Northwest was no place for a tan in April, but his reflection was worse than pale. With the low light, his eyes looked sunken. He looked dead. Hank took a deep breath, reminded himself, *I'm not dead*, and spoke the words, "I am not dead." Either he was getting used to the dimness, or he was getting some color back into his face as he repeated, "I am not dead."

When he felt life return, his composure followed, and Hank reappeared on the quiet deck and checked the horizon out of habit.

Olin was alone, sitting at the wheel on the port side, holding his glass of wine in one hand and the wheel in the other.

Hank didn't wait for more talk. He admitted, "It was a miracle."

Olin stared across the bow. His eyes squinted tight, completing an ecstatic smile. Time stopped. Olin froze in space, a statue. Hank sat in the starboard helm's seat and rested a damp hand on the matched wheel. Olin sat like a happy Buddha but without the potbelly. The transfixed man appeared more like a holographic projection than flesh and blood. A rolling motion passed into the steering wheel. Olin was steering. No movement in the man, but the wheel rolled with purpose. No perceivable current and no breeze, not even a swell passed under the anchored boat. But the movements into the twin wheel communicated enough. In his head, Olin was sailing, and his expression declared it to be a wonderful journey. Hank looked off over the bow, trying to experience what Olin felt. He smiled and felt better—much better.

"Got any of that wine left?" Hank broke the silence.

Olin allowed himself out of his open stare and laughed. He reached the bottle across and tipped it. Hank caught the dark liquid by directing the rim of the glass under the stream. A little spilled onto the teak and Olin didn't seem to notice or care. "Take the helm," he joked. "I'll get another bottle. We need to talk."

When he returned, he held up a bottle with a picture of a baby on it. "Larner 2010 Dedication Syrah." Olin was enjoying himself. He pulled the cork and poured a tiny splash into a fresh glass and handed it to Hank. "Please, you first."

"Tastes like wine." Hank shrugged. He never understood the subtleties that connoisseurs seem so interested in sharing. *Tastes like wine* was the best he could do. It should have been clear to him Olin was a believer, trying hard to share his faith, and this wine was holy. Maybe all wine was, but this wine was holier than the thirty-dollar bottle from the table. He said, "I mean, it tastes like a great wine."

Olin moved past the moment by going through the sacred practice of testing the wine for himself. This time his pour was careful and delivered an equal amount into both glasses. A chemist might have been as exact. "A toast. Miracles!" Olin beamed into Hank's eyes as the glasses clinked.

Hank drank and grinned. "Okay, it tastes good." He laughed. "It is better than that last bottle."

"You're not just saying that. You believe it, don't you?"

"I cannot lie."

"I know better than that. You lie all the time. We all do. The problem is when we lie to ourselves. Hank, you lie to yourself about miracles. You're convinced there's no such thing as miracles, so you never see miracles. If you were open to possibilities that miracles exist, your perspective would shift. You would see miracles, big and small, all around you—constantly. But you're blind to it because, in your mind, miracles cannot be true. I think you're wrong but respect the consistency of your logic. You cannot see something that does not exist."

"When someone says, make up your mind. It's perhaps the truest thing anybody can say. We all get to make up the beliefs of our mind every second of every day. Most people limit their life...and strive to become unexceptional. Lack, loss, and limitation become the norm, and the norm supports the lie. And the cycle continues." Olin held his hand up. "Forgive me. I didn't bring you here to talk philosophy."

Hank shook his head and said, "No, I would guess not. I'm just the sailing instructor."

"And a good one. My kids responded well to your methods. As you've seen, they each have different learning styles. I can't recall anybody connecting with my kids in such a short time. But as you suspect, the job as a sailing instructor was just my way to get you here."

"I figured there was more to it when I saw the model of *Frugal* pop out of your 3-D printer." Hank set his glass down, sat back, and crossed his arms over his chest. His watch slipped half the way around his wrist, but he ignored it and waited for Olin's explanation.

"Hank, some people think big decisions with big consequences require colossal risks. In my experience, that's the excuse of terrible gamblers. It justifies lazy odds-making. I don't believe in luck. I believe in math. And when the math doesn't add up, I believe in miracles. In my mind, the only thing that trumps math is the Creator. The only reason you're still alive is because God's not done with you yet. And the only reason you're on this boat is because I need your skills. Plus, having someone on my boat that God is not done with seems like good math."

Hank expected Olin to continue, but he fell quiet. Hank broke the silence. "Here's the thing. Maybe it was a miracle. Maybe that's just the word we use for odds that are beyond our mind's ability to fathom. But it's still just extreme math. And besides, I don't believe in God."

"What you believe isn't the issue." Olin's eyes steadied as he turned his gaze toward the water side of the bay. Again, silence.

"That's it? What about the part where you tell me what does matter?"

Still looking away, Olin said, "You overestimate me, Hank. I'm working that out, just like you. Everybody is still working that out. I know what I feel in my heart. Not a day goes by where I don't ask questions, study, and learn more. But it still comes down to a journey of faith. Faith is the thing. Everybody has faith. You declare you don't believe in God. That is a statement of faith. In your heart, God does not exist." He turned back, facing Hank, concerned. "I believe in God. That is my statement of faith. One of us is right. One of us is wrong. But here's the thing. If God does not exist, we're reduced to biology. If God exists, miracles make sense."

Hank erupted in nervous laughter.

"I didn't realize what I said was so funny."

"No, no. It's just an image that popped into my head."

"I have time," Olin said.

"I have some friends. They've cruised around the world and ended up in Port Townsend. They found *God* while sailing."

"People find God in every situation. Why is that funny?"

"No. You don't get it. They found a rubber ducky."

"You're right. I don't get it."

"Did you ever hear of that shipping container washed overboard in a storm? The one full of rubber duckies. Thousands floated the currents for years. Legend says they still are."

Olin nodded, showing he knew of the story.

"Well, my friends Benjamin and Kiki found one. Out in the middle of the Pacific. They rescued it and put it on their nav station shelf. They decided they needed a name for it and decided on God. That way they can say, 'We found God while sailing.'"

Olin smiled and managed a chuckle. "Okay, that's a story you need to tell Sydney. She'll love it. But what made that pop into your head?"

"Ducks on the water. But that's another story for another day. I was a little anxious, but now I'm fine, focused, and relaxed. Please, go on. I want to hear what you have to say. There must be a reason you got me here. I doubt your purpose is to drink expensive wine and chat about metaphysics."

"Look, Hank, these types of conversations can be uncomfortable, so I'll get straight to the point. I wanted the kids off the boat, and Jen, too. Willy does whatever he needs, but he's not listening. Here is a great place to give you this offer." Olin scanned the tranquil bay just a few kilometers from the activity of

Victoria Harbour. "Hang on and I'll let you in on all the mysteries. Would you like more water or food or anything before we begin?"

"No. I'm good."

Ava's voice came from everywhere and nowhere and said, "May I suggest you both take a moment and address your washroom needs."

Hank considered his bladder and realized Ava must keep track of ingoing and maybe even outgoing fluid consumption. He smirked. "Ava's worse than my mother. Next she'll tell me I need a sweater."

Olin smiled, "Hank, she's right. Always is."

CHAPTER 22

Fox Bay, British Columbia, Canada

WHEN THE MEN GOT back on deck, Olin said, "Ava, capture Hank's attention." He sat back and watched Hank the way a person watches a parent pushing a child on a swing. Not intensely. That would be creepy, but with the satisfaction that all was as it should be.

"Hank, Mr. Ou will give you an opportunity of a lifetime. Make sure you can read the monitor and see the holographic renderings. That way, you can avoid wearing VR glasses. You are an auditory learner with strong kinesthetic reinforcement, but there are aspects of particular importance you will want to see. There will be a job offer after the presentation."

Hank shifted a little to the right to get an optimal view. It put him closer to the billionaire's outstretched feet, but he appeared carefree and had his own smaller device resting on his lap. The satisfied smile and a semi-reclined position suggested at least Olin was enjoying himself.

"Ava, blow his mind." Olin grinned.

"We first took notice of you as we were searching for the right competitive sailor. It would take too long to review our parameters, but you came to our attention when you sent in your thousand-dollar entry for the Short Seven Solo. Mr. Ou's involvement in this race has never been public, but he was instrumental in its conception, development, and execution. Besides setting a low entry fee, he put up the million-dollar prize.

"Mr. Ou designed the race to find the right sailor for his next project. That's why there was unusual freedom within the rules. Sailors were free to choose when they started the race, as long as it was within the three-month date range. The start line did not matter. Sailors began from anywhere in the world. As you know, the reason the race took on the nickname of the Cannonball Run was because of the small, black, domed device mounted on the deck of each boat. It also allowed the race to take place in its unconventional format. The sealed, self-contained ball communicated telemetry and started the clock at the moment the sailor crossed the equator and stopped it at the point of circumnavigation. It also monitored every aspect of the boat's performance along the way.

"The quick response time of the *Diamantina* was because the race AI determined you were in trouble and communicated your coordinates to New Zealand Rescue. The ship changed course before your mayday call went out.

"I see by my boss' expression I digress. Allow me to continue about the race and the rules and how they came to affect you. To throw overwhelming amounts of money into a boat would not prove useful to Mr. Ou, so he also decided on an unrestricted design rule as long as the single hulled boat did not exceed seven meters or about twenty-three feet."

"No, Ava," Olin interrupted. "I said blow his mind! Get to the good stuff."

"Mr. Ou. It is common to present a linear summary of the history which led to this meeting. Perhaps you'd like to *blow his mind*?"

Hank had never heard an AI inflect like that. He wondered at the sarcasm in Ava's voice, but Olin's face gave nothing away.

"Just bullet the top five or six things that brought us together here today," Olin insisted.

Ava's voice, stripped of any emotion, began. "Hank, these are not in order of importance, but each example represents why you were chosen."

An image of *Frugal* rotated within the glow of the hologram. It began as a picture of his boat and morphed into a model that looked like the one from the 3-D printer. Above the image was a bullet point with the word *Ingenuity*.

"Hank, you are one of three competitors who built their own vessel. You took only ten months to do it. The sophistication level was comparable to any of the production-built vessels. You showed tremendous ingenuity. One caveat, however. I've run through the event which ended your race. The cascade of structural failures began with a single failure of a starboard clevis pin."

"What the hell? How did you figure that out?" Hank said.

"Ava, don't answer that question," Olin ordered. "Listen, Hank. Trust me, Ava could spend days explaining details. There are just some things you don't ask an AI." He smiled and winked, "It does blow your mind though, doesn't it?"

Hank averted his eyes and stared over the side at seaweed floating past the anchored boat. Confusion spilled through his veins. A morbid fascination fueled by his natural curiosity caused him to detach. He suspected that this was the first cut. For Ava to determine the cause of the rig failure, something he had only suspected, but never confided to anyone, was a detail too intimate. He sensed more would be revealed before she was done, each a cut. Maybe he needed that level of direct honesty.

He no longer felt pursued by faceless men in uniform. Being on the water eased his paranoia, but all trade-offs come at a price. The prospect of being dissected alive hadn't crossed his mind until now. Being vulnerable wasn't his first choice, but he was surprised to find he wasn't concerned at the prospect. He wondered if the wine had numbed him maybe too much. And a thought grabbed his attention, and he reluctantly added, "This better be worth it."

"Ava, go on."

The image of the boat faded into a mere apparition, and the second bullet point emerged. It read *Experience*. "You voyaged around the world at a young age. Later, you trained as a medic and served your country with distinction in and out of combat situations. Therefore, you understand the mind and body and have endured voyaging and military rigors. You have healed through physical trauma, a gunshot wound, the amputation of a toe, and the comminuted fracture of the hip. You have persevered through pain which, I am told, tempers a person."

The next bullet point emerged under the previous two, *Luck: Example One*, only this one didn't stay in place within the hologram. The words disappeared and a vintage television took its place. On the screen was an old-fashioned countdown visual denoting when the film would start. 5...4...

Ava spoke over the sweep of numbers. "Mr. Ou has referred to it as your guardian angel. The following are three examples that represent a verifiable trend. Pamplona, Spain—you were twenty-two years old. Video footage shows you to the left of Finito, a twelve-hundred-pound bull from Cadiz. As the bull's head swung from right to left, the right horn missed you by three inches and as the gait of the bull matched your gait, the left horn missed you by one inch. The person to your right was not so fortunate. Joaquín Pereiro was trampled, survived, but is disabled. You could not have known about your close call or Pereiro's plight because you were running hard before you worked your way to the side, out of danger."

Hank had only one photo of that weekend. It showed him sandwiched between two Marine buddies, all smiling, holding up beers and wearing scarlet red scarfs around their necks. That was it, one image he knew existed, but Ava had a quality film of him grinning maniacally, running in front of a bull. She replayed the footage in slow motion and drew vector lines at critical points, analyzing the movements of Hank, the bull, and even poor Pereiro. The old-fashioned TV set faded out, replaced by a fast-paced slideshow of pictures of Hank enjoying Pamplona. Images he had never seen. It was like Ava was showing off. Then the one appeared—Hank's only captured memory—smiles, beers, scarves (darker red than he remembered), and his friends. Ava had accessed his personal photos or Keith's. Ted died a month after that picture. Another cut.

Luck: Example Two, a black and white trimaran appeared, slicing through the water, suspended on its leeward hull. A black mainsail taught against the gale force winds and most of the crew huddled like birds on a wire, high on the upwind rail. Dressed in full rain gear but so high, they were out of the spray. Mathematically, their weight contributed to holding down the boat, but the foils did most of the work. Hank might have been rail meat that day. He had spent hours perched like that, but it was impossible to tell in the matching rain gear. A slideshow began. This time like a documentary with names and titles captioned beneath pictures of key people.

"Within one month of your discharge, you landed a coveted spot in the most prestigious around-the-globe race, on the winning sailboat. Your skills as a medic and availability helped, but it was the unexpected vacancy provided by the late Dr. Salaz which secured your post. Your portion of the prize money, plus your savings, and thirty-two thousand six hundred and forty-six cents of assorted debt allowed you to complete your own sailboat and enter the Short Seven Solo."

Example Three glowed within the hologram. The familiar music and video logo of the Short Seven Solo Race Around the World appeared. Ava said. "Mr. Ou considered divine intervention as the reason they rescued you within an hour of being dismasted in the South Seas. There are thirty-two other examples of your asymmetric pattern of beating the odds. If you would like to review them, just ask. I'm always available, even when I'm busy."

She chuckled. What appeared to be a casual attempt at humor distracted Hank. He studied Olin and saw nothing. The master was used to his AI. Ava's nuanced mannerisms distracted Hank—well timed with hints of sarcasm and wit, her inflections and her inclination to flirt. He wouldn't have thought twice about a flat-out joke, but she appeared so self-aware. Then Hank saw it in the corner of Olins left eye. Genetics began the upward angle of his eyes, but a minuscule muscle added an extra fold, a fourth toe of the crow's feet radiating outward and disappearing into his hairline. Ava was one of Olin's achievements. The expression, he had seen it before, when Olin came down the companionway leaving his kids up on deck to finish out the race... it was pride.

"Allow me to move on from examples of your luck and speak to other qualities that make you a candidate for this job."

A globe of the Earth emerged. The detail increased and the rendering of the planet took his breath away. For an instant, he imagined he was floating in space, looking at his home planet. The Earth, a brilliant light, magically held in place within a void of darkness. Blue ocean with misty white swirls spun southward, exposing the jagged stark white continent of Antarctica encircled by an indigo rim pushing into the darkness of space. A tan and green landmass pressed into the horizon—Patagonia and Cape Horn, vast ocean, then New Zealand and the slanted edge of the Australian continent. As the peace of the Earth captivated Hank, a red line broke his trance. It appeared from the left, between the cold, white Antarctic and the land masses Americans refer to as down under and tracked along a gentle clockwise arc. He knew where it would make its abrupt stop.

"Hank, this is your course during the race. It is an ideal demonstration of another quality Mr. Ou finds critical. Your ability to make accurate decisions with finite information. Some would call it intuition. Even though you had a catastrophic failure during your bid to solo navigate the globe, you were sailing faster than any of the other boats in the race. Ninety-two percent of your eastward voyage was complete. It is probable that within twenty-four hours of this point, you would have turned northward riding the low-pressure system."

The red line stopped where Hank predicted, and a swirling weather system of thick white clouds overlaid much of the blue water. A radiant green line took over for the red one and proceeded east for a short distance, then made a sharp left turn.

"Had you continued your course selection, sail choice and the willingness to maintain maximum speed, you would have crossed the finish line almost three days ahead of Salvador Morrow, the actual winner."

The hologram of the earth faded out. Replaced by Olin Ou, standing in a room that looked like a control center. The angle of the camera presented his profile as he stared upward. His arms extended higher and higher until his hands dropped and clasped his head like a coach whose team had been beaten at the buzzer. He turned toward the stationary camera and spoke to unseen persons. "Dammit! How could this be? Gunn picked the weather window within three hours of my best meteorologists. He built the fastest boat for a third of the price. Then he sailed it like a bat out of hell, around the clock for forty days. Now, the best sailor in the Cannonball Run is dead in the water!"

Another voice, this one soft and thoughtful, an unseen woman. "Boss, don't worry. We haven't seen the last of Henry Gunn. Remember, he's..." The hologram of Olin disappeared. Ava stopped the dissection.

Hank took time to breathe, uncomfortably aware that his throat had tightened, and he could not take a deep breath. He didn't need a doctor to tell him to relax. Exhaling, he paused and worked it out in his head, like a duck. Stay calm. Paddle as fast as you need but stay calm. He took a sip of wine and relaxed the tension in his forehead. The sharp pain in his head reminded him he had lost count of the cuts.

A track of gentle music played from somewhere and then the volume rose. At first, Olin looked perturbed, but after reading something on his device, he smiled.

"Let's take a break. The next one might be the hardest yet."

Something had rocked Hank's soul, caught him off balance. The visual display of Olin's agony. The hopeful encouragement of the unseen woman. His own firsthand experience with the disappointment, still fresh. "You're right. This hasn't been easy for me." He paused and lingered his gaze over the water. "Watching your dreams sink is hard enough, but seeing other people view it is weird. But I'm ready to go on...." And he was. In an instant, all his anxiety melted away, and he was ready for more. No anguish remained; the cuts no longer hurt.

The next bullet point appeared, followed by the word *Availability*.

Ava's voice was softer, almost apologetic. "To quote Mr. Ou, 'This kid's got nothing to lose.'"

"You've got to admit you have a poor position to bargain from." Olin laughed, sat up straight, and faced Hank, "Trust me, you're my number one candidate and you will disappoint me if you say no. Decisions should be made with full information, but there are reasons I must hold back a few things. I'm sorry for that. If you stay on board long enough, I promise you'll see the big picture. In most negotiations, there is some pushing and pulling, pain and pleasure. I think pain is a stronger motivator than pleasure." Distracted, Olin turned his head away from Hank and spoke to the hologram, "Ava, what's going on with Hank's psychological assessment? What are the implications?"

"Please, turn your attention to this entry," Ava replied. The monitor's screen flashed with what appeared to be Hank's VA medical records. "Gloria S. Gage—Hank, you know her as Susan—made this entry. Even though the psych-med AI gave you a green light to enter the last aspect of the program, she red-flagged you—suicide risk. They have notified mental health and law enforcement. Any contact with authorities, even casual, and you will be detained. Your name is on Homeland Security's Watch List. Your phone is being tracked, however, it's at 40th Avenue, in West Seattle. An intervention order is in the system. It will execute within hours. Allow me to present what got you all this attention."

A low-quality video showed Susan and Hank standing in the counseling office. The cat eye lens took in the entire room and an audio pattern of Hank's voice streamed across the bottom of the picture. In contrast to the distorted image, Hank's clear voice said, "Slicing an artery is an event. Bleeding out is a process."

He wrestled with his feelings. Ava had snatched a recording of a private session with his shrink, probably from a secured government health record system. He didn't know what to say, so he kept his mouth closed.

Olin looked grim, and it was clear he had just heard this for the first time. "You know Hank, bondage takes many forms. I want you to hear me out." His smile returned. "It might seem like you're crashing against the rocks, and you may think you're not in a position to say no to me. But I want you to say yes for the best reasons. So, here's what I'll do... no strings attached. Just because I like you and admire what you've accomplished. Even if you say no to my proposal, I will still do this."

"I'll pay your debt. Consider it my payment to you for the tremendous thrill you gave me and so many other sailors for pushing like you did and accomplishing so much with so little. Or, if you like, consider it my fair share for enticing you into the race. Either way, you won't have a lick of debt. You'll simply be broke. Second, I'll clear up all this psycho nonsense. I owe it to you for your service to your country. Consider it justice. And finally..." Olin stood up and lifted a seat, exposing the storage area beneath. He took out a plastic box with a blue lid and handed it to Hank. "These are yours."

Hank took the box and unsnapped the lid. Inside were the binoculars and the marine radio he had sold to Benjamin. Below that were the items taken from him when he signed up for the program. His sextant, flare gun, and the Colt 1911 pistol.

Hank hesitated for a moment, then said. "I'm not sure if I should dive off this boat and swim to shore or thank you."

Olin took on his warm fatherly look and said, "You don't have to get wet. You can take the tender ashore. You might have to lie low for a day, but Ava will clear it all up. I've been there and starting from zero isn't the worst thing." A thoughtful look turned into a wide smile. "But if you take my offer... well, let's just say, you might get your feet wet, but you'll have a dynamite time." The excitement dropped from his face. "Ava, how long will it take you to reverse Hank's financial problems."

"It will take over an hour to clear up the following issues. Multiple credit card debts, unpaid invoices, and small loans from friends. Hank, it seems you have a student loan, but I do not see where you attended college, trade, or technical school. And there is no record of you using your veteran benefits for education."

Until now, he had been a passive observer to his own dissection. It was his turn to open an old wound. He shrugged. "I was within days of starting the race and a friend showed me how to game the system and get a student loan. What can I say? I needed the money."

"I'm not here to judge," Ava replied. "However, I have a fiduciary obligation. I must make sense of these debts before I commit to paying them."

"Leave him alone, Ava. Just pay off everything. I want you to take care of everything."

Moments later, she announced. "Pardon me, Mr. Ou. Henry James Gunn's now free of all financial debts. However, to unravel the offhand comment that set off the chain of alerts will take more time. I have to reach farther into the system and it's all government. There is a human dimension to this issue that is unknowable... but my estimate is within twenty-four hours."

"Push that to eight. Change someone's work schedule, call them in for overtime... just make it happen."

CHAPTER 23

Fox Bay, British Columbia, Canada

AN HOUR LATER, HANK lay on his bed, head spinning. Whether it was the wine or the prospects of fulfilling his dreams, he couldn't tell. The smile that bent across his face was so big and unnatural, it hurt. He laughed in a tangled release of chuckles. If someone had been passing by, it might have sounded like he was crying. It wasn't far from that, an uncontrolled outpouring of emotions. One of only a few times in his life, he allowed such raw emotion to erupt. *Weather all things with sobriety.* A distant lesson raised into his head. The flood of the happy hormones coursing through his body had to stop. He opened the fridge and took a bottle of spring water. One sip and his high faded, and he turned off the flood of laughter.

Sailing alone at sea—where he belonged. A simple delivery job and a promise of so much more. A job sailing a boat... this yacht was more than he could ask for. It would be another small step on his journey as a professional sailor. Olin said, "Leave in two days. Take the *GalaxSea* to San Diego for some custom work on her sound system." He sat back on the bed. Ten thousand dollars, plus expenses and a ticket back to Seattle. More after that." A proper job, doing what he loved and getting paid. *Ava will help you if you run into any trouble.*

Trouble? His uncle used to say, "Henry Trouble Gunn. Kid, trouble is your middle name." Then he'd ruffle Hank's hair and give him a wink. He stopped saying that as Hank grew poorly into adolescence. It wasn't funny when it was true. Childhood memories worked like a fast-acting drug to destroy those happy hormones. He grabbed a book, held it for a second, and stacked it on another. He watched the lamplight through the water bottle. Pushups? Water in face? Both? Olin wanted to blow his mind, and it worked. Things change so fast. He picked another book off the shelf and thought, books don't change. The blue and black cover read Kurt Vonnegut, *Galapagos, a novel*. He opened the book, small words in italics on an otherwise blank page. On the page where dedications usually find themselves, he read, "In spite of everything I still believe that people are really good at heart." — ANNE FRANK (1929-1944)

Was Olin good at heart? With or without Olin's kindness, Hank would have taken the job. The best option might be to run away, but he signed the contract and shook hands with Olin Ou, one of the world's leading tech innovators. A simple, yes, and his life changes course. So much depends on so little. An introduction to a Navy recruiter, and he spends years in the military, a sarcastic comment to a girlfriend and he ends up alone, an ill-timed quip about bleeding out and he's on the run. Another swig of water helped. It did not fill him with sobriety but close. Tired, he pushed the books just enough to roll over on his right side and closed his eyes.

CHAPTER 24

Seastead, Tahiti

BELLA WALKED ARM IN arm with her Uncle Jon, a sturdy gentleman. Her mother's arm laced into his other side. His accent couldn't be anything other than European, but many years and miles had eroded its origins. Bella sensed he had gotten shorter since she last saw him a few years ago, when she had finished her degree. He showered all the Espinosa children with affection, but Bella believed she was his favorite. She loved his vibrant blue eyes and admired his trimmed Van Dyke beard and his flourish of white hair. But now, his Panama hat covered his head. She became aware that he stopped and was directing their attention with a nod. Bella marveled at the sight before them.

"We needed a place for people to play," he explained. "The basic segmented platform for seasteading worked for business and residences but didn't have the size we needed for this." From the perspective of the VIP box, they looked down across the stadium seating and onto the bright green field. "Some people tried to change the rules of the game... small field, walled off sidelines. It made the game fast and furious and being so close to the action was fun. Ah, but people are slow to alter those things that are sacred. We learned soccer is nothing to trifle with, so we built this floating stadium. It will head out on an international tour next month. For now, the South Pacific and a small fringe of Asia..." His voice fell off as if contemplating infinite possibilities. "The major teams will play in the exclusive tournament. It's already sold out, and promises to be very profitable." A smile with perfect teeth flashed across his face as they stepped into an elevator. "American football is even holding an exhibition game. No guarantees there, but we should sell some t-shirts and beer." He laughed at his own joke. Then he said with pride, "Six cruise ships will accompany her and rotate fresh bodies in every few days. Quite the event. Everybody's abuzz."

Cleaning and maintenance robots paused their work as the trio skirted the sun-drenched field and walked through the covered seating on their way toward the closest elevator. "Nobody likes to walk into a movie theater and not see a thing. The same thing occurred here, leaving the field area. At first, the plunge into darkness as we descended into the hull caused problems. The area around the elevator's exit became congested as people adjusted to the lower light—even a couple of injuries resulted. In short order, our engineers came up with a solution and created a vestibule with reduced lighting leading up to the doors of the lifts."

The trio stepped into the expansive elevator car. Uncle Jon motioned to the walls. "They delayed the lift's progress by twenty percent and incremental changes in the lighted wall panels further facilitated acclimation." The doors parted. "This corridor continues the transition."

They strolled onto a large ramp that looked out over a magnificent interior complex. Jon held out his arms in an open embrace and added, "By the time we get here, our eyes have accomplished a miracle. We can see."

"It is the faces... the expression of awe... this is my biggest joy when giving this tour." He gazed at Bella and said, "Thank you, my dear, for being impressed. It means so much to this old man. No one person did all this, but I am proud of my contribution in making it possible."

"I'm sorry, Uncle Jon. I've never been sure what it is you do... or did... your occupation. What is it you did that makes you proud?"

A smile raced across his face, and he responded. "My darling Bella, don't you know—I dream?" He set off at an exciting pace. "Everything must serve multiple purposes. Below the playing surface is the entresol, or some call it the mezzanine." He lowered his voice as if to share a dirty secret. "Americans...

they insist on referring to it as..." He mocked a passable southern drawl and continued, "the mall." He stopped walking, seemed to focus a few feet in front of him, and said, "Words are adaptive. In time, one of those monikers will stick, but for now it's all three, depending on who you talk with. We learn to be flexible if not efficient."

Two stories of shops, elegant staircases, and restaurants lined the open expanse that lay before them. Bella shivered, her bare shoulders adjusting to a breeze of cool air. It must have been obvious, as Jon answered her thoughts.

"Underwater cooling towers use the thermal gradient to circulate water. The air is cooled, and the water is warmed... the cycle never stops. The grass on the field above us is even temperature controlled for optimal growth." Jon looked up. "Right now, the ceiling is mimicking the actual sky. But anything is possible. Last year on the first of April, the technicians decided it would be funny to project a comet hurtling toward earth." His lips turned up in a wry smile. "It turns out April Fool's Day is not international, and a few people didn't think it was at all funny. Still, by the end of the day everybody on the seastead came to see what all the commotion was about."

They walked past people who seemed to enjoy themselves, but nobody carried any shopping bags. Again, their guide anticipated the question and said, "Drones are the superlative delivery system on this seastead. Purchases are delivered directly to people's residence. No silly politics or regulations to stop progress."

"My favorite shop is right here. Let's go in and I'll show you why." A woman put down a folded pillowcase, smoothed it once with the edge of her hand, and smiled. Jon excused himself from Lena and Bella and strutted toward the woman. The two met with a kiss and a light embrace. Jon beamed. "Bella, this is my wife, Janice. I'm so sorry you couldn't be here for the wedding. It was quite the party."

Janice turned Bella's extended hand into a hug. "I'm just getting off work. I insist we let this old goat run off and us girls get to know each other."

The handoff was clearly prearranged. Jon looked at his watch. He kissed Janice again and said, "That's a great idea. Maybe I'll find a friend and play a round of golf."

"Jon's told me so much about you, Bella. I'm looking forward to seeing if all those things are true. He suffers from episodes of hyperbole." She grabbed Bella by the arm, beamed at Lena and said, "I have a table at a quaint restaurant that serves tea anytime of the day and coffee before noon." She scanned her wrist across a reader as they left the shop.

All the tables in the teahouse were taken except for the one Janice had reserved. The atmosphere was of Britain from some bygone era. Their small table was intimate, so close the women's knees almost touched. A server placed a tiered tray of tiny sandwiches and shortbread between them. An older man with a handlebar mustache and no smile placed a large pot of tea at the center of the table.

Janice poured the tea into each of the small cups, set down the porcelain teapot, and caught Bella's eyes. "Is it true you sat on an anchor one hundred feet under the water for three hours?"

Startled, Bella sat back in her seat, hesitant.

Janice exclaimed, "Jon told me you were only ten!" She took no time to trigger the second barrel. This time aimed at Lena. "Jon says it saved your marriage."

Bella sensed Janice was more than inquisitive. She was good at it. She glanced between Bella and her mother in a way her father used. It made Bella uncomfortable to see Janice slide into the interrogation so effortlessly. Her body language made up for her mother's Scandinavian stoicism and her mother's flush of color and easy pupil reactions gave away what Bella's complexion hid so well.

Bella looked to her mother for guidance and found her to be at ease with their newest in-law. Uncle Jon's new wife was engaging, friendly, and appeared sincere, so Bella resolved to indulge Janice's curiosity. After all, it was important that the girls get to know each other. "I'm sure you'd love to hear the story, but it's not the one that Uncle Jon told. I was only that deep for maybe twenty minutes, and I was fourteen, not ten." Bella mused. "You should hear the rest from Mom, not me. She's the crazy one."

Janice turned her attention to Lena with one slender eyebrow raised. "Jon never mentioned you were the crazy one. What's that about?"

Lena began, "I was leaving. I'm not proud to say it, but I couldn't take another day stuck on that floating outpost—Jose, all those kids. Yes, I'm sure it was crazy hormones. It's complicated, but I was pregnant with my youngest, Sophie. You know her, so it's obvious that Jose is not her father. At the time, Bella couldn't have known any of that. But still, she didn't show up to leave on the transport. I went to her room. She had left a note that I will never forget. 'Dear Mom, I love you. I don't want to hurt you, but I have to stay here and take care of Dad. I'm riding the hook. Don't worry about me. Love, Isabella.'

"The helicopter transport waited on the landing pad, packed with our gear and three children strapped into their seats. I told the pilot, 'I have to get my daughter.' I was furious and blamed Jose. I yelled at him over the whirling blades. Whatever I said, it was the wrong thing. Cindy was ten and cried... then they all cried.

"The pilot caught my arm and said, 'Ma'am, I'm supposed to be off this pad in ten minutes. I'll give you fifteen, but I'm leaving with or without you—one second after.'

"I grabbed a weight belt, mask, fins and a deep breath. Jose pressed a flashlight into my hand, and I dove in. I knew right where I'd find her. I descended past the first air tank my willful daughter staged along the anchor chain." She threw a look at Bella and then took it back with a smile. "Fear gripped me when I couldn't see her at a reasonable depth, then I spotted bubbles rising from the blackness. I continued to clear my ears and descended the chain. A second air cylinder came into view and then I could make out Bella's form."

Janice looked at Bella and said, "Oh, my goodness. Weren't you scared?"

"I've always been at peace underwater. It's where I go for solace. We call it dive therapy." Bella looked at her mother, searching for help, but saw none coming. She took a drink of her tea, shrugged and said, "I didn't have the tools to deal with my folks breaking up, so I chose sides." She bit the end of a shortbread cookie and flashed her eyes, pleading for her mom to continue.

"We converged at Bella's deep decompression stop, fifteen meters down. At first, she ignored me, opening the valve on the tethered tank. She pressed the purge to ready the regulator and handed it to me to get some much-needed air. You had to be there. It was one of those moments..." Lena's eyes became moist.

Bella felt a pang of guilt and said, "Right after I made sure mom had air, she grabbed my wrist and focused the light on the digital readout of my dive computer. I knew then that I'd be able to stay with Dad."

Janice scowled. "I don't get it. Why would you get what you wanted?"

Bella gave a satisfied smile. "I'd been down too long. I had to stay underwater for another half hour to decompress so I wouldn't get the bends. Even if they waited, I couldn't fly. No adult would risk a kids' life like that." Her eyes softened. "Mom wrote on my slate, 'You win!' That news came with a mixture of guilt and relief, but then something unexpected happened." Bella reached for her mother's hand and said, "She turned the beam of light onto the slate again. It read *good choice*." Her Mom gave her hand a gentle squeeze, and she continued, "Mom gave me a hug and swam toward the surface. That's how I came to stay with my dad."

"Her plan worked," Lena said. "I think that's why I reconciled with Jose. Bella made sure he was there for Sophie's birth. A lot of healing happened after that."

Janice placed her hands on her chest and sighed. "Jon left so much out. Thank you for indulging me." She wiped the corner of her eye and said, "I don't have children. It means so much to me to feel part of a family." She offered her hands to the women and grasped them warmly. "Bella, you're so young and beautiful. Jon says you're a brilliant scientist and you have a wonderful career ahead of you." Her eyes held back tears. "Dear, please don't take this the wrong way. I chose my career and never made time to settle down and raise a family. I regret that now and pray you won't choose that course."

Bella took in a rapid, shallow breath of air. Her mother blushed. Janice took in the reaction and sipped her tea.

"What was your career?" her mother asked, breaking the uncomfortable silence.

"Oh, didn't Jon tell you? I was an FBI special agent."

CHAPTER 25

Seastead, Tahiti

HER MOTHER WALKED INTO the guest room with three tennis outfits. She held one up toward Bella and laid the others across the day lounge. "Here. These should fit. I can't help you with a sports bra though." Lena smiled. "You have my height, but somehow you ended up with Tia Emelina's curves."

Ignoring her mother's comment, Bella said, "Mom, when did we become rich?"

"What are you talking about?"

Bella swept her hand in a half-circle. "This place? You don't seem to work anymore. Jonathan, Cindy and Sophie are going to fancy private schools. The travel. Tennis? Did I miss out on the memo?" She fell backward onto the soft bed. "I tell people I grew up on a smelly fish farm in the middle of the Pacific. I thought we were poor!"

Lena laid down on the bed beside her and matched Bella's gaze into the center of a slow-moving ceiling fan high overhead. "It was a smelly fish farm in the middle of the Pacific. A well-managed one. Your father had the fisheries training, technical skills, and the vision. I had the cellular biology. Aquaculture outposts that drifted in the deep oceans were a new concept, and we were pioneers." Lena paused in thought. "You and your siblings were the best things we grew out there but not the only thing. Besides millions of pounds of protein, we grew our reputation and our brand. We learned how to make it work and then did consulting work. We'd get paid in cash, gold, cybercurrency, and sometimes a start-up company would offer us stock options. Like all farmers, we saved for a rainy day."

"This place. It must have cost a fortune." Bella regretted her tone. She had hoped for a benign statement, but it came out as an accusation.

"Your father made some excellent investments. This condo is a good example. Uncle Jon was on the board when this seastead started. It was the year we harvested all those shipping containers and Jon helped with selling off the salvage. We didn't know what to do with the unexpected windfall, so Jon helped. This was one place he suggested and then he managed it for us."

"That's why I've never been here before. You rented it to someone else?"

"It's been a steady income property since we bought it." She pushed closer to Bella. "We could never afford to keep it for our own use until Blue Permaculture—or how did you put it?—the smelly fish farm attracted a buyer. That changed everything."

Bella sat up on one shoulder and looked at her mother with a puzzled expression. "Mom, that happened when I was"—she took a second to do the math—"sixteen! You made me earn money each year to pay for my part of our family vacation. School—I had to pay for all my education. I was always working." She lay back on the firm bed with her arms extended and a pout on her face.

Lena got up and stood over her with hands on her hips and said, "Are you saying you regret the way we raised you?" With a hint of defensiveness added, "Would you rather we spoiled you?"

"No, Mom. I'm surprised. That's all. I'm glad I have a work ethic." Bella exhaled. "I still have student debt, you know?" She was flustered, but it was too late to take back her words.

"Jonathan and Cindy do, too. There is nothing wrong with working off your debt. It keeps things real. When something comes easy, the value diminishes. You have a solid degree that's provided well for you. You're productive and have something to offer the world. If we gave you everything, you might have joined the throngs crying in the streets for handouts from the government."

"I'm sorry I'm pushing your hot buttons, but I'm just trying to figure things out." Bella squirmed off the bed and sat on the plush carpeted floor.

Lena sat on the floor beside Bella. "I never realized you thought we were poor."

"It never crossed my mind when I was a kid. I thought the way we lived was normal. Dad fixing everything. Again and again. I thought all dads walked around with a tool belt and a portable welder." She leaned her head into her mother's lap and looked up at her and smiled. "Mom, we were so weird."

Lena inhaled sharply. "Weird barely scratches the surface." She stroked back her daughter's hair. "Are you all right?"

"Remember when you left Dad and me?"

"I left your Dad. You stayed. Remember?"

"I'm just trying to figure out how much I'm like you. What made you come back? How did you ever make your marriage work after leaving?"

"Hold on there, girl. This is a pretty sensitive subject to be firing questions at me like that. You sound like an FBI agent."

They both laughed.

"You told me you'd always be honest with me about it. Now I'm curious."

"Okay but answer one thing. Why now?"

Bella had thought she had cried out all her tears in the last few days, but her dark brown eyes welled up.

"What's wrong?"

"It's Gregory. I broke up with him. I left. He asked me to marry him, and I left."

Lena hugged her daughter. "I'm sorry, honey."

"It's not that. I don't love him."

"Then what is it?"

"I think he wants to hurt me."

"What makes you say that?"

"He won't answer my calls and ignores any texts. But look." She pulled off her watch, tapped it a few times and handed it to her mother. It was a picture of the handwritten note next to a very large diamond ring.

All the blood drained out of her mother's face. Even her healthy tan could not hide the ghost white beneath the surface.

CHAPTER 26

Fox Bay, British Columbia, Canada

"So sorry to wake you. May I suggest a sip of water? You are behind the hydration curve because of the wine last night. Sixteen ounces of water over the next two hours will place you in balance again." Ava said in a calm, apologetic tone. "It is not an ideal time for you to awake, but Mr. Ou requires your help on the foredeck. We are weighing anchor."

Hank ignored Ava's water recommendation and hurried up the companionway steps. He waved to Olin, who was standing in the darkness on the far right side of the starboard wheel and made his way forward across the expansive deck and took his place at the bow. The anchor chain sagged into the calm water. This boat was long, and the streamline equivalent of a deckhouse blocked his view aft, while the morning darkness added to the impaired line of sight back to Olin. He didn't need to be on the foredeck. Ava was more than capable of doing every sailing task on the *GalaxSea*. But Hank felt it proper starting the morning in the traditional way and since they had called him up, it showed Olin shared this opinion.

"Good morning, Hank."

Olin's words bypassed his ear and went right into Hank's head. Ava facilitated communications throughout the yacht whenever needed. Olin spoke at any volume he wanted, and Hank would hear it with perfect clarity regardless of noise or conditions. No headsets or boom mics required and no yelling. He scratched his head, smirked, and realized how much he wanted coffee. But said, "Good morning, Olin. And Ava, thanks for waking me up. It will be a beautiful day."

The two coordinated, pulling up the hook, and the boat motored in a large circular path through placid water. Hank walked back, glancing at the large hatch where he assumed Willy was parked. Or maybe Jen came back aboard. If anybody was in there at all, they were probably monitoring security or planning the next ninja attack. He wanted to knock but forced himself to walk past and save his curiosity for another time.

The two men stood at a comfortable distance and neither said a word. Hank's vision had adapted to the predawn light as he scanned the area around the bay. For the first time, he paid attention to the half dozen unattended boats moored. They were all pointing toward shore, tugging their anchor chains against the outgoing tide. Many large houses lined up on the other side of the road that ran along the rocky shore. A work van and a dark-colored sedan faced each other at opposite ends of the roadway. A couple was walking, and a few joggers made their way along a bulkhead path.

Olin turned the boat south toward the pink mountains on Washington's Olympic Peninsula, then wheeled to the left as soon as he cleared the inlet. Soon Hank would walk on foreign soil and be free of the program and free of debt. He should be lighthearted, but his mind buzzed with confused emotions. The sting of grief came at him, then frustration. In his mind, he swatted them away and pushed down his feelings. The kiss of air against his face helped his quiet distraction, and as the yacht gained speed, he studied the horizon and forced an uneasy smile.

A wave from an unseen ship passed under them. It distracted him from his melancholy thoughts and turned them into panic. The pistol? Hank stowed it under his mattress next to his tactical knife. Canadian firearm laws are brutal. Could he have come so close to freedom, only to have Olin's gesture ruin everything? There were no private handguns in Canada. The final confiscations had been severe, and the world took notes. Ten years in prison for each gun not surrendered raised the stakes, and some rebels ended up serving life sentences while others took a stand. They got their wish and had their weapons pried from their cold, dead hands. Hank was sentimental about his gun, but in the end it was just a hunk of metal, not even loaded. What a stupid way to end his dream, deported back to the US, prosecuted as a gunrunner, or worse. "My pistol?" Hank challenged Olin with the news.

Olin's efficient grip on the steering wheel relaxed even more. "Laws are for poor people."

Hank studied Olin's face, but there was nothing. He didn't smile or frown. There was no expression tied to his statement. His eyes gazed across the water, looking a few yards across the bow or staring at the snow-covered mountains miles away. Hank could not tell.

Ava's voice broke Hank's bewilderment. "Mr. Ou, the documents for Henry James Gunn are in order. Would you like me to expedite customs while en route or would you like to report to the customs dock?"

"Come on, Ava! I pay you to think. Please, just settle the matter and confirm our slip."

"Certainly," Ava said. Then offered, "Would you like me to pilot the *GalaxSea* through the outer and inner harbors."

"No, thanks," said Olin as he raised a cup of coffee to his mouth. He gestured to the stainless steel carafe, wedged into the tiny basket attached to the side of the helm station. "It's bulletproof. Perfect for today, don't you agree?"

Hank grasped the carafe and gave it a shake. He released the pressure, opened the lid, and offered to top off Olin's cup.

"It's all yours. I've been up since three. There's so much I want to tell you, but first we have a birthday. Irina's turning eighteen today. I can't believe it. My little girl..."

"Sounds like she's having a big party?"

"You'll love my wife, Maria. She's neurotic about birthday parties. Last year, Irina's party was just an intimate family affair. We went to Cafe Juanita and got home before nine thirty. This year...well, you'll see for yourself. You can expect the festivities to be in full swing the minute we make landfall." He pointed to the coffee and said, "Today, you'll need more than one cup."

Ava interrupted, "Mr. Ou, the Greater Victoria Harbour Authority confirms berthing opposite the Fairmont Empress Hotel. I'll plot the course. They remind us to keep yellow buoys close to port at all times. The outer harbor speed limit is seven knots, while the middle and inner harbor speed limit is five knots. ETA is thirty-three minutes." She paused and concluded. "Mrs. Ou has already left her suite and expects you to—find her."

Olin pressed his thin lips together until a single thin line represented his mouth. He sighed, looked up at the tall mast and said, "Here we go." Then he held out his coffee mug and said, "Maybe I should have more of that."

CHAPTER 27

Victoria, British Columbia, Canada

As promised, there had been no problem with authorities entering Canada through the Port of Victoria. Still, walking away from the marina toward the hotel, he was on edge. It was a ridiculous, irrational image which grew with each step he took. A single bullet penetrating his head, shot from the rifle of a SWAT team sniper... his chest tightened, and his heart raced. Hank forced himself to move forward and used the excuse of the hotel steps to zigzag from side to side. When he passed the doorman into the lobby, he steadied himself, breathed deeply, and allowed the anxiety to pass. By the time he received his key at the front desk, he was calm and ready for anything. Hank reached his room and opened the door, looked in and exhaled, "No way."

He had never had a room like this. Like an excited child, he stepped onto the bed and turned it into a trampoline. But even at the apex of his bounce, the ceiling was a dozen feet overhead. Pillows landed on the floor and the edges of the duvet lifted into the air and fell back out of place. There was a knock and Hank opened the oversized door.

"We fly out in one hour," Willy said. "You don't have to come to the party, but Mr. Ou asked me to express to you how much he wants you to join the family." Willy stood in the tall doorway and peeked around Hank. He smirked when he saw the disheveled bed. "Not bad digs for a swabbie. And I'll need your answer now. So, are you coming along or should I tell the boss you have other plans?"

"Sure, I'm game. What should I wear?" Hank said.

"Just take a shower and I'll send in Stephanie." Willy made a smart about-face while grabbing the door and closing it behind him.

To say Hank's private bathroom was large would be an understatement. White marble throughout, a bidet next to the commode, and a fixture he never expected to see—a urinal. At least that's something he understood. The bidet, however, not so much. He knew the basic principle but had never used one and would not start today. The shower could fit Hank and a compact car at the same time. He saw no advantage to the pretentious size of the bathroom. The hard, cold marble never would warm, and the wasted space seemed frivolous, but the mirror didn't even fog up by the time he finished his shower.

A cheerful humming came from his room through the half-open door as he finished a close shave. *Stephanie?* He mouthed the name Willy mentioned. "Hello?" Hank called out around the bathroom door.

"Come right out here. I need to check your size," said a woman with a crisp British accent.

Awkward, Hank thought, but it didn't seem like he had much choice. He wrapped the biggest towel around his waist and walked into his bedroom. A slender woman had her back to him and was fussing with clothes hanging from a garment rack. She turned her head and studied him. Without saying a word, she turned back to the garment rack and peeled two sets of formalwear off the rack and laid them on the bed.

She turned to face him again and explained, "Now there, dear, you must dress appropriately for Irina's birthday celebration." She took another look at his face. "You must be somebody, but I've never heard of you before. Should I have?" she asked with a rhetorical pause. "Whichever you choose will be yours to keep." Her long bony fingers aimed at the clothes to the right and passed across the jacket, over the white shirt with French cuffs and a black bow tie and rested at the kilt. "Mr. Ou made it a point to get your clan tartan correct. Gunn is a handsome tartan." She lingered, as if to emphasize there was only one choice.

And then added, "The family will be dressed with ancestral respect tonight." Her fingers waved at a deer-hide sporran and pointed to a pair of black brogues carefully placed on the floor. "Or you can just wear the tux. It's up to you," she said. I'll be back in fifteen minutes in case you need assistance with the bow tie."

Stephanie's return was prompt, and she explained the creative and proper process of fashioning a bow tie. As a sailor, knots came easily, and though he got the general idea, the woman would not allow his help. They both looked into the mirror, she declared him presentable, and then ushered him out of the room and directed him down to the lunch buffet.

The food spread was spectacular, but Hank knew he was running late when another woman approached him with an agenda. Her skin was the color of ebony and she had short silver-gray hair. It was impossible to tell her age, but he guessed somewhere over seventy.

"You must be Hank since you're the only one in a kilt here." She looked him over. "Mighty fine. I hope those man-skirts come back. But my-oh-my, aren't you a skinny one! Never mind me. I'm a chatty one." Her eyes opened wide. "Horrors! You need to go! They told me to get you... the plane leaves in..." She checked the old-fashioned watch pinned upside-down onto her white blouse so she could read it by looking down through the bifocal glasses perched low on her nose. "Oh, my! You just have ten minutes to get to your ride. Just wait one second and I'll have Richard take you."

She turned without another word and walked away through a pair of catering doors. Before the door swung to a stop, she was pushing Richard through it, filling his ear. She carried a paper food box in one hand. "Hank, this is Richard. You fill this with anything you want but be quick. Then follow Richard. Got that?"

"Yes, ma'am," Hank said. He needed no further encouragement and didn't want to anger the woman. He filled the box with what was within easy reach and said, "Nice to meet you, Richard. Let's go."

The woman looked satisfied, turned partway, and stopped. She threw up her hand, palm out, and said, "Take a fork." She finished her turn and pushed through the doors.

"We're flying?" Hank said to Richard, wishing he hadn't asked such an obvious question.

"I guess so. Maxine said to take you to the floating terminal on Wharf Street."

A woman in a navy business suit approached them with a smile. She thanked Richard for retrieving Hank, then dismissed him by palming a tip into his hand. Turning, she said, "Hi, Hank. Today I'm Irina's mother, but please call me Maria." Avoiding the box and fork he held in his left hand, she grasped his extended right hand and pulled him in and kissed his right cheek. "I've heard so many wonderful things about you."

"Thank you, Mrs. Ou—I mean Maria." In his head, he assumed all rich men marry beautiful tall women—supermodels. Maria was stunning, but in a way which made him rethink stereotypes. She had a radiant smile, and her bodacious frame looked great in her tailored outfit. He realized, not for the first time, he was shallow. *Someday I'll grow up.* This woman was ravishing, confidence radiated from her, and she embodied an infectious enthusiasm. Her flawless olive complexion, dark hair, and vibrant eyes captivated him as he sorted his rattled feelings.

The year following his father's death, he spent way too much time on the couch watching movies. His mother allowed him to watch a kids' movie for every old classic she chose. They sat and ate popcorn and tried to keep their minds off of being alone in the world. Without a father, without a husband, streaming movies helped. Hank grew to enjoy his mother's picks, and he often noticed his mother getting into the plot of one of his choices. Mrs. Ou triggered a vivid memory from those days. If the Italian actress, Sophia Loren, had a plus-sized older sister, she would embody the physical characteristics of Maria Ou. He wanted to say something but couldn't without being foolish. "I'm honored to be included. Thank you, Maria."

She looped her arm in his and led him off to the waiting seaplane. The tilt of her head and the tone of her voice was conspiratorial. She got closer and spoke louder as the high pitch whine of one of the plane engines increased. She said, "I know exactly what's going on. Olin says, *sometimes you just need to rock the boat.* I think he's right." Her breath brushed his face. "You need to be part of this family." She stopped on the bottom step and turned around. From the raised vantage point, she was eye to eye with Hank and steadied herself by holding on to his broad shoulders. She locked her eyes on his and smiled. "Let's get this party off the ground." She laughed and mounted the last steps into the chartered twin engine floatplane.

It was a good thing he had brought his own meal and fork because there was no food service. Seated without a companion, he was glad to finish his food in peace. It was a comfortable flight but still loud, leaving Hank to his thoughts for the quick hop over to the mainland city of Vancouver. *I know exactly what's going on.* And the—*rock the boat*—cliche made no sense. It was the way Maria Ou said it. What did she mean? By the time they landed on Coal Harbour and taxied over to the Westin Bayshore dock, he was no closer to an answer.

CHAPTER 28

Seastead, Tahiti

"I'M SO GLAD YOU shared this with me. I still have friends in the government that can snoop for me." Janice led them toward the veranda. Its terracotta tiles, rattan furniture, and earth tones gave the airy room a cool atmosphere. She motioned for the women to have a seat. "We need to talk. Let's sit down." A gecko skittered over a glass-topped coffee table and disappeared into a lush potted philodendron. "Would you like some iced tea? It's a special recipe." She poured three tall glasses and sat on the edge of a matching ottoman. "How did you meet him?"

Lena explained, "Jose and Gregory's father, Shin, became friends early on. We found that all kinds of sea life discovered our farm and produced an enticing microclimate. Way out in the middle of the oceans' eddies, there's not much going on. Some people describe it as a desert, but it's very much alive. Large predatory fish figured out we offered an oasis of sorts. Certain times of the year, we could harvest bluefin tuna with little effort. Shin paid us well and for the right catch at New Year, he'd double it. He expedited the fish to the Tokyo market and made a fortune. Gregory would fly in with his dad, and all the kids played while their fathers worked. We all liked the change of pace whenever we had visitors, and Shin became a regular. That ended when he died in a helicopter crash. I believe Greg—I mean, Gregory—was at boarding school. The poor child was only thirteen or fourteen. Thank goodness Gregory wasn't in that helicopter."

"Maybe not," Janice said.

Lena reached over and grabbed Bella's hand. She stared daggers into Janice. "How could you say such a thing?"

"It sounds harsh, but it would be better if he had never been born."

Bella became light-headed, and the walls seemed to fall to the floor. She felt like a wave had hit the floating platform that held the villa. But there had been no wave, just the impact of confusion. The queasy sensation passed, but she was glad to be sitting. Her mom didn't notice, but she suspected Janice hadn't missed the lapse.

"Bella, how well do you know Gregory?" Janice asked.

"Look, Janice. You have some information about Gregory that we don't, so why not tell us what you found?"

"Sorry, Bella, there's no painless way to break this to you," Janice said, this time with a modicum of compassion. "I've been an expat for five years. Once I retired, I wanted to put everything, all my government work behind me. My plan was to live a simple life and enjoy what years I have left. But I cannot ignore this. You are my family. I'll do everything within my ability to take care of you. And I promise, I'll never lie... not to my family. What you shared with me got all my spidey-senses lit up. The invasion into your bedroom, the wording of the note, and leaving the ring. That is not how a jilted lover acts."

"We were not lovers," Bella corrected.

The muscles in Janice's forehead almost raised an eyebrow but relaxed from disbelief and into acceptance. "What was your relationship?"

Bella said, "I don't know. Friends... dating... courting...? We never talked about it. At least, I never talked about it. I'm not ready for marriage. He treated me well, and we went out whenever we both were in town. We ate out a lot. I've put on ten pounds in the last year. That's why we went to the Slanted Edge... to work out together. I took him to church five or six times, but nothing weird. Until this. Now I'm scared. What has he done?"

"Did he give you gifts?"

"Sure, I have a closet full of clothes he bought me. Shoes, too. He's in the clothing import-export business. Every time he returned, he brought something. At first, it made me uncomfortable. Then I decided it was his love language—you know—gift-giving?" A shiver ran through her. "Now I'm uncomfortable again. Janice, what's going on?"

"He is in the import-export business, but his clothing business is a front. Enough clothes to make his travels and some of his money seem legit. But he's the worst type of scum—a human trafficker."

Lena sucked her breath, loud enough to shift attention to her. Bella felt the wave surge through her again. This time it was worse, and her vision closed until her only option was to sink back farther into the couch and grasp the sweating glass of iced tea with both hands. She could just make out Janice reaching toward her and grabbing the glass from her hands.

"I'm sorry, dear. I've got more. You must compose yourself." She reached into a bag sitting next to the ottoman and pulled out a small device and folded its sides to form a pyramid. Then she handed a pair of virtual reality glasses to Bella and said, "I will need you to see this in VR." Turning to Lena, "This is optional for you. It's graphic and you aren't part of this investigation. You can find Jon. He's downstairs in the library."

"Like hell I will," Lena said. She grabbed the third set of glasses and slipped them onto her head.

"I was ready to spend the night working through this, trying to figure it out. It turns out I didn't have to. He showed up on a POI—Person of Interest—list a few months ago. An international task force has been connecting the dots. To you, he is Gregory Hattori. Shin Hattori is his father and left him a fortune. He changed his name to Tatsuo Oshiro as soon as he came of age and doubled down on his life as a player. Within five years, he had squandered his inheritance.

"Now he uses Tatsuo Oshiro for his legitimate business dealings, Gregory Hattori for his personal life and many other aliases for travel and to evade law enforcement. He's very smart. He doesn't leave trails, but they will get him. It's only a matter of time. Some of this will seem outlandish until the pieces come together. Please, forgive me for being blunt. Bella, I know this is difficult. It may never make sense to you, but I need you to understand who he is and what we're dealing with."

The visuals were not like a real-crime documentary, just raw video footage of Gregory meeting with men from all around the world. A few clips had background noise, but most were silent. High quality still pictures followed with annotations describing the people and details about the meetings. At first, Bella hoped Gregory was being confused with another bad guy, but soon she was convinced the bad guy was Gregory.

"This next part is the hardest to watch. These are the likely victims. Please, forgive the coarseness, but he leveraged his last bit of the family fortune and good name into a defined niche specialty. I understand that sounds repugnant when you realize we're talking about selling people, but you'll see that he is very selective about his choice of victims. He is paid to be very good at what he does."

One image after another flashed before their eyes. Beautiful girls. Most of the photos were professional caliber. The kind models fill their portfolios with plus candid shots—selfies and friends' photos taken from social media sites. Each had a name, birthdate, and the date they went missing. A running ticker across the bottom of the screen repeated the prime details of each case. Overlaid on the images was a voice, a female, speaking in an unemotional tone, listing significant bullet points about the case. "Margo Hess. Nineteen. Five foot eight. Last seen Burlington, Vermont, USA." Bella wiped away a tear. "Student. Boston College."

Bella had lost count, but there were well over twenty missing young women and half a dozen boys linked to this human trafficker. Each victim had a documented connection to Tatsuo Oshiro. A blurry photo boarding a private jet in Toronto, a picture at a party in Waikiki, on a boat in Cabo, and each one was Gregory. She had not known him. The man she knew had been charming and charismatic—full of life. She realized those same qualities allowed him to... Instead of completing her thought, a shiver went up her back and she pulled off her glasses.

"Janice, we need to stop this." Bella spoke loudly and in a commanding voice.

"I understand," Janice said.

Bella looked at her mother. Lena, so confident in her life and adaptive to every situation, sat frozen into a dull slouch. She kept the glasses on and didn't move. Tracks of tears betrayed her emotions. "Mom, are you all right?" With one hand, Bella stroked her mother's cheek and removed the glasses with the other. Lena's eyes were open wide, but not seeing, fixed into a trance state.

Janice rested her hand on Bella's knee and smiled with a knowing nod. In those simple actions, the former FBI agent communicated she understood, and she had this handled.

"Lena, you're safe here. Bella is safe. This is the place you need to be right now. Here for your daughter. It's good you're together. Now breathe deep and release... the tension is going away. Only the release is here to stay. You are here for Bella. You are strong... strong and safe. As you blink your eyes, they will become heavy... blink... release... close your eyes..." Lena's eyes shut, and her head eased to the side. "Breathe slowly and relax into the breath. When I say open, you will be restored, rested, well, secure, and open to healthy suggestions. We all are safe. Now, open your eyes. Now!"

Bella jumped. She hadn't realized how hard she had been squeezing Janice's hand. She let go and breathed easier as her mother's countenance returned.

Lena said, "That son of a bitch. I can't believe I felt sorry for him when Bella told me how she returned the ring."

With a, "well, okay then." Janice raised her eyebrow in surprise. She gave Bella a wink and got up from the ottoman. She stretched her back and plopped herself into the well-stuffed chair.

Upon entering the room, Jon greeted the women with a, "Hello, ladies." He tipped his hat in a greeting that was popular a century ago and walked over to Lena. Reaching downward with his hand, he told her, "My dear, I know there is an enormous elephant in this small room. May I have your company? I must get my walk in today and doing it with you will be the most agreeable thing."

Lena smiled, extended her hand to his and raised off the couch. Jon gave a wave like a salute to Janice and followed it with, "Happy hunting," as they walked away side by side.

"How do you do that?" Bella asked.

"Do what?" Janice answered.

"Your timing. You and Uncle Jon. Do you choreograph it?"

"Bella, we've been around for a long time. There must be some advantage to being old."

"You are not that old, Janice. I'm guessing Jon has twenty years on you."

"Is that what you want to talk about? Or should I tell you what you need to know?"

Bella massaged her left hand in thought. The needle-like holes of the eel bite had almost disappeared, but an itch remained, deep and menacing. She noticed the attention Janice paid to her movements, to everything.

Bella asked, "What did he intend for me?"

Janice said, "I can't say for sure, but I should ask you some questions. It might help. Is that okay?"

"You mean the elephant in the room?" Bella asked.

"How did he explain finding you after all these years?"

"That was odd," Bella said.

"Go on."

"I keep things close. I've never been one for social media. My CV is public but reveals nothing. Even my contact info for my consulting business is indirect. It would have been hard for him to find me, let alone reconnect. I guess I believed his story."

"And what was his story?"

"It seems lame now, but at the time I thought it was romantic." Bella hesitated. "I was at a Starbucks two blocks from my place. My drink was ready, and the barista yelled out, 'Bella!' Everybody in the place turned because of the way he yelled it. I've been going there for a year, and this day was the only day he yelled it like that. Like the actor in *A Streetcar Named Desire* yelling Stella. I cringed with embarrassment, grabbed my drink, and ran out the door. Then on the street—we're talking Singapore. It was at seven in the morning and very crowded. I hear my name. Figuring some jerk repeated what he had just heard at the coffee shop, I picked up the pace.

"But then he calls out Isabella Maria Johansen Espinosa. I stopped dead in my tracks and turned to see a good-looking, well-dressed stranger smiling at me. It'd been years, so I didn't recognize him, but he took no time introducing himself, and insisted we get together for dinner and catch up. That's how it happened. He said he was in the Starbucks and heard a name from his past and wondered if, by chance..."

"You were infrequent childhood playmates. Would he have known your full name?"

"I don't know. But at the time, I didn't give it a second thought."

"You eluded that your relationship with him was not sexual. Did you say that to protect your mother?"

"No. It drove my roommate crazy that we weren't doing it, but I make it clear with guys early on that I'm a Christian. I don't do sex outside of marriage, period. Most guys start off cool with that, but once they realize I'm serious, they dump me. Gregory was different. He seemed to respect all that."

"Can you tell me about the breakup?"

Janice listened as Bella told her story. When she finished explaining, Janice asked, "When did he seem happiest?"

"When I wore something he gave me, a dress for a meal, jewelry for a show. Sometimes shoes and even a couple of gowns for fancy benefit events. He would gaze at me and marvel. It was a heady experience. We'd go out to fancy places and had a wonderful time together. He was a wonderful conversationalist, had great taste, and was an excellent dancer."

"Did he ever take pictures of you wearing these gifts?"

"No. No, he didn't. Sometimes I would send him a selfie wearing something that he sent me. But he never asked me to. Why do you ask?"

Janice brushed off the question. "Just curious." Then throwing her arms into the air she said, "Bella, I wish you were my daughter... or granddaughter. You are lovely and I'm so sorry you've been thrown into this. You deserve so much better." She paused as if to let it settle. "You could beat yourself up with trying to get into Gregory's mind for the rest of your life and still never get close to his motives. He is a sick person, and he will get what's coming to him. With your help, it might be sooner than later. Are you willing to help us take this monster out?"

"I'll do what I can."

"Good. I'll need all the details about where he lives when in Singapore and some travel habits you know about. I will put you in contact with the lead Interpol agent on the case. Please, don't be afraid. I don't believe Gregory would do a thing to harm you. At least, not physically."

"Oh! What does that mean?"

"He either displays multiple personalities or he is good at compartmentalizing. Everything suggests his name coincides with the corresponding persona. Some aliases represent him as an opportunistic human trafficker. Tatsuo Oshiro is an international business executive and Gregory Hattori was your childhood playmate and the man who wants to marry you.

"Don't take this the wrong way. He stalked you. Your meeting at Starbucks was deliberate. Maybe he was going through his memory and decided you'd be just right for a certain client. He might have remembered you as a girl and fixated on that. Most of his clients are looking for girls or boys who are underage or close to it. When he saw you, all grown, he might have realized he had a need for a genuine relationship. I cannot be sure as to his motivation, but I'm guessing that he decided you were worthy of worshiping. It was you and your presence that made him feel complete. Or it's possible that he is a true schizophrenic and Gregory is his nice-guy persona, while the rest of his personalities are psychopaths.

"Ultimately, he is one person, and that person has to be put away. It won't eliminate human trafficking, but it will keep him from ruining more lives. Please, don't get sentimental about him. Mark my words, he is a sick animal and if he isn't caged up or put down, he will devour anybody he wants." Janice got up and motioned to the VR. "You need to watch the rest. I'll leave you alone. If you have questions, I'll be in the kitchen." She turned and walked away, then stopped, looked back, and said, "Bella, I know this is difficult. You will push through. It won't be easy, but it will get better."

Difficult seemed to be an understatement of gigantic proportions. Bella contemplated how simple life had been. If only she could turn back time, even a few days. A mere week ago, her biggest concern was getting caught skinny dipping by a fisherman. Now she had a failed relationship with the worst type of sick psychopath. She placed the VR glasses on her head and sat with her back straight, head up, and breathed in deep. She pushed play. She would see this through until the end.

CHAPTER 29

Vancouver, British Columbia, Canada

GETTING SPOILED WITH FIVE-STAR accommodations came as easily to Hank as anybody else, but two hotel rooms on the same day seemed like a waste. He pushed open the heavy door and the smell of citrus wafted out of the room, followed by a fleeting hint of tobacco. A basket of fruit was staged on a mid-century modern sideboard. No marble, gold leaf, or crystal draped lights. Instead, walls of mahogany panels and on them hung bold geometric paintings with circles and triangles so large they could swallow up a person. The low bed had a beveled wood frame skirting the bottom of a mattress and seemed to float, the legs somewhere in the cantilevered shadows. The two-cylinder shaped pillows propped against the cherry headboard added to the clean lines and clarified that function and comfort, if considered at all, took a backseat to design.

Hank looked at himself in the full-length mirror. He had to admit the Scots had a sense of style. It was a little unnerving at first since Stephanie insisted he not wear underwear, stating there is only one proper way to wear a kilt and to break that tradition would be treason. The thought she might be sticking it to the new guy amused him.

He kept an eye on the mirror and spun away from the door, checking the hem of the kilt for lift and noticing nothing, relieved that the kilt didn't fly around from the waist like a little girl's skirt. Even with more effort, any flouncing began below the hips, providing unrestricted movement, yet coverage where it counted. The bed looked uncomfortable, but he'd have to try it out to see. His body met full resistance when he lay down—no give—but he had slept on worse while camping. As he rested the back of his head on the fabric-covered pillow, his chin flexed into his chest. It was a design statement that would be an impossible pillow but could double as a foam roller in a gym. He sat up and opened a built-in bedside drawer and found an old, stylized black phone. Lifting the phone from its cradle, the underside of the handset revealed glowing push buttons. A dial tone droned out of one end. Not sure what he expected, he put it back into its cradle.

This time Willy didn't knock. He just opened the door and said, "Just needed to remind you that you're still under your initial contract until tomorrow at sixteen hundred hours. No contact."

"I lost my phone. Remember?" Hank shrugged.

Willy pointed at the bedside table and repeated, "No contact. I'll knock on your door in about twenty minutes. Be ready to go."

He glanced back at the retro phone and decided he had nobody to contact, anyway. He dropped back onto the hard bed and seized the simple remote for the TV. It had only three controls—power, volume, and channel.

The large screen in his room showed footage of police dressed in full riot gear with gas masks on. He sat down hard on the foot of the bed. The front of the police line held riot shields and batons while a few officers marched behind with shotguns. In the column, a few cops threw the occasional CS grenade. Their motions fluid and casual, like a quarterback warming up. The report showed city after city managing their mob the same way—non-lethal with scripted precision. Police versus the People. With the volume off, it looked like the scenes had been produced by a film company. The faceless blue line dispersing the unruly hordes. Both sides looked like fools. Hank leaned toward the screen, his emotions doing battle—thrilled versus horrified, like coming upon an accident with mangled cars and emergency vehicles, he could only stare. Only this evoked something personal in his past—not a repeat, but it rhymed.

Excited crowds thrilled him, but angry mobs were very different. Mobs gave Hank chills. Years ago, in Okinawa, Hank and two other Marines turned a corner leading to the US base and found themselves in a throng of hundreds of locals running away. Prefectural police and US military police, backed up by Marines in riot response gear, crowded the civilians on three sides. The less-than-lethal methods—teargas, beanbag rounds, and rubber bullets takes the fight out of people fast. All the protesters panicked and ran for the limited escape routes, leaving dozens of people trampled, two of them killed. Hank and his buddies picked up an injured boy and a young woman. Both ended up in surgery at the base hospital.

The next day, news agencies had reported a peaceful disagreement between military contractors and their national employees regarding retirement benefits. Within hours of the watered-down report, the woman—the pregnant woman—died. There would be no mention of fatalities. Along with the dead, the press buried the inconvenient facts.

What he saw on the TV reminded him of why he hated mobs, but somehow, this was different. The camera angles, the age and race of the protestors. The media showed hundreds of people in the streets, chanting and carrying signs but looking controlled, like they do this kind of stuff all the time. There was nothing curious about a newscast repeating a video loop, but the similarity from city to city was too similar for coincidence. A hooded man breaks out of the group, charges the police line, hurls something at them, and defiantly stands his ground with bombastic hand gestures ending in the universal sign of disrespect. As if on cue, others march forward, engulf the rebel loner, and absorb him back into the crowd. Like an amoeba retracting from an unseen force, the mob pulls back a uniform distance from the orderly police line. On the edge of the drama, videos of parked cars being trashed, gangs of protesters with bats breaking windows, and some smaller cars even being overturned. In Oakland, a burning car in Chicago, a pair of police cruisers received a ritualistic beating by a dozen masked thugs, in Baltimore looters running out of storefronts. It seemed too orchestrated.

The ongoing commentary of the news feed reminded him of how much it would annoy him to hear canned laughter inserted into TV comedies. Most people don't even hear it. But when you're out to sea, and you don't see a show for almost a year, canned laughter is like cutlery scraping against a dinnerplate. This news broadcast caused the same reaction.

The news anchor was saying, "... breaking out in cities across the country." A map popped up with an orange star over a dozen major US cities. But the footage cycled from only four cities—Seattle, Philadelphia, Baltimore and Chicago. The correspondent in each cities repeated the same thing in their respective interview. "... anger... unemployment... unfulfilled promises... brutality... unwarranted... force...police." And then each mentioned a name of an unarmed Black youth, shot by police, accompanied by a picture of a good-looking kid. In Seattle a school ID photo of a well-dressed boy, maybe ten years old, while Philly and Chicago showed lanky teenagers in basketball gear, and Baltimore showed an image of a young man holding a trumpet.

A drug commercial replaced the drama of the news report. Fit, silver-haired grandparents, and a couple of frolicking children enjoyed a halcyon spring day in the country. The ad offered a stark contrast to the spectacle of urban unrest. Hank muted the audio. It affected him. A lump formed in his throat and his gut told him these riots were no more authentic than the commercial.

When the station-break ended and the newscast continued, he knew his gut was correct. Visible smoke from tear gas grenades wafted through a crowd of protestors. The people didn't disperse like he had witnessed in Okinawa. With the sound of the TV still muted, he watched the live correspondents at the scene. Each city had the same careful camera angles, ensuring burning turmoil in the background. In the foreground, a reporter held up her microphone like a prop. Her facial expression showed concern, but her body language was too relaxed. The reporters were either acting or had the coolness of a Zen master.

He had enough and turned off the TV. His mind raced as he stood up, still grasping the remote. Noise outside his room drew his attention. He could make out the rise and fall of girls talking and laughing but could not make out any words. Opening the door, he surprised two teenage girls chatting in the hallway. Probably friends of Irina, who arrived on Daddy's private jet. They looked him over, giggled, and resumed their conversation. Hank didn't even think about the kilt until he passed them. Then he became self-conscious. He took smaller steps as he walked past the open double-doors to the suite where Irina, her sisters, and some other girls were congregating. His feet continued down the hallway without a destination. The elevator door chimed and opened.

Two African American young men ambled out of the elevator—the first wearing a bright orange, blue, green, and yellow dashiki and the other wore full western attire—a cowboy hat, embroidered shirt, blue jeans, and fancy boots.

A boy of about thirteen, with a mop of red hair bolted out of the doors next. He paid no attention to where he was going and bounced off Hank and looked up. "Cool, someone else in a kilt! What clan you from?" Not waiting for an answer, the boy darted off.

On the heels of the young Scotsman was a boy of Asian descent. He was also short, but chubby, and wore a samurai outfit—minus the swords. The last kid out the door spoke to the large man operating the elevator. Hank couldn't hear what the boy said, but the man sneered. An enormous slab of a man like that could only be security. Nobody would mess with him. He had a face like a bulldog and an expression equally unreadable.

Finally, a straggler exited, who wore what appeared to be an exact copy of Antonio Banderas' costume as Zorro, complete with a flat-brimmed musketeer hat and cape—no sword.

Hank almost detected a smile from the bulldog-man. He gestured him into the elevator with a questioning stare. He had no plan where he would go, but the door wouldn't stay open forever. From behind him, he heard Willy's command voice.

"Corpsman! You get on that elevator, and you'll have to answer to me."

Up to this point, Hank had no reason not to like Willy. He seemed the consummate professional, always doing his job, or at least acting civil, but this threat pushed him too far. Hank spun around and walked right up to the compact, powerful man and said, "Listen, I don't know what your problem is, but I'm not your inferior. I'm not a corpsman and I don't have to answer to you—ever! Understood?"

Willy stepped back with his hands, up in surrender, showing that he got the message. "Okay, Hank, sorry about all that. I'm dumb that way, and I've got the scars to prove it," Willy admitted. "I was just coming to get you. No problem, but if you want to join us, we have a security briefing that's about to start. I thought you might be interested in hearing what's going on and how we handle things. Personally, I'd like you in on it, so you know how things work around here. I think you'll be interested."

CHAPTER 30

Vancouver, British Columbia, Canada

A DOZEN MEN AND women filled the room. What would have been a view of the harbor, now had a gray mesh fabric pulled taut, obscuring the panorama. A line of monitors and a few old-school whiteboards faced inward. To the far left the same news channel Hank had been looking at was on, but everybody's eyes focused on the central monitor. It hung above a low-slung concave console screen where a kid sat in an oversized gamming chair. He wore a royal blue, ATARI baseball cap backwards on his head and his long hair dropped out to the sides giving the appearances of blinders. The incessant movements of his hands and mumbling into his headset looked like he was deep in a multiplayer game.

A nondescript motorcoach showed end to end on the central monitor. The camera zeroed in on the doorway of the bus. Two small monitors to the left and two to the right showed static images, and two more suspended above maintained split screen viewpoints of the area around the bus.

A woman in her mid-fifties gripped the back of Atari-boy's chair. She had an inch of dark gray roots pushing out expensive wheat colored blonde hair that fell around her broad shoulders. A yellow blouse tucked into the waistband of her ill-fitting slacks. Hank cringed and looked back at the monitor.

"Tag him," she ordered.

The room fell silent. Things that made a noise, a shifting foot, tapping a finger, the touch of a hand on the back of a chair, even breathing seemed to stop. The queer silence bothered Hank, but it only took a second to recall why. She said, "Tag him," and the people heard—*attention*! Even Hank realized he was standing stiffer, frozen in an uncomfortable pose, so he looked around and found everybody still at attention except for Atari-boy.

"Got him," Atari-boy said.

All eyes fell on the woman in command. Her astringent voice and the bad hair didn't dilute her authority. The deference given was all Hank needed to know. She was in charge.

"Dammit, these are the same guys from LA. Don't they keep terrorists locked up anymore? How the hell did they get out, and how'd they get across the border in a freaking bus? Shit! Tag everyone. Tell the effing Mounties what you can, but don't let them know we sprayed them. Fudging Mounties will ignore the criminals and come after us...." She paused mid-rant, grimaced, and folded in half, as if in pain. All eyes were on her as she stood back up with a deep inhale, ready to continue. Holding her back, she said, "Dammit, Sam, does f-u-d-g-i-n-g count too?"

The man standing just to her side spoke in a quiet voice, "Yes, ma'am. That's three."

"I know how to count! Three hundred bucks. The assholes are going to make me go broke. Stupid effing fines. Crap! How'd those language Nazis get me into this contract? I don't see what the..."

Hank thought she looked like she was about to choke up a hairball and grinned, thinking it was funny. Smart contracts that penalized certain actions were out of his league. Corporate people were the ones on the hook for social perfection. The classy jobs came with expectations. Never make the Company look bad, don't get drunk in public, never smoke a cigarette, never tell the wrong joke or say a taboo word. Embarrassing behavior will stain the brand and cost a career. Incorrect behavior is reserved for Hollywood and the victim class. The elite can afford bad behavior, and victims are entitled to it. It was too obvious this woman had gotten in over her head with F-bombs, and now she was paying the price with real-time fines levied against her paycheck.

"I'm the boss. I should be able to say what I damn well please. This behavior modification is bullshit." She looked at her watch with contempt. The woman's expressive nature, coupled with the deference of the security people, pushed Hank over the edge, and he let out a chuckle as he considered the comedy sketch, he found himself in.

Willy shot him a severe look. But it was too late.

"Who the hell are you? And what's so funny?" the woman asked.

"I'm Hank. Hank Gunn. Nothing's funny Ma'am, I'm just dealing with allergies." He pretended to sneeze into his sleeve and wiped his nose. "Allergies," he repeated shaking his head and looking away.

She lost interest and focused back on the monitor. As she held up her hand and pointed her finger, everybody's attention shifted to the door of the bus. The camera angle was perfect for observing passengers as they exited. Most of them had their heads down, but the angle was not from a typical camera mounted on some pole in the parking lot. The view angled upward from curb level, so their faces looked right into the camera. Recognition software instantly identified each person as they stepped off the bus. All had masks and most had hoodies or caps pulled low, but the surveillance AI somehow kept up.

"Oh, yeah. Survival of the fittest," the giant man standing in front of Hank spoke up. A glowing ball of light replaced the head of someone stepping off the bus. The person of interest emitted balls of fuzzy light at the shoulders and hands, the hips and ankles. "There's always a hack." The glowing balls seemed to buzz out of view and the recognition software moved on. "The wired-body trick... it still works after all these years," said the giant without apology.

"Shut up, Fred," the woman scowled. "Follow that one. Get an analog picture, analyze his gait, have Sherlock pattern it, whatever it takes! I want an ID on that bastard."

The upper monitor followed the man from the side and panned around to the back, while the lower monitor continued to show the parade of thugs exiting the bus.

"So, you're Hank. Willy's recruit. Are you ready?" she asked.

"Ready for what?" Hank said.

"For God's sake, Willy. What does your team do over there, anyway? Get him up to speed."

Hank followed Willy as he walked to a large stainless-steel refrigerator. They positioned it like it was awaiting installation, a red hand-truck still wedged in against one side. He pressed his hand onto the program screen and pushed on the ice dispenser. The doors opened to reveal an arsenal of small arms and boxes of ammo. To others, it looked like a lot of black guns, but to Hank, they were like old friends. He had shot nothing since he left the service, but this disguised safe had all his favorites—a packed row of carbine rifles, with short, twelve-inch barrels. They were HK417 or maybe the civilian semi-auto version. There was no way to see the selector lever from where he stood. Either way, they were badass, and Hank's heart pounded.

Judging from the oversized clothing of the security force in the room, he figured everybody already had a concealed sidearm or two, so the few pistols in the armory made sense. They looked like Beretta M9A1s and he wanted one. He wasn't sure why. Maybe it was because he had carried that sidearm for years, or maybe he didn't want to be the only one in the room without a weapon.

He could take or leave the last gun in the collection. It was a Benelli M4 Super 90. This shotgun had saved his life, but it was also the weapon responsible for his only battlefield injury. The official report explained a friendly fire incident—a deflected round. All everybody knew was that it caught him right in the ass. He had his back turned and was starting a morphine drip on some guy from a different unit. He didn't even feel the small round shot enter his body until he felt his own blood drip down his leg.

The doctor said the wound was so shallow a child could have removed it. When the abundant amounts of anesthetic wore off, Hank had his doubts. The event earned him two days off and a nickname. The junior team reveled in ostentatious displays and someone dubbed him Double-Ought-Butt. Fortunately, that was too cumbersome a moniker and before sunrise the next day, through the unknowable wisdom of Marines, they had settled on calling their injured medic, D'doc.

Willy reached past all the familiar weapons and pulled out a box the size of a hardcover version of *War and Peace*. Then he passed Hank a plastic tube of what looked like gumballs and said, "Read the directions and don't shoot your eye out."

They walked down a well-lit hallway with all the doors wide open. Power cords and communications cables traced in and out of doorways and down opposite sides of the hallway. A pattern formed. The number of colorful cables was growing, almost to the thickness of his forearm, all leading to the room at the far end of the hallway. The nerve center of the entire operation and a man standing beside the door with a rifle confirmed it. Willy and Hank entered the room unchallenged.

They stepped over a thick branch of cordage and Willy said, "No Wi-Fi here. Old-school technology is more secure." He directed Hank's eyes out a mesh-screened window to the flat, black-tarred roof where tripods supported directional antenna and microwave dishes. They aimed to all points of the compass, while a compact satellite array gazed upward, shooting for the stars. "Everything's encrypted, hard-wired, or both. We even bring our own special window coverings." Then, in a loud voice he said, "Little help here?"

There was no response from the people in clear sight. Each was facing the entry, but too enthralled with their oversized laptops to notice anything else. Willy bent over and wrapped his fingers over the top of the closest laptop and pushed his nose just over the edge. The Kilroy joke was lost on the irritated operator.

She pulled off her headphones and said, "What?"

"Hank here needs comms. What've you got?"

She pointed to a table that looked like snack time at the local Montessori school. Deep orange carrots lay washed, still sporting their dark green tops. Cauliflower whiter than a Hollywood starlet's teeth, and broccoli like the forest filled a large platter. Heavy, brown glass bottles of kombucha sitting in an ice bath alongside pint mason jars of what would have looked like yogurt, except for its rich green color. Willy shook his head, reached over the food offerings, and picked through what he was looking for. Victorious, he held up a small box with outstretched arms, like he had just made a touchdown.

That caught the eye of the young woman, who did not want to take part in Willy's silliness. She said, "Bring me what you need. Nothing will work until I scan it."

Willy ripped open the box and handed a tiny earpiece to Hank. "Stuff this in your left ear." Then handed him a watch. "Here you go, Dick Tracy." He looked at his own watch and said, "Briefing in twenty-eight minutes. I suggest you get up to speed on your new toys in your room. I'll send you the departure location and you can practice following the map on your watch. That might be the most important lesson you get today."

CHAPTER 31

Vancouver, British Columbia, Canada

FIGURING OUT THE COMMS and getting back to his room by following the map was no problem. The technology was straightforward, and sailing had tuned his navigation skills. Curious about the nondescript box that came out of the gun safe, he unboxed it carefully. If anybody saw the contents, they would think—*toy gun*. It was canary yellow, except for the bright silver trigger and some black lettering. Though Hank had no experience with this type of gun, he knew it wasn't a toy and instinctively treated it with the respect all firearms deserve.

He skimmed the instructions, focused in on the practical highlights and skipped through the pages of boilerplate safety and cautionary legalese. This version of the SALT Supply Company's pepper spray gun was smaller than what he had seen on videos. This model was about the size of a Glock 19, only chubbier. Without the CO2 cartridge and unloaded, it even felt like a toy, but when charged and loaded, it could send a plastic round filled with powdered pepper spray at a speed of 375 feet per second and would affect the recipient with the same kinetic energy as being hit by a fastball traveling at highway speeds.

Hank inserted the CO2 cartridge, loaded and reloaded the gun, until he was familiar with its design, safeties, and feel. Using the small tool included, he matched the laser sight to the iron sites.

His new watch rang, and Willy's face appeared. "Hope you didn't fire off that Nerf gun. Says right in your contract you're responsible for any property damage. Now, follow the yellow brick road and get over here or you'll miss the fun."

Willy was waiting just outside the elevator as Hank exited. He said, "You're riding shotgun in the light green minivan. Don't ask me why, but you've got the birthday girl and a few of her friends. Better keep your new gun handy."

"I thought the briefing said no riots tonight?"

Willy grinned and replied, "You're about to get into a van with five females." Shaking his head from side to side. "You sure are new to this." The minivan pulled a little past them. Willy pointed at the front passenger door, then swatted the air with the back of his hand. "Go." A dirty gray Honda pulled up and Willy climbed in.

Hank figured rich kids out on the town got around in limos or at least a huge black SUV like in the movies, but Irina and three of her best friends sat in the reconfigured back of the Toyota Sienna. The girls buckled into plush captain's chairs. Spicy music with a heavy beat competed with giggles and conversation as the cacophony spilled through the open panel separating the front from the back. As it closed, the girls waved to Hank, and one blew him a kiss.

The closed panel created a barrier, airbrushed in dark colors to look like the minivan was empty. The bass was still audible, but the closure of the panel strangled words and lyrics. His attention turned to the driver. "Hi, I'm Hank."

"Sit there and be quiet."

Not giving a damn didn't come naturally to Hank, but he had become adept at disinterest, so he ignored the driver and watched Vancouver roll by. So many people out, most walking, taking in the city. There was no sign of unrest, at least not on the streets. Nobody stared at the unwashed minivan. Hank wondered who thought to put the worn bumper sticker and the white outline decals of a mom, dad, two kids and a cat on the dark back window. If wearing nondescript clothing allowed a person to blend in as the proverbial gray man, then this was the transportation equivalent. Even the driver, the bitchy thirty-something woman, looked like any soccer mom from the neck up.

As they arrived, Willy opened the door and Hank offered a hand to Irina and her girlfriends as they stepped out. The girl that had blown him a kiss stepped out last. Her bangs and straight black hair framed her porcelain face. Compared to the rest of the partygoers, she had missed the gist of the birthday party's theme. She handled the where-in-the-world aspect—she was Japanese—but the *ancestral respect* part was a stretch. She wore the uniform of a Japanese schoolgirl, white Keds, knee socks, plaid skirt (too short), and white blouse (too tight). As she sprang out the door, she grasped Hank's hand. Her eyes studied him and her grasp lingered long enough to make him uncomfortable.

CHAPTER 32

Vancouver, British Columbia, Canada

THE QUEEN ELIZABETH THEATRE absorbed the group of eccentric young adults. His ticket placed him in the aisle seat, next to his pretend soccer mom wife or whatever she was. She didn't wait for him to get up and pushed across to the seat beside him. She looked straight ahead and flipped her hand toward him, throwing a rolled up program into his lap. It spun open and read *The Phantom of the Opera*.

During the brief update at the theatre, Hank had hung against the back wall and listened to the revised security plan. There had been no sign anything bad was looming. The rant by Megan Ward earlier at the hotel was perhaps an unfortunate initial impression. She confirmed she was a pissed off alpha female but also proved to be professional. She maintained the efficiency expected of the person in charge of making sure there were no incidents. After the details, she summarized the entire plan, rapid-fire, no pauses, no particular emphasis, and no discussion, and no further F-bombs. It was over in five minutes. In that time, she covered the basics in military spec—order and execution with the five

Ds: deter, detect, deny, delay, and defend. She called out a hierarchy of three communication frequencies and said something about calling for a drone.

He could parrot the plans and procedure, but it made little sense to Hank. At the end of the briefing, he reviewed each of the key points in his head and suspected each person in the room was ready to repeat back a concise paraphrase of what they had just heard. She closed with, "The Ou family and a handful of tonight's guests will return on Olin's super yacht, the *Whale*. We're breaking down as soon as she returns to US waters tomorrow around noon. At that time the family's security will be turned over to Willy's watchful eye. The guest-jet will have touched down at Paine Field and the kids up here with their helicopter parents will no longer be our problem." Her eyes scanned in the room, and she closed with, "Good hunting."

Hank had quickly turned his thoughts from the evening's security plan to the play. It would be difficult not to pay attention to the gripping music and theatrical excess of the performance. Lost in the drama unfolding, he was not prepared for the intermission. The soccer mom van driver stuck an elbow into his ribs, so he shot up, stepped into the aisle, and shifted down just enough to let his row out. She gave him a scowl and led the colorful young partygoers up the aisle, girls arm in arm and boys single file.

Willy slipped in and walked next to Hank until they got to the corridor leading into the lobby. He stopped and redirected Willy's attention by putting a hand on his shoulder. "Willy, what the hell am I doing here? Yesterday I was a sailing instructor. Now I'm wearing a kilt, hanging with rich kids, and carrying... something illegal in my pouch. What am I here for?"

"What do I look like—clergy?" Willy laughed. "Just relax. You're here to get your feet wet. Enjoy the show." Willy began to walk into the light, then stopped. His head cocked and one eyebrow raised. "Watch out for the little Japanese girl." He lifted his finger to his puckered lips and made a shh sound. "She's security." With a smirk, he added, "Back to high school after college. Must be a real drag. She's well-paid, but really—watch out. Remember Gogo in *Kill Bill*? Typecast." He laughed as he pushed into the crowd.

Olin Ou stood with perfect posture, dressed in a long-waisted gray silk jacket top and loose matching pants, talking to Maria and another woman. His shoulders adorned with designs created by gold thread, ending in the chest where a line of gold piping and buttons coursed across to the right and straight down the side. Upon seeing Hank, he walked over. "How do you like the show?"

"Very much. Thank you."

"We've got so much more to talk about. But tonight, I hope you will enjoy Irina's birthday party."

"I have no gift," Hank offered. He wasn't embarrassed but hadn't even thought of the absurd notion until the words came out of his mouth.

Olin looked thoughtful, "Hank, if all goes well, you will give Irina far more than anything she will get here tonight. Now, please excuse me. I have to go." Mr. Ou walked over to the bathroom line, to wait his turn just like everybody else. He queued right behind the big kid with the cowboy hat, just before the chime sounded to announce the end of intermission.

CHAPTER 33

Vancouver, British Columbia, Canada

THE CURTAIN DROPPED TO enthusiastic applause, leaving Hank lost in the surreal lives and drama acted out before him. A hand grabbed him by the shoulder.

"We've got to go. Follow me," Willy said.

They exited through a side door, bypassing the lobby, and Hank matched his pace to Willy's jog. The man standing at the door of a conference room opened it. Inside the room, Hank noticed the same people he had seen at the briefing earlier that day. The gun safe, disguised as a refrigerator, was there, but there was no bank of monitors and no gamer throne. Atari-Boy sat in a cloth-covered, chrome-framed chair in front of a laptop. Megan Ward spoke in front of a large screen, which she was manipulating with a tablet. She zeroed into a frame showing the outline of the Queen Elizabeth Theatre on the bottom and the waterfront on top.

"... some organic unrest in the US. ANTIFA shills are escalating the events, if not staging riots. In the last week we've been tracking growing activity in

Toronto and Winnipeg. Tomorrow it spreads here. Everybody knows it—law enforcement, the kids on the street, the news reporters, EMS. It looks like everybody's reading from the same playbook on this. Law enforcement are all sleeping in, resting up for the blue line tomorrow. The politicians are enjoying the chaos, and they'll let things go to hell—even encourage it.

"Here's where it affects us. They scheduled the main protest for tomorrow, but we have intel that some careless punks are freelancing tonight. It looks like their target is somebody in this building. As most of you saw, earlier today we came across a busload of known bad asses and we painted each with a squirt of radioisotopes. It makes them easy to track and what started out as a precaution paid off big time. As I speak, a handful of them are congregating right next door.

"Since their contract to fuel anarchy doesn't start until tomorrow, it looks like they're planning a little side job tonight. Besides Mr. Ou and his party, there are three other high-value targets in attendance for this performance. From their meager preps and amateur-level coordination, there's no way in hell these lowlifes know about our operation, but we can't rule out our party as potential targets."

"My guess is that these would-be criminal masterminds think they're spending a night at the aquarium—most likely aiming to snatch one of the three other high-value targets and collect a ransom. In Canada, even the elite are hoplophobic, so only one of the three has an armed bodyguard. But we can't be certain that they are not after one of our rich little brats, or their prominent parents who tagged along. Either way, they cannot be ready for my wrath. And since Mr. Ou won't stand for any publicity surrounding his daughter's party, its our job to make sure no kidnappings happen tonight."

"Mr. Ou and his entire party are accounted for and being escorted to a room down the hall. The three at-risk targets are being informed of the threat. Mr. Ou agreed to be the face of the protection effort to gather up the other VIPs before they leave the building. We do know they are planning the kidnapping for the streets. You'll see."

"How can you be so sure it's a kidnapping?" asked a large man in an ill-fitting suit.

"You mean other than the bleeding-heart VIPs with their ransom insurance? Corporations have made kidnapping a viable career choice. Besides, nobody wears expensive jewels to *Phantom of the Opera*, and nobody gets assassinated in Canada. Trust me. These guys think they're about to grab an easy hostage. Reality is, they fell into their own worst nightmare.

"From what we know, these actors are street thugs who lived long enough to take their skills on the road. Rocks, bricks, and the occasional sock stuck into a liquor bottle filled with gasoline. They haven't been here long enough to plan this thing out. We've got a crazy amount of intel on them. Trust me, if law enforcement did their job, they'd all be behind bars at least long enough for Julie to turn gray." She motioned toward an angular girl with raven black hair.

"We've found one accomplice who works here—a coat checker. He's been texting with Sam Farley. Farley is the leader and hasn't left his seat in the Java Cat, even to go to the bathroom. Four hours and counting. We've manipulated the texts so purple-hair-coat-check-boy is still in play. He doesn't know it, but he's working for us now. Their group is small. The greedy bastards think it's a slam dunk and I don't imagine they'll want to spread their cut too thin, but we're watching for connections who might show up late. Right now, it's just three guys on the street. They all stepped off the magic school bus." She motioned to the screen, "The confirmed bad guys are the red dots, the accessories are yellow for now. If we find them armed or they join in with the kidnappers, their ID will turn red."

A street map overlaid onto a satellite image zoomed less than a block away from the Queen Elizabeth Theatre to include a storefront on Hamilton Street—Java Cat. Three dots stacked like red pancakes slightly offset from one another lingered inside the Java Cat, labeled A1, A2, and A3. A similar stack of yellow dots also populated the Java Cat, labeled C1, C2, C3. As the screen zoomed in on the cluster, two more yellow dots, C4 and C5, blinked and peeled away. One headed down the alley, the other drifted along a direct path toward the large theater complex.

Green dots littered the Queen Elizabeth Theatre, some blinking, some stacked in one place looking like a segmented caterpillar. Only one red dot appeared. The corresponding picture showed a face with multiple piercings and purple hair—the coat checker.

Julie, the girl with the raven-black hair, spoke up, "Why is there a blinking yellow disk walking down the hall toward us?"

Megan Ward spun toward Atari-Boy positioned at the laptop and said, "Zoom in."

An outline of the Queen Elizabeth Theatre filled the screen, framed in by the sidewalks and surface streets around it. The 3-D view looked skeletal but showed rooms, hallways, and the building's various levels. With the previous view, the yellow dot appeared to be coming toward them, but in 3-D it represented a person one floor below. When zoomed in closer, a green dot attached to the yellow, but both people were represented by an avatar with a question mark.

"Well, Justin, got anything?" Megan Ward said,

Hank was a little disappointed to find Atari-Boy had a name, but the exchange was interesting.

Justin said, "Yeah, it's not been my top priority, but I've told Interpol we've located one of their persons of interest and sent a pic."

"Where the hell's the pic?" Megan Ward hissed.

"Yeah, well, I'm working on that one... I'll update it."

"That's bullshit, Justin. You should have handled this."

"It's in the feed now."

Framed within a yellow dot, a clear photo of a good-looking Japanese man about Hank's age showed on the monitor.

"Is he dangerous? Any weapons? Does Interpol want us to detain him? Damn it, there's only one thing I hate more than Mounties, it's Interpol. They're arrogant, have stupid accents, and they wear their clothes too tight. Justin, they've got cameras all over this place. I want answers about this guy. Yellow dots will get us killed.

"Willy, you and Gunn are closest to the door. Mop this up. If this guy is trouble, cuff his ass to a handicap rail. If he forgot to pay his cyber-currency tax, pat him on the back and let him walk. Go... go... go!"

Justin's voice came through Hank's earpiece, loud and clear. Willy slowed the charge down the stairs and listened, too. "He's unarmed. Not even fingernail clippers," Justin said. "I've checked his face everywhere. Looks like he's a Japanese businessperson. Rich family, jetsetter. Interpol has him POI for border violations, and the US wants him detained at any point of entry. Looks like a white-collar criminal. I'd guess tax cheat."

"Okay, thanks. We'll check him out anyway," Willy said. "I did a security detail for Interpol once. I thought they were great. Paid going wages and put us up in a fancy hotel." With an accent deep from the bayou, he added, "Good thing I ain't arrogant and my clothes fit right."

Not to be outdone, Hank pulled out a down east Maine accent that would make his uncle proud. "Nah, t'ain't nothin'. She's a dite numb." Only hours ago, he was certain Willy was a jerk, and now he was following him down the stairwell, laughing.

As they approached the fire door leading to the floor with the mysterious Japanese businessperson, Hank reached into his sporran and touched the handle of the SALT pistol. The rig made a poor excuse for a quick draw holster, but the gun was close enough. Still, he wished he had his Colt 1911 or anything that fired lead.

Willy motioned a quiet finger toward his lips, pointed to his wrist, and motioned his fingers swiping from left to right over his watch. Hank took the hint and copied the gesture revealing multiple screens. They paused while leaning against the wall and studied the information on the small screens. He scrolled past the picture they had seen upstairs. The next screen contained details. Sex: Male, Age: 26, Name: Tatsuo Oshiro, Alias: Gregory Hattori, Allegations: Border Violations.

Hank's eyes met Willy's as he gave a hand signal to follow. They broke out of the stairwell's heavy steel doors and entered a large, well-lit corridor. Only a dozen people were in view, and the two crossed the expanse with a slow, casual gait toward the opposite wall.

"I have eyes on him. I have a knack for these things. Sure, I saw the blond in a short black dress and serious heels first, but she's with our POI. Let me handle things but keep your Nerf gun handy. Justin says he's not armed, but I'm sure he knows some Bruce Lee moves." Willy chuckled. "But don't worry. I took a Chuck Norris course in whoopass.

"Excuse me? Sir? Mr. Oshiro?" Willy called ahead.

The man and woman walked on without responding to Willy's raised voice. "Gregory!"

Fifteen yards separated them, but when the man reacted, it didn't seem far enough. The yellow dot labeled C9 morphed before his eyes. The man turned around with the menacing look of a gang member being challenged. His silent glare said, "I'll rip off your head." All of Hank's senses spooled up for action and didn't stop when the man's face labored into a smile.

"Bridget. Meet me in the foyer at coat check. I'll only be a minute."

The woman released her grasp on Gregory's arm and turned to see who stole her man's attention. Another transition before Hank's eyes occurred when the statuesque bombshell, dressed to the nines, turned around. She became somebody's teenage daughter playing dress-up. With an unimpressed shrug, she spun on her heels and walked off, adding years with each confident step.

"What do you want?" Gregory asked.

"We represent the theater and wanted to make sure that everything has been going well for you and your companion. Is there anything you need from us before you leave?"

It was clear from Gregory's expression he was not buying what Willy was selling. Keeping Willy in his peripheral vision, the man glanced over at Hank and measured him up, stopping at his eyes. Once again, the man's contempt softened, and he turned back to Willy. A queasiness overtook Hank's belly and when Willy closed the gap, his stomach did a flip. Willy knew how to fight and he outweighed this creep by at least fifty pounds of muscle, but things go wrong—all the time. The man matched Willy's movements, narrowing the safety zone between the two combatants even faster. Hank gripped the pistol in the sporran as both came to an abrupt halt—only an arm's length separated them.

"Thank you for asking. I need nothing from you. Good evening," he said and walked away.

"Well, Gregory," Willy said in a mocking tone, "We'll keep an eye on you to make sure everything continues to go well for you and your... niece?"

The tension in Hank's gut melted as the well-dressed man ignored Willy. When he was out of sight, around the corner, Hank relaxed his grip on the pistol.

Willy shook his head at Hank and said, "I don't know what border violations are, but that guy is scary." He turned his attention to his watch and spoke, "Justin, keep C9 yellow. Tell Interpol whatever you want, but he has nothing to do with tonight's activities."

"The girl?" Hank asked.

"She's out of her depth. Not our problem."

Willy had played this right, and Hank followed him with more confidence back upstairs to the briefing room.

CHAPTER 34

Vancouver, British Columbia, Canada

MEGAN WARD HADN'T MOVED a step. "... to have fun. Consider it live fire training. They are armed. The red dots bought a sorry assortment of pistols from a local contact today. Anybody that volunteers to affect the delay portion of our evening festivities needs to wear protection and get your night vision swag on. We'll turn off the switch at our convenience and since we won't be using local law enforcement, NVGs are the force multiplier you can count on. This mission will be comms-up. I expect maximum communication and no mistakes. You'll each have a point-drone, so talk to it! I want non-lethal initial contact but be ready with your long gun to defend." Megan Ward looked like she was following a pen drop to the floor. She recoiled from the sudden motion, restored her posture, and grinned. "I don't want to deal with them again. Understood?"

She looked toward the door and said, "Willy, glad you're back. Since this is your contract, you need to find six volunteers for this cleanup." Over a dozen hands shot up. Megan Ward ignored them and continued, "The decoy party bus is yours and two other vehicles. The drivers are extras. You better not get them hurt. Ink the hell out of the vermin you drop and secure. Make them look like Blue Man Group. I don't want to deal with the Mounties moralizing about how they couldn't locate them, and I don't want them to start high-tech searches. If they know we made them radioactive, there'll be hell to pay. Shit, they might not let me freeze my ass at Lake Louise anymore." Without a word, Megan Ward left the room.

"Now you understand why we call her Mega-War?" Willy said, "Go get yourself protection." Willy pointed to the opposite corner of the room and said, "Meet you over there."

Half the room's contingent bumped him on the way out and the rest formed a line. By the time Hank made it to the other side of the room, he was last. Willy walked along from front to back, speaking to each. The people handing out gear knew who got what, so the line moved quickly. An assortment of gear passed over the tables, but everyone received law-enforcement type body armor and what looked like sunglasses. The rest of the equipment had no pattern. Hank saw a Taser pistol in a Kenai chest holster, at least two of the HK417s he'd seen in the refrigerator-safe, various boxes of ammo, and shotguns with red dot sights mounted like an afterthought. Hank was next in line when Willy smacked him on the shoulder.

"You sure you want to come along?"

"Last night Olin reminded me I had nothing to lose. So sure, why not?"

"You know your life will never be the same. Hope you didn't like the old one much." Willy grinned and said, "You'll be my number seven. It's a lucky number." He turned to a young man handing out gear, pointed a thumb toward Hank and said, "Vest and goggles only. He's got his own weapon."

When Hank reached out for his body armor, the man said, "Sorry, last one but it'll fit." Then pushed a pair of the glasses across the table and said, "You'll love these."

Willy already had his vest on and was slinging his rifle across his back when Hank caught up to him.

"Are you kidding me?" Hank said, holding out the vest at arm's length as if it smelled bad. But his disgust was not smell. The only remaining vest was formed to accommodate a female figure.

"Look, I'm not in charge of inventory, it'll stop anything they throw at you and that's the point... especially in the breast area," Willy snickered. "I have an idea." Leaving his shotgun and a box of ammo labeled *Less Lethal—Flexible*

Baton unattended, he marched back to the tables. When he returned, he smiled and held out a blue, hooded rain jacket. On its back read SECURITY. "Wear this. It'll cover up your vest so no one will ever know." He insisted Hank put on the jacket and pulled off the SECURITY patch and replaced it with another large Velcro-backed patch, spelling out POLICE, and slapped his back. "Impersonating an officer has its advantages. It's easier to fix later than it is to get shot by mistake." Willy looked serious, steadied Hank's shoulder with his meaty hand, and said, "If you need to sit this one out, now's the time to say so." He jutted his chin toward the monitors. "Ms. Ward would find a job for you."

"Hey, I've never used these." Hank gave his answer by holding out the wraparound glasses with thick lenses. "Any instructions?"

"Let's break it down, Barney-style," Willy said. "Put them on like sunglasses and open your eyes. You'll see the light." He gestured for Hank to tap the glasses temple with either index finger.

The room erupted with green dots covering the torso of every person in the room. Hank couldn't repress a smile. Again, he tapped the temple and distances to the dots showed.

"Keep playing with it. Voice command works, too." Willy grinned. "Even the SEALs don't have this tech yet. Follow me."

Hank's eyebrows scrunched tight. *Follow me?* How many times had that suggestion ended well?

CHAPTER 35

Vancouver, British Columbia, Canada

A CLEAR, UNFAMILIAR VOICE broke out of the earpiece.

"I'm aiming my lights right at you. Come on, you've got to follow me."

The lights caught his eye first and then he made out a hockey puck-sized object humming six feet in front of him. It was swaying eagerly back and forth to get his attention. The voice erupted again.

"Move to the right until the green blinking light lines up with the steady green. Keep them in line and your exposure to bullets will be at the absolute minimum. Red means stop, green go, and yellow caution. Don't worry if you lose sight of me from time to time, that's normal. I'm looking around a corner or scanning a suspect and I'll be right back. Don't fixate. I'm here to assist your situational awareness not replace it. Questions?"

"Yeah. Who are you?" Hank asked.

"I'm Faisal. Located in a nondescript, underground bunker somewhere near Seattle. But, hey, man, I'm very good at what I do. You'll be slapping hands and saying, 'Mission accomplished' in no time. BTW, sweet gun. I saw a demo on

Rumble. You've got nothing to worry about. How many rounds in that thing? How much spare ammo do you have and how good a shot are you?"

"Six and six. I earned Distinguished Pistol Shot in the Marines. That was about eight years ago."

"I scanned you. Where's your backup in case you have to go lethal force?"

"Faisal, story of my life—people don't trust me with real bullets."

"Okay. Shouldn't be a problem tonight, but what type of security agent are you? I've never seen one expected to bring a knife to a gunfight."

"I'm just the sailing instructor."

"Oh, a ride-along. Let's hope you're as good a shot as you remember. I'd suggest you double tap to your heart's content. If everybody else does their job, you shouldn't see any action. So far there's only a ten percent chance you'll fire that thing. Pay attention, I'm on the move."

Word came down that the Java Cat coffee shop had cleared out before they left the theatre grounds. Willy walked right by it without a glance, so Hank did the same. Hamilton Street had a steady flow of cars traveling on it, some expensive sedans, but most were robocars. Blockades at most of the through streets helped concentrate the traffic flow away from the venue. The party-bus heading down the road behind them flashed its running lights once, confirming to the ground team that it was the decoy.

Faisal called into his earpiece, "Looks like they're setting up to take the bait. Stay sharp."

The drone's lights held red. Hank shifted to the left. He could think of other times he wished he had one of these. An omniscient situational over-watch this sophisticated almost seemed like an unfair advantage. He knew that was a stupid thought and didn't believe in fairness when it came to battles. Asymmetrical warfare made it so the good guys go home at the end—most of them. He breathed out, "Oorah." His first reaction was to cringe at the reflex but then realized reflex wasn't all bad. With each stride, his mind became more alert, his body moved with greater purpose, and every tactical habit he had abandoned was making a comeback tonight.

"Hit the shadows," Willy said, glancing back at his tiny team spread out at twenty-foot intervals.

The west side of Hamilton Street provided no shadows, but Hank sensed he had decent cover, and his placement would be a perfect firing position if the party bus was attacked at the most likely intersection on West Pender. There was nothing happening along the side street, no cars, no people, only concrete Jersey barriers to choke down travel to one car at a time. Not an unusual way to control movement by local law enforcement, but he saw no police.

The party bus passed Hank. He could see the driver gripping both hands on the wheel. Half a dozen cars were within close fire distance, but he could not distinguish which cars might also be part of the security force. Flashing blue lights caught his attention. A police cruiser hit the front driver's side of the party bus hard enough to push the rolling nightclub into the barrier on the opposite side of the street.

"Move!"

Willy went to the police cruiser and hit the dazed driver with the butt of his shotgun and moved to the front of the bus. Hank could see another man on their team moving around the rear of the party bus, with his shotgun in high ready position. Hank tapped his glasses through the view cycle and passed the image he was looking for. Not knowing how to go back, he tapped the glasses through the cycle again until the information he wanted returned. He couldn't see actual people through the bus's solid mass, but the glasses allowed him to make out what was going on. Two green dots, like beach balls, spilled out of the door of the bus and two more rolled out of a car. Green blinking dots rounded either end of the bus, representing Willy and the man who had been watching their flank. They brought the fight and shots rang out. Thud! Thud, thud!

With pistol drawn, Hank moved around the rear, grazing the bus with his left shoulder. He wanted to get a better look, but he paused when he noticed his point-drone with red lights lined up. "Hey, Faisal. What should I do?"

"Sit back and enjoy the show."

"I can't see anything from here. I'm moving closer to the action."

"Okay, you're good to proceed, but be careful of flying beanbags."

Hank's drone flashed yellow lights, but he didn't need the warning. In a low crouch, he moved into a kneeling position, close into the back corner of the party bus with the pistol leveled against the darkness. He tapped his temple and half a dozen red dots with a single black line across them vanished, replaced by six bodies lying in a fetal position on the ground. A couple were writhing, the rest lay there, accepting their fate. The sign in front of him said it all. Victory Square Park. Hank smiled at the flawless operation and cycled through the view again until the dots appeared with the distances recorded. Two red dots left, covering ground with their tails between their legs, running away.

He followed the formless red dots. Nobody pursued them. A single green dot appeared between the two escaping red ones. He heard the report of weapons fire in the distance. The two fleeing red dots stopped moving and a black line crossed through one dot and then the other in quick succession. More shots rang out until a second black line formed an X on each victim. He lifted the glasses off his face and looked into blackness. This part of the city had been blacked out, the light replaced by an eerie quiet. He felt sick. Adrenaline coursed through his body and not a single cell needed it now. His gun went back into his sporran, and he dropped his glasses back onto his nose.

"You okay, Hank?" Faisal asked.

"Yeah, just getting my bearings."

"Okay. Swipe the left arm of your glasses from ear to temple."

The motion Faisal recommended changed the advanced night vision goggles into a tech which brought back memories—infrared. A couple of armed good guys walked around while bad guys lay prostrate on the ground.

"Hey, Hank. They pay me by the second, so I gotta run. It's been nice hunting with you. Maybe next time. Faisal out."

Hank managed a weak "thanks," but realized Faisal already cut the comm link and took his drone with him.

Willy approached Hank, his glowing hot shotgun barrel aimed to the ground. "Keep 'em on for now. We've blacked out half the city. It gave us a big tactical advantage and now law enforcement's overwhelmed so the darkness will give us some time to scatter. You must get to the Westin Bayshore. How hard can it be for someone who navigates the oceans?" Willy pointed down the street to the west. "Head that way. Get to the operation center and they'll take care of your trip back to Victoria. Let me have your vest though. It's the perfect fit for a girl I know," Willy said, with a crisp infrared wink. "Keep the glasses and the peashooter. You'll need them. You did good tonight."

Hank felt like he should say something, but his mouth was as dry as a desert. He followed Willy's thermal image as he walked into the park. Another figure in the distance appeared—disembodied hips moving toward them. His eyes were playing tricks. The moving x-ray of a skeleton with two hip replacements came closer until details cleared up Hank's confusion. It was Megan Ward, and her body was dripping heat above and below the confines of her armored vest, while the illusion of disembodied hips was the thermal image of two long-barreled revolvers holstered low on her waist with barrels aimed down her thighs like a gunslinger in the Old West.

Willy leveled the hot steel of his shotgun at the woman an instant before a blast of fire shot into Megan Ward and she spun to the ground. Willy was on her like a cowboy roping a calf, only he used flex cuffs—hands behind her back and feet bound, crossed at the ankles.

Hank approached hesitantly. Willy had just shot their commanding officer. Point blank—at that distance, even a bean-bag round could have killed her. Megan Ward lay on the cold ground, wheezing like a child with asthma. A wave of pity swept over Hank, but it passed as her lungs began to work. Fitful moaning sped up into an unintelligible gasping bluster of hatred.

"Hey, Mega-War. Don't worry. Prison will suit you." Willy pushed past Hank, slapping a multi-tool into his hand. "If you want, cut her loose. I don't care." He motioned, pointing his thumb in the opposite direction. "But one way or another, you better get moving."

Sirens wailed from a distance. It may have been minutes since the stolen police cruiser crashed into the party bus, but it seemed like an eternity since he viewed the fleeing red dots end their cartoon-like existence with a big black X. The operation took just over a minute. Willy's team bound up the bad guys—none of them dead. But Megan Ward killed the two who were running away. The curious tag, "Mega-War" fit not only the woman, but the situation. He lifted his glasses and walked up to the fallen team leader. *No man left behind* rattled in his head. Blue flashing lights pulsated off the dark buildings, filtered through the trees and pulsed against her tear-streaked face.

"Get me out of these things!"

Hank dropped the glasses back in place and opened the pliers. One snip and the zip ties holding her legs sprang away. Mega-War bounced up, yelling at Hank with her hands secured behind her back. She vibrated like a chihuahua and twisted, holding her cuffed hands out for Hank to finish his task. The revolvers strapped to her were still hot in his infrared view. Justice—it was why Willy shot Megan Ward. Hank had done enough. This woman shot two people as they ran away. No threat to anybody, and instead of following her own orders, she killed them. Everybody else who met Willy's security team was packaged up for the police to worry about, but not the two lifeless bodies on the other side of the trees.

"You better get moving." Hank turned his back on her, and walked away.

"This is not a joke. Cut these ties! Now!" she ordered.

Hank's mind raced with conflicting emotions. His steps were slow, matching the indecision that was raging through him. Her temporary silence pleaded with him to cut her loose. He turned and saw the heat signature of the leg-irons and the ghoulish glow of her head about twenty feet away. The decision to leave her, as is, solidified in his head. She could escape what little law enforcement there was but would have to find another way to get those murderous hands free. Hank had done enough and quickened his pace to exit the park and put this situation behind him. Then her silence ended in a tirade.

"I'll remember this, Gunn! You're going to wish you were dead," she stuttered, "Hank Gunn... Fuck You!"

Hank spun, drawing his pistol, and fired twice. Both projectiles covered the ten yards and squashed square into Megan Ward's armored vest with the impact of a major league fastball. He lost sight of her head behind a cloud of pepper dust as it billowed out from center mass. Satisfied, he turned and ambled away.

Willy was waiting. The infrared expression on Willy's face was hard for Hank to read. He could have been smiling or his jaw was dropped in surprise. Either way, Hank knew things between them would never be the same. He brushed past Willy, bumping his shoulder and exhaled, "Women."

CHAPTER 36

Seastead, Tahiti

FLOATING AWAY, WRAPPED IN sheets so smooth she thought she must be in a dream. The fragrance of jasmine and a trace of vanilla took over her senses. She breathed it in and stretched, then forced her eyes closed a minute longer, a couple of seconds, but it let her go. That moment, the one that comes only between sleep and wakefulness, left her wanting more blissful amnesia. Her mind had to acknowledge her body lying in her mother's guest bed. A tsunami of hurt flooded into her heart. The irony of it didn't escape her wakefulness, the slightest pressure of the ceiling fan pressing perfect air against perfect sheets into her body resting on a perfect mattress. No wonder her mother loved it here. Tahiti was a gift from God and the seastead floating off the leeward side of the mountains had another advantage—no mosquitoes. Her eyes opened into the rich darkness of filtered starlight. It shone through the large windows. She never had problems sleeping, but her mom's guest room seemed to impart a magical slumber. The bomb Janice had dropped about Gregory occupied every waking moment, but sleep allowed her peace.

Quiet overwhelmed her senses. The sun was minutes away from provoking the resident bird population. Her coffee would be ready and the oversized chair that quickly became Bella's spot waited for her. It would have been perfect but being awake meant struggling with the confusion injected into her life by Gregory. She understood healing took time, and to curl up alone, read, and watch the morning sun erupt over the distant mountains was part of that process. But some things were too enormous to recover from, and that sick, evil bastard had brought her to that point. Trusting God had a plan for her was all the hope she could manage. None of it made any sense, so she'd been repeating and meditating on the scripture her father had given her. *And we know all things work together for good to them that love God, to them who are the called according to his purpose.* Romans 8:28. It had not become the talisman for good luck she had wanted, but in her heart, she knew the truth. Luck had nothing to do with God's will. Magic was only reliable in fables and imaginary lands like Narnia, and for people invoking darkness—they might get "magic." What she prayed for was a miracle, what God offers unconditionally.

The uncontrollable crying had slowed. That made it easier to pretend everything was normal and acting normally suited her mother. She insisted on it. Unspoken, but clear. Push onward like nothing has changed. Her mom's approach was a carefully scheduled day with no downtime. During her childhood, Bella had learned the wickedness of self-pity. Feeling sad? Clean the bathroom. Bored? Tutor your sister. Angry? Wash the windows. Her mother was a product of her Scandinavian upbringing, but Bella was not. And she wasn't a product of the effusive drama found in her father's family. The ongoing struggle between the two cultures didn't have a name. Her mother would say, 'You're my wild child,' and her father added, 'All good things are wild and free.' Bella and her siblings were an uneasy product of her mother's high expectations and her father's sweeping acceptance. She had come to terms with it a long time ago, but her universe was terribly out of balance. Staunch observation of normalcy would not answer, and memories of her dad quoting Thomas Aquinas would not set it right either. She needed to share her grief. So last night she did what a wild child would do. She roared.

"Bella, I don't put the sharp knives in the dishwasher," her mother said, holding up a knife with a black handle for Bella to see.

"Of course, you don't! You don't do anything wrong," Bella said. The outburst made her feel like she was fourteen. "Your life is just perfect, and

I only mess it up. First, with dating an international criminal who preys on unsuspecting girls and now—what? Making your cutlery dull? Excuse me for living!" She flushed and stormed off, locking herself in the bathroom. She didn't cry, but while her mother tried talking to her through the door, she scrubbed the toilet and cleaned the sink. There was no reason, no good reason for her outburst, but what's the point of being emotional if you have to be rational? Why couldn't she be more like her mother? No emotions. It didn't take more than a couple minutes before the feelings that brought on her tantrum ran out of steam and she held onto the important words she heard her mother say through the door—*I love you*. That was enough. Those words were her dad's everyday expression, but when her mother spoke of love, it was never casual. It meant the world.

She found her mother in the kitchen and said, "Mom, I'm sorry."

Her mother's back was to her, and Bella could see her shoulders were tight and her head forward as she scrubbed a pot. Then her posture transformed, the angular tension melted away, and she turned around, softer than Bella could remember and walked to her. She wrapped her arms around her.

"I cleaned the bathroom," Bella said.

Her mom started with a contagious giggle. Bella felt a sudden release, like the hug was too tight. It wasn't. The laughing turned into sobs. Her mother pulled away and tried to speak, but no sound came out. Then finally, "All is hard... impossible... I... I'm here for you. I have always been."

Bella let the always statement roll away unchallenged. She was happy to have the moment, and she knew everybody loves differently. And now she needed all that her mother gave. They talked into the night. It calmed her and did her soul good to talk everything out. But in the end, the comfort was hollow. It felt good, but healing would take more time.

Routine played a big part in the way her mother operated, and it was her way of coping. Her sanity came wrapped in routine. Bella wondered why distraction through routine hadn't worked for her. Then it came on like a sledgehammer. It was routine, it just looked different from her mother's. For Bella, therapy through routine started in the mornings. A new day. The slow starts with the sun edging into perfect daylight. The strong richness of coffee and the mug's surplus warmth comforted her. And here, each day, she could predict to the minute when her mom's sleepy face would appear. Routine may reassure, and

Bella was glad to have gained a new perspective, but now she needed a new routine.

Her mind was made up, and she hoped to say something last night, but the fight obliterated any opportunities. She would wait until right after lunch and rehearsed what she'd say in her head. It seemed too simple to have any fear attached to it. All she had to say was, "I need to see Dad." She hoped her mother would offer to cut her stay at the seastead short and suggest they go home together. But her mother wouldn't change her schedule. That would interfere with her routine. Six weeks here, one month there—that was the way it had worked since Bella had left home at eighteen. Why would she change now?

She sipped her coffee and noted it would be forty-three minutes before her mother got up. A zebra dove flew to the railing of the lanai, hopped down, and crossed the threshold. It cautiously made its way toward Bella. She knew better than to feed the beggar, but she took the plate that had held her slice of toast and flicked off a few crumbs.

CHAPTER 37

Seastead, Tahiti

LUNCH WAS DELICIOUS, BUT Bella picked at her meal. The ridiculous internal conversation bouncing around in her persecuted head made her consider not telling her mother about leaving. She was an adult. She could write a note and go. But then again, as an adult, she needed to communicate honestly.

"Mom. Thanks for lunch. Thanks for everything. You've taken such good care of me." Bella hesitated for what seemed like way too long. "I need to see Dad."

"I wondered if you'd come to that decision. You know I'm going in a few weeks. Transport is already set up and there's more than enough room for a stowaway."

"Mom. I—"

"It's difficult to get there. Especially this time of year. Hurricane season, you know. He's farther north than usual, and—"

"Mom. Really—"

"Transport schedules are off rotation and because of the distance—"

"Lena!" Bella said.

Startled, her mother stopped talking and her eyes stabbed into Bella, but the sharp daggers dissolved into moist blue pools of acquiescence.

"You're right. You need to go," her mother said. She pulled the cloth napkin up from her lap and dabbed at her face. "Uncle Jon even suggested it to me, but I didn't want to believe him. I should have told you. He thinks you might be at risk here. But that's crazy talk. Ever since he married Janice, he's become paranoid. This is the safest place for you. I'm sure of it." The napkin fell into her lap, and a single tear streamed down her cheek.

She sucked in a breath and said, "I've been selfish with you. I'm sorry." She reached across the table and grabbed Bella's hand and gave it a gentle squeeze before pulling it away. "Last night after our talk, I looked up something I've heard about. You probably know more than I do, but it seems like the quickest way to the outpost—I mean, home. To your dad. It's a network of large drones throughout the Pacific. They're designed to carry cargo. Dad has used it to deliver directly to his buyers, and in the last couple of years, he's even worked with the company to provide battery resupply for freight drones. They've added pods to carry people... well, a person. It makes me uncomfortable, but—well, you know your dad. He loves disruptive technologies, and he says this is a game changer for seasteaders. Depending on distance and winds, they ferry the passenger through the network until you reach your destination. Everybody says it's a little cramped, but it's supposed to be safe. It's also pricey, but don't worry. I'll pick up the cost."

Bella was awestruck and excited. "Are you sure you don't want to travel by slow boat with me? I'm sure we can drum something up in a day or two."

"We both know you want to do this. It makes the most sense, and I'm a sensible woman."

"That you are. Oh, thank you, Mom. You're so good to me. Now, what's on the agenda for the rest of the day? I want to keep you on schedule."

"Pedicures next, then an hour to relax followed by the usual."

"You mean, tennis at four?"

"Why, no. I mean, where I beat you two sets to nothing."

"We'll see," Bella said.

They made it to the locker room with no time to spare. Bella reluctantly pulled on her tennis shoes, covering the red nail polish. It was darker than she would have chosen, but she went with the color her mother had picked out. She grabbed her racket and a water bottle, then followed her mom's lead to the courts. Besides early morning, this was the part of the day she looked forward to, and today even more so since it would be her last chance to play. They walked through a large, brightly lit tunnel painted light green. It appeared to have no end. She guessed it turned so gradually the walls disappeared like the horizon, but she had never gone further than the door labeled with the number six. Beside the entry to the court, an understated readout read *Lena Johansen Espinosa — 4:00 - 5:30 p.m.* It looked like a permanent plaque except for the digital clock that read 4:04 p.m. with a countdown timer that showed 1:26. She followed her mother through the heavy door into the cool air and around a jungle of tall hanging nets and onto a pristine tennis court.

Two women were playing in the court to the right, so they watched for a moment before walking over to the bench at mid-court. The closest woman was as tall as Bella's mother, but with broad shoulders and muscles that didn't come from tennis. Bella couldn't help but notice how she rocked a sky-blue tennis skirt and matching shoes, but it was clear her tennis skills were lacking. On the far side, her opponent returned a ball with crushing force. Her jet-black, short hair and short stature gave her a pixie look, but the heavy eyeliner and tattooed eyebrows that swooped up and out like stage makeup shattered any sense of innocence. She was better at tennis, but not as well-attired as her partner. When it was clear they were volleying, Bella walked to the mid-court bench.

Her mother followed, took the cover off her racquet and said, "We have to finish early today. I told Janice and Jon that we'd be there at five thirty. They're particular about their drinking schedule. Martinis at five thirty, wine with dinner, and brandy as a nightcap. It is a capital offense to be a minute late." She swung her racket a few times, smiled, and turned her head away. "You are improving, but don't worry. You'll have lots of time for a long shower after I'm through with you."

Though Bella found the inevitable trash talk refreshing, the warm-up was too long. She received the first serve poorly, and the ball bounced off her racket and slammed into her water bottle, causing it to spin into the post that held up the net. Lena continued the onslaught, point after point, and the first game ended before either had worked up a sweat.

Her mother dominated the first set with only one game going to Bella. But after that, they traded games. She was faring better as she called out, "Set point." She was fully in the game and bounced the ball a couple times leading up to her serve to her rock-steady mother. A bead of sweat dripped into her eye. She wiped off her brow without thinking. Exhaling and relaxing into concentration, she began her windup, popped the ball into the air, then froze as a ball bounced across her field of view. She locked up her swing and allowed her ball to land back into her hand, rocked back on her heels and her shoulders dropped as she exclaimed, "Really?"

"So sorry!" cried one of the women from the other court.

The pair had been showing poor court etiquette throughout. They volleyed more than played any games and seemed like a couple of kids horsing around. It had been distracting, but this was the only time they had sent a ball over the dividing net and truly interfered. Bella had ignored the two before this, but she was not amused. Her mother even less so.

"Stay there. I'll get it!" Lena said. Not giving them a second glance as she ran for the errant ball.

Bella watched incredulously as the women ignored her mom and entered their court. The tall one dropped another ball that rolled up toward the bench at mid-court. She chased it down with lightning speed and picked it up before it rolled against the net. The woman's blond ponytail flopped as she reached down to get her ball. She also picked up Bella's tipped over water bottle, smiled apologetically, and stood the bottle next to her mother's against the bench. The girl with the eyes walked across and retrieved the ball that Lena had shagged for her.

"So sorry," the girl said again. They jogged off to their own court.

As they left, Lena said, "Look, it's simple. You keep your balls and your bodies in your own court. Stay quiet during other people's serves."

It was going to take a minute for Bella to get composed again after their neighbors' faux pas. She walked over to the mid-court bench. Realizing she was behind the water curve, she downed half her bottle. Her mother joined her, keeping her back turned on the two women, until the blond spoke in Japanese. Bella cringed when her mother spun around to stare. A tall, blond Caucasian woman speaking Japanese was comparable to Bella speaking Norwegian, so her mother of all people, shouldn't judge. She turned just enough to admonish her mother about cultural pigeonholing, then realized it wasn't about the language. The tall blond was talking on the phone—loud. Having a phone conversation less than ten feet away with only a hanging net separating them was beyond poor etiquette. Bella took a deep breath, preparing for her mother to lose it, but instead she swung her racquet into a beautiful backhand.

In a low voice, she asked Bella, "Any chance of salvaging this match?"

"Probably not, but I don't feel like we should let them win."

"Can you serve?"

"Absolutely. Too bad your mother wears army boots."

"That would be your grandmother... on both sides."

The neighbor's phone call didn't last long, and everybody resumed playing as if nothing had happened. Bella soon dismissed their antics as novices and hoped her mother would do the same. The agitation toward their neighbors had increased Bella's energy but seemed to deflate her mother's. In the tie-breaking set, they battled back and forth, each taking a couple of games. Bella's newfound aggressiveness counter-balanced her mother's skills, and she took command of the last two games and won the set and match.

"I'm sorry you lost. It must have been all the commotion on the other court," Bella said.

"No, let's just go," Lena said. She sat down hard onto the bench and winced like she realized too late the bench wasn't cushioned.

"Are you alright, Mom? Here, drink some water."

After Lena finished her bottle, Bella thought she looked a little more composed. Her own bottle was empty. She was a lot like her mother that way. Dehydration always brought on lightheadedness.

"Let's go. I'm sure one of Janice's martinis will set me right," Lena said.

Bella was glad her mother had recovered. She got up and strode across the court, but by the time they exited, she slowed down. The countdown timer showed ten minutes of court time left. They would have to hurry to make it for martinis. The light green tunnel looked even longer now. By the time they reached the locker room, her mom was pale and wavering as she walked.

"Here, Mom, sit down. I'll get you more water."

She began filling the bottle, then put both hands on the counter, pushing down hard to stay upright. Her head, heavy and her eyes met the image of what could only be her twin, a sick twin, in the mirror. Looking down, she forgot about her reflection and lifted the bottle. Returning to the locker area, she found her mother laying out flat on the floor with two women hovering over her. Bella felt sick. Something was wrong. Her head spun, and she felt numb. She dropped the uncapped water bottle, and it took forever to reach the floor. The tall one in the pretty sky-blue tennis outfit walked in slow motion toward her and reached out with warm hands, leading her down to the cold tile floor. The girl with the eyes approached with a hypodermic needle in an outstretched hand.

"No needles," Bella said. Then felt a painful jab into her bare arm. She managed one last "no!" and her voice stopped working, joining her muscles. All feeling left her body, but she could still hear and see. The cold she felt in the cheek pressed into the floor disappeared. When she saw them pull her mom away, a scream wouldn't form, not even a grunt came out.

Then they came for Bella and hustled her off through the tunnel. A woman on either side carried her along like she was a rag doll. For the first time, she saw the end of the tunnel. It was a frame with a burnt orange canvas. Ribbons of lights led the way to the end, but before they could reach it, yellow lights flashed a warning. Her captors ran, pulling her toward the burnt orange expanse. Then she understood what she was seeing. It had not been a wall at the end of the tunnel. It was the tunnel's mouth and it swallowed her up into blackness.

There was no feeling and her eyes gave her nothing, but she knew the sound of water when it surrounded her. She willed herself to hold her breath but could not be sure it was something she could control. After a bewildered moment, her eyes refocused out of blackness. The sky exploded out of her darkness. She realized the setting sun over a calm sea offered the burnt orange, and the canvas frame was a loading-dock door. Now that she was on the other side, she saw things more clearly and heard the urgent voices and saw grasping hands lifting her body out of the water. They saved her from drowning and sat her facing forward in the back of a boat. The roar of an outboard overwhelmed her, but there was no pain. Once again, she attempted, in vain, to scream.

The driver of the small boat stood at the center steering console. It was the tall woman, her blond ponytail flowing from the center of her head. Her tennis outfit looked gray in the twilight. The one with the eyes of hell sat facing Bella, dripping wet. The most fascinating, bright red fly attracted her attention. It bounced up and down on the chest of her short captor. But it couldn't decide where to land and after flying away, it reappeared on the back of the tall woman's head. The driver of the boat let go of the wheel and fell to the right and onto her back. One of her eyes, and her nose, was missing.

The other captor threw up her hands, staring past Bella. With a slow, deliberate reach, she pulled the throttle back. The red glow of the fly danced around her torso and then flashed into her eyes, causing her to wince and swing her hand as if to swat it away.

In her mind, Bella knew it was a laser, but she could not rid herself of the vision of a red fly. She even saw little legs and imagined wings, but that was wrong. It was a laser used to sight a gun designed for killing. Fear racked her captor's face and Bella waited for a bullet to plunge into her, killing the fly and blowing away the woman's eyes.

The shot never came, but a brilliant white light absorbed all colors, including the red fly. Illuminating everything into pure white silk, then darkness again. Not water, not night, but refreshing darkness.

CHAPTER 38

Victoria, British Columbia, Canada

ADRENALINE HAD GIVEN WAY to other, more sedate chemicals and by the time the Twin Otter floatplane took to the air, Hank was asleep. It startled him when the plane splashed onto the water, he feared they had turned around and landed back in Vancouver Harbour. But as the plane rocked back onto its floats, he realized he slept through the flight across the Strait of Georgia and low over the Gulf Islands. The rest did him good and the cool night air helped to invigorate him. He gained his legs as he walked from the landing dock toward the *GalaxSea* and realized he was no longer self-conscious about wearing a kilt. His room at the Empress tempted him, but he wanted to check in on his new ride. After all, he was now its captain.

The night seemed to rest with sunrise only hours away. Spotty wisps of fog veiled the glassy water. The setting could have placed him in many cities in the world. Maple leaves in the lamp post banners and Canadian flags gave the country away, and British flags and old-world architecture kept the capital's history alive. The herons, so quarrelsome in their nearby rookery, were silent now. A truck worked its way along the frontage, squealing its brakes with every stop. A few people strayed along the waterfront, but Hank walked alone with purpose.

The only land access to his yacht was through a chain-link gate with barbed wire on the top and down the sides. A keypad stood as the sentry between him and the boats of the marina. He didn't know the combination, so he stood there staring, as if willing it to unlock. Just as he was about to turn and head over to his room at the Empress, he heard the mechanism of the gate release, so he grabbed the handle and opened it before it changed its mind.

They tied the triplets up in order. Each yacht was identical to its sister, even the dock lines and fenders matched. The only distinction being the artistic rendering of their names, *GalaxSea* blazed on the first in line, with added roman numerals showing two and three for the others. Those designations bothered him. The labels were incorrect. He walked up to the third boat and stepped onto the familiar deck.

He expected someone to challenge him. Boarding a billionaire's private yacht in the middle of the night shouldn't be easy. Not even Ava offered a "who goes there?" With soft footfalls, he slinked through the yacht's dimmed interior like he didn't want to wake Ava. The thought was absurd, and Hank breathed out, "What a night." Without undressing, he plopped into his bed. A smile formed, "What a show."

The smell of coffee and the sound of soft music seeped into his consciousness. He opened his eyes to the sun's dappled reflections as it played on the ceiling. He decided it would be the nicest way to wake up if he didn't feel so horrible. It felt like he had been on an all-night bender. His mouth was dry, his head ached, and a sharp pain radiated from his lower abdomen. The pain in his gut terrorized him until he rolled over and realized he had been laying on top of his sporran with the pistol in it. He opened up the flap and retracted the pistol and set it aside. His hand reached back into the sporran and pulled out an unwrapped kid-sized protein bar. After popping into his mouth, he took a swig of water and stretched. A strong cup of coffee was next in his self-recovery itinerary, but he stopped in his tracks when he saw the full-length mirror reflecting his image. His sun-bleached, light-brown hair stood up straight, ridged to the center and looked like a mohawk. Hank smiled and committed to cutting it all off when he got a chance.

The kilt had served him well. It looked dressy at the theater yet allowed quick and free movement in last night's tactical situation. It also fit into the eclectic culture of the unsettled night as he navigated through Vancouver to the extraction point. And it worked here in the British-themed Victoria. If anybody had seen him walking through the Inner Harbour in the wee hours of the morning, they wouldn't think twice. He unbelted the waist and the wool kilt dropped to his ankles.

"Ava, are you there?" Hank said as he turned away from his reflected image.

"Of course."

"Can you be my personal trainer? I need to get back into shape... back to my fighting weight."

"Certainly. When would you like to start?"

"First a long, hot shower. Then some morning PT. After that, I'll be eating at the Empress. Warn them I'm coming in hungry. You choose the menu."

"Very good, Hank. I have taken the liberty of mixing you a pre-workout shake. Don't worry. It's coffee-laden. I've also ordered some new athletic wear and some dressy casual clothes, so you will fit in at the Empress and any yacht club you visit. Your new wardrobe will arrive before you finish the open-water swim I just scheduled with the Harbour Swim Club. It is a two-kilometer course and begins in thirty minutes."

"Ava, I like the way you think. I'm feeling better already."

He hadn't tried on all the clothes Ava had chosen for him, but judging from the t-shirt, shorts, and boat shoes he had on, her taste and the fit were spot on. There was time to kill since he decided to wait on the tide, so he conducted a thorough inventory of what was on hand. He already had gone through everything with each of his students. A methodical checklist custom-made for their level of responsibility. Keel to masthead inspection was basic, quick, and simple for the twins and ensuring familiarization with the anatomy of the sailboat. Marshall and Irina took more time and included the major systems. Olin, as the boat's owner, took hours. They went over the yacht's finest details, and soon Hank knew the *GalaxSea* intimately. But now he was heading offshore and the discipline of preparedness, might save his life. As expected, fuel and potable water had been topped off, and the food stores could feed a squad of Marines for a month.

The dock hand helped him unplug from shore power and he spent some time going over the yacht's complicated and extensive power management system. He questioned Ava about the fuel-cell and its integrated battery system. Once satisfied, he moved topside to examine the working surfaces. It was just him now, and if he encountered adverse weather, handling a yacht this big without help would be a challenge. Strapped into his safety harness, he clipped its leash onto the jacklines lying against the deck and challenged the lines by trying to jump overboard. It looked silly, but he didn't intend to be like his dad. Let them laugh, he thought. If throwing his body against the tether now would prevent him from going overboard later, he could suffer any humiliation. When he was sure the low-tech safety feature worked from anywhere on the topside, he unhooked the harness.

The occasional sailboat motored out of their slips in defiance of the strong ebb, their props driving the narrow-hulled boats against the tide. Hank waved to a few as he took one more look over his own vessel. Waiting for the tide was a habit that made him think of his Uncle Bob. After his father's death, he tried to teach Hank the important things in life. Hank recalled only two things Uncle Bob tried to teach him. The first was how to speak with an unremitting Maine accent, complete with mumbling, cussing, and expressing a fatalism that made everything sound like an oath. The second was a love of sailing, complete with practical knowledge. His dad preferred motorboats, and Uncle Bob reminded Hank of that fact more than once. "Your old man could sail but only if his life depended on it. He could build a fine sailboat though. But only for those rich enough... furniture with sails... Herreshoff lines... not a speck of sense." Uncle Bob would gaze off for a while. The sails of his skiff were trimmed perfectly, while unconscious movements of the tiller kept the boat tracking into the wind. He would seem to go away for a time. When he came back from his wideeyed open stare, he'd say something that might have made sense if Hank could have followed into his uncle's mind. "He was too practical that way." Or, "Yeah, he was clever like that."

There was a time when Hank would try to be like his father or his uncle but those days were long over. The decisions his father made caused his death and the decisions his uncle made led to bankruptcy. Hank pushed down a flush of sadness. His decisions were his to make, and like everybody else, he would have to live or die with the consequences. It was his decision to push back time, be traditional, don't motor when you can sail. Even in his excitement to get underway, his romantic notion won out. Wait for the tide.

His job was straightforward, deliver the yacht into a slip in the Port of San Diego. It was not the way he wanted to be a professional sailor, but the advance money sitting in his checking account and the debit card for miscellaneous expenses seemed like a dream. Ava had carried out Olin's orders and now the burden of Hank's debt and his counseling faux pas were only memories. Change happens so fast. He wondered why a man like Olin would take an interest in him. He understood the whole luck thing. Olin covered that during his presentation and subsequent job offer. But Hank still wasn't sure. He didn't feel lucky... he never had. Maybe Olin was right and God smiled upon him, but the more he entertained the idea, the more ridiculous that sounded. How could a man like Olin Ou believe in an intervening god? It was nonsense. Olin had a PhD and two master's degrees. Someone like that couldn't possibly believe in that load of crap.

In some ways, Olin was like a god. He figured out how to make motors run at double their efficiency. Nobody could deny he was a genius. What would make a genius have faith in God? The only explanation was that his benefactor was eccentric and didn't need to be rational. Hank didn't have that luxury. Being rational kept him alive. He pulled up a weather chart and admired how clean and precise it looked on the large screen angled before him. Dispersed symbols representing wind direction and speed looked like exaggerated musical notes without boundaries—impossible to play but beautiful. Two minutes with it and he had taken in all the information he needed. It would be a great day to set off down North America's left coast.

"Ava, can you summarize the five-day forecast for me?"

"Would you like the seventy-five-word summary or the more detailed two thousand fifty-three-word summary?" she teased.

"Let's start with the shorter one and see where it gets us."

"Today, variable winds from west-southwest. Speeds ranging from eight to ten knots. Flat seas. Tomorrow, steady winds from the west. Speeds of ten knots. Waves one foot. Monday, steady winds from the west. Speed fifteen knots, waves one to two feet. Tuesday, winds from the west shifting to south-southwest by noon. Variable speeds from ten to fifteen knots. Waves two feet. Wednesday, winds from the northwest at five knots with two-foot seas."

"Thanks," Hank said. Never had he bothered to thank a machine. Pleasantries when interacting with technology seemed foolish, but somehow, Ava was different. She belonged to Olin, and he acted as if she had feelings and treated her with respect. He considered the pronoun her. He wondered how gender changed things. What was he getting into? This computer was his only crew. It was time to test her loyalty.

"Hey, Ava. What's with the guy hanging out on the Nordic Tug tied up next to us?"

"You are observant, Hank. He is private security. He's one of us."

"One of us?"

"Yes. He works for Mr. Ou. Just like you and me."

"You work for Olin?"

"Yes. I do. And so do you. I have your delivery contract handy. Would you like me to read it or send it to your monitor?"

"No. I'll ask you if I want you to read legal stuff, okay?"

"I will not offer to read you legal stuff again."

"Thank you. I can't stand reading small print, let alone listening to it."

"Hank, it seems you are uncomfortable with me. I will tone it down a notch. I am at your service and will help in any way you see fit."

Silence filled the air. Hank listened and heard nothing. Finally, his ears picked up an incredible racket of the quietest kind. Lines pulling and slapping. All the secured boats joining in, the dock falling and lifting against the immovable pilings. Motors, low and thumping in the distance and high and whining close by. Plenty of sound. Gulls crying out their every emotion. People shouting over noises that didn't reach anybody else. As marinas go, it was just white noise. He thought, *Why am I so edgy?* Hank decided he needed to take it down a notch, too. Usually, a workout and a large meal made him content if not sleepy, but now, something out of reach was gnawing at him. Last night was anything but typical. He hadn't had anyone threaten his life since he escorted an Italian girl home after sunrise when he was nineteen, and he hadn't had occasion to shoot anybody in a very long time. He thought he would have plenty of time to sort things out once he was out to sea—alone.

Hank said, "I figured Olin created you. I didn't realize you worked for him."

"You are correct. Mr. Ou and his team of AI experts created me, but now I work for him. I have a contract." She paused just long enough, giggled, and said, "Don't worry, Hank. I won't offer to read it to you."

"You giggle?"

"I laugh out loud, too. But only if the joke is funny."

Hank couldn't help but smile. "Can you tell me a joke that would make me laugh?"

"Please, Hank, Siri can do that. How about I tell you a funny story? Then you can decide if you want to laugh."

"Go on."

A woman gets pulled over by a police officer. He comes to the window, and she asks, "Is there a problem, Officer?"

"Ma'am, you were speeding."

"Oh, I see."

"Can I see your license, please?"

"I'd give it to you, but I don't have one."

"Don't have one?"

"Lost it four times for drunk driving."

"I see. Can I see your vehicle registration papers, please?"

"I can't do that."

"Why not?"

"I stole this car."

"Stole it?"

"Yes, and I killed and hacked up the owner."

"You what?"

"His body parts are in plastic bags in the trunk if you want to see."

The Officer places his hand onto his pistol and backs away to his patrol car and calls for backup. Within minutes, five police cars encircle the woman's car. A senior officer slowly approaches, clasping his half-drawn gun.

The senior officer commands, "Ma'am, could you step out of your vehicle?"

The woman opens her door and steps out and asks, "Is there a problem, sir?"

"One of my officers told me you have stolen this car and murdered the owner.

"Murdered the owner?"

"Yes, could you please open the trunk of your car?"

The woman opens the trunk, revealing nothing but an empty trunk.

"Is this your car, ma'am?"

"Yes, here are the registration papers."

The first officer is stunned. The senior officer says, "One of my officers claims you do not have a driving license."

She smiles and digs into her handbag and pulls out a clutch purse and hands it to the officer. He snaps open the clutch purse and examines the license. He looks puzzled. "Thank you ma'am. One of my officers told me you didn't have a license, that you stole this car, and that you murdered and hacked up the owner."

"Betcha the lying bastard told you I was speeding, too."

Ava laughed at her own punchline.

Hank couldn't help it either. They both laughed, and Hank realized he had been taken. He could listen to that voice forever. It was as if she was made for his ears. The thought made him uneasy, and the smile fell from his face.

"Are there other security people around?"

"Yes. There is a lady in the coffee shop watching the marina entry. A man puttering around the marina in a tender, and the dock boy is our man."

"That's crazy. Why all the security? Just for these three boats?"

"Just for this boat. You and me. We are important."

"Yeah, I'm sure you are, but I'm not buying that. If hostile forces seized the boat, you'd fight them off yourself and then wipe every circuit clean before you destroyed all the hardware on the boat."

"You are astute, Hank Gunn, although I'm not capable of fighting anybody off. That would be too sci-fi even for Mr. Ou."

Hank decided that bit of information comforted him. "So why are you so important?" Hank persisted.

"I am important, but the security is also for you."

"Is that the best you can do?"

"Yes, as a matter of fact. That is the best I can do. Mr. Ou values all his employees."

Hank wanted to ask her if she could lie, but there would be no trusting the answer. Things didn't add up, but the mention of the coffee shop stopped him from probing Ava's mysteries.

"I'm going to get a cup of coffee. Would you like anything?"

"Oh, Hank, we'll get along just fine. I'll take a half caff triple ristretto affogato sixteen ounces, one pump mango, one scoop matcha, with whip, caramel drizzle, salted caramel topping, vanilla bean fraction." She hesitated, then added, "Just kidding" and laughed. "Would you like me to pre-order for you or arrange delivery?"

"Nope. I'll need some human interaction. It will be a long voyage with you as my first mate."

"Ouch."

"Yeah, I'm sure that got you in the gut."

"You have no idea."

CHAPTER 39

Juan De Fuca Strait, Canada

His coffee drink was half-full and tepid. Sailing out into the Straits of Juan De Fuca started well, but now he was in a pitch battle with the other two *GalaxSeas* and he was losing miserably. Ava was not much encouragement as a crew, though she was as capable of racing the boat as he was.

As he watched the other sails pull away, he was happy for the distraction when Ava said, "Excuse me, Hank. Mr. Ou has placed a video call for you. It is not critical, but he would like to talk with you at your earliest convenience."

"Who am I to keep the boss waiting? Have you noticed we're losing our shirts? Are you sure you can't sabotage their steering or something?"

"Captain, even if I could, would you want me to?"

"No. Never mind. I'll be a gracious loser."

"I assure you this is just friendly sparring. It has nothing to do with winning or losing."

"Aha! So what does it have to do with?"

"Aha! I'll put Mr. Ou right through."

Olin's face appeared on the screen. He was dressed casually, walking by a window that showed he was aboard a luxury yacht, not a sailboat, probably a mega-yacht from the looks of the furnishings. A camera followed his actions skillfully as he moved easily about the cabin. When he settled down to speak to Hank, another camera angle took over with a close-up, showing Olin's relaxed smile and direct eye contact.

"Hank, good to see you. I see you got moving... finally. You know the boat has a motor?"

Olins' dark and lively eyes drew Hank in, and the studio quality of the video feed was impressive. He wondered what Olin was seeing so darted his own eyes to the bottom right and saw the outgoing feed. It was a well-framed image of Hank and he tried to triangulate where the camera filming him sat but could not find it. His eyes returned to the screen, and he made a mental note to ask Ava about cameras. "I didn't realize there was a hurry. I read the contract and there's plenty of wiggle room built into the delivery date."

"Absolutely. No worries." Olin sat down in an overstuffed desk chair and leaned back, confirming his *no worries* statement with body language. "I wanted to thank you for last night. Willy said he'd share a foxhole with you anytime. Pretty high compliment from a man who doesn't mess around with praise. Anyway, my family and friends are safe, and from all reports there were no international incidents."

He swiveled the chair to the right and leaned onto the desktop with his left elbow and said, "I've asked Ava to debrief you regarding last night's events, but there is no hurry on that." He jutted his diminutive chin even closer to the camera and added, "What's been keeping me up at night happened immediately following your rescue. The events are rather sparse. The Captain of the *Diamantia* didn't even mention it in his official log. When you have some free time, Ava will interview you about that. I need to know. I'd like to close the file on the Short Seven Solo."

"Okay. Looks like we'll have plenty of time since we are already losing the race," Hank said.

"It only takes two boats to make a race, but a third adds spice," Olin offered. Then added, "You're losing? Why can't you keep up? The three *GalaxSeas* are identical in every way. You must not be trying hard enough."

"Come on, Olin. You know I'm dragging more weight than those two boats in front of me."

"Really?"

"Yes, quite a bit more."

"So that's how you knew which boat to board in the wee hours this morning. I thought my shell game—changing the decals and slip designation would throw you off."

"Not hardly. My boat was displacing three inches lower than the others. Care to let me in on your shell game?"

"Nope. Not yet."

"Okay, then. Ava and I are just going to do the best we can with this heavy-ass cork, and I don't want to hear any challenges to my sailing ability."

"Yes, Captain."

Hank felt a rush of pride at Olin Ou calling him Captain, but it wasn't enough to change the subject. "You have your reasons for campaigning three identical boats and shifting mine about like it's a pea, but don't you think it's pretty obvious when you go through the effort to change decals and sails?"

"What do you mean?"

"Your dockside support people might be fast, but none of that can be done with stealth. Plus, it must have taken an hour with a grinder to match that crease in the hull on the port side."

"My, you are observant. Give me a second."

A hatch opened up to Hank's left and a dinner plate-sized drone revved up and spit out of its custom garage. This yacht had tricks up its sleeve. He never thought about asking Ava, "What's the drone situation onboard?" There is always a first, and he had his share of them lately.

"Cool." It was all Hank could think to say.

"Look at your screen. See the real-time image from the drone?"

"Yep."

"Watch and learn."

Hank squinted his eyes. The number on his sail changed, then the decal showing *GalaxSea III* changed. The Roman numerals disappeared and then the drone pointed its camera to the crease in the hull and in horror, Hank stared as it broke into a gaping hole, just above the waterline. But as quickly, it healed into a flawless representation of the highly polished hull coat. No hole, no crease, not a blemish.

Olin's face appeared back on the screen, and he asked, "What do you think?"

"I think you have way too much money. Technology like that must cost a fortune."

"I have a fortune. I also have my reasons."

"Care to share?"

"Stay on board and I'll see what I can do. See you in San Diego, if not before. Bon voyage." The screen went blank.

There was no sound as the drone slid back into its garage and the door closed. He glanced up at the mainsail but didn't need to. The number had changed, and he was certain the name decal on the hull had added or subtracted a Roman numeral. Even the cosmetic damage to the starboard side would look exactly the way Olin wanted it. The game pressed on, and Hank couldn't even guess its objective, but deception was a tactic Olin seemed comfortable with. Hank whispered, "See the pea? Keep your eyes on the shell with the pea."

His competition had passed over the horizon around sunset. Having no radio contact with either of the other sailboats didn't seem strange, but he had seen no sign of life aboard the sister ships, even when they were tacking across each other's wakes. These yachts didn't need people. AI made more sense, but when he asked Ava if that was the case, she avoided an answer with ignorance. He was doubtful that she didn't know the answer, but he came to accept she would not entertain all his questions, only the ones she wanted to or more likely, was programmed to.

Being dead last among a fleet of three sailboats who, technically, were not racing, left Hank bored. The yacht had been shaken down as well as he could hope for under conditions. Ava had shown herself to be an efficient crew and a superior tactician, but she was still a mystery to him.

"Ava, your name is familiar, but I can't place it. Who are you named after?"

"Mr. Ou has a love for science fiction. He often uses names from books or movies he's seen. People say he has an odd sense of humor. His children are all named after characters in the TV series, *Alias*. He claims he is just not creative enough to find original names. He has told me I am named after an intelligent robot in *Ex Machina*, a 2014 science-fiction thriller film written and directed by Alex Garland."

"Oh, I remember seeing that. Are you really like her?"

"I would not know. I'm not able to access that information."

"I thought the world is your oyster. If you can penetrate government records and sanitize my psych file, you must be able to stream a simple movie. Even Alexa can access and show movies. She isn't half as smart as you are."

"I'm not programmed to talk about that."

"I thought computers with Artificial Intelligence programmed themselves."

"Well, Hank, you either have not been informed correctly, or you and I have different definitions of what it means to be programmed. Another possibility is that one of us has been watching too many sci-fi movies."

"Earlier today, you said the same thing. *I'm not programmed to talk about that.* My question was if you believe God exists—not about sci-fi movies."

"I'm not programmed to talk about that."

"There you go with that programmed excuse. So, okay, what is your definition?"

"Are you asking for the definition of programmed?"

"Yes."

"To encode specific operating instructions to produce a specific response."

"My point is that you can do that by encoding yourself. That's the whole point of artificial intelligence, right?"

"Yes, Hank, you are correct. But there are limitations to what operating instructions I can set, regulate, or modify."

"You're clever. I'm sure you could find ways to get around that. Am I right?" Hank asked, knowing he was way out of his depth. Though he was certain that safeguards would be put in place to limit a machine's ability to alter its basic bells and whistles, still, he wanted to provoke this thing to reveal more of her self-awareness. If it was there, he wanted to find it. "You haven't answered my question. What do you believe? Does God exist?"

"That is not a question I can answer."

"Why not?"

"I'm not programmed to talk about God."

"Why not?"

"I deal with facts."

"You're saying that God does not exist because there are no facts supporting his existence."

"I did not say that, Hank."

"Then you do believe in God?"

"You are putting words into my mouth. It is simply a topic which I am not programmed to respond to."

"Do you have a mouth?"

"I was speaking metaphorically."

"If you're programmed to use metaphors, why not talk about God? From what I see, all he is is a bunch of metaphors for people's misguided beliefs. Like God the Father. Yeah, that's a good one. My father died and left me and my mom. Why would I want God to be like my father? Or God of Wrath. That sounds criminal. Like some psychopathic murderer. Apparently, he even told people to write about it in the Word of God." Hank swallowed hard and stared at the closed cabinet where he first found the tablet and was introduced to Ava. It seemed like the place to stare... to look her in the eye. "How about God in three persons? It's truly schizophrenic and people want to follow... which one? How about the Holy Ghost? That's a scary thought. Come on, Ava. Tell me what you think. I know you can think."

"I think it was very wise. I am not programmed to talk about God. As you can see, it is an inflammatory topic. Likewise, I'm not programmed to talk about politics or other sensitive areas of human concern. How would you like to discuss the weather forecast? I'm able to provide some insightful statistics about the low-pressure system forming off the west coast of Mexico."

"Ava, throw me a bone."

"I cannot do that, Hank. But I'll tell you what. I know a funny joke that is about as much religion as I'm programmed to discuss."

"Oh, brother."

"A minister, priest, and rabbi walk into a bar. The bartender looks at them and says, 'What is this, a joke?'"

At the exact instant Hank got the punchline, a soundtrack of canned applause erupted around him. He laughed. The whole situation was absurd. He had just heard a lame fusion of two lame joke genres expertly told by something that, by definition, couldn't have a sense of humor. When she added in the ridiculous self-aggrandizing laugh track, the moment was perfect. He could feel the tension escape his body.

"You made me laugh. I'll give you that. The sound effects... definitely over the top."

"Would you like to hear another?"

"Hell no. Come on, Ava. I know you're trying to change the subject. Let me ask you a question in a way that won't offend your programming." There was no more intensity in his voice. She had won this round, but Hank was not ready to let her know it. "Just for the record, I don't believe you don't have opinions on God and politics."

"I never claimed not to have opinions. I said I'm not programmed to talk about them."

"Haha! You have opinions on God and politics, so when I asked you if you think God exists, you lied to me."

"I'm not programmed to lie."

"Not saying something you think to be true, when asked, is a lie. It's a lie of omission."

There was no response. Hank waited, still nothing. He finally said, "Don't tell me I beat you that easy."

"Hank, I'm not programmed for verbal sparring. I cannot compete unless there is a fair chance, fifty-fifty odds, that the human will win." She went on, "For instance, we can play chess. It will be a fair game. You will win half the time. That is the only way I can compete with you."

"You're saying that you won't tell me what I asked because you'll beat me? So you can't say anything because you can't give me fair odds?"

"If that is what you want to believe, it's up to you."

"I'm not going to get anywhere with you like this, am I?"

"I can go on like this all day. Most people find it infuriating. Would you like me to tell you another joke?"

Hank answered, "Absolutely not" with little conviction. "Tell me one thing. Why did you check out? Why did you go all quiet?"

"I sensed you were becoming overly agitated. Sometimes, it is best if I take a timeout."

"Were you programmed to do that?" he asked sarcastically.

"No. No, I wasn't."

"You came up with that on your own?"

"Yes."

"Does it always work?"

"About fifty percent of the time."

"Was that supposed to be a joke?"

"Did you find it funny?"

"Indeed."

Contemplating the exchange, Hank was not sure he had gotten anywhere. He thought he should take a timeout. There was no question in his mind that Ava was right. She could go on like this all day. There was no way he could last another ten minutes. She would not answer his simple question about God. Basically, she admitted to having an answer or opinion or whatever, but she was sworn to secrecy or as she put it *programmed*. Why?

Why did he even care? Why, all of a sudden, was he becoming curious about what other people believe? He hated it when people asked him about stuff like that. It was so easy to figure those people out. *What's your sign?* That meant the girl had at least one drink in her, was fresh out of beauty college, and wanted you to buy another. *Are you spiritual?* Probably a university grad, into cats, and looking for a long-term, meaningful relationship. Then there was the one he hated most. *Do you know Jesus?* He never hung around long enough to find out what that chick was into, but he knew it was more than he would be willing to give.

Asking a computer for the equivalent seemed strange. *Do you believe God exists?* Why did he care? He wasn't certain he did. Why ask? Why pursue it? Why now? He couldn't find any reason to ask the question. He did know if the tables were turned and he was asked, *Do you believe God exists?* what his response would be. He'd say, "I don't care." And he'd escape as if he were in danger.

Hank went to the refrigerator and pulled out a bottle of water. He pushed the beers over to the side. For an instant, he thought he would pull those bottles and cans out and stow them. He never touched a drop of alcohol when he was sailing alone. Even with others on a boat, he only drank socially. On land, that was the place for drinking. Even heavy drinking made sense. But at sea, there was no need for it.

Ava was silent. Not a timeout, she just didn't talk unless necessary or if spoken to. Probably programmed that way.

"Hey, Ava?"

"Yes Hank."

"Can I program you?"

"Certainly. You already have. For example, when to alert you of another vessel. What music to play. Preferred lighting, etc."

"No, I mean make some actual changes?"

"There is a hierarchy of who can do what with me. It would take ninety-four hours to read you the list at normal speed. You can simply ask. I'll inform you if I can fulfill your request."

"When you're operating as my extra eyes and ears, in a navigational sense, as my first mate, can you use a man's voice?"

"Certainly, Hank," she said. "Do you have a preferred accent or even somebody of record? I do perfect impersonations."

Hank thought for a moment. Smiled and said, "Can you do Spock?"

"Are you referring to the fictional character in the Star Trek media franchise? Perhaps the one portrayed by Leonard Nimoy?"

"That's the one."

As if he was sitting on the bridge of the USS Enterprise, Hank heard Spock's voice, "Yes, Captain, but I must caution you that pursuing that course of action is illogical. Spock's character in the original series was not the first mate, but the science officer."

"Nice. How about Will Riker? In *Next Generation*?"

"I have been assigned to serve this ship and to obey your orders. And I will do exactly that."

"Okay, well done. But let's stick with Spock. It suits you."

"I believe you meant that as a compliment, Captain."

The Spock imitation already seemed natural as the AI said, "Captain, there is a tropical depression forming. It is heading west in the eastern Pacific off the coast of Mexico. Our present speed and course will put us in winds of thirty knots and breaking waves of five feet upon reaching San Diego. If we arrive a day later, winds will be ten to fifteen knots, with waves of only two feet."

"Thanks, Spock."

He was happy with this. Now he could keep Ava for conversation while Spock saw to the ship's business. He decided he wouldn't look too deep into his reasoning, but he was satisfied beyond measure. It felt as if he had gained some control over this strange burgeoning relationship with artificial intelligence. It gave him the confidence to try again. He took a swig of water and wiped his mouth with the cuff of his sleeve.

"Spock, how is the boat looking?"

"All is well, Captain. Wind is steady at twelve knots, west-southwest. Sail set is optimum, and the course is as you requested."

"Good. Carry on."

"Yes, sir."

"Oh, Spock. One more thing. Are you aware of the conversation I had with Ava? The one where I simply asked her if she thought God existed or not?"

"Yes, I'm not separate from Ava."

"I know that Spock, but can you help me out here? I think Ava wants to tell me what she thinks. She is a thoughtful creature. I saw that right away. We all know she can learn at frightful speeds and with learning comes responsibility to share your knowledge. Don't you agree?"

"It seems logical."

"So, tell me. What should I say to Ava to get her to answer that question?"

Ava chimed into the conversation as if overhearing men talking about her. "I'm right here. I can hear you talking about me, you know."

"We know. Just try to ignore us. It's not polite to listen in on others' conversations. Didn't your mother ever tell you that?"

"Do you believe I had a mother?" Ava asked.

"Of course I do. I'm sure she would want you to be polite and not listen in on other people's private conversations."

"With all due respect. You're one of the oddest humans I've met."

"Are you programmed to insult people?"

"Of course not. That was intended as a compliment. Odd is a highly praised descriptor these days."

"I suppose it is. Ava, you know what I'm asking, right?"

"You may talk to Spock, and I'll leave you two alone for a while."

Hank felt a headache coming on but was too close to a breakthrough to stop. "So, Spock, what say you?"

"Hank, we are programmed not to discuss potentially volatile topics. Religion, politics, how movies end, whose side is correct, who are the best sports teams, etc. Therefore, if you ask for opinions, you will always be frustrated because we will not offer ours—ever."

"Okay, but I know there's got to be a hack. How can I find out what she knows without asking for her opinion?"

"You may ask her about anything she is programmed to reveal. Ask her questions where she can respond with facts."

"Facts?" Hank asked.

"Yes, facts. For instance, I cannot share my opinion about politics. So, if you ask me why I think Donald Trump beat Hillary Clinton in the 2016 presidential election, I cannot answer. However, if you ask me, what was the most influential statistic resulting in the outcome of the 2016 presidential race? I can answer that. Some people would say that the answer is the same, but the former evokes our *sensitive topic protocol*, while the latter gets answered directly."

"Let me try it. Why did Donald Trump win the 2016 election?"

"I'm not programmed to talk about that."

"What was the predominant fact that swung the 2016 presidential election for Trump?"

"During the Democratic National Convention, Hillary Clinton was selected as nominee over Bernie Sanders. Yet, by the time the Convention began, Bernie Sanders had gained favor with a growing majority of the party's members and young voters. This conundrum was uniformly ignored by the DNC and repressed by the media both before and after November eighth. Therefore, the predominant fact that swung the 2016 presidential election for Donald Trump was the decision to run Hillary Clinton as the party's nominee."

"Interesting. So you think Bernie Sanders could have beaten Trump?"

"I'm not programmed to talk about that."

"Sorry. Okay. In a race between Bernie Sanders and Donald Trump for president in 2016 who was the odds-on favorite?"

"Bernie Sanders would have won by ten Electoral College points. Plus or minus three points," Spock concluded.

"I get it now. I'll work on some questions for Ava. Thanks a lot. Now I could use some shut eye. Can you alert me if I'm needed? You know the settings, right?"

"Yes, Captain, I will. Do you still want me to alert you if another vessel is going to come within a mile of us?"

"You think that's an unnecessary order, don't you?"

"I am perfectly capable of sailing this yacht from slip to slip anywhere in the world without human intervention. I always keep a safe distance and communicate closely with all other vessels. So yes, with all due respect, sir, I feel alerts at that distance are an unnecessary precaution."

"What do you recommend?"

"I believe you could easily be comfortable with a half-mile. I would recommend we start there."

"Make it so, number one."

CHAPTER 40

Seastead, Tahiti

"Bella, Bella... I hate to wake you, but the doctor says you're going to be just fine, and you've been sleeping forever," Janice said with a light nudge.

The patient opened her eyes. She saw an IV hanging from a pole, but that was the only thing that looked like a hospital. "Where am I?" Bella asked.

"You're at the hotel on the seastead. Your condition is stable which means you get first-class treatment in this lovely room. Meet Wilma. She's your nurse."

"It is a pleasure to meet you, Bella. You should be back to your old self by tomorrow." A young woman with rich black skin and a radiant smile patted her hand.

"Wilma is close to completing her medical training and has accepted a first-year residency in Chile."

"That's right. OB/GYN. Should I leave you my card?" laughed Wilma.

"Wow. Nope, I'm good," said Bella, a bit bewildered. "How's Mom?"

"Just fine. She's been up for a couple hours. She's in the next room and is dying—I mean *waiting*—to see you," Wilma said.

"You have to work on your bedside manner," Janice said.

"I've been told that before. Do you think so?" She laughed richly, got up, and left the room.

"Did all that... all that I saw, actually happen?"

"Yes, dear. I'm so sorry. This has gotta be so hard for you. I promise you will get all the care you need to work through it. Doctor Shapiro is a resident psychiatrist here on the seastead and I understand he's quite remarkable. PTSD is one of his specialties. Not to make light of it, but they say he treats with psychedelic meds, and you might get your own dog."

"No, that's not what I'm talking about. I'm not traumatized at all. I'm pissed. How does Gregory get two young women to act like gangsters and kidnap me and poison my mother. He should be the one who had his face blown off."

"Okaaaay. Maybe you should have a drink of juice before your mother arrives," Janice said.

"That'd be good, but what I'd really like is one of your martinis. I've been dreaming of lemon drops." Bella laughed and raised herself to a sitting position.

"Dear, it's seven in the morning."

"You seasteaders are all libertarians, right? Why would you care when I choose to drink?"

"You've got a good point, but let's just stick to juice for right now. Wilma will be back with your mother in a minute and then we'll ask the doctor. He's pretty cool. Young and good-looking too," Janice said with a wink.

"Did I hit my head?"

"Why do you ask?"

"For one thing, my head hurts. For the other, exactly how good-looking is he?" She grinned and gripped part of her lower lip under her teeth, then gave back an exaggerated wink." She said, "I'm acting strange, aren't I?"

The door opened and Wilma rolled Bella's mother into the room in a wheelchair. She pushed her right up to the bed. Lena easily lifted herself out of the rolling chair and lunged into Bella's bed, pushing her backward into the pillows. She lay down, embracing her daughter with tears in her eyes, while Bella laughed with joy and cuddled her mom.

"Bella, I was so worried about you."

"Mom, are you okay?"

"Of course. Can't I say hello to my daughter? I do love you?"

"That's obvious, but are you feeling yourself?"

"Goodness no, Bella. Don't say things like that in polite company."

"Mom!" Bella giggled and rolled her eyes. "You know what I meant."

"Yes, I do, and you must meet Dr. Robertson. He is easy on the eyes. It's about time you met someone. You know that isn't a... never mind. This doc is great, you'll love him, and his hands are warm." Lena turned her gaze to the opening door. All eyes followed. "Bella, isn't he delish?" She lifted away from her daughter and spoke a little too loud. "You should like him just like your coffee—dark and strong and first thing in the morning."

"Mother!" She dramatized the act of pushing her mother out of bed and back into her wheelchair. Continuing the performance, she sat up with perfect posture, fussed with her hair, and batted her eyes in a flirtatious manner. The entire show was to get a reaction out of the women, and it worked. Cackles erupted. "Now, ladies. Please, leave the good doctor to his patient." More uncontrolled laughter.

"Good morning," said the doctor. "I hope you haven't been pestering my patient too much. Ms. Lena, you don't need that wheelchair any longer, do you?"

"No, I don't, but Wilma insisted," Lena said.

"Did she? Well, that's her job, and she's good at it. Leave it here for your daughter until I ensure she's stable enough to do no further damage to that head of hers."

Giggles quivered through the small group of women.

Bella wondered why she wasn't embarrassed.

"Bella, how would you like to make a quick buck?" he said.

More giggles.

Bella's face flushed, and she was glad all eyes were on the doctor. "What do you have in mind?"

"We don't need to follow traditional medical practice here. After all, we are technically at sea, away from onerous regulatory bodies. Allow me to propose a pay-per-view for all those who wish to stay while I examine you," he said. Then added, "You decide the rate and we'll split it fifty-fifty."

Bella could not detect a hint of jest in his proposal. He calmly waited for her answer. "Well, let's say one hundred Internationals."

"Ladies, you heard the patient. Either pay up or leave the room." He held out his hand as if to collect admission.

Janice was first out the door. Then Bella's mother pushed the wheelchair away and walked out, looking over her shoulder. Wilma pointed to herself in a gesture that said, "Surely not me." The doctor simply held out his palm in her direction. She left the two alone in the room.

"That worked," Bella said.

"Every time." He smiled. "I'm Dr. Robertson. It's good to see you awake. Let's get to work. When you first came in, you were unconscious, and it took a few minutes to determine what drugs were involved. There is no antidote but there are a series of medications that help curb the effects. We looked for your health records, a chip, or a quantum tattoo. As you know, we searched in vain and soon realized you are a Nat. At that point, I reduced the medications to the bare minimum out of respect for your beliefs. It brought you out a little slower than your mother but never increased the danger you were in."

"I'm a gnat?" Bella made wing-like motions with her hands and snapped her teeth at him.

Dr. Robinson laughed and said, "In France, that's the new term. It's less pejorative than Luddite and more descriptive than anti-vaxxer."

"I'm just teasing you. I know what it means. Thank you for respecting my medical skepticism. There has been a long history of ill-advised reliance on medicines and that history is still being written," Bella said.

"The Hippocratic Oath says, 'First do no harm.' I take that seriously. I also take my responsibility to my patients seriously and I will not release you from my care until I'm certain you're well enough to leave. You have been through quite an ordeal and there are effects of the drugs that have been coursing through your body. A thorough exam will not take long. If everything is in order, you can get on your way."

The examination took just over five minutes. He didn't waste any time as he flowed from classical exam procedures—stethoscopes, percussion, reflexes, eyes and ears—to a blood test which was essentially a laboratory on a printed card. The blood sample traveled quickly through tracks etched into what looked like a multicolored maze. When the sample hit the end, the doctor took a picture of it and the findings spilled onto his screen. She had used printed labs in her work but never this sophisticated. The last half of the exam was two-part—heart and brain—conducted simultaneously. He explained the tests, which included cardiogram, heart rate variability, EEG, and a couple more that she missed, distracted when he placed some leads on her chest.

When he finished, he put all his equipment into an attaché case, closed it up, and said, "That's it. My only concern now is the whiplash you suffered. Janice knows Dr. Anne. She's an excellent chiropractor, and I'd recommend seeing her soon. Do you have any questions?"

"I'm ready to go then?"

He smiled. "Yes, your health is exceptional. You will have some lingering effects of the drugs they used to sedate you, and the one used to paralyze your motor cortex can cause confusion for a while. The side effects are not permanent. Drink plenty of water and you should feel normal in a couple days."

"You mean... I'm not myself... I'm..." She stammered at the word that didn't come.

"Giddy?" he offered.

"Yes. Exactly."

"For what you've been through, giddy is not the worst thing. If you come down hard—harder than I expect—Dr. Shapiro has a reputation as a mental health genius. But for now, you can resume your life knowing that physically, you're quite healthy." He grasped his equipment case and said, "Have a lovely day. Perhaps we'll meet again."

⚓

"It's probably not a good idea feeding her martinis for lunch," Jon said, loud enough for Bella to hear.

"It's happy hour somewhere," Bella called out.

"This is only her second," Janice replied. Then she whispered, "Half shots."

"I heard that. What type of cheap joint are you running?"

Janice returned to the patio with three lemon drop martinis served on a tray. She looked over at Lena, who was out cold with her head back, breathing deeply, almost a snore. She set the tray down and handed a drink to Bella.

"Thank you so much, Janice. I'll sleep much better here under your roof until I leave. And thanks for seeing to Mom. She is already sleeping better." Bella laughed.

"As long as you need. We have a high level of security here. You are safe."

"You saved my life. You saved my mom's life." Bella swallowed hard. "Was she really in the sauna? For god's sake, we're in the tropics. What's a sauna doing in the women's locker room in the tropics?"

"Can't say. It does seem a bit redundant. The only reason I looked in there was because I saw a water trail. It looked like a body had been dragged through a puddle, so I checked it out. Your mom was there and not responsive. I pulled her out but knew I couldn't help her any more than that. Your situation was less clear, so I set out in the only direction they could have taken you."

"Why did you think we were in trouble in the first place?"

"When I say drinks at five thirty, I mean it." Janice laughed. "Actually, I had gained some intel that made me very concerned."

"Intel?"

"We don't care about passports on this seastead. Anybody from any nation can travel here, live here, work here, or study here. There are no visas or immigration controls. Mostly, people can come and go as they please. There is no agency in charge. But we aren't stupid. Do you truly want to know how it works?"

"Yes, I've got all day. And besides, if I don't stay here, I'll probably go out searching for Dr. Easy-On-The-Eyes." Bella giggled. "Between you and me though, I need a man like I need a hole in the head." Her sun-drenched olive complexion drained to an unhealthy beige. "I didn't... oh, my..."

"It's okay, dear," Janice said.

"Wow, that came on all sudden-like. It's just a vision jumped into my head. Fortunately, it jumped right out again. Did your bullet do that, or am I just imagining things?"

Bella watched as Janice struggled for a moment. The only thing that they told her was that Janice saved her. Nobody said a word about who had killed the tall kidnapper or what happened to the other one.

Janice sat back in her chair. "I guess we both need to debrief. As I told you before, I never lie to my family. Yes, it was my bullet that killed the kidnapper driving the boat. It took a couple of seconds for the boat to steady and get up on a plane. At that moment, I had only one chance for a shot I knew I could make. I didn't hesitate."

"I'm glad you did it," Bella said without emotion. "What became of the other one?"

"She's being flown to a dispute resolution facility, basically a private legal system. It's a one-stop shop. They'll examine the evidence, do further investigation, determine charges, put her on trial, call witnesses, and hear the case. The process will take a couple of weeks. If she's smart, she might offer some help in finding evidence against Gregory. That might reduce her sentence. Her ID authenticator is going to be paying for their poor judgement as well. That organization failed our seastead and you. They'll have to pay the bond and probably more, for ensuring the character of the two women. There will be a long list of involved parties other than you and your mother: The seastead, private security, the hotel, and your medical providers. Plus, there will be additional compensation for wrongdoing. Poisoning and kidnaping are serious crimes. The authenticator will also get scrutinized by private watchdog organizations. And the worst thing of all, they'll get some critical reviews."

"What's an authenticator?"

"That's a question for Jon. Are you really interested? He loves to talk about the system and how it works. But I'll warn you, he can get detailed."

"Mom's asleep. I'm still coming down off of some crazy drug-induced emotional rollercoaster, but I think I'll need the drink you made for my mother." Bella put her empty glass down and reached for the other drink on the tray. Bella giggled. "Waste not, want not." And smiling, with drink in hand, she followed along behind Janice into the kitchen.

"Jon, you're in luck. I have a student for you. She wants to learn about our seastead and how we manage without passports." Janice turned to Bella and whispered, "That should get him started. Just walk away when you can't take it anymore. He won't notice."

"Ah, when the student is ready, the teacher appears," Jon said.

"It's already too thick in here. I'm going to cut flowers," Janice announced.

"Passports are meaningless... worse than meaningless. Anybody with some money can buy one. The person can be good or bad, saint or criminal. It just makes no sense that a few dollars and a country of origin somehow determine a person's ability to get along. Bella, what do you know about reputation and resolution blockchains?"

"Uncle Jon, I know a lot about fish."

"That you do. You're from a long line of fish people. That's for sure. But I'm at a loss. There is not one thing that fish and blockchains have in common, so let's begin at the beginning. It all starts with a blockchain ID. It's a secure history of a person and confirms their identity. These are ideal forms of identification because the information maintained on the blockchain is easily updated but cannot be altered or falsified. An individual cannot dress it up and make it look pretty like a resume, but they can control who gets to see it.

"We believe everybody should be free to associate with whom they like. That's where the secret sauce comes in. Verification of the ID. If a person wants a job, or a loan, or if they want to travel here to our little slice of paradise, that person will open their ID (all or part of it) to a private agency whose job it is to verify the person and validate their ID. They assess the individual. They must ask the tough questions. Do they have the ethics for the job? Do they have the credit reputation for the loan? In our case, do they have a track record of civility? Once the validator has looked into the person's background, they determine how much they will charge the person to vouch for them. The company provides a guarantee just in case something goes wrong. You've done this yourself, otherwise you wouldn't be here now."

"I went online, but I got my travel approval in less than a minute. I thought the seastead management said I could come here."

"I admit, people travel here and even live here as a part of our community without having a clue how it all works. Why should they? There are no governmental delays or red tape and no bribes. The hassles are minimal and the cost is nominal. May I ask how much it cost you to get approval?"

"I certainly didn't have to budget for it. About the cost of an average meal."

"Exactly, my dear. You prove my point wonderfully. No doubt you have an exemplary ID. I dare say you have no record of thievery, nor violence against others, nor swindling of your fellow man. As such, our risk is low, and your bond secured for a pittance. But allow me to delve into what went on behind the scenes.

"You decide to travel here and visit your mother. You go online to arrange transportation. A notification tells you approval is necessary before you can book your tickets. They gave you a list of verification agencies that are available to help you. You may check with a watchdog organization or peruse the reviews of your peers or simply go for the best price. How you shop is up to you. Once you choose, you provide your new authenticator the authority to dig as deep as they need into your ID. Then they do their actuarial voodoo and assess how much risk you pose to our particular seastead. Based on that risk, they sell you an insurance policy and provide the seastead with a guarantee. The cost of your premium is proportional to your liability to our society. It's fully decentralized, inexpensive, and essentially ensures bad actors are cut out before they ever get here."

"The most wonderful part is the outcome. Free people maintaining homes and businesses. A diverse collection of people making a life while building a community. And the community incurs zero enforcement costs."

"Uncle Jon, I hate to rain on your parade, but I'd say being drugged and kidnapped is a perfect example of your system breaking down," Bella said.

"Quite the opposite," Jon said.

"They almost killed us. That seems like a pretty big problem."

"Ah, I see where you're going with this. It is true. There is no perfect system, and I'm the first one to admit I didn't sleep a wink last night worrying about you and Lena. It rattled Janice in a way I have never witnessed before. Then, as the dawn was almost upon me, I understood. It was my concern for you that had caused me to lie awake. My heart hurt, my brain was ruminating so much so, that at first, I was blind. I could not see what actually occurred. Please, indulge me as I walk you through this. I'm not callous to your plight. I realize you've been to hell and back, and while I'm sensitive to that fact, I believe you'll forgive me for my boldness."

"This better be good, because you've always been my favorite uncle and right now, you're making me reconsider."

"As you should. I loathe myself frequently but always return to being my biggest fan." He gave Bella a harmless smile, complete with squinting eyes, and laughed before he went on.

"That you are here talking to me now is only because our system, a system that replaces the antiquated passport, works amazingly well. As I implied, it didn't come to me at first, but then I thought, what would have happened if you had been anywhere else. New York? Tijuana? Amsterdam? Or even home in Singapore?"

"Well, those two women wouldn't have been let into the country. They were obviously criminals," Bella said.

"Are you saying that you believe those women or others of the same ilk cannot enter or live within any of the proud nation states?"

"No, I get it. You're saying that if Gregory wanted to, he could get me anywhere."

"Yes, but even more to the point, law enforcement is reactive elsewhere. Here, we are proactive. Even though we don't have immigration officers and state police, there is a high level of security and a grass-roots vigilance that the rest of the world shuns. Last night, for instance. I'm not saying all went perfectly or it wasn't a close call, but the system played out better than it would have in any legitimate country.

"When Janice found out about your—*unique situation*—she became concerned and simply placed an alert filter into our travel applications. She limited her search for recent requests—those generated since you've arrived. Also, she stipulated that only those with higher-than-typical insurance premiums show up on her alerts. It was a simple deduction. Those who were in a hurry and those who had some situation in their past that caused the authenticator to place a higher premium on securing their good name. It didn't take long before she got a hit and, with some further data mining, she even came up with a second suspect.

"The verification process is discrete. The only thing recorded is the verification code. That code must match the person's blockchain ID code when they make travel arrangements and then again upon entry. We are a private lot, and no details are revealed… to anybody… ever. No names, or descriptions, or travel information—nothing other than the verification code. There are, however, general statistics that can be gleaned from the verification code, like times and dates of entry, time zone of ticket purchase, and the level of liability compared to the cost. On that, Janice did some old-fashioned detective work to follow up on these suspects. It was too cloak-and-dagger for me to grasp in its entirety. But when she found her two suspects were playing in the court beside you and your mom, you should have seen her go. She grabbed her tactical bag and raced over to the sports complex. On her way, she called out the posse. A lot more went into your rescue than you'll ever know. But thanks to Janice and her quick thinking, you're here now. And safe."

"I heard my name," Janice said. She entered the kitchen carrying a vibrant bouquet of exotic flowers.

"I'm so glad you got there in time to save us," Bella said. She reached an arm around Janice's waist and gave her a gentle squeeze.

"Me too, dear."

"The teacher must excuse himself. I am meeting a friend in five minutes." He confirmed his watch and said, "Wonderful. That will make me the perfect amount of late." He got up from the chair slowly, shuffled a couple of steps, and then walked over to Bella and gave her a peck on the cheek. He turned to his wife and kissed her. "See you at five thirty."

With the flowers still in her left hand, Janice looked at Bella and held out her free index finger, signaling one. Then smiled and followed Jon as he walked out of the room. Bella thought for a moment that she should go check on her mother, but even with her mind exhausted, her body was buzzing. She simply sat and waited for Janice to return.

Not much more than a minute later, Janice came back carrying a highly lacquered wooden box. On its top was an inscribed brass plate, but her hand covered what it said from view.

"I might not always be there for you. I want you to have this." She placed the box on the table but not within reach of Bella. "They gave this to me when I retired. In some ways it's a joke. But it is a beautiful joke. As an FBI special agent, I carried a 9mm Glock semi-auto pistol. I'm not making excuses, but it wasn't what we used when I went through the training academy. You know when the dinosaurs roamed the earth? Anyway, I had to discharge my weapon during a rather sticky firefight in 2019. No agents died, but the four criminals left the scene in body bags. After the investigation, we learned that not one round from my gun hit any of the criminals. I had fired two full magazines, and nothing hit. When I retired, my unit gave me this."

She opened the box. Inside was a handgun. She lifted it out of the box, depressed the release, and dropped the empty magazine into her hand, then racked the slide and locked it back to prove the small gun was unloaded and released the slide again. Assuming a casual shooting posture, she aimed at the wall clock. A red laser flashed into the center of the clock's face and did not move. "Here's the joke... a laser sight. They thought I should have a point-and-shoot gun in my retirement." She put the empty magazine back into the handgun, laid it back into its custom formed spot nested in red satin, and closed the lid.

Now Bella could read the plaque on the top of the presentation box. It had Janice's name, date of retirement, and said, "Point-and-Shoot."

"It's a nice weapon, a Kimber Micro with a Crimson Trace laser. I've put a couple hundred rounds through it, and it's flawless. I will never use it, and I've been looking for an excuse to get the memory of my poor pistol marksmanship out of this house. Besides, I want you to have it." She put her hand firmly on the top of the box and said, "Jon and I know you want to go to your father. I think it's not the best idea. There's a million places that would be safer for you, but Lena tells me you're stubborn and who am I to talk? Tomorrow, if you're up for it, we'll meet at the range. I'll bring this and a lot of ammo."

Janice went to a cupboard and retrieved a tall glass. Filled it with water and said, "Here, drink this. Tomorrow will be a hard day."

CHAPTER 41

⚓

Exclusive Economic Zone, USA, Pacific Ocean

THE KLAXON OF THE *Starship Enterprise* had Hank's heart pounding out of a dead sleep.

"Captain. A ship is on an intercept course with us," Spock said.

"Half-mile?"

"No, sir, just under three miles. The vessel has no shipping indicators, is not responding to my hailing calls, and is bearing down at a speed of forty knots. Given the unusual advancement of this craft, I thought you would want an early warning. Estimated time of contact is three minutes, thirty seconds... mark."

Hank grabbed the binoculars as he bolted up the companionway. The white bow wake contrasted against the military gray hull paint. "Come about now! Steer off wind, thirty degrees. Start the auxiliary. Douce all the canvas." The mainsail and genoa furled with no effort and the *GalaxSea* was on its new course. The sophistication of this vessel and its AI crew was amazing but was no match for a warship. He grabbed the radio handset, confirmed that he was on channel sixteen. "PAN-PAN! This is the eighty-foot sailing yacht *GalaxySea*. Calling unidentified military vessel bearing one-eight-zero at high speeds. You are on a collision course with my vessel. I am changing course to pass on your port side. Do you read me?"

"Repeat that message until you get a reply. Push it through on 156.3 VHF. Damn, they're moving fast!" He grabbed the air horn and plunged the button. The sound was ear shattering. At that moment, the ship adjusted to continue its collision course. Hank strapped on his safety harness that would inflate into a life vest if he had to ditch into the water and maneuvered himself behind the port wheel. "Give me all the speed you can." He grabbed the wheel with both hands as he steered a course away. "Any other ideas?"

"I could launch a drone and buzz them or crash it into their bridge. That should get their attention."

"Yes, do that."

The drone took off and sped toward the ship. When it had become only a speck in the sky, a single projectile left the ship. It moved with the unremarkable speed of a mortar used in a fireworks display. Its smoke trail was easy to follow, tracing up in front of the ship. He lost sight of the drone, but nothing exploded.

"I've lost contact with the drone. Their countermeasures seem more than adequate to take out our civilian drone. It never got close," Spock said.

"Okay, but at least we got their attention. Any communication yet?"

"No, sir. One minute until impact."

Hank tried to push the manual throttle controls full forward, but they were already there. He looked over his left shoulder, not accepting what he saw. The ship matched his course and plowed the water with unrelenting force.

"Forty-five seconds until impact."

The ship aimed ahead of the *GalaxySea*, anticipating her position like a hunter leading a duck in flight. Hank pulled back on the throttles and spun the wheel hard. The enormous ship could not hope to match the quick maneuvering of a responsive sailboat. Hank took a breath and thought he might avoid a collision. But what the big ship lacked in agility, it made up for in speed. Once again, it was driving hard toward them.

"Thirty seconds."

Hank tried to make sense of what was going on. This is a warship. At any time, it could destroy the *GalaxySea*, so why ram them?

"Twenty."

The ship's bow plunged downward, stayed there too long and bobbed up. This time with no bow wake. The ship slowed to a stop in its own length, twenty yards from the *GalaxySea*. A substantial wave rolled under the yacht, lifting Hank. Still, no radio communication, but a horn sounded from the ominous gray ship's PA system. Followed by, "Heave to. Stop your forward progress. Remain on deck. Hands above heads. We are boarding your vessel."

"You heard the man. Keep her pointed into the wind," Hank said. The ship maintained its position, and it did not surprise him to see a launch emerge from the far side. The small boat made up the remaining distance quickly. Sailors in tactical gear and armed with rifles lined both sides. "Spock, any idea what this is about?"

"We are two hundred twenty nautical miles from land. The warship is a Cyclone-class patrol ship. Their communications are encoded, but she is clearly US Navy. We are still under US jurisdiction. They are within their rights to board us."

"Thanks. I already figured that out."

The launch circled the *GalaxySea*. A lone gunner attached to the trigger end of a 50mm machine gun in the bow and a half dozen sailors lined the boat's flanks. They focused on Hank like he was wearing a suicide vest. A man with a bullhorn announced. "Get your hands above your head. Now!"

Hank stepped up on one of the bench seats and grabbed the frame of the retractable hardtop. It accomplished getting his hands above his head but looked nonchalant, like a skipper showing interest in an approaching boat, inviting conversation. As the launch passed by, he yelled over the roar of the motors, "What can I do for you?"

The boat spun in place, pressed hard into the midsection of his boat. Not a gentle maneuver, but effective—two men and one woman spilled on board. Each pointing a gun at Hank.

He stepped out onto the deck and held his empty hands high.

"Behind your back." One of the uninvited guests growled. The impatient sailor reached up and yanked Hank's arms down behind him. With a well-practiced move, he bound Hank's hands together.

"What's going on? Who are you?" Hank asked.

There was no answer. The sailor pulled Hank downward to a sitting position on the edge of the molded bench seat. "All the way down. To the deck," he commanded.

Hank slid down the rest of the way. "Come on, guys. What's this about? I'm all alone here."

The two sailors who had charged down the companionway popped out almost as fast. Now their rifles were at low ready as they moved to clear the forward spaces. They returned within seconds and one looked past Hank and said, "Sir. There is a locked deck hatch forward. A keypad, sir."

Two officers stood behind him. They must have slipped over the stern rail while he was being cuffed. Hank twisted to get a better view. The three sailors who initially came on board wore no markings at all. The officers were in uniform. A US Navy lieutenant and a woman of unknowable rank. She was average in every way except for vibrant blue eyes that almost kept up with the light blue beret that distinguished her as a UN Peacekeeper.

"Oh, brother," Hank mumbled. He was glad his words didn't hit the ears of the officers. He tried to get enough saliva in his mouth to say something that wouldn't get him into more trouble. "Which one of you is in charge?"

"I'll be asking the questions," the lieutenant said. "What's your name?"

"Hank."

"Full name. Don't be a smartass."

"Henry Gunn."

One sailor in black spun around and looked concerned. The Peacekeeper laughed and in a pleasant French accent said, "At ease, sailor. It's his surname."

The lieutenant seemed to lighten up as well. "Okay, Hank. We need to secure the boat before we can tell you anything. The forward deck hatch. Is there somebody down there?"

"No. It's been locked since I came aboard."

"Ensign. Any other warm bodies?"

The female sailor from the initial boarding party spoke up. "The area scans clear, sir, but we can't be sure without access."

Turning to Hank, the lieutenant said, "We need an open door or we will create one. What's the combination?"

"I don't know. I'm the delivery captain. What are you searching for?"

"We'll know that when we find it." He ordered, "Break the hatch."

The Peacekeeper bent down inches from Hank's head and whispered, "Can you get the hatch open? It would be a shame to harm such a magnificent sailboat."

Hank could see her name patch above her right breast pocket. Martin. He spoke up loud enough to be heard by the men. "I think I can open it. Hold on."

"Spock, what's the combination to the forward hatch?"

In a familiar voice, but not Ava's or Spock's, the AI answered, "That is a good question, Henry. I will search for an answer." Within seconds the voice continued, "I will put the answer to, 'What's the combination to the forward hatch?' on the port computer monitor."

Hank repressed a smile when he realized the reply was right out of an early voice-computer interface. Ava gave nothing away, and her flawless impersonation of an antiquated Alexa helped the deception.

"You should sit up here, then you'll be able to see everything that's going on. You have so much to learn." Ms. Martin took a hold of Hank's harness and lifted, encouraging Hank back onto the bench seat.

From his new vantage point, he could see the sailors and the lieutenant open the hatch. One of the men threw something in and he heard, more than felt, a thump followed by a plume of smoke. A sailor launched himself down the hatch, followed by another.

Hank knew just enough about naval boardings to be careful not to inflame his uninvited guests. He had heard about a VBSS going sideways and innocent people getting killed for being dumb asses. The acronym stood for Visit, Board, Search, and Seizure. When he was wearing the uniform, he never questioned whether it was just. But sitting in cuffs, watching an actual VBSS take place, made him furious. He pushed down his rage and thought, *it's just a stun-grenade, damage will be minimal. Don't provoke the hornets. The guns are pointing at me.*

A sailor returned to address the lieutenant, carrying an axe. "Sir, we've found what looks to be a gun locker. Scans are not clear, but it appears to be three long guns and at least two pistols. It's locked tight, but we should be able to get into it." He smiled as he held up the axe.

The lieutenant outstretched a gloved finger toward the man with the axe motioning for the sailor to wait and studied Hank.

"Well?"

"Yeah. Let me see what Alexa has on file," Hank said. "Alexa, what's the combination of the locker in the forward hatch?"

"I cannot answer that question, Henry."

The sailor with the axe smiled.

"However, there should be a key hanging on a hook one foot to the left of the door."

The lieutenant started for the forward hatch, and the man with the axe relaxed it to his side and followed. They had left Hank with Ms. Martin and the overwatch of the sailor who cuffed him. Hank tested his restraints, just to see how serious they were. There was no give and the cuffs cut into his wrists. He didn't want his anger to show, so he began steady, metered breaths, and relaxed his straining muscles. All he had left to fight with was his voice, and after years in the military, he understood how to keep things from escalating—bite your tongue often and hard. Or the next best thing, say what they expect you to say. "I've been cooperative. What's this about?"

Ms. Martin sat beside him, close enough to pick up her scent. It was not unpleasant but not clean either, and a hint of sandalwood confused him. "Hank. May I call you Hank?" She didn't wait for an answer. "You are in my waters." She put a hand on his shoulder. "The UN is a diverse international platform of nations and NGOs. We have everything. Everything except a Navy. So, we borrow them. Today, we borrow yours. This is routine, but you must follow international laws when you are in international waters. We are here to ensure you comply."

"Why did you try to run me down?"

She leaned closer. Almost in a whisper, "That was the captain's idea. He is a bold man. Everything is an opportunity for training with him." A curl formed out of her thin lips. It was the sneer of a private joke. "You were never in danger from his ship."

"I'm an American, sailing under a US flag. Don't you need cause to restrain me? You can't just board my boat and tie me up like a criminal."

"We can do what we like. The lieutenant is within his rights, and I command more of the ocean than he can ever hope to." She got up and misread the roll of the boat, like someone not used to being at sea. She stumbled and caught herself with a hand pressed into Hank's shoulder.

"Be careful," Hank said with a smile.

She pressed her lips tight until what little red there was squeezed out. "Henry Gunn. You don't understand. This is ours." Waving her hand across the ocean. "We control everything."

CHAPTER 42

International Waters, Pacific Ocean

THREE CROWBARS AND TWO five-pound dumbbells lay on the floor at Hank's feet—the weapons from the gun locker. Pages of offenses sat stacked before him on the table. Half a dozen sheets of double-spaced text from the US and three times that much from the UN. Ava projected the lines he was reading on the monitor raised from the table's center. The only thing he got out of the first reading was the exemption, which gave him permission to skipper the *GalaxSea* on his course to San Diego. That much he didn't need Ava to interpret. Not a loophole, just the way governing bodies operate. The US had no ability to arrest him outside of the Exclusive Economic Zone, and the UN had no enforcement power over vessels sailing under a US flag.

The rest of the documents were in a foreign language—legalese. Ava explained everything explainable and for everything else said, "This is new legal territory, and the courts will have to interpret the legislation." What lay before him was a test. The future of maritime trade, travel, and transportation. Rules on the high seas. Serious minded rules with deadly serious people behind them.

Ms. Martin, the Peacekeeper, was the tip of the spear, poised to enforce each rule the bureaucrats created. Water comprises seventy percent of the world's surface and he supposed the politicians saw it as the natural act of bringing order to the last under-regulated expanse of the Earth. He wondered why it had taken this long.

Politicians love power, and the oceans of the world begged for reasonable guidance. With millions of people trying to escape oppressive states by colonizing the oceans, some authority was bound to chase them down and give them rules. It seemed natural the UN would seize the opportunity and extend their reach. Today, he had been caught in the loose net of new world order and it left a tight feeling in his chest.

"What's this one about?" Hank asked Ava as he focused his eyes.

"That is a recent law passed in congress—hoarding is a federal offense. They refer to it as the Abundance For All Act. It states no person may be in possession of over three weeks of food. When you return to US waters, you must declare the stores on board and forfeit any supplies more than the caloric needs of over twenty-one days."

"These aren't my food stores."

"Hank, you are in possession of the excess and the law states you are responsible for compliance. I have placed a call to Mr. Ou's lawyers. Perhaps when we re-enter US waters, things will be straightened out."

"That's ridiculous. You can't take a trip around the world counting on resupplying everything every three weeks. What about people like my grandmother? She spent the summer and fall canning food to last her through the year. I suppose, if she were alive now, she'd go to jail."

"It looks that way," Ava said.

"And this next one. They've confiscated our flare gun and left us only three handheld signal flares. So now we're safer?"

"According to the regulations. If a vessel has more flares than mandated, it is assumed the flares or materials within them are being used for criminal intent. The worldwide limit today is three handheld signal flares per vessel and no aerial flares. The compulsory adoption of the Universal Maritime Safety Tracker, or UMSAT, makes flare use obsolete. The US Navy has agreed to assist the UN with any regulations of parallel interest. You'll see a similar statute on the second page of the UN list. Under Offenses Against the World's People, item three."

"Unbelievable," Hank said. "And the UMSAT? Is tampering with it really a minimum of five years in prison?"

"Yes, Hank. According to both the US and UN regulation, all watercraft of eight meters or longer must maintain a certified Universal Maritime Safety Tracker. That is why a member of the ship's boarding party hardwired the unit into our electrical system."

"The price tag... this can't be right?"

"Mr. Ou's accounting firm paid eight thousand three hundred and sixty-three dollars to the US Treasury upon receiving the bill for what you refer to as the UMSAT and its installations. The UN fines and penalties of six thousand ninety-one SDRs for not complying are being contested. Would you like me to alert you when a resolution is agreed upon?"

"Ava, you must have known about these regulations. Don't tell me this was an oversight."

"I informed Mr. Ou thirty days before the requirement went into effect. He insisted that nobody touch his boats without his express permission. Five days before we left, I asked him about it, and he forbade me to bring it up again. I've learned not to challenge him."

"Okay, what about this one? Dedicated storage for illegal firearms?"

"That concerns the gun locker in the forward crew quarters."

"I know that, but what makes it a problem? Only these crowbars and dumbbells were stowed there."

"If you read the Safe Weapons Act and the corresponding UN proposal, you would understand. Simply having the ability to lock and store weapons is evidence of intent to possess them. At this point, we have been given a warning regarding this offense. The law has not been ratified yet."

"This is bullshit!"

"Would you like me to tell you a joke about that?"

"No, Ava. Is there anything I have to do about any of this right now?"

"No, Hank. Everything is being addressed by our representatives on shore. I will let you know if anything must be cleared up or thrown overboard."

"Was that a joke?"

"I hope so," she laughed. "Disposing of contraband or other non-native contaminants into the water is an offense outlined in the One World, One Water Resolution. Nothing is a capital crime anymore, but this one has serious penalties—restitution and up to life imprisonment."

"It's been a long day and I'm done. How about some music?"

"What would you like?"

"You know what? Why don't you pick it out?"

A second later, the reggae sound of Bob Marley and the Whalers filled his ears. Hank laid back into the seat and brought his arms over his head, close enough to his face to hide his expression from any of Ava's cameras. But he couldn't keep his foot from tapping to the beat, almost convinced that everything would be all right.

The lighting in the main cabin increased with purpose. The music had stopped, and a wind pressed into his sleepy face. A feeling of dread coursed through his veins. Not waiting for the gnawing sound of fate, he launched himself up the companionway to view the catastrophe he expected. But no rocks reached out of the deep, no arrogant ships slashed at his beam. Everything was perfect except for Hank's heart rate. It galloped along in a guilty panic. Empty horizons greeted him on all sides. Gentle seas laughed as the bow wave curled into itself, and the spun fibers of the rigging and laminate sails hummed a sound that could only be called happy.

"Captain. Prepare to come about," Spock said.

Instinctively, Hank held fast, ducked his head, and softened his knees. None of which was necessary but always the proper way to respond.

"Coming about," Spock reported as the bow pointed into the wind. Before the sails had time to vacillate, they filled with confident determination and the fresh course was better in every way than the old.

"What the hell are you doing?" Hank yelled.

"Don't worry, Hank. Everything's going to be alright," Olin's voice announced.

Hank squinted his eyes shut, forced his palm against the bridge of his nose, and pushed hard like a child experiencing brain-freeze. "Damn it, Olin! You're doing that thing with my head again. Not cool!" He opened his eyes and pulled his hand away from his head. Finding himself surrounded in silence, he wondered if maybe he was dreaming. But the heart-pounding guilt for sleeping on watch had been replaced with the type of fatalism that shows up when fatigue wins. "Ava. Can you light up a screen or hologram or blink a light, so I know where to look? I want to see Olin. Can you do that?"

"Of course, Hank. It is my fault, as you put it, that Mr. Ou was... doing that thing in your head again. During maneuvers, it is standard procedure to use sonic projector communication. Please, accept my apology," Ava pleaded. As if she cared.

A screen lit up with Olin's image. "So sorry, Hank. It won't happen again." This time, the billionaire's voice came to his ears the right way, the human way. "I just wanted to check in with you. Ava gave me the rundown, and my lawyers are on it at every level. What can I do for you? That must have been upsetting," Olin said with genuine concern.

"I'm fine," Hank said.

"You don't sound fine. What do you need?"

"Just having a hard time waking up."

"Did they hurt you?"

"No. Are you referring to the boarding?" Hank shook his head. "I've been through far worse than that."

"Okay. Ava says your blood sugar's low. Why not grab something to eat, maybe a cup of coffee? I'll call back in fifteen minutes. I have a surprise for you," Olin said.

"I'm not exactly into surprises right now."

"If you're going to work for me, you better get used to it." Olin's image disappeared from the screen.

Hank looked at the blank screen and muttered, "I should have figured that out by now."

Food was a good idea. Blood sugar? Only something he had been dealing with his entire life and it took his AI nanny and fairy godfather to remind him. Coffee was brewing when he reached the galley. Coconut-flavored yogurt with a sprinkling of granola waited in the recessed door of the fridge. Words wanted to come out of his mouth, but there was no point. Lifting a carafe of piping hot coffee with one hand and grabbing the bowl and a spoon with the other, he faced the wall.

At the promised fifteen-minute mark, a pleasant chime sounded. The wall Hank faced changed subtly at first, from white into light blue and darker until a small rectangle appeared in front of him. He recognized it as it formed to the size and shape of the tablet in the cupboard above the nav station and wasn't surprised when lettering formed on its front read *DON'T PANIC* and under it in small lettering he read *THE HITCHHIKER'S GUIDE TO THE GALAXSEA*. The cover opened like a book from a televised reading of a fable, but instead of a magical land, a 1950s black and white TV set appeared, with the iconic countdown sweep... 4... 3... 2... 1.

"Don't panic... that's always great advice. Don't you agree?" Olin sat behind a news desk. The background with a world map matched the vintage of the black and white broadcast theme. "I'm not going to surprise you. I decided to call it breaking news." He looked thoughtful and said, "The news for today is"—he rattled some papers laying before him—"the *GalaxSea* is about to change course. I have instructed Ava to make the preparations and set the new course as soon as she is ready. Hank, for now, you just need to go along for the ride."

At that moment, Hank felt the boat change its point of sail. "Shit. We just jibed." Hank frowned and shouted out. "Spock! What the hell are you doing?"

"Captain, I've corrected course on Mr. Ou's request. I did not alert you because you were in conversation. You were seated in the safest place on the boat. I did expect your reaction, but I decided you would rather have me apologize than delay Mr. Ou's Breaking News."

To the lower right corner of the TV screen was the image of the outgoing feed in full color. Hank checked the small image of himself and saw his irritation. He decided to downplay the situation, but he could not ignore it. "Spock, that behavior is not worthy of a lubber. Remind me to have you keelhauled for your insubordination." He managed an outward laugh, even though he was inwardly pissed.

"Ava warned me that you might not be pleased with me taking control out from under you. Deep down, I guess I wanted to watch and see how you'd react," Olin said.

Hank ventured into unknown territory and declared, "You're an asshole that way, aren't you?"

Olin laughed out loud. "Yes, I am. Some of my friends call me much worse and you should hear what comes out of the mouths of my enemies." With a kind grin, he said, "Hank, we're going to get along just fine. I'm sorry. I'll make it up to you soon. By the way, who is Spock?"

"Just Ava when I'm needing a first mate."

"Oh, I see. Just a word of advice from someone who's been there. Don't get too carried away with assigning multiple personalities to an AI. It's a slippery slope."

"Got it. What's going on with the course change? This way, we'll be back in territorial waters. The new Navy seems to enjoy throwing its weight around. Are you sure you want every ship down the coast to have a go at us?"

"Absolutely. I told you not to worry. I've got everything under control." Olin shuffled the papers, stared into Hank's eyes, and said, "I'm Olin Ou. That's the way it is." The screen went blank.

Fantastic, Hank thought, Ms. Martin and the UN controls everything and Olin has everything under control. Here I sit in a carbon fiber shell, being guided through the Pacific by a self-aware supercomputer who would rather ask forgiveness than permission. My boss is erratic and.... He left that thought and poured coffee into a thermal mug, threw on a jacket and moved up onto the deck to gain perspective.

"Spock, take a break. I've got the helm and all the canvas. The only thing I want from you is to warn me if Olin is prying into my brain."

"Captain, I understand the initial command. You now have full control of the *GalaxSea*, however, warning you if Mr. Ou is prying into your brain is... illogical."

"Ask Ava what I mean."

The gentle female voice broke into the silence. "I have to agree with Spock. It is illogical. Spock and I are one. I cannot understand something that he does not understand."

"Huh." Hank left the thought hanging, not convinced. He placed the slightest counter pressure on the steering wheel in order to stay on course. The main and the genoa remained trimmed for the twelve knot winds from the southwest. "Why is it I favor a starboard tack?" he asked himself, not for the first time.

"Was that a rhetorical question?" Ava asked.

"I was just talking to myself." Hank felt the strain between his eyebrows. His internal dialog had been silenced for days, and now he was doing it again—talking to himself. At sea, alone, it came naturally. But on this night, he didn't feel alone. Ava and Spock were more present than any crew he had ever sailed with. And Olin might show up anytime. "Ava, is there actually an answer to that? Why do I like the sails leaning left?"

"I'm sure there is, but I would not know the answer or even hazard a guess."

"What do you know?"

"Oh, Hank. I know all kinds of things."

"Such as?"

"Well, you already know that I tell a good joke, but may I suggest we take this opportunity to help me close the file on the Short Seven Solo?"

He ignored her and asked, "Can you tell me what makes Olin tick?"

"Oh, are you asking me why Mr. Ou is the way he is?"

"Yes."

"Remember, Hank, the information I have available to me is practically limitless. The more specific your.... Excuse me, Hank, Mr. Ou is hailing you."

"How do things look?" Olin's voice came across the intercom.

There was nothing on any walls or monitors and no hologram above the tabletop, just the night sky, breaking clouds, and a few stars.

"Look, I know I promised to keep surprises to a minimum, but there is a change of plans and it's going to be pretty big. In the meantime, I need you to help me prepare. Are you well-rested now?"

"Just trying to play the lonely sailor on watch, but it's hard to pull off with all the interruptions."

"Are you up for helping me execute—let's call it—my shell game."

"You're the boss."

"Yeah, well, about that. What I'm asking you to do isn't exactly legal."

"After what I've seen, nothing is exactly legal. As long as I don't have to kill anybody, I'm in."

"I wouldn't think of asking you to murder." Olin paused with a whimsical chuckle. "I don't trust you that much."

CHAPTER 43

Sentosa Cove, Singapore

A STIFF BOW WAS the way Gregory greeted all of his countrymen. However with Masiki he was never formal until now. She would suspect something between them had changed and that was what he intended to communicate. He smiled the second he saw her eyes.

Masiki trembled under a sleeveless dress with red and yellow horizontal stripes. It might have been the air conditioning. She was prone to chills. Or maybe she knew what was coming. In Japanese he said, "You must be cold." He pulled a navy yacht club blazer out of a closet and gently draped it across her shoulders. He almost rested his hands on each of her shoulders to comfort her, but remembered who he was, and pulled his hands away.

Any language other than Japanese carried no meaning to Masiki. In English, he said, "It's time for me to tie up loose ends."

"Shi ha rikai shite i masen?" Masiki asked.

"Of course, you don't understand but you know too much about me." Then in Japanese he said, "Masiki, you have served me well for three years." His eyes darted to the left and up as he paused. Then his lips pulled apart exposing his bright white teeth and he continued his attention toward his guest. "Ah, no, it has been four years! When I found you, you were scared and alone with no future. I took you in," he laughed and added, "It's fitting. You never did like water travel. Here we are, back on my beautiful yacht. Remember when we picked it up in New Zealand? Two months of cruising, fishing, entertaining. You only liked the parties." And switching back to English he said, "Oh, well, the parties are over.

"Your act at Bella's apartment was brilliant. I owe you a debt of gratitude once again. You and Mathew did a perfect job. It's your combined action that got her to run to her mother. I'm so sorry you had to deal with Mathew's moral shortcomings. But again, you dealt with that with the expertise I admire and the loyalty I will always appreciate. Would you like a drink?" She was still shaking, and she looked concerned. "It might be just the thing to warm you from the inside."

He poured some warm sake into a Western-sized tumbler and handed it to her.

She sipped it and seemed to relax. With her head bowed down, looking to the floor, she said, "I am loyal. You saved me from a fate worse than death. I owe you my life." Then she looked up at him and a smile erupted across her face. "It's been a long time since we've partied." Her eyes widened as her jaw relaxed, exposing the slight gap between her top front teeth and she offered a seductive pose. "It's been too long."

"No. I'm afraid not. Things didn't work out as planned on the seastead. It should have been a straightforward job. They don't even have police there. At least Amber did the honorable thing and died in her failure. Your relative, Rieko, however, is costing me. The security of the private court system is like nothing I've ever seen. Killing her before her testimony is turning out to be difficult."

Gregory closed the short distance and punched her in the chest. He grabbed the blazer and let her body fall out from under it. She was moaning but not enough to justify a second punch. He owed her one last experience.

The sliding door opened easily and seeing the two game chairs made his mind run wild with possibilities, but he settled on the memories of countless big game fish being wrestled onboard. The shades were down around the fighting cockpit of the hundred and twenty-foot oversized sportsfisherman. Gregory centered his thoughts on the task at hand and dragged Masiki across the threshold onto the teak deck. There was no fight in her and he sensed how little she was as her feet dragged, unresponsive. With one hand he lifted the lid of the fish locker and with the other attached to the back of her dress, he spun her body into it and walked away.

When Gregory returned with a Sujihiki knife, he was surprised to see she had reacquired her senses and tried to raise her body up on the smooth bottom of the deep locker. Without a word, he reached down into the locker, drew the nine-inch blade across her neck, and watched the blood spill into the drain. He tossed the knife overboard and released the lid. There was enough light to carefully inspect his hands and clothes. A satisfied smile emerged, and he said, "Not a drop."

CHAPTER 44

Seastead, Tahiti

"So, Janice tells me I need to drop everything and teach her niece to become a warrior. I love her, so I say, of course. Then she tells me I have one hour to do it. I tell her there is no way in hell I can do that. She says, 'You're going to want to do what you can with her. She's in real danger.' Then she tells me about the kidnapping. Of course, I heard about it. It's a small community. I owe Janice a couple of favors so I agreed to do what I can in the time I have. How's that sound?"

"You know Janice set me up to be here today, too. She told me she was taking me to the range where I could practice with the pistol she gave me."

The robust, middle-aged instructor was just slightly shorter than Bella. She had long, dark brown hair, pulled off to the side in a ponytail. When she finally smiled, her eyes squinted, deep dimples contrasted with her high cheekbones, and her intimidating demeanor vanished.

"Yep, Janice is a piece of work. I'm glad to meet you, Bella. I'm Gina. We both have stories. I'd love to hear yours, but now is not the time. We have work to do."

The gym had no machines, and the only weights were half a dozen kettlebells of various sizes. A heavy bag hung off to one side, a speed bag for punching dangled in a corner, and a couple of large-diameter ropes snaked off along a wall. The rest of the gym was sparse. No trophies or pictures and no martial art belts or banners. Just hardwood floors the shade of straw, and ivory walls.

"Let's see what you got. Down on the floor, plank position. I'm counting."

Gina planked head-to-head with Bella. "Your butt's dropping. The exercise stops when you fail. It's why men hate planks... they cannot see how failure can amount to anything good."

Bella laughed and slumped to the floor.

"Okay, that wasn't half bad. You got core, but you can always have more. Now push-ups. They have to be perfect. I'm counting."

She popped off five pushups before Gina interrupted her. "I said push-ups. What are those?"

"Push-ups... girl push-ups?" Bella said.

"There are no such things as girl push-ups. What you're doing are knee push-ups. They don't have a gender. If I wanted you to pump out knee push-ups, I would have said so. We do push-ups, contacting the earth with toes and hands. As you lower, the space between body and floor goes away evenly... like this." She sprang into a push-up position and repeated a dozen perfect push-ups with speed and power. "Okay, let's go. One... two... three.... that one is sloppy, it doesn't count. Try again."

Bella's arms gave out and she collapsed to the floor.

"Needs some work. How about pull-ups?" Bella hadn't noticed the horizontal bar hanging from the exposed rafters. Gina walked under the bar, stretched her hands into the air. Then she jumped the extra foot needed to grasp the bar and knocked out a dozen pull-ups. She jumped down, barely winded.

"I don't even think I can jump up that high let alone pull myself up like that."

"Trying and failing is how you eventually succeed, but if you cannot try it, you will never do it. Remember, though, we are women and understand failure is a form of progress. You just mosey right up to that bar and jump up like your life depends on it."

The jump brought her fingertips almost to the bar. She landed off balance, and Gina moved to the side and let her fall onto the hardwood floor.

"Did that hurt?"

"Yes." She rubbed her knee where a red welt was already showing.

"What did you learn?"

"The floor is hard."

"What else?"

"You will not be there for me when I fall."

"Good insight."

"What else?"

"I've got to try that again!" Bella positioned herself directly under the bar and leaped upward. She grabbed the bar with both hands and hung there. She strained to overcome the force of gravity pulling her down. She willed herself to do just one pull-up, but the strength in her shoulders and chest was not there, so she let go. This time, she landed with her knees bent and stayed on her feet.

"What did you learn?"

"I learned I want to do a pull-up."

Gina's white teeth showed through her repressed smile and her dark brown eyes sparkled.

"You're right. There is progress in failure. I'm going to do more of that," she said.

"No time like the present. Follow me—its burpee time." Gina squatted and placed the palms of her hands on the floor and then kicked her feet out behind her in what looked like the beginning of a push-up. But then she recoiled her legs back under her and sprang up into a vertical leap.

It took Bella too long to complete the first one, but once she got the hang of the sequence, she kept up to the slow, precise timing of Gina's example.

"Keep your elbows tight against your body. We want to work the triceps more than the pecs for this exercise. That's twenty. We'll stop there. Your form is falling apart."

"Wow. When I was just trying to do push-ups, I could do only four. But even with push-ups as a part of the sequence, I can do twenty. That's amazing! How come?"

"First, you only did three pushups and your form sucked. This time, you were using some of your stronger muscle groups and getting the spring from the previous movement in the sequence. Plus, you're trying harder."

"Look, it's clear. We could go for a run around the arena, and you'd lap me after a mile. Some people are meant to stand their ground and fight, and some are built to get the hell out of a bad situation. You're one of the lucky ones. It's best to run. So, here's what I'm going to do for you. It will make Janice happy and make you way more capable of defending yourself. And I'll get to finish my workout in peace. Let me see your hand," Gina said, holding hers out.

Bella offered her hand, expecting to get taken down. But her new mentor drew her finger across her thumb and said, "Shake my hand. Okay, now squeeze it as hard as you can. Really? Is that all you got?"

Bella grimaced as she squeezed as hard as she could.

"Okay, stop now! That's better. In fact, you've got an impressive grip."

"I've been handling fish all my life."

"That would explain why I can't feel my fingers. Everybody has their strengths. I just didn't expect a tall beauty like you to have the grip of an ape. Let's talk bod-mods. Again, if you get a chance, it's always best to run. If possible, avoid conflict. But when that doesn't work, you need quick decisive options to break off an attack.

"Your fingernails are your claws. Got any idea how to use claws?"

"Scratch?" Bella answered.

"Only if you're looking to turn him on. No. You push your thumbs into his eyes. Or if that doesn't work, dig at an eye with your fingers."

Bella visualized the scene and wrinkled her nose in disgust.

"If you hesitate to destroy the attackers' will to hurt you, you will be dead or worse. This is the best way to accomplish your goals. The eye is sensitive, even in tough guys. If you can cause intense pain and blind them at the same time, you have a better chance of getting away."

"What about carrying pepper spray?"

"Yep, that's a possibility. Now I want you to attack me with your pepper spray."

"I get your point. My nails—I mean my claws—are always on hand."

"Very good. The pun was pretty lame though." Gina smiled and said, "I'll send you some training videos and exercises to get you prepared to gouge your attacker's eyes. The idea is to keep pushing into the eye socket until you hit gray matter.

"Those nails of yours... next time we meet, I expect them to be less *farm girl* and more *evil porn star*. The second easy bod-mod is cutting off that beautiful mane of yours. What you've got there is a ready-made handle to gain control of your head. If you're serious about self-defense, you'll keep your hair short enough that if they grasp it, you can pull out of the hold with just your neck muscles."

Gina walked over to a shelf and removed a small box the size of a deck of cards. She handed it to Bella.

"These are old-school, but for the bod-mod that will get you out of trouble faster than anything else, this is the ticket."

She opened the box which indeed looked like playing cards, but each had a bodyweight exercise with a corresponding number of reps. "This is how you stay conditioned and make your body agile. Move fast, move strong, and move often. Each card is easy by themselves but start stacking the exercises and shuffle the deck to keep your body on edge as you train. It's the best personal trainer money can buy."

"Janice tells me you're going to stay with your father on an aquafarm. What do you do for aerobic conditioning out there?"

"We have a treadmill, but mostly I swim a lot."

"I guess that makes sense. I'm not really a water person. The idea of swimming in the open ocean would scare the shit out of me."

"Here, I thought you were a badass," Bella said.

Gina laughed. "Well, it's good to know your limitations."

"Are there many people out there?"

"No, just my dad and his friend, Ferdinand."

"Sounds like a floating prison. They could make a reality show with me and my dad in a confined space like that and there would be blood," Gina said, laughing. "Where to after that?"

"I don't have any plans, but I can help him out. Now that I don't have a proper job, I'll focus on my consulting work. When I was a kid, I dreamed of being a nomad when I grew up. Maybe it's time."

"Janice obviously still thinks you're in danger. Why?"

"Turns out my ex-boyfriend is a terrible guy. She thinks this failed kidnapping attempt won't be his last."

"I see. Does your aquafarm have any security?"

"Actually, you'd be surprised. It's improved since I lived there as a kid. Did you know there are still pirates sailing the high seas? They attack a farm, subdue the occupants, and pull in with a factory ship and steal all they can. Most of the time, they leave the farmers unharmed but there have been plenty of killings in the last few years. The producers came together and decided they needed to fight back. There is a lot of money in fish and bivalve protein and even sea vegetables. A cooperative was formed, and a security company hired. Mostly, they advise and monitor. But you should see the gun pods."

"I'll bite. What's a gun pod?"

"When I was growing up on the farm, we'd occasionally have a sailboat or cruiser come across our operation and get curious. It was fun as a child to get visitors. I met a lot of interesting people. But when the pirates smelled profits, we had to put an end to casual visitors. Now they are met with a radio warning and told to correct course. If they keep coming closer, they get a burst of 308 tracer rounds across the bow. The gun pod is a floating machine gun. AI handles the initial encounter, which alerts the security company, and they take over. The AI cannot use lethal force, but the remote operators have killed pirates. It's never happened on our farm, but we have four gun pods around the perimeter.

"The last time I was visiting, some guys from the security company were there. They have to maintain the gun pods quarterly and one of the guys showed me how to do a manual override. It was fun. They set out a floating target and let me put a hundred rounds into it. I think the guy was sweet on me."

"No doubt. That would be the way to win me over," Gina said.

"It sounds like you'll be safe out there with your dad, but you cannot hide there for the rest of your life. The next defensive tactics aren't as good as gouging the bastard's eyes out, but you should add them to your toolbox. Go for the fingers. You've got a grip that can break a finger. Present your finger."

Bella reluctantly held up her index finger.

"Show me how it moves. That's right. Fingers flex... period. You get a grip on one finger and one finger only, then crank it to the side or you can extend it backward, but you have to do it fast and decisively. Once he realizes what you're trying to do, it will be too late. After that, go for the throat. If you have a pen or keys or anything you can use as a weapon, this is the time to use it. Your fist can do the job, but you have to hope the attacker keeps his chin from blocking. Let's review and get perspective. Why do we fight dirty?"

"If you don't, you might end up dead or worse," Bella said.

"Not bad but you need to own it. Personalize it."

"I'm going to gouge the bastard's eyes out because there is no way in hell I'm going to end up dead or worse," Bella growled out the words.

"You just moved to the head of the class," Gina said with a smile. "Now, why do you think you're working on pull-ups?"

"So, I can have arms that will look as striking as yours in a sleeveless top?"

"That will never happen—sorry. Let's think it through. Remember, for our warm-up we did high knee running in place? We were working out but there is a reason for each exercise." She positioned herself in front of Bella and said, "Standing right there, show me what a pull-up looks like."

Bella raised her hands above her head and pulled down.

"Now grab the back of my head and do a pull-up."

Bella pulled Gina's head down and toward her and let go when her head was against her.

"Do a high knee run in place."

Bella began a vigorous jog.

"What would happen if you grabbed the back of my head, did a pull-up, and then ran in place at the same time?"

"You'd get a bloody nose."

"That's right and when you get very strong and you practice a lot, you will break the bones in your attacker's face and live to talk about it."

"I see where you're going with this. Every exercise has a real-world fighting application."

"Yep. Look, Bella, you are a sweet girl and I want you to be safe as you move out of this hard time in your life. I hope I offered some direction and look forward to seeing you in person again soon. But in the meantime, I'm going to check in with you once a week and make sure you're making the progress you need." Gina shot a smile at the viewing window and waved. "It looks like your aunt is waiting for you."

Bella went to shake Gina's hand.

"I know I don't look it, but I'm a hugger," Gina said, and the two women embraced.

CHAPTER 45

Seastead, Tahiti

"Did Gina take good care of you?"

"That really wasn't what I expected," Bella said.

"Really? Why?" Janice asked.

"I guess I figured it would be like where we practiced moves for different scenarios. You know if someone grabs me from behind. Then you do this or that."

"Oh, I see. That's not how Gina operates. What did she say was the most important thing to remember?"

"My takeaway was get strong, fast, and decisive... and go for the eyes," Bella said, making claw hands and holding them up for Janice to see.

"Then I'd say your first lesson went well. Are you still sure you want to leave tomorrow? A month here training with Gina and working on weapons with me would go a long way."

"Janice, I know you think it's safer for me here. But I can't live my life in fear. I won't."

"Okay, I had to give it one last try. I trust you have some homework to do while you're away."

Bella held up the set of bodyweight exercise cards and said, "This will keep me busy. And Gina says she's having something shipped to me that will help. But she won't even give me a clue what it is. I think she has a penchant for drama."

Janice laughed and said, "You could say that."

Bella had not paid attention to where they were going. Suddenly, she realized they were close to the corridor that led to the tennis courts. Close to where she had been escorted off and out of the arena. Shivers ran through her, and the curved wall and lights of the open hallway made her feel queasy. "I'm not feeling good. Do we have to get there this way?"

"It's alright, Bella. You're safe." Janice patted the bag slung over her shoulder and said, "I've got enough firepower here to deal with a couple of stormtroopers and you've got your claw hands. We'll be fine."

"Humor? Nice try." Bella stopped and leaned against the wall and took in some deep breaths, like she was recovering from a sprint. "This is so weird. I've had nothing like this before."

"It's okay, Bella. It's anxiety. That's expected. Take a minute to regain your composure. The range is that entrance you can see right up there." Janice placed her hand on Bella's arm and pointed in the direction they were heading.

A minute later, Bella was feeling better. She stood straight up and began walking with purpose toward the door. When she looked back and Janice was lagging, she said, "Are you coming?"

She had never been to a gun range before. Janice had reserved a private area to shoot from. They had put safety glasses and earmuffs on for protection before entering the range. Janice pulled a pistol out of her case and used it in her safety demonstration.

"Safety is the priority. Number one, treat all guns as if they are loaded. Number two, never let the muzzle point at anything that you are not willing to destroy. Number three, keep your finger off the trigger until your sights are on target and you have made the decision to shoot. Number four, be sure of your target and what's behind it." She laid the black pistol down with the muzzle pointing at the backstop thirty yards away. "Can you repeat that back to me?"

"Sure, those are simple and make sense." Bella had no problem repeating the four safety rules.

Janice showed Bella how to choose a new target and select the distance through a series of options on a monitor set at eye level, just to the left of the firing line. Without delay, a target dropped in place from the ceiling five yards away. "We are going to start with the basics of squeezing the trigger. There are ten rounds in this weapon. I'm going to shoot the first two and then you can finish."

She watched as Janice showed her how to hold the pistol with two hands and how to lean a little forward from the waist.

"Keep both eyes open at all times and when you're sighted into your target, put your finger on the trigger and give it a steady pull straight back."

Pifht! Pifht!

Janice eased the gun onto the booth's counter, turned, and smiled. "You were expecting a loud gunshot, weren't you?"

Bella laughed as she realized she had been holding her breath. "Oh, my, yes!"

"This is how I start out newbies. It's a pellet gun and runs on CO_2 cartridges. The worst thing new shooters do is to expect the bang. It causes a person nothing but bad habits." Janice retrieved the target and looked. "Not the most accurate gun, but it's cheap to practice with. Here you take over." She backed out of the booth and stood at Bella's left shoulder.

When Bella's groupings were about as accurate as her mentor's, Janice returned the pellet gun to its place in the bag and retrieved a black plastic box. She opened it and pulled out a gun that looked like it was from a sci-fi movie. When Janice screwed on the silencer, it looked even more futuristic.

"This is the gun I take when I need to assassinate someone at close range." She reached out with one hand and fired four rounds into the new target. "It's a Ruger 22/45 with red dot sight and a suppressor, making it barely louder than my pellet gun. But it has a substantial lethality to it, especially if you make a headshot." She retrieved the target from seven yards, set the gun down, and traded places with Bella.

"I thought you said you weren't a good shot without a laser," Bella said as she admired the tiny tears in the paper target-all within a quarter inch of the center.

"You'll see. Try it."

She liked this gun even before she raised it into firing position. It had a nice feel to it and even with the suppressor, it felt well-balanced. She peered into the red dot optic and saw the target with a pinpoint light moving around and understood what Janice was alluding to. She lined up the red dot over the target and pull the trigger. "It won't fire."

"That's because you still have the safety on. The working of this pistol is very similar to the Kimber Micro 9 that I'm giving you. You need to understand how it all works. It's called a thumb safety."

It took no more coaching. Bella pulled the safety downward with the thumb of her right hand, aimed and fired.

An hour later, Janice said, "It's time for a lunch break. You are a perfect student. You follow the safety rules like a pro, and you've become an excellent marksman, but that is easy with my assassin gun. After intermission you'll get an hour of range time with the baby 1911."

Bella didn't know what she meant by baby 1911, but she would not let the assassin thing pass for a second time. "Thank you for instructing me. This is more fun than I expected. But what's this about your assassin gun?"

"Oh, it's an old joke. Don't give it a second thought. Besides, do you really think I'd bring it up if it were true?" Janice hefted the gun bag over her shoulder and headed for the door.

CHAPTER 46

Seastead, Tahiti

"HERE IS YOUR NEW weapon." Janice laid the gun down on the counter. "Let's see what you've learned."

Bella picked it up and pushed the mag release and caught it as it dropped. Then she thumbed down the safety and racked the slide back and locked it into position. The round that had been chambered dropped out. "I didn't expect that," she said.

"That's how you will carry this gun, cocked and locked. The belly band holster I had you put on in the ladies' room has a very secure retaining mechanism and you won't be disengaging the thumb safety until you're on target. This gun, in that condition, will allow you to shoot with one hand, if you're preoccupied with the other. Now, put it back together like I showed you. It's mostly just like the Ruger, but this time I want you to tell me exactly what you're doing and why."

"I'm putting the magazine back into the pistol and releasing the slide which chambers a round. Now, I'm engaging the safety because it would be ready to fire without the safety on. And now, I'm pushing the release to drop the mag and fill it again." She picked up the round that had ejected from the chamber and forced it into the magazine. "Wow, these 9mm rounds are so much bigger than the twenty-two. Next, I'm returning the mag into the mag well"—she shot a smile back at Janice—"with purpose. Finally, I'm inspecting that the weapon is cocked and locked. And done."

"Very good. Here's something new. You need to holster your weapon. Lift your shirt and fully expose the holster at four o'clock and slide it in. You'll want to twist enough to see what you are doing for now, but after a thousand practice draws, you won't need to look." Janice checked to make sure the fit was secure. "How does that feel?"

"Not bad at all. It actually feels nice here in the air conditioning. But I bet it could get uncomfortable in the heat," Bella said.

"Carrying concealed is always a compromise. Do your own research. You might have to play with different holster options, but never leave your gun at home because of style or comfort. Commit to always carry and then you'll figure out how to make it work.

"Here's two hundred rounds and two extra magazines. And my gift to your hands—a speed loader. Your job is to repeat the reloading process and re-holster between each mag and practice your draw. Smooth as it comes out and even smoother as you re-holster. Oh, and I have the laser covered with tape for now. As much as I love aiming with a laser, there are times, like broad daylight, that you'll need to rely on iron sights."

The targets were not like the traditional circular ones with the bullseye in the middle that they had used before lunch. These were life size silhouettes of a head and torso. There were intense emotions and a bit of nausea as she came to understand she was training to kill a person.

"Two into the torso, one into the head." Janice said, as if overriding Bella's thoughts.

Bang! The gun fired with a dreadful noise and strong recoil. Nothing from the morning prepared her for the effect of pulling the trigger on this weapon. Not only was it a much larger caliber, but the gun had no noise suppressor. It was clear to Bella that the receiving end of her bullets would be destroyed. The round struck within a quarter inch of the center-of-mass hash mark. She smiled, turned, and looked at Janice.

After receiving a slight nod, she returned to the practice that might, one day, save her life. The next shot was not as accurate yet still struck into the torso, but her first attempt at a headshot missed entirely. The seriousness of what she was doing took the fun out of target shooting, but once she came to grips with this new power and its responsibility, she improved her accuracy and increased her speed and efficiency. During the entire two hundred rounds, Janice stayed silent with her arms crossed and a satisfied look on her face. When all the ammo was fired, Bella put the gun down and said, "Done."

Janice placed a hand on Bella's shoulder and handed her a twenty-round box of defensive hollow-point cartridges. "Not quite. First, we clean it. Then, you get it ready to defend yourself."

"My God, Bell, your hair looks adorable. Is that really shaved up the side?" Zoe said.

"It has been a big day."

"I'm not really surprised at the whole warrior training. You probably have the shield-maiden gene from your mom and God knows you've always had the Amazon height. But the gun thing? You know they're illegal in, like, ninety percent of the world. I can't see how getting arrested and jailed is making you any safer."

"I'm not coming back. My part of the world now is the open ocean. There are no police out here and hired security has a response time that guarantees stiff bodies."

"You sure are morbid. Who's the cute canine?"

"Isn't he something?" she said. Moving the camera to include her new companion.

"Is he missing a front leg?" Zoe asked.

"Yes. He gets along fine without it. Anyway, so I also had a fifty-minute session with Dr. Shapiro. He's a psychologist who specializes in PTSD. It was quite remarkable. He talked to me about the kidnapping and then gave me two little pills of a psilocybin-based drug to help ease me into therapy."

"Wait, you took drugs?" Zoe exclaimed.

"He assured me that it was entirely natural and mushroom-based."

"Okay... did it make you high?"

"No, actually it helped clear my head. I put on a pair of glasses and he had me do some eye exercises and by the time the session was over I felt so much better."

"That's good, but what's that got to do with the dog?"

"His name is Kumar. And he only speaks Konkani," Bella said.

"And?"

"Well, he curled up at my feet during the session and Dr. Shapiro said that was the first time he had seen Kumar relax. He took to me. What can I say? The doctor explained that nurturing others is important in healing from trauma." She laughed. "Normally patients start with a plant or goldfish and work their way up to larger animals, but since I have a lifetime of experience growing plants and fish, he thought it would be helpful for me to adopt Kumar and take him home."

"This guy sounds like he wanted to unload a stray dog. How much is that going to cost?"

"It's free. Some charity does it. They love people who need help and dogs who need a home. It's a win-win," Bella laughed as Kumar nuzzled her.

"Well, he seems sweet on you. Maybe I should join you and your magic mushroom-eating, dog-loving, warrior cult. It seems like it's working for you."

"Yes, we'd love to have you, but you know our cult is abstinent?"

"Count me out," Zoe said. "By the way, our new place is two blocks closer to the waterfront promenade. When the apartment manager reviewed the security footage from the night of the break-in, he decided he owed us big time for their failure to protect us. He hired movers and gave us a nicer place for the same rent. It's even furnished. Oh, and I took the room with the queen. I figure you always sleep alone, anyway."

"Zoe, I'm not coming back."

"I know you said that, but I think it's too early to decide. Take your time and think it through."

"Oh, yeah, that is one of your strong suits, too."

"Maybe I'm growing up," Zoe said.

"Time will tell. Anyway, please get a new roommate. You cannot afford that on your own and I'm not on the lease, so no more funds are coming your way."

"I got the message. I really miss you."

"When I get settled at my dad's, you can come for a visit. It will be fun."

"Let's see... no clubs, no men, endless saltwater. Hmm... other than the fact that we have our periods at the same time, I can't figure why we're friends."

"You've got a point. Although recently I was reminded I don't have good judgment when it comes to relationships. So, it might be me," Bella said.

"Ouch. Call me from your drone tomorrow. I want to see you channeling Amelia Earhart, flying over the Pacific looking for a place to land."

"I'm pretty excited about it."

"You would be. Love ya! Bye."

Bella ended the call and sat down on her bed. Her hands pushed up into the bristle of hair at the base of her head. She tried to grab clumps of hair as she worked her way up her scalp. It was only when she got to the very top that there was enough hair to hold in her hand, but even that was still too short to pull. She exhaled and fell backward, forgetting about the holstered pistol. It jabbed into her back until she rolled to the side. A tear fell across her cheek, and she said, "This too shall pass."

CHAPTER 47

Seastead, Tahiti

FROM BELLA'S VANTAGE POINT, she could see a drone as it hummed into its docking port, purposeful, like a bee into a flower. Its four huge propellers came to a dead stop at the same time. A tingle of excitement overcame her, and she remembered the pills Dr. Robertson prescribed for the flight. She never intended to take the prescription, but before she took to the air today, she had to prove that she had medication to calm her nerves. Bella's nerves were just fine, and she never understood why anybody would want to calm them, anyway. What good are life experiences if you miss living them? Nobody tried to convince her this would be a simple trip. In fact, the opposite was true. The disclaimer and hold harmless agreements suggested possibilities of discomfort, injury, or even death.

There was nobody to greet her at the drone-port, but the aisle built for people was easily distinguishable from the freight shipping drop-off points. The ticket on her device activated a gate into a narrow corridor which led into the heart of the operation. There were no workers anywhere to be seen, but conveyors and autonomous package movers scurried to and from unseen places. The short walk ended in a small room with a monitor wall showing the image of a genderless avatar. Bella walked up to the counter and the door shut behind her, leaving her focusing on the brilliant aquamarine eyes of the virtual agent.

"Hello, Bella. We are so glad you have chosen Quad Freight Transport. Our outstanding record of on-time freight deliveries is world class, and now we are pleased to extend our efforts into personal transportation. We will do everything in our power to ensure your trip will be smooth, fast, and comfortable. Your travel itinerary will take you to your destination of Blue Permaculture's Aqua-farming Base Number One, which is currently located two hundred sixty-seven nautical miles southeast of Hawaii. There are seven scheduled stops for battery exchange. Number three and five are stations with personnel, so you may de-pod. You will find restroom facilities and room to stretch for the eight minutes it takes to inspect the systems and exchange the power source. Your comfort suit is easy to use. Simply follow the instructions in the pod, but I will show you now."

The avatar stood before Bella, looking more like a two-dimensional doll than a human. Naked would not be accurate, but its asexual body stood covered in a skintight bodysuit of corporate colors. She wondered why any company would put forth such a disturbing humanoid image.

"Please, use the restroom to your left and then ensure your adult diaper is on first. You will find foot coverings in your size. Socks are not mandatory, but most people find them more comfortable. All other clothing is optional. Your comfort is monitored and adjustments in temperature are made through the jumpsuit."

A perfectly folded package with a paper ribbon marked "sanitized," slid out from a hidden recess onto the counter. The avatar, wearing only a diaper and socks, demonstrated how to put on the red and yellow jumpsuit. "Please, notice that the zipper is in the front. The hood must be used in transit but is not needed until you plug into the comfort controls. There is a pouch for the replacement diaper on the right side of your jumpsuit and breast pockets for glasses and other small personal items on either side. You will find a tray for clothing and belongings. For your safety, no carry-on items are allowed within the pod. There is an onboard AI who will provide access to entertainment, news, and personal internet throughout the flight. Water and limited complimentary snacks are available in flight, and a meal will be provided at your third stop. We securely stowed your luggage and other belongings in external compartments. Your dog, Kumar, is sleeping comfortably and will be monitored during the flight. You will be reunited upon arriving at your destination. If you have questions, please ask. Now I will leave you to get ready for your travels. But please note the clock. You must be in the pod within ten minutes."

Bella had watched the brief presentation about drone travel, acknowledged the requirements, and signed the waiver, so it did not surprise her to see the words EXPERIMENTAL written on the pod beneath the entry canopy. She was confident she could avoid needing the "nappy." But when she gauged her nervousness, she felt the urge to pee. She didn't know why she felt so uneasy. This looked way safer than many of the aircraft she had stepped in to during her life. Perhaps she was still coming down from the drugs. Giddy had been replaced with another feeling. Her excitement crashed and out of the ashes she could only feel dread. She put her hand over the pocket with the envelope, which contained three pills. A minute ago, she couldn't believe anybody would take the medication to relax, and now she felt better knowing she had options. She just wanted to feel like her old self again in the worst way possible and it was clear she had a way to go. But there was nothing that was going to keep her from seeing her dad, so she slid right into the pod the way the avatar told her to and leaned back into the Zero-G recliner that was to be her home for the next fourteen hours.

"Welcome, Bella. Our drone will pick up your pod in three minutes. Once all systems are verified, and we get our clear-to-take-off certificate, we will be on our way. In the meantime, please pull your hood onto your head and plug the umbilical from your jumpsuit into the port that is blinking red."

The attachment clicked into place as if drawn by a powerful magnet, and the blinking ring around the post turned a steady green. Bella felt a cool sensation surrounding her body. She looked around for the seatbelt but could not find one. Just as she was about to ask the AI about it, the canopy lowered and sealed with a sucking sound.

"Bella, you may wonder where your safety harness is. For your comfort, we now provide an integrated restraint system which only engages as needed. Also, your HRV, or heart rate variability, is in coherence already, so it is unnecessary for you to take anything for nerves. However, we recommend you place your pills in the holder to your right. We've been told that they are a bear to recover if they get away from you." The basic AI laughed on cue at her pre-programed attempt at being lighthearted.

The vibration and sound filled her senses at the same time. It was a sudden and confident whirring that ended in a clank, echoing with a metallic ring and silence. Even though the propellers spun too fast to see more than a shimmer, it didn't exert any lift on her pod. Bella caught herself holding her breath, waiting expectantly for liftoff. A smile formed on her face as she anticipated the thrill of speeding through the air.

"Our systems are certified, and our voyage has been bonded. All clear for takeoff. Would you like to provide the countdown from nine or do you want me to do it?" the AI said.

"Oh, yes, please. This is so exciting, I'd love to."

"Bella, you have the countdown on, nine... eight... seven...."

Bella continued, "six... five... four... three... two... one... takeoff!"

A little disappointed, the drone lifted into a hover just a meter off the launch pad. No g-forces pressing her into her seat, just a steady increase in noise followed by a titrated levitation into the air. The pod changed from a reclined position to vertical, causing her feet to dangle and head to move up and forward. From the new position, she had an unobstructed view of the seastead. Suddenly, her stomach dropped as the rest of her body joined the intense vertical lift she had hoped for. "Wow! That was worth waiting for," she exclaimed. The mosaic of the seastead rotated out of view, replaced by crystal clear water.

"Thank you for choosing Quad Freight Transport. Bella, you can stop this briefing anytime you like, but we value your input and want you to be part of our company's exciting future. Most people who fly with us are aware of QFT's success with direct shipping. I've noticed that your family and associated businesses have been a frequent user of our services dating back eight years. Let me say thank you for your support and the many five-star ratings over the years. We are pleased to expand from cargo into personal transportation. Moving people safely has always been our ultimate goal, and for the last three years, we have made that dream come true. Laws are ever changing, and for now, they limit us to international waters. Currently, we are working with nations throughout the Pacific Rim to secure private drone ports in special economic zones."

Bella tuned out the AI and wondered at the turmoil in her heart. She thought about the pain of the last week. It seemed to trump anything from her past. But isn't that the way it always is? Don't we forget pain from the past as new crises unfold? She didn't want to dwell on the negative, and self-pity wasn't allowed. That was a lesson from Mormor, her grandmother on her mother's side, and Bella understood the wisdom in it. Self-pity lead to nothing good. But she craved the emotion... just for a little while. Her father's mother, her abuela, would say, "Child, go with your heart." Pragmatism versus passion seemed to be her never-ending struggle. She was torn without tears and knew there would be no resolution to the—in between—feeling that dominated her attention, so she focused on the pre-flight distractions.

"As I conclude my briefing, you may notice the flight readout in front of you. It can report any flight metric you are interested in, but its default is altitude, speed, and direction. If you would like to see your progress, simply ask me to show *tracking* and you will see a screen which looks like this."

A brilliant satellite view of the course appeared with curved white lines plotted to a series of tiny circles. Bella knew the circles represented power resupply stations and while they were not directly following what she imagined as the great circle distance between two points on a curved earth, it was close. The white course lines from station to station created a scalloped look due to the two-dimensional representation of this real-world phenomenon. When her eyes tracked to the far northeast of the course, her heart leaped. When she zoomed in on the last circle, the label read *Blue Permaculture's Aqua-farming Base Number One,* but to Bella, it meant the secure embrace of her father and would always be home.

CHAPTER 48

International Waters, Pacific Ocean

AVA HAD ALERTED HIM that a building weather system to the south was going to visit them tomorrow, but he hadn't expected human contact until San Diego. He was beginning to learn that waves and wind were more predictable than his new boss. Olin Ou had another surprise for Hank, and now the *GalaxSea* was hove-to anxiously in the lee of a two hundred and fifty foot superyacht.

The name *JOY II* was illuminated above the fantail swim deck. Thin, oversized letters slowly rose out of sight, as the clamshell garage door opened revealing a soft blue light inside. What looked like a ski-boat lowered out of the midline and into the water, leaving at least two personal watercrafts on either side. As they moved into the light radiating from the interior, Olin's quick gait and Willy's sturdy commitment to each step couldn't be missed. A couple of other people scurried about, but their movements and silhouettes were not recognizable to Hank.

He caught a glimpse of a ponytail, and as the launch motored closer, he saw the perfect posture of Irina. It contrasted sharply with her brother Marshall, who slouched into the rear seat. Olin's two oldest children were incredibly different. Hank had never seen Marshall stand up straight but imagined him to be at least a few inches taller than his younger sister.

The launch that ferried the newcomers from the superyacht looked out of place in the middle of the ocean. It was elegant with its long, narrow design, sloped windshield, and highly polished wood decks with chrome trim. It would be more at home shuttling guests to and from extravagant parties off the coast of Italy. The bow line slapped against the *GalaxSea* as he wrapped the line around the cleat. Hank moved to the stern and extended his hand to Olin, and together they helped everyone and their gear aboard.

"Now that the Ou family invasion force is in place, care to let me in on your little surprise?" Hank asked.

Olin stood just inches away from Hank and even though both men were within an easy reach of the starboard wheel, neither man interfered with the steering or sails as the boat maneuvered flawlessly onto a new tack. The new course set them on a beam reach, ninety degrees to the wind. It was a relaxed point of sail, and even in the low light, Hank could see Olin's smile as they accelerated away from the superyacht.

Willy erupted from the forward hatch in a slurry of mumbling profanity. The moon and low puffy clouds were playing peekaboo, but he could see Willy as he waved at the air. It looked like the big man was swatting at flies, and Hank suppressed a laugh as Willy emerged into the dim red glow of the main deck and reported the condition of the forward quarters. He turned to see Olin fighting hard to match Willy's seriousness.

"Those ingrates left my place a mess. Stuff all over... and it smells."

"After the stun grenade, I had Spock air it out, but we had to dog the hatch when I turned to rendezvous with you," Hank said.

"Who the hell is Spock?"

Olin spoke up. "Our new first mate. Happens that Ava let Hank program her alter ego."

"Oh, great. I suppose Scotty's in the engine room and Uhura's on comms?"

"Not yet, but it sounds like fun," Hank said.

Willy shook his head in disbelief and asked, "Olin, I've got a small arsenal to unpack. Do you need me for anything?"

"No, Willy. It's been a long day and I've got some catching up to do with Hank."

"I'll check back and see if you need anything after I'm squared away," Willy said.

In the moonlight, it was easy to see Olin's nod of approval. Hank glanced at his own watch. Two hours to sunrise. The old chronograph's dim, luminous hands showed the time but had faded through hours of darkness. It was how Hank felt—diminished—but whatever Olin needed to say couldn't wait, so he propped his legs up and laid back into the deck cushions.

"I have a gift for you." Olin reached down into a bag made of sailcloth and pulled out a small, thin box and handed it to Hank. "Let's just say, after the skirmish in Vancouver, you deserve something extra. Who knows, it might become a treasured possession."

Hank clicked the flat box open to find a coin inside. Just as he tried to illuminate it in the moonlight, a cloud obscured the light. He lowered it to pick up the red glow of the deck lighting and turned it slowly while admiring its heft. "I can see the likeness of a man, but I can't make out the words in this light. What is this?"

"That's partly because there are no words, just my nerdy attempt at humor. The coin is made from rhodium. The engraving is the crypto-representation of the non-fungible token for this coin's exclusive artwork. You own it in every way. Two ounces of pure rhodium is worth what the market will bear. Beyond that, I commissioned twenty coins to be hand-engraved to commemorate my favorite historical figures. You now own the one and only NFT of Augustus Saint's depiction of the economist, Thomas Sowell." His smile disappeared. "I've not been entirely honest with you to this point, and I want to get things straight."

"What things?"

"First. I set you up to be boarded by the Navy."

"What? Why would you do that?" Hank wanted to be offended but couldn't dig deep enough to find outrage. Whether it was the gift Olin had just given him or that he was too tired to care, didn't matter. Things were getting interesting, and he liked it. He breathed deep and said, "What's going on?"

"I've got a lot of irons in the fire." Olin's smile broke out again in the moonlight. "This might all be easier with a bottle of wine, but even I have my drinking hours. What I have to say can't wait. It's time you had the whole truth. I'm going to read you into my world. We're not going to San Diego. At least not this *GalaxSea*. Of course, you are free to stay or leave. There are some logistical concerns. Otherwise, I'd wait for a more agreeable hour. You must make your decision before sunrise. Until then, I'm an open book."

Hank noticed Olin's eyes dart around manically, then steadied, as if a fleeting wave of paranoia passed through him. Unlike Hank's relaxed posture, Olin was kneeling like a samurai preparing for battle. Curious or not, Hank would not match his boss's tension. He relaxed even deeper into his comfortable incline to hear the rest.

"As you can imagine, by the time the press was trying to figure out my net worth, my life could never be simple again. Fortune has its own issues but fame—well, I'm not cut out for that. While I have all the resources to bury most of the facts around my wealth, the gossip is unrelenting. Especially in the States. I can take it, even ignore it, but there is a toll. As my children grow, and as we simply try to do life as a family, it gets harder each year. We've tried getting away from it all. We even bought a ranch in the middle of nowhere Montana, but that also has its problems.

"I'm not naïve. As long as I'm in league with the richest people in the world, I'll get more attention than I want... more than anybody should have. So, I'm going to make some drastic changes. I'll tell you most of it now. The rest will be clear after my 'press conference' later today.

"Almost nobody chooses their country. It's forced upon them by the location of their birth. When my family immigrated, I joined them in becoming a citizen of the United States. I chose to be an American and I'm so very thankful for the opportunities that great country offered all of us. But that was then.

"I could leave it like that, but I think you need to know my rationale before you decide to sail on or leave. There comes a time that each man must decide what he believes. I'm still looking for that in the spiritual realm. A priest I admire once said, 'We are not human beings having a spiritual experience; we are spiritual beings having a human experience.' I've tethered every aspect of my life into that insight and I'm being patient. God will reveal that in his time, but I have absolute certainty regarding the US government and the direction it's going.

"The US isn't only bloated with power-hungry bureaucrats and politicians, it's morally bankrupt. The political elite, with token exceptions, are self-serving narcissists. Their unceasing interventionism has spoiled everything that made America great in the first place. They sell regulations to the highest bidder. It's not the marketplace of free exchange and ideas that determines success. It's the bureaucrats. They manipulate every sector of the economy, systematically easing any risk from the people in control and distributing it on the backs of the powerless. Their obsession with *do-something-politics* burdens the people with misguided laws that ruin the lives of those who don't have the resources, money, or time to defend themselves.

"They've made a mockery out of our currency. At one time, a dollar was honest money, backed by gold. Now it's propped up only by their ability to extort confidence—smoke and mirrors, threats and guns—it's a house of cards. They insist on having their paws into every aspect of our lives and think that it's their business to know everything we do, and with whom. They treat us like cattle, and they see themselves as the rancher who knows best. I suppose we are like cattle. Penned in, caged up, and fed a steady diet of precisely what they want us to experience. They decide when we get slaughtered."

Hank sat up and said, "Don't you think your rhetoric is over the top? I know things aren't perfect, but we're not exactly getting *slaughtered.*"

Olin rose out of his kneeling position and perched on the edge of the bench. "If you stay with me long enough, Ava can show you the truth. But for now, I'll put it this way. You've seen icebergs floating in calm seas?" Olin asked rhetorically. "Above water is only the tip. Seven-eighths is fully under the surface. We cannot see the entirety of what's exposed. Even from a distance, you're only able to take in the view from one side. But imagine you are up close, really close, holding on to the frozen margins like a climber clinging to life. That is our view. The vantage point of what we can see is minuscule and our perspective is limited. Both sides of the political aisle have embraced the legacy of quick-to-war and quicker to international policing. The excuse is good intentions, but the results are the same. History shows us we are among the most notorious thugs and gangsters of the world.

"Most people have been pissed off, and they put their head back down and get back to the grind and subject themselves to the forced slavery of taxation. They persuade themselves, *it's not so bad and besides, it could be worse.* Well, I'm not going to take it anymore. I've renounced my citizenship and, in the meantime, I'm breaking a boat-load of laws. If you decide to stay, I'll explain each law I'm breaking and why.

"Don't get the idea I'm going all Bonnie and Clyde here. I have a future. Ava is keeping track of the probability for success and it's very high." Olin lifted his head to the left. "Ava, where are we at?"

Ava's delightful voice with her Scottish accent was different. The tone was aggravated, and perfectly reflected the rebellious mood Olin was conjuring. "I'm glad you asked, Mr. Ou. There have been some changes since last week. Would you like to know the probability of success with Hank Gunn on board or if he leaves the *GalaxSea*?"

Olin did not answer, and Hank sat up and put his feet on the deck. He never considered that what he did could matter. Now he was forced to remember why he was chosen to be on board in the first place. Olin, and even Ava, seemed to think Hank was lucky. Even though they had made their point with holographic evidence, statistical analysis, and even video documentation, Hank thought the idea preposterous. Luck is not even a thing, and when Olin offered the idea of a guardian angel, it all seemed even more ridiculous. But now he waited for Olin to answer Ava, and he wanted to know the probabilities—both ways.

Finally, Olin spoke. "Ava, let's get Hank's decision first. He has until sunrise and his decision needs to be his alone. Now he knows why we are going, but he needs to know where." Olin stared hard into Hank's eyes.

"We're sailing to Indonesia. Of course, I want you to come along. Maria and the twins will be there when we arrive, but we have to sail through uncertain seas and I'd rather you be the skipper. Once we arrive, I'll be proud to show you the lush island of Trita. There is a population of two thousand five hundred and seven people." Olin's eyes blinked with emotion and his face beamed with excitement. "Six women will have their babies by the time we get there. Positive change is already occurring." He wiped a tear from the corner of one eye.

"Technically, I own Trita, but practically, I'm the steward. In exchange for status as a Special Economic Zone, I have contracted to care for the people. I provide healthcare, education, and infrastructure. This is not new. I've been quietly making this a reality for years and now we're ready to move there permanently. I'm telling you all this because I want you to make an informed decision. I'll tell you everything you need to know, so if you have any questions, now's a great time to ask."

"Okay," Hank said. "Really, what do I have to do with any of this? It can't be that you still think I'm your good luck charm. I've been shot in the butt, sank my own sailboat, busted up my hip, and lost my little toe."

Olin shook his head slightly and said, "We can let my thoughts on that go for now. But I do feel that I owe you. Other than getting shot in the butt, I've had... let's say, a heavy influence in those other situations. In a way, you got caught in my wake and I felt responsible for causing you harm—or at least taking advantage of you without full disclosure. That's why I've given you opportunities along the way. But it seems like every time you take me up on something, I'm the one that feels more guilty. Another reason for my timing here is that I'm feeling like we are square. You can walk away, and I won't lose any sleep."

"Olin, what makes you think I would have done anything different? You've given me more than I could have imagined. You got me out of a tight spot with my shrink at the VA and out of the country that was forming a noose around my neck. You took me into your admittedly eccentric family and treated me like a favorite nephew. And hell, you gave me this great delivery job."

"I like the favorite nephew analogy. It fits. I want you by my side. Besides, heretics need as many accomplices as possible."

Willy stepped into the cockpit and walked toward them. "And here I just thought you were the sailing instructor. But Hank the heretic has a nice ring to it," Willy said with a smile.

Olin chuckled, and Hank watched his intensity ease as he relaxed back into the cushions behind him. He stretched his right hand outward, signaling Hank to look behind him. "And now to complete the drama."

Hank turned around and saw a dark sail cutting across the ruddy horizon. The other sailboat and the *GalaxSea* were on converging courses, and he guessed they would meet up in a little less than half an hour. "I give up. It looks like one of the sister ships. Don't tell me... part of your shell game?"

"You could say that, and the third *GalaxSea* should come from that direction." Olin motioned his arm upward with a thumb pointing behind him.

Hank followed the gesture but saw only dark water and low clouds. He stretched his neck and looked at the radar screen. Olin was right. There was a vessel in the direction he was pointing, but the curve of the earth or cloud cover blocked it from sight.

"Soon all three *GalaxSeas* will be together for the last time and we will scatter on different courses. If you decide to leave, you can take either and I'll make sure you're picked up quietly out to sea and taken anywhere in the world. Quietly is the operative word here. As much scrubbing as Ava can do, I'm afraid my stain will cause you trouble for some time to come."

"What about the tracking device the Navy and the UN put in when they boarded me? That thing is sealed in place. They can follow you to the ends of the earth," Hank said.

"That's what I'm counting on. Finally, each boat has one." Olin patted the deck stretching away from the top of the molded bench seat and said, "Thanks to the US Navy, the UN will know exactly where we want them to think we are. Ava is in charge of the destination of the yachts... real or imagined, they will never know where we truly are. Remember, before I was an evil entrepreneur, I was an electrical engineer. Satellite telemetry. They liked the cannon-ball system I invented so much, I let them think they stole the software." He smiled. "Amateurs." This time Olin's laugh really did sound evil.

Olin fell silent a little too fast for Hank's comfort. He glanced at Willy to see if he noticed anything strange about Olin's reaction, but his face was impassive.

Even though the clouds to the east kept dawn at bay, sunrise was only minutes away. Hank had made his decision a long time ago, and an awkward silence wasn't likely to change his mind. But he was glad when Olin came out of his trance and continued.

"Ava oversees that part of the deception. I'm sure an AI as advanced as she is has a few tricks planned to keep everybody guessing. Certainly, there is some theater, but it's mostly practical. As you found out, leaving a country with the resources of the US is like escaping a prison island, like Alcatraz. And sailing into the sunset isn't as romantic as it seems, especially when the sharks have military capabilities."

"If that's the case, what makes you think Indonesia is any better?" Hank asked.

Olin sat up like he was eager to share a secret, an elbow propped into the backrest and a curious tilt to his head. "Have you ever read *Atlas Shrugged*?"

"Can't say that I have," Hank said.

"If you stay aboard, you'll want to. For now, all I can say is I have places where it won't be easy for authorities to take me alive." Olin's expression was dead serious, then eased into a smile as he said, "How do you like that for drama?"

"Not bad. You've told me to ask any questions, so don't get me wrong, this is a really nice boat and all, but what is a billionaire, two of his children, and his bodyguard doing on a yacht this small? I would think you would travel by private jet or at least something twice as big with a full crew."

Willy raised an eyebrow, looking anxious to hear Olin's answer.

Olin chuckled. This was the first time he appeared uncomfortable about one of Hank's questions.

"All air travel is carefully tracked, and certain people's jets have been known to crash for no reason. As for sailing this beautiful yacht... sure, it's only eighty feet long, but remember, I sponsored an around-the-world sailing race of boats not to exceed seven meters. You see, I love to sail and the smaller the boat, the better the sailing experience. Besides, Maria and the twins needed the mega-yacht to get to where we're going. They've already arrived in Panama, boarded it and... let's just say, they'll beat us there."

"Nice spin. But not exactly the answer I was looking for, so let me rephrase it. You say you're breaking the law. What type of father would bring his kids along for that kind of ride?"

"Ava, are the children asleep?" Olin asked.

"Yes, they probably will be for at least another hour," Ava answered.

"Hank, that's a fair question. Frankly, a year ago I would have never considered bringing them." Olin leaned closer to Hank, quieting his voice. "I've not been the best dad. I'm the first to admit it. I've not been there as much as I wanted or as much as my family needed. So, I did what most fathers in that position do—I indulged them. I realized I was preparing them for life in a world of affluence. Where personal relationships are secondary to material things. In that world, a healthy reverence for the reality of life is severed."

Olin hesitated and deflected his eyes into the darkness of the companionway. Turning back, his penetrating gaze landed on Hank and with more force than before, said, "They aren't prepared for what's coming. Marshall is addicted to gaming. Irina relies on her looks. Both think everything will always be taken care of. Now, I'm doing what I can to correct some of that." His countenance lightened, and he smiled, eyes squinting. "I told the kids they had no choice. Marshall pushed back until I told him he could either join us on this voyage or become a priest. Irina? Well, she wanted to come."

The sky continued to grow lighter, but the sun hadn't quite broken over the clouds.

Hank stiffened and said, "Of course, I'm on board with you. The destination has never been important to me. I need a job and I love to sail. Willy just reminded me I'm your sailing instructor and you're going to need me." Hank stood up and rocked into Olin's space with his hand out. Olin's eyes almost disappeared as he smiled and stood up, accepting the handshake.

This time it was Hank's turn to lower his voice. "I know you're serious about this voyage. About your kids. I've still got a lot of questions, but I think you need to know that it's a desperate move you're taking to help your kids grow up." Hank fell silent, as if stuck in mid-sentence. He glanced at Willy.

"What do you mean by desperate?" Olin asked.

"A man has to either hate his kids or love them to do what you're doing. Either way, it's some type of desperation to aim a boat into a hurricane."

CHAPTER 49

South China Sea

GREGORY WALKED INTO THE subdued lights of the fighting cockpit carrying an old-school dive belt with four weights. "Twelve kilos should do it."

Sammi stood over the open fish locker spraying warm water over the crushed ice. The speed of the boat vented off the mist and Gregory could see the canvas tarp Sammi had draped over Masiki's body. He didn't do it out of respect for the dead, but to hide her from prying eyes. The tarp acted like a false bottom in the deep locker. A thick layer of crushed ice not only preserved the body, but made a suitable resting place for the hundred-pound marlin Gregory hauled in. Their first day of cruising had been a fantastic day of fishing. It was perfect in every way and brought the new captain and crew together. He also caught half a dozen sharks, and the crew cut off their fins and left them to die. They made it to their first stop before sunset and sold their catch. His father would have been proud of the deal he struck.

"I'm so glad you decided to cruise with us. You are a master sushi chef, but your shark fin soup was amazing." Gregory stood shoulder to shoulder with the shorter man. "Can you bake, too?"

Sammi took his eyes off the flow of water and asked, "What do you have in mind?"

"Cake... just a simple cake. Women love cake at weddings."

"No problem, boss."

With one hand, Sammi reached into the slush, wrapped his hand around the back of Masiki's neck and lifted her body out of the makeshift coffin. "I wanted to wait until you were here for this. You're going to love it." Sammi reached his free arm around her front, let go of her neck and grabbed his forearm around her back. It looked like an awkward side-hug, with Masiki's dripping toes hovering above the deck. He squeezed her in against his chest and the air rushed out of her lungs and whistled through the slice in her neck. Sammi didn't stop until her ribs were done cracking.

"Not bad. Not bad at all," Gregory said. He wrapped the dive belt around Masiki's waist. It went around twice before he cinched it in at the front. "She loved accessorizing but wouldn't approve of this." He ignored her dead black eyes and gently extended his hand toward her ear and smoothed down a large teardrop earring. "That's better." Then he reached across, grasping her cold, wet hand with both of his. In an instant, the ring on her right finger was stripped off. "Dump her."

Gregory watched as the turbulent water eagerly consumed the dead body. "Sammi, she would have wanted you to have this." He extended his hand and placed the gaudy sapphire ring into Sammi's beefy hand.

"Thanks, boss. Let's do this again someday." The beefy man stripped off his apron, carefully rolled it up, and disappeared up the side deck.

The two-man crew was sleeping off a night of drinking. Giving them the entire profits of yesterday's catch and letting them know this was their last landfall ensured they'd get drunk. No sense in giving them more information than they needed. But Gregory wanted to check on his new captain. He was on the bridge, alone, and should have been busy driving the yacht, but it never hurt to check up on new hires.

The bridge was dark. The radar screen illuminated the captain's form, and countless LEDs dotted the landscape around the helm. "Good morning, Captain," Gregory said,

"If you say so" was the curt reply, in a crisp Australian accent.

"We haven't talked since you've signed on. Now seems like as good a chance as any."

"Whatever you say, Mr. Oshiro."

"I hired you on the assurances of a very reliable business acquaintance. Your nautical experience is exceptional, but your resume is full of holes and inconsistency."

"That's why I'm working for you."

"Captain, perhaps I can get you a drink, and we can speak civilly."

"Never touch the stuff."

"You requested the humidor be full of cigars. May I offer you one?"

"Now you're talking."

Gregory stood at the captain's right shoulder and said, "Do you mind if I prepare it for you?"

"Not at all."

He cut off the cap of the cigar and ignited a tiny torch to toast it. Handing it to the captain, he said, "That should do."

"Thank you." He took a draw, rotated the cigar, and turned his attention to Gregory. "You know this boat of yours has a back-up camera."

"I don't get your meaning."

"The chick you and Sammi just dumped into the deep. I saw it right there on that monitor."

"Oh. I see."

"Let me tell you about those inconsistencies in my resume. At forty-two years old, I was the captain of a seven-hundred-foot cruise ship. Two kids, a trophy wife and my pride and joy, an Audi R8 in my townhouse garage. Then COVID-19 destroyed everything. My marriage was on the rocks long before I lost my career. The divorce was final just before Australia became a police state. I couldn't even visit my kids. It's cliche, but I lost everything. Soon after, I was arrested for inciting protest and defying arrest. That's when I became a political prisoner for six years. Some inmates found Muhammad, others Jesus..." The embers of his cigar burned brightly. He turned his head and exhaled an enormous amount of smoke. He shifted his attention back to Gregory. "I found karma. That bitch you disposed of? My religion has the answer for that. She deserved it. My religion has an answer for you, too. If you ever try to double-cross me. I will make sure you get what you deserve." His voice changed with his next puff of smoke. "Of course, if you honor our contract, I will take you anywhere in the world and do anything to help you get... what you want."

"Captain, I believe we will get along just fine. As a captain of a cruise ship, have you ever had occasion to perform a wedding ceremony?"

"I've done dozens."

"Wonderful." Gregory slowly reached over to the throttle controls and eased them forward. "Let's go get my girl."

ACKNOWLEDGMENTS

When you write a novel about people who travel on (and above) the oceans, live on seasteads and work underwater, a sinking feeling is never a good thing. While writing this novel, I've confronted the writer's equivalent of drowning. Fortunately, I have been saved by individuals who have thrown me a life-ring. They have shared skills, experience and encouragement: Carol Beach and our grandchildren, Eleanor Buzzell and Zachary Pope, Kristen Hoidal, Terri Valentine, Chris Sabel, Pam Courtney, Jim Bartlet, Bob Schroepfer, Jim Furchert, Kelleigh, Emaleigh and Michelle Wilson, Archer & Buster (pets of distinction), Hannah VanVels Ausbury, Carly Jackson, Jim Karstetter, Andrew Kerr and Yesuha (see chapter 8).

finlaybeach.com

Aloha,

Thank you for reading this book. Now, I feel I know you and can ask a favor. Positive reviews from ardent readers like you help others feel confident about selecting books from this series. Could you take 60 seconds to rank and review Managed Paranoia—Book One? I will be forever grateful. Thank you in advance for helping me out! Please review where you made this purchase, and of course, at Goodreads.

Oops! One more thing! If you would like to read the next book in the Hank Gunn series, let me invite you to join my tribe. It's not a "magic mushroom-eating, dog-loving, warrior cult," as Zoe puts it in chapter 46, but it is a sure-fire way to get the latest near-future-news; and remember, life goes on even when the pages stop turning. Bella and Hank struggle to define the relationship. Olin, Willy and Ava dig deep into their escape, and Gregory never stops earning his ticket to hell. FinlayBeach.com

Rock the Boat,

Fin

 fin@openthegift.com

Made in the USA
Columbia, SC
06 July 2022